THE
ENEMY
TOM WOOD

sphere

SPHERE

First published in Great Britain in 2012 by Sphere
Reissued by Sphere in 2014, 2021

1 3 5 7 9 10 8 6 4 2

A CIP catalogue record for this book
is available from the British Library.

ISBN 978-0-7515-4535-7

Typeset in Sabon by M Rules
Printed and bound in Great Britain by Clays Ltd, Elcograf S.p.A.

Papers used by Sphere are from well-managed forests
and other responsible sources.

MIX
Paper from
responsible sources
FSC
www.fsc.org   FSC® C104740

Sphere
An imprint of
Little, Brown Book Group
Carmelite House
50 Victoria Embankment
London EC4Y 0DZ

An Hachette UK Company
www.hachette.co.uk

www.littlebrown.co.uk

Tom Wood is a full-time writer born in Burton-on-Trent who now lives in London. After a stint as freelance editor and film-maker, he completed his first novel, *The Hunter*, which was an instant bestseller and introduced readers to a genuine antihero, Victor, an assassin with a purely logical view on life and whose morals are deeply questionable. Like Victor, Tom is passionate about physical sport, being both a huge boxing fan and practising Krav Maga martial arts, which has seen him sustain a number of injuries. He has not, however, ever killed anyone.

By Tom Wood

The Victor series
The Hunter
The Enemy
The Game
Better Off Dead
The Darkest Day
A Time to Die
The Final Hour
Kill For Me
A Quiet Man

Ebook short stories
Bad Luck in Berlin
Gone By Dawn

Other Fiction
A Knock at the Door

For Michael, brother and friend

CHAPTER 1

Bucharest, Romania

It was a good morning to kill. Impenetrable grey clouds obscured the sun and the city beneath was dark and quiet. Cold. Just how he liked it. He walked at a relaxed pace, in no hurry, knowing he was making perfect time. A fine rain began to fall. Yes, a particularly good morning to kill.

Ahead of him a refuse truck made its slow way along the road, hazard light flashing orange, windshield wipers swinging back and forth to flick away the drizzle. Refuse collectors followed the vehicle, hands buried under armpits while they waited to reach the next pile of trash bags on the sidewalk. They chatted and joked among themselves.

He interrupted the group's banter as he passed through the spiralling cloud of exhaust fumes condensing in the spring air. He felt their gaze upon him, taking in his appearance for the few short seconds before he'd gone.

There was little for them to note. He was smartly dressed – a long woollen coat over the top of a dark grey suit, black leather gloves, thick-soled Oxford shoes. In his left hand he carried a metal briefcase. His dark hair was short, his beard neatly trimmed. Despite the cold, only the bottom two of his four overcoat buttons had been fastened. Just a businessman on his way to the office, they would assume. He was a businessman of sorts, but he doubted they would guess the nature of his uncommon profession.

Behind him, a trashcan clattered into the road and he looked briefly over his shoulder to see black bags split open and refuse spilling across the asphalt. The garbage men groaned and rushed to gather up the trash before the wind could spread it too far.

After a short walk, the businessman arrived at a large apartment complex. It stood several storeys taller than the surrounding buildings. Balconies and satellite dishes jutted out from the dull brown walls. He made sure not to appear rushed as he took the half-dozen steps up to the front door. He unlocked it with his day-old key and stepped inside.

There were two elevators, but he opted for the stairs, climbing twenty-two flights to the top floor. He reached his destination with little trace of fatigue.

The corridor beyond the stairwell door was long and featureless. Spaced at regular intervals were numbered, spyholed doors. Dirty linoleum lined the floor. The paint on the walls was faded and chipped. The cool air smelled of strong detergent. Somewhere a baby cried softly.

At the end of the corridor, where it intersected with another, was a door marked *maintenance*. He placed his briefcase down, and from a pocket removed a small packet of butter taken from a nearby diner. He unfolded the wrapper and carefully smeared the butter on to the hinges of the door. He placed the empty wrapper back into the same pocket.

From inside his coat, he removed two small metal tools: a tension wrench and a slim, curved pick. The lock was significantly better than most, but the businessman unlocked it in less than sixty seconds.

A door opened behind him.

He slipped the lock picks back into the pocket. Someone said something in gruff-sounding Romanian. The man with the briefcase spoke several languages, but not this one. He stayed facing the door for a moment in case the speaker was talking to someone inside the apartment. A slim chance, but one he had to play nevertheless.

The voice called again. The same guttural words, but louder. Impatient. His back still to the speaker, the businessman reached inside his coat. He withdrew his right hand and kept it out of sight by his hip. He turned side-on, to the left, to look at the resident, keeping his head tilted forward, eyes in the shadow of his brow.

A heavyset man with several days' worth of stubble was leaning out of his front door, fat fingers white on the frame. A cigarette hung from thick lips. He looked over the man with the briefcase and removed the cigarette from his mouth with a shaking hand. Ash fell from the end and on to the marked linoleum.

He swayed as he spoke again, words slow and slurred. A drunk then. No threat.

The businessman ignored him, picked up his briefcase and moved down the adjoining corridor, walking away from the drunk before he made any more noise. When a door clicked shut behind him, he stopped and silently retraced his steps, peered around the corner, saw no one, and placed the 9 mm Beretta 92F handgun back inside his overcoat. He reset the safety with his thumb.

Total darkness enshrouded the room on the other side of the maintenance door. Water dripped somewhere unseen. The businessman flicked on a slim torch. The narrow beam illuminated the room – bare brick walls, pipework, boxes, a metal staircase along one side. He negotiated his way across the space and ascended the stairs. His shoes were quiet on the metal steps. At the top, a padlock secured the rust-streaked roof access door. The lock was marginally harder to pick than the previous one.

Eleven storeys up, the icy wind stung his face and every inch of exposed flesh. It subsided within a few seconds as the pressure equalised between the stairwell and roof. He crouched to reduce his profile against the sky and moved across the roof to the west edge. The wind was pushing the clouds northward, letting the glow of the rising sun spread across the city. Bucharest extended out in front of him, slowly awakening. Present location aside, a particularly beautiful city. This was his first visit, and he hoped his work would bring him back before too long.

He turned his attention to his briefcase, unlocked it, and opened it flat. Inside, a sheet of thick foam rubber surrounded the disassembled Heckler & Koch MSG-9. He removed the barrel first and attached it to the body of the rifle. Next, he fixed the Hensoldt scope in place, followed by the stock and finally the twenty-round box magazine. He folded down the bipod and rested the weapon on the roof's low parapet.

Through the scope he saw a 10x magnification of the city –

buildings, cars, people. For fun, he positioned the crosshairs over a young woman's head and tracked her as she sipped her morning coffee, anticipating her movements to keep the reticule in place. She passed beneath the branches of a tree and he lost her. Lucky girl, he thought with a rare smile. He took his eye from the sight, repositioned the rifle, and looked through the scope once more.

This time he saw the entrance to the Grand Plaza Hotel on Dorobantilor Avenue. The eighteen-storey building had a modern façade, all glass and stainless steel, appearing both strong and sleek at the same time. The businessman had stayed in several hotels of the Howard Johnson chain while plying his trade around the globe, but not this particular one. If the Grand Plaza met the reasonable-to-high standards of the rest of the franchise, he imagined the target would have enjoyed a pleasant stay. He thought it only fitting that the condemned man should get a good night's sleep before his morning execution.

The man with the rifle took a laser rangefinder from his brief-case and aimed the beam at the hotel entrance, finding it exactly six hundred and four yards away in central Bucharest. Well within acceptable range, and only six yards under his estimate. He rotated the elevation wheel to correct for the distance and elevation.

Outside the hotel entrance, a craggy-faced doorman revealed his bad teeth by yawning. Close to him, tied to a nearby street-light, a purple ribbon fluttered in the breeze. The man with the rifle watched it for a moment, calculating the wind speed. Five, maybe five-and-a-quarter miles per hour. He adjusted the Hensoldt's windage wheel, wondering how long it would be before someone realised the significance of the seemingly innocuous ribbon. Maybe no one ever would.

He adjusted the scope's power ring, decreasing the magnification to see a wider view of the hotel. There were few other people nearby. Some pedestrians, the occasional guest, but no mass of people. This was good. His marksmanship was excellent, but with just seconds to make the kill, he required a clear line of sight. He had no compunction about shooting whoever was unfortunate enough to stand between the bullet and its true mark, but such killings tended to give targets advance warning of their own impending demise, and as long as the target wasn't mentally deficient, they moved.

The man with the rifle checked his watch. Today's unfortunate subject was due to appear shortly, if the itinerary included with the dossier was accurate. The businessman had no reason to doubt his client-supplied information.

Another adjustment of the scope and he saw the entire width of the hotel's front side and two-thirds of the way up its single tower. Light from the rising sun reflected off the windows of the top three floors within the scope's view.

The rain had ceased by the time a limousine pulled on to the hotel's drive from the adjoining road and stopped outside the main entrance. A large white guy dressed in a beige overcoat and dark jeans climbed out and ascended the steps with the brisk efficiency of a bodyguard. His head swept back and forth, fast but efficient, gaze registering every nearby person, assessing for threats and finding none.

The man with the rifle felt his heart rate begin to speed up as the time grew rapidly closer. He breathed deeply to stop it climbing too high and negatively affecting his aim. He waited.

After a minute, the bodyguard reappeared and took up position midway down the steps. He looked around before gesturing back up at the entrance. In a few seconds the target would come into view. According to the dossier, the target – a Ukrainian – typically travelled with several bodyguards who would naturally have stayed at the same hotel. The bodyguards were all ex-military or ex-intelligence, who would no doubt surround the Ukrainian and make an otherwise completely clear shot difficult.

The man with the rifle had selected the MSG-9 because it was semi-automatic and would allow him to fire several times inside of just a few seconds. The 7.62 × 52 mm full metal-jacketed rounds carried enough power to pass through a human body and still kill someone standing behind, and these particular bullets incorporated a tungsten penetrator to account for the body armour the target and his guards would likely wear. A wall of flesh two armoured-men thick could shield the Ukrainian and he would still die.

Before the businessman could zoom in closer to prepare for the shot, a tiny flicker of light from a window of the hotel's thirteenth floor caught his attention. He quickly raised the barrel of the MSG-9, angling up the scope to check out the light source. He feared a guest was better enjoying the view of the city through a telescope or pair of binoculars. From an elevated position they might inadvertently spot him, and if so, he would have to forget about the contract and make a quick escape. No point completing the kill if the police apprehended him afterwards.

Once the reticule centred over the window he increased the magnification of the scope, and saw the source of the flicker was not the reflection of sunlight on the lenses of binoculars or a telescope but a rifle scope like his own.

A suppressed muzzle flash transformed the businessman's surprise to alarm for the two-thirds of a second it took for the bullet to reach his head.

Pink mist swirled in the air.

CHAPTER 2

Victor watched the body fall out of sight and took his eye away from the scope as the crack of the shot slowly faded into nothingness. The rifle's long sound suppressor had negated the muzzle report but could do nothing to stop the sonic boom emitted when the bullet broke the sound barrier. Though a person with the right ear would know a shot had been fired, without the accompanying muzzle blast and flash its point of origin would be all but impossible to decipher. Subsonic ammunition would have eliminated most of the sound, only it was windy in Bucharest, and at a distance of six hundred yards, Victor didn't trust the slower round's accuracy.

The hotel-room window hadn't opened far enough for his purposes so Victor had unscrewed the pane. As a result it was cold inside the room, but the flow of air would help disperse the tang of cordite. Shooting with the rifle barrel outside of the window would have helped with the smell, but it would also have helped give him away. Only amateurs operated like that.

Quickly, but not hurrying, Victor unscrewed the suppressor from the rifle's barrel and disassembled the weapon. He placed the individual parts back inside the foam rubber insert of a leather briefcase. The process took less than fifteen seconds. Using a handkerchief, he retrieved the hot brass shell case from the floor and placed it in a pocket. He then moved the armchair he'd been sitting on away from the window and back to its original corner. With his foot, he rubbed the depressions from the carpet where the chair legs had rested near the window.

He screwed the windowpane back in place and used a small piece of sandpaper to smooth the heads of the screws. He surveyed the room for signs of his presence. It was contemporary, neat and very clean. Neutral colours. Lots of stainless steel and lightwood. No personality in the décor but no offence either. He saw nothing to be concerned over. He hadn't used the bed or the bathroom, or so much as turned a tap. Hard as it had been to resist the pull of 300-thread-count sheets, the room was a strike point – nothing more – and tasting its comforts wasn't worth the implicit risk. Sleeping in the same place where he fulfilled a contract was simply not how Victor conducted business.

Happy he'd left no physical evidence to tie him to the room, Victor placed the briefcase inside a larger suitcase, closed it and exited the hotel room. His pulse was two beats per minute above his resting heart rate. He didn't have to worry about fingerprints as a clear silicone solution covered his hands to prevent oil from his skin leaving prints on anything he touched.

He walked to the stairwell to avoid the security camera near the elevator and descended to the first floor. He passed through the lobby, ignoring the commotion, with his head angled slightly downward so the cameras there would only see his forehead and hair.

Near to the hotel entrance, a tall, wide-shouldered man in

jeans and a beige overcoat was speaking frantically to a similarly sized but older man. Both looked Eastern European, Slavic – Russians or Ukrainians maybe. The older man appeared to be in his late forties, clothed in a fine black pinstripe suit that was perfectly cut across his large, muscular frame. He had short-cropped black hair that was grey at the temples, and a clean-shaven face. He stood left side-on to Victor and the jagged line of scar tissue forming the bottom of the ear was clearly visible. There was no earlobe.

Four other men surrounded the two Slavs. All were pale-skinned Eastern Europeans, all in dark suits, all muscular but not overly so, all with the bearing of ex-military high-end body-guards. They formed a tactical screen around the man in the beige overcoat and the older man in the pinstripe suit, each looking in a different direction – overlapping fields of vision, alert, good, primary hands hovering near their waists, ready to earn their pay cheques.

As Victor approached the desk he heard the large man in the overcoat explaining in Russian why the man in the pinstripe – the VIP – needed to wait inside. Victor pretended not to understand the topic of conversation as he reached the front desk and stood at an angle so the nearest camera would only catch the back of his skull.

The receptionist behind the desk looked flustered, staring at the group of Slavs, and didn't notice Victor's presence until he held a hand across the guy's line of sight.

'Sorry, sir,' he said in Romanian-accented English, 'how can I help you?'

'I'd like to check out early, please.'

Victor gave his details, handed back his keycard, and waited

11

for the receptionist to finish doing whatever receptionists had to do, all the while listening to every word of the conversation between the head bodyguard and his VIP.

As he checked the bill and went to sign the paperwork, he heard heavy footsteps approaching. Normally, Victor never allowed anyone to walk up behind him, but conscious of the security camera, and in the process of signing out, he couldn't reposition himself without drawing attention to what he was doing. And the bodyguards looked observant enough not to let such telling movements go unnoticed.

As a result Victor stood still as he finished putting his alias's signature on the bottom of the form, and received a predicted shove to the shoulder from the bodyguard as he arrived at the desk to bark orders at the receptionist. Victor didn't dodge and he didn't resist the shove – again to preserve his cover as a forgettable guest – but the bodyguard had to weigh two hundred and thirty useful pounds and Victor stumbled. He recovered his footing easier than a surprised businessman might have, but only to stop himself crashing to the floor.

Before he could make an expected angry – but not too angry – comment, he heard the man in the pinstripe suit shout, '*Nikolai*.'

The guy in the beige overcoat turned from the front desk to look at his boss. Victor looked too.

The forty-something VIP stormed towards his head bodyguard, the other four guards rushing to maintain a full screen around him, five paces out, no corner of the lobby not covered by at least one set of eyes.

'Nikolai, you disrespectful brute,' the man in the pinstripe said as he drew near, 'apologise to this man immediately.'

He gestured to Victor, and Victor recognised the rural Ukrainian accent.

The bodyguard called Nikolai looked at Victor and said, in inflectionless English, 'Sorry.'

'It's fine,' Victor said back.

The Ukrainian in the pinstripe suit turned to him. 'Forgive me, please. My friend here has yet to be civilised. More primate than human. I do hope you're not hurt.'

'I'm okay.'

Victor took a step away, eager to end the interaction with the man whose life he had saved. Each second here increased his risk of exposure exponentially. The Ukrainian looked at Victor with a curious, almost intense gaze.

'Oh, no,' the Ukrainian said as his gaze dropped, 'your suit.'

Victor looked too, seeing the small tear in his right jacket sleeve. It must have caught on the corner of the front desk as he stumbled.

'It's okay,' Victor said. 'It can be fixed.'

'No, it's ruined.' The Ukrainian turned to Nikolai, and said in Russian, 'You stupid fuck, look what you've done.' He faced Victor again. 'I'm so sorry. And that's such a nice suit too. I can see you are a man who cares about how he dresses, as do I. I would give you money for a replacement, only I don't carry any quantity of cash, and who has a chequebook these days?'

'There's no need, really,' Victor said, thinking he'd have drawn less attention to himself if he had back-flipped out of Nikolai's way.

'There's every need.' The Ukrainian reached into his inside jacket pocket and produced a business card. He handed it to Victor. 'I'm afraid I'm in the middle of a crisis at the moment,

13

otherwise I would take you for a new suit, but here's my card. Call me and we can work something out. If you are ever in Moscow I will have my tailor make you a suit so fine it will make you weep.'

Victor took the card. In both Cyrillic script and English, it said: *Vladimir Kasakov*. There was a phone number and a Moscow office address.

'That's very kind of you, Mr Kasakov,' Victor replied.

'Now, before my employees can do any more damage, you must excuse me.'

Victor nodded and headed to the front entrance. He didn't turn around, but he felt eyes watching him the whole time.

Outside it was cold and the doorman looked far too frail to be still doing the job at his age, especially in this weather. Victor's gaze drifted to the eleven-storey building whose ugliness was all too apparent even at over six hundred yards. The assassin had been right to shoot from there. Other buildings were closer, but not as well positioned to command an uninterrupted view of the hotel entrance. Victor would have used it himself, had their roles been reversed. He would have been more careful not to die there, however.

Victor saw his reflection in the hotel's glass doors and noted that he didn't look too dissimilar to the man he'd shot. He wore a charcoal grey suit with a white shirt and sky blue tie underneath his black overcoat. Perfect urban camouflage. His dark hair was short and not styled, his beard trimmed short. He looked like a stockbroker or lawyer, one that kept a smart but unremarkable appearance. He blended into the background, seldom seen, rarely noticed. Unremembered.

In a taxi, he unwrapped a stick of peppermint chewing gum and folded it into his mouth. He'd read gum made a good substitute for cigarettes, but no matter how much he chewed he couldn't inhale any smoke from the stuff.

He had the driver take him to Gara de Nord station where he purchased a ticket to Constanta and boarded the train seven minutes before it was set to depart. He left his seat six minutes later and disembarked five seconds before the doors closed and locked. He left the station by a different exit, climbed into another taxi and told the driver to take him to Herăstrău Park, where he walked leisurely through the park before exiting and entering the Charles de Gaulle Plaza. He took a seat in the lobby and read a complimentary magazine while he watched the main entrance.

With no one registering on his threat radar after five minutes, he stood and descended the stairs to the lowest level of the underground parking garage. One of the high-speed elevators then carried him to the top floor. He went back down in a different elevator to the fourth floor and used the stairs to return to the lobby. He left the building by a side entrance.

He walked to the closest metro station and stayed on for thirty minutes, switching trains and doubling back on himself before changing routes and leaving at the University of Bucharest station. After a pleasant walk through the campus, a taxi took him to Elisabeta Boulevard near to City Hall and from there he walked the short distance to the entrance of the Cişmigiu Gardens.

The park was quiet and peaceful. He passed few people as he made his way to the circular alley of the Rondul Român where he spent some time looking at its twelve stone busts of famous

Romanian writers while he finished his counter surveillance. His precautions were as essential a part of fulfilling a job as squeezing the trigger. The successful execution of a contract depended on remaining unnoticed and untraced. Nearly anyone could kill another person, but few people could get away with it once, let alone time after time.

For years, Victor had plied his trade with complete anonymity. Working freelance, he'd killed quickly, efficiently, silently. Those who employed him had no idea who he was. No one did. He had lived in near isolation – no friends, no family – no one who could betray him and no one to be used against him. It hadn't lasted, and in hindsight, it was inevitable. He of all people should have known nobody could remain unfound for ever.

When Victor was satisfied he was not being observed, he left the Rondul Român and walked to the centre of the park where a man-made lake was located. He paused on an ornate footbridge, removed the briefcase from within the suitcase, looked around to make sure he was alone, and discreetly dropped the briefcase into the lake. The rifle weighed just less than fifteen pounds and sank straight to the bottom.

Victor left the park via the south-eastern exit and caught a bus. He took a seat on the top level, at the back, disembarking after half a dozen stops when he was sitting alone with no other travellers nearby. The suitcase remained on the floor by his seat.

His thoughts turned to the man whose life he had saved. When Victor had received the contract he'd been given no information on the assassin's target, only that he had to survive. Had the incident in the hotel lobby not taken place, Victor would have thought little else about him. But now Victor knew his name, and it was a name he had heard before. Few people in Victor's profession would not have known it. Vladimir Kasakov was one of the biggest arms dealers on the planet, if not the biggest. He was an international fugitive. Normally, Victor cared little about the motives behind his jobs, but he couldn't help wondering why his CIA employer would be so keen on saving the life of such a man.

It started to rain again and Victor increased his pace to match those of commuters around him. No one paid him any attention. On the surface, he knew he seemed just like them – flesh and blood, skin and bone – but he also knew that was where the similarities ended.

You know what makes you special? someone had once told him. *People like you, like me, we take that thing inside us others don't have and we make it work for us, or we stand by and let it destroy us.*

And he'd spent his life doing just that, making it work for him. But his carefully maintained existence had fallen apart six months before and in the following maelstrom he'd fantasised about retiring, about trying to make a normal life for himself. A fool's hope, but that had been then. Now, even if Victor wanted to, there was no chance he could walk away from what he did for a living.

He knew his new employer would retire him permanently if he tried.

CHAPTER 3

Tunari, Romania

Steam rose from the washbasin. Victor turned off the hot tap and lowered the razor into the water. He'd already used scissors to trim his beard, and he shaved with the grain of his stubble – neck first, then cheeks, chin and finally upper lip. He was slow, careful. He couldn't afford to walk around with a cut or shaving rash. After smearing his skin with aftershave balm, he used a set of clippers to cut his black hair to an even half inch.

When he'd finished he looked notably different from the man who had supposedly stayed in room 1312 of the Grand Plaza. The blue-coloured contact lenses and non-prescription glasses he'd worn had been disposed of before checking into his current hotel. It was a busy establishment located near to Otopeni International Airport. Far too busy for anyone to notice one particular guest had checked out with shorter hair and minus a beard. Victor didn't put much faith in elaborate disguises. Unless prepared by a make-up artist they were seldom completely convincing, especially at close range. Wigs and peeling latex were more likely to draw attention than divert it.

He performed an intense thirty-minute workout routine consisting of bodyweight exercises and stretching. After he'd bathed, Victor sat down at the bedroom's small desk. He picked up a 9 mm P226 SIG Sauer and stripped it down, cleaned it methodically, and reassembled the weapon. The gun was already clean, had never been fired, but it relaxed him to do something so familiar.

His CIA employer had supplied the SIG, like the rifle – a Dakota Longbow. Both had been waiting in the trunk of a plain sedan left for him in the long-stay parking lot of Otopeni International.

Though Victor had to admit it made his work considerably easier not to have to source and move his own weapons, he found the convenience outweighed by the sense of control he relinquished in doing so. For years he had answered to no one but himself, completely self-reliant. Now, being dependent on any person or organisation felt like a weight chained to his ankle.

More importantly, it put him at far greater risk. His employer not only knew whom he was going to kill and when, but also how and where he picked up the tools to do so. With such information a route could be cut straight through his defences.

For the time being he had little choice but to do things their way. The terms of his employment required him to do exactly as told, when told. In return, he was well paid and his CIA handler created a barrier between Victor and certain parties, including the rest of the CIA, who could make his life extremely difficult before extinguishing it. Victor was also prohibited from taking contracts from other sources and had so far honoured that condition. His freelancing days were over. He was now a CIA contractor. An expendable asset. Nothing more than a slave with a gun.

His left arm ached and he rubbed it gently. He had two thin scars – his most recent additions – one on top of his forearm, and one below, where a blade had plunged through his flesh. It had healed well, with no loss of dexterity, and a cosmetic surgeon had ensured the scarring was minimal, but occasionally the wound still caused him pain.

Protocol dictated that windows remained shut and locked, and shutters, blinds or drapes closed at all times. Therefore, to look out of the window, Victor gazed out through the slim opening between the drapes. It gave him a narrow view of the world outside – a glimpse of what he had given up and could never recapture.

When he realised he was thinking about someone he'd told himself he had to forget, he removed a small bottle of vodka from the mini bar and downed it. It took all his willpower not to have another.

Victor moved the SIG to one side and got out a compact laptop computer. After it had powered on, he entered his password and opened an internet connection to check his Cayman Islands bank account. He was pleased to see a very large sum of money had recently been deposited. Victor had been paid the same amount two days prior, when he'd received the contract. It was the way he always used to operate – half before, half afterwards. This time the fee was higher than the initially agreed terms of his employment to compensate for the job's short notice.

Up until two days ago, Victor had been preparing for what should have been his first assignment for the CIA. He had been told to expect a second and maybe third job soon after the first's completion, but then the Bucharest contract had arrived unexpectedly – killing an assassin before he could kill a man his employer wanted to keep alive – with its strict deadline. Victor hadn't hesitated in accepting it, glad for the chance to get back to work and shake off the rust. It had gone perfectly. His first job in half a year.

In less than a second the gun was in his hand and he was out of the chair.

He'd heard a scream. Female. Victor moved to the door, checked the spyhole. No one. He remained absolutely still, listening intently. He waited ten seconds, hearing nothing further. Keeping the SIG out of his sight down by his side, he opened the door, looked left then right. Clear.

After a minute he sat back down, surprised by the strength of his reaction. The scream could have been for any reason; someone in an adjoining room spilling coffee on their lap or startled in the shower by a spider. Either that or it had only been in his head and he was one more step along the road to insanity.

Keeping the gun in his right hand while he used the laptop's touch pad with his left thumb, he navigated to the email account created to receive and send communications from his employer. Untraceable, he'd been assured. He had no reason to think otherwise. His employer didn't want the NSA or GCHQ intercepting his emails to an internationally wanted contract killer. If nothing else, the account seemed to be immune from spam and that alone was enough to make Victor happier than he'd been in a long time.

A message from his employer sat in the inbox. He memorised the number it contained and entered it into the laptop's VoIP program.

The laptop's speakers played an imitation dialling tone for the nine seconds it took for the call to connect. The throaty baritone that answered through the computer speakers said, 'Nice to hear from you again.'

Victor remained silent. He heard a click of a tongue.

'Not a man to waste words, are you?'

'Evidently.'

'All right,' the control said. 'We can dispense with the small talk if you like, Mr Tesseract.'

Victor had met his employer only once, nearly seven months before. It had been in a hospital room where the choice to work for the CIA had been offered to him, though it hadn't been much of a choice at the time. The guy who'd come to see him had been fat, pushing two hundred and fifty pounds, average height, mid-fifties, greying hair, sharp eyes. He'd had the confidence and bearing of a high-ranking official but with the manner of a former field operative. He might as well have had a badge that said Clandestine Services. He hadn't given his name and neither had he asked for Victor's. Their conversation had been brief, and Victor full of drugs, but he never forgot a face.

'I don't like that code name.'

'You don't?' The voice sounded perplexed, almost offended. 'I'm quite partial to it myself. Despite the history it carries.'

'It's the history I don't like.'

'You've never struck me as the prone-to-nightmares type.'

'You have to dream to have nightmares,' Victor replied.

'But like you said, that code name has history. It's been used before. Therefore it's compromised. That's why I have a problem with it.'

'Ah, I see,' his employer breathed. 'You shouldn't worry, my man, everyone who knows its connotations is dead.'

'I don't worry,' Victor corrected. 'And what you said is inaccurate. You're alive.'

'But you can trust me.'

Victor remained silent.

'You know,' his employer said, 'you'd find our arrangement a lot more palatable if you lost some of that paranoia. I might just be the one person in the entire world you can actually trust.'

'Trust is earned.'

'So it is possible for me to earn your trust?'

'Let's not get ahead of ourselves.'

A moment of silence, maybe to accommodate a smile, before the voice said, 'I think you're forgetting the circumstances in which we met. You were wrapped up in so many bandages you should have been in a sarcophagus, not a hospital room in the back of beyond. If I'd wanted to, I could have sent you to the morgue there and then when it would have been quiet and convenient.'

'Interesting,' Victor said, 'because at the time you told me you had no backup.'

'Didn't think I'd meet a lethal assassin all on my lonesome, did you?'

'Didn't think I wouldn't notice your janitor friend with his bought-that-day toolbox, did you?'

After a pause, his employer said, 'I think this conversation has taken an unnecessary turn for the worst. Let's reset.' Another pause. 'All I wanted to do was congratulate you on your good work this morning.'

'Noted.'

'I know it was a rush job, and I want to apologise for your lack of lead time. Not that it seemed to be a problem for a man of your skills.'

'I told you before, my ego doesn't need massaging. Who was the target of the assassin I killed?'

'He's not important.'

'If he's not important, why don't you tell me his name?'

'Because you don't need to know.'

'I thought you might have been more original.'

'It's a cliché for a reason, my man. You concern yourself purely with the job at hand and I'll concern myself with everything else. So, let's get you back on the Farkas contract as soon as possible, okay? There's a supplier I'd like you to liaise with.'

'I take it you can tell me this name.'

'I only know him as Georg. He's German. Operates out of Hamburg.'

'Never heard of him.'

'Is that a problem?'

'If I had heard of him it would have been a problem.'

'He's not Agency, and he's not an asset. But he is a fixer, and he deals in what you need. I've just sent you some supplementary materials. Should be in your inbox any second.'

'I have them.' Victor opened the attachment and began absorbing the information.

'Good. Georg is expecting your call, so read the files, and drop him a line.'

'It says here I'll need to meet with him in Hamburg.'

'Is that an issue?'

'One, I never meet anyone directly connected with what I do for a living unless I also plan to kill them, and two, Hamburg is Georg's turf. I've never heard of him, you know nothing about him. Me going to him gives him the perfect opportunity for dishonest trading.'

'I can assure you of Georg's quality and reliability.'

'Yet you only know his first name.'

'He comes highly recommended.'

'I prefer to reserve my own judgement.'

'I hate to break this to you, pal, but you don't work for yourself any longer, and the kind of jobs I need doing will require you to come from under your rock once in a while and interact with the world. I'm not paying you to just pull a trigger.'

'Which is good, because if you pull a trigger you're going to miss. You want to hit your target, you squeeze it.'

'Putting the correct use of firearms to one side, I need the Farkas contract fulfilled in a very specific manner. To do that you're going to have to meet Georg. If you don't like that, you're shit out of luck.'

'Don't curse in my presence.'

'Was that a joke?'

'When I make a joke you won't have to ask for confirmation.'

'All right,' the control said with a breath, 'I didn't figure you as the conservative type, but I guess I can watch my language.'

'No blasphemy either.'

A laugh. 'Now I *know* you're joking.'

Victor remained silent.

'Okay,' the control said, drawing the word out slowly, before adding, 'No swearing, no blasphemy. I'll work on that. You work on your attitude. But if being employed by me is so problematic for you then after you've completed these three jobs we can go our separate ways. No hard feelings.'

'Very charitable of you,' Victor said. 'But with the inclusion of the Bucharest job it will have been four contracts, not three.'

'True,' the voice agreed, 'and if that's how you're going to be, then I should remind you that after the little circus show you partook in last November there are a lot of folks out there who would like nothing more than to see your head atop a spike. Considering the lengths I've gone to in order to keep you out of the crosshairs of several intelligence services, not least of all in Russia and the US, I would have expected a little more gratitude.'

'I would have sent a card, only I don't have your name or address. Would you like to give me your name and address?'

His employer laughed briefly. 'For some reason I don't think that would be a particularly smart idea, do you?' He didn't wait for an answer. 'If protecting you isn't enough, I guess you've forgotten that I've already scratched your back at the beginning of this arrangement in handing over a certain individual.'

'I haven't forgotten,' Victor said through a tight mouth. He tried, without success, to stop his thoughts taking the inevitable path.

'Good, because now it's time to return the favour.' A long pause. 'Or was I wrong to take you as the kind of man who honours his word?'

Victor answered, 'That's the only way left in which I have honour,' and disconnected the call.

There was no need for goodbyes. Such courtesy was the benefit of friends alone. And years had passed since Victor had anyone who could be considered a true friend. The last person who had approached that mantle had helped organise an attempt on his life. Victor would never make that mistake again.

But when his employer knew so much about him and his enemies, Victor had to be careful to keep his paymaster happy. He also knew that when these kind of jobs went wrong the people involved in them tended to prematurely expire. Victor was well aware that his usefulness could run out without warning and any arrangement made for him could be a potential ambush. But Victor had been honest about keeping his word. He would pay off his debt.

Outside the hotel, he walked for a while until he found a payphone. He dialled the Hamburg number he'd been given. A woman answered in German. She had the voice of a long-term heavy smoker.

'Yes?'

'Georg, please,' he said.

She coughed and thirty seconds passed before a male voice spoke. 'Yes?'

'We have a mutual acquaintance,' Victor said. 'They tell me you have something for me.'

'At nine p.m. tomorrow get ferry line sixty-two from Landungsbrücken to Finkenwerder. Take a copy of the *Hamburger Abendblatt* with you. Keep it in your left hand. Stay on the top deck, port side. Don't bring any weapons.'

The line went dead before he could respond.

Victor replaced the receiver. He did not conduct business this way. If arrangements could not be made without a face to face,

27

they should be conducted in a neutral location. A ferry could be construed as neutral, but the meeting wouldn't take place there. Someone would get on and lead him to where Georg waited. That would certainly not be a neutral location. Alternatively, if anything went wrong, the ferry would be a floating trap.

Back in the hotel room, Victor reset the chair wedged under the door handle, checked the SIG was loaded, tucked it into the front of his waistband, and, fully dressed, lay down on the bed atop the covers. Three more jobs and he could have his life back. Whatever that equated to.

He thought about the scream until he fell asleep.

CHAPTER 4

Athens, Greece

At the same time, approximately nine hundred and fifty miles south-east, Xavier Callo was trying to hide his growing erection from the six feet of blonde Norwegian hotness he'd somehow managed to pick up. The American had set the trap perfectly and she'd fallen straight into it. He'd been sitting at one of the bar's tables, sipping Krug and tipping the waitresses with a fifty-euro note every time they so much as wiped his table. It was one of his best tactics. Waitresses liked tips, and they liked ridiculously huge tips even more. When such tips came along, they told people about them. People told other people and before long every gold-digger was looking at the small, balding guy sitting alone in the corner.

The bar had a load of modern art on the walls that looked like something Callo's niece might make after too many E-numbers. There were no chairs around the tables. Instead there were cushioned stools that were as uncomfortable as they appeared. Behind the bar itself was a huge array of bottles neatly aligned and backlit. They glowed hypnotically to Callo's ever more inebriated brain.

Before the blonde had arrived, Callo had let a couple of skanks swoon over him, but when the statuesque Viking goddess appeared through the bar's door he shooed them away. Callo liked tall women, which he knew was a good thing being much closer to five feet than six, but most of the girls he ended up with only had a few inches on him. In stiletto heels, the Norwegian beauty dwarfed him.

She was on the seat next to him solely because of the money he was flashing, but Callo didn't care. What mattered was that she wanted him. She was a good talker too, classy, and she loved that he was American. She wanted to hear everything about him. Where did he live? What did he do for a living? Did he have a family? What was he doing in Athens? What did he like to do for fun?

'I'm a diamond merchant,' Callo slurred. 'I live all over. I've got an ex-wife but no kids. I'm in Athens to unwind and I like doing all *sorts* of things.'

'Oh, wow,' the blonde said, inching closer. 'I love diamonds. They're so sexy.'

Her English was flawless and she didn't have a Norwegian accent that Callo could detect. Not that he knew what one sounded like. She liked her champagne too and had Callo order another magnum, but he seemed to be doing most of the drinking. He'd only known her for twenty minutes but he was sure he loved her.

When she whispered into his ear and asked him if he wanted to go back to her place, he knew he was in for the night of his life. He followed her out on to the street. The bar was in downtown Athens and overlooked the sea. Callo loved it in the Greek islands and always visited after a big diamond sale.

He let the blonde hail a cab while he kept an arm around her slim waist for support. Taxis were usually a bitch to get late at night in this part of town, even at weekends, but one pulled up in front of them straight away. He remembered his manners and held the door open for the Norwegian. She slid on to the seat elegantly and Callo stumbled in after her.

The driver didn't ask where they were going and the blonde didn't tell him, but the taxi pulled away regardless. Callo tried to put his arm around the blonde but she shrugged it off. She opened her purse and took something out.

By the time Callo realised it was a hypodermic syringe, the Norwegian was already stabbing him in the thigh. She gave him an angry stare.

'Pervert,' she hissed.

'*What the . . . ?*'

He tried to keep speaking but the words wouldn't come out. His head felt heavy and flopped forward. He couldn't move his limbs.

He remembered nothing after that.

CHAPTER 5

Hamburg, Germany

Hamburger Kunsthalle was open until 9 p.m. on Thursdays so Victor spent an hour perusing the art hanging in the various galleries while he checked for surveillance. When he was sure no one was watching him, Victor lingered in the Gallery of Old Masters for his own pleasure, before buying a takeout coffee at the Kunsthalle's tastefully decorated Café Liebermann, and left.

The art gallery sat overlooking the Elbe and Victor walked the short distance along the river bank to the ferry port.

He boarded behind an elderly couple who moved slower than he would have believed possible, waiting patiently until he had room to walk past. He took the rolled-up newspaper from a pocket of his overcoat, unrolled it and kept it in his left hand. In his right hand he held his coffee cup. After climbing the steps to the top deck, he found a spot on the port side from which he could watch the steps without being obvious. He counted twenty-two passengers.

The vessel was just under ninety feet long and twenty-four

feet wide. Smaller than he'd expected. Good. Too small for anything to happen. If there was an ambush waiting for him, it wouldn't take place here.

The waters of the Elbe were black like the sky above them. The horn sounded and the ferry pulled away. Victor pretended to be just another uninterested passenger while he studied the other people onboard. He was dealing with criminals, not trained operatives, and he saw nobody who could be either.

At each stop, he watched who embarked. The ferry was used by a range of people, some on their way back from work, others on their way out for the night, tourists, a few on the way to the night shift. He paid attention to anyone who wasn't young or old, but no one gave him reason enough to watch closely. A couple sitting across from Victor had no inhibitions about expressing their affection for one another. He did his best to ignore them.

At the fifth stop three people boarded, of which a lone man registered on Victor's radar. The man ascended the steps and with no subtlety paused to look around at the other passengers. He wore loose jeans and a long leather jacket. His square face was etched with purpose. After waiting too long to avoid being noticed he sat down in front of Victor.

'Get off at the next stop and follow me,' the man said without turning around.

At least you did that right, Victor thought.

Victor disembarked at the next stop. He abandoned the newspaper and switched the coffee cup to his left hand. In the distance, moonlit clouds silhouetted the harbour's tall metal cranes. The air was cold. Victor's suit jacket was unbuttoned. He had no gun to draw but it was easier to fight or run without a jacket than with.

The man in the leather jacket didn't wait for him. He was already walking along the riverside in the direction of the harbour. He walked fast, his strides as purposeful as his face had been. Victor didn't follow immediately but spent a moment observing the area. No one nearby.

Victor followed at the same pace as his guide to maintain the distance between them. He didn't know where he was being led to or what awaited him when he arrived, so a little space between them was a necessary precaution. When his guide reached their destination, Victor would have some time to analyse the situation while he caught up.

They turned away from the river and along a canal that ran between huge warehouses with tall, arched windows. There were few streetlights and the area was quiet and dark. The sound of traffic was in the distance. Victor's gaze swept back and forth, down and up, continually evaluating the environment for signs of an ambush and advantages to exploit in the event of one.

Working on the assumption that the guide was right-handed like ninety per cent of the world, if he drew a gun, he would naturally turn around in the opposite direction of his dominant hand to shoot at someone walking behind him. It was quicker that way. So Victor walked behind and to the right to maximise the turning distance, and therefore his own warning.

Up ahead the man stopped near to a wide alleyway. He turned to face Victor and waited for him to catch up. Victor decreased his pace, watching, listening. When he stopped before his guide, the other man gestured to the alleyway. Victor waited.

'Down there,' the man said. His hands were in the pockets of his coat.

Victor didn't move.

The guide remained stationary for a moment. 'I said down there.'

'I heard you the first time.'

The purposeful face showed understanding. 'Don't like people walking behind you?'

'No,' Victor admitted.

The man nodded thoughtfully. 'That's smart.'

He took his hands from his pockets and walked first into the alleyway. He didn't look back. Victor followed after a few seconds. There was nowhere to run or hide in the confined space of the alleyway so Victor stayed close his guide. If he pulled a gun, Victor wanted to be near enough to grab it.

Fifty feet down the alley, the man stopped again. He used a key to unlock a metal door set into one of the warehouses. Hinges squealed.

'Here we are,' he said.

The guide looked at Victor, gave a knowing smile when Victor didn't move, and then stepped through first.

Victor followed.

Inside, fluorescent ceilings lights illuminated a vast open space full of stacked crates and boxes. The air was cool and damp, smelling faintly of mould, rotting wood and marzipan. Victor stayed close to the guide. There were no people that he could see or hear.

The guide led Victor to the far side of the warehouse, heaved across the metal shutter of a freight elevator and stepped inside. He closed the shutter after Victor entered and pressed the button for the third floor. It took a few seconds for the ageing machine to come to life and squeaks and clanks accompanied their ascent. They left the odour of marzipan behind but the smell of mould and rotting wood deepened. Victor tilted his head to the left and then right to crack his neck.

He saw their legs first. Two pairs of boots and faded blue jeans standing near each other. He could hear one part way through telling a joke – something about a prostitute and a vacuum cleaner. He stopped speaking before the punchline as Victor came into view. Of the two, he was obviously the muscle, six-four and around two-twenty or -thirty. An even layer of stubble covered his head, chin and cheeks.

A woman stood close to the muscle. She was in her forties, five-nine, average build, lank black hair hanging over her ears. Her weighty duffel coat was buttoned all the way up. Victor smelled cigarette smoke and felt his mouth water. Four stubs lay crushed out by their feet.

The shutters clattered open. Victor stepped out, surveyed the level. Fewer boxes and crates than the ground floor, more open spaces. Empty metal shelving units, metal pillars. Old cement sacks lay in one corner, a stack of dust-covered plastic sheeting near the woman. The air was damp.

Three banks of fluorescent strip lights, of which only the middle bank was switched on, hung at regular intervals from the ceiling. There were no covers, just bare tubes, some burned out. Just enough light to illuminate the centre of the warehouse level. The floor to Victor's left and right faded into darkness except where the arched windows were set.

Victor noted the ways in and out. On the wall on the far side of the woman and the muscle, a sign above a half-open metal door denoted it as a fire exit. Along the same wall, near to a stained stainless-steel sink, another opening led through to an adjoining room. Sickly green and flaking paint covered the far wall. Dirt and grease smeared the bricks and filled the gaps between them. In places long cracks cut through the mortar.

The guide stood near the elevator. Victor walked forward. The flooring was narrow planks of wood. Some were cracked, loose, warped or missing entirely. Victor felt soft, rotting boards under his shoes and took a step to more solid footing. He positioned himself so he could keep the guide within his peripheral vision while he faced the woman.

For a long moment no one spoke. Victor assessed the woman and her hulking friend, as he knew he was likewise assessed. What they made of him, he didn't know. Victor was careful with his body language and facial expression to convey no threat while projecting no weakness.

'You must be the buyer,' the woman said eventually.

Her voice betrayed a measure of surprise. Whatever the woman had been expecting, Victor knew he wasn't it.

He nodded. 'And you must be Georg.'

'Not my real name, of course.'

'Of course,' Victor echoed.

Georg said, 'You're not what I was expecting.'

'I know.'

The overhead lighting created deep shadows under Georg's cheekbones, nose, bottom lip. Her eyes were almost invisible in the darkness of their sockets.

'Are you carrying any weapons?' she asked.

'Not unless you count my coffee.'

Georg's thin lips stretched outwards slightly. 'That's good,' she said. 'But I have to say I'm more concerned about firearms than I am hot beverages.'

'I have no gun.'

'You'll have to forgive me if I don't take your word for it.' She raised a gloved hand, motioning to the muscle while her gaze stayed locked on Victor. 'Make sure he's telling the truth.'

The huge guy next to Georg strode towards Victor, eyes narrowed, thick jaw clenched, elbows bent outwards as though he was so laden with muscle he couldn't walk any other way. The effort to intimidate was basic at best, especially when as he got closer it became apparent that a quarter of the bulk was made up of fat. Victor kept the observation to himself.

He stood still as large hands patted him down around the legs, arms and torso. He noticed the muscle had a .45 calibre Colt tucked into his jeans, hidden but not well enough. He gestured for Victor to raise his arms, and he did. When the search had finished, the muscle walked back over to Georg.

'He's clean.'

'I'm glad to hear that,' Georg said to Victor. 'It would have been very bad for you had we found anything.'

'I can imagine.'

'Your German's excellent,' Georg said, taking two steps closer. 'But you're not German. What are you, American?'

'Sometimes,' he answered.

Lines deepened in Georg's forehead. 'You're really not what I was expecting.'

'You said that once already.'

'Let me explain myself.'

Victor brought the cup to his lips and swallowed.

'In my line of work I meet all kinds of people, all different, but what I get for them tells me a lot about who they are. Let's take you, for example. You don't have to say what you do for a living as what you're buying might as well be a business card.'

Victor remained stationary and silent. He didn't know where Georg was headed, and he didn't care, but it seemed polite not to interrupt.

'I'm not sure what the correct euphemism is these days but I've dealt with your kind before,' Georg continued. 'Not often, but more than a few times. And when I have I've always been able to analyse that person completely within seconds of us meeting. It's not difficult. They try so hard to make out they're fearsome when they're actually not, else they really are that scary and they don't need to try.' She paused. 'But you're neither.'

'I'll take that as a compliment.'

'I'm not sure I meant it as one.'

'I'll still take it as a compliment.'

Georg stepped closer and stared hard at Victor. Her eyes were bloodshot, pupils dilated. On something stronger than just nicotine. 'I'm really not going to find out who you are, am I?'

'No,' Victor said. 'And you wouldn't want to.'

'A shame.' Georg sighed and perched herself on a crate and used a hand to wipe something from her jeans. 'Let's do some business.'

Victor nodded. 'I take it you have all the goods on the list.'

Georg counted off on her fingers as she said, 'Russian army blasting caps, nine-millimetre pistol with threaded barrel, silencer, pick gun, and fourteen pounds of cyclotrimethylenetrinitramine with the bits to make it go ka-boom. Did I pronounce that right, by the way?'

'You did,' Victor assured. 'I want to check everything.'

'Of course, my boy, I would have expected nothing less. You're a professional, after all.' She drew out the words. 'But so am I. And I'd like to see the money first.'

With his free hand, Victor slowly reached into an outer pocket. He did so while closely watching what the muscle and the guide were doing. There were no tension-relieving gestures, no shifting of weight, nothing to suggest they were waiting to put a pre-planned course of action into play when he showed he had the money. Satisfied this wasn't an ambush, Victor withdrew the slim bundle of hundred-euro notes.

Georg dropped down from the crate and inched closer. She stared at the money. 'That doesn't look like enough to me.'

'It's half of it.'

Georg's eyes rose to meet Victor's. She spoke quietly, menacingly. 'Then you've not only wasted my time but insulted me. And neither is a very wise move for a man in your position.'

'After I have the goods you can come with me to pick up the rest of the money,' Victor explained. 'Or send one of your men to do so.'

'That's not how I do business.'

'And ferries, empty warehouses and guards with forty-fives aren't how I do business,' Victor countered. 'This is the price you pay for how things have been conducted thus far.'

The muscle touched a hand to his gun. His expression was half-surprised, half-annoyed. Georg considered for a few seconds.

'What's to stop me taking that money and having the location of the second half beaten out of you?'

The guide and the muscle both stiffened in readiness for what might follow.

Victor kept his gaze locked on Georg. 'One, you'd lose a valuable future customer. And two,' he said, voice calm, emotionless. 'I'd kill you and your men inside ten seconds.'

The muscle didn't like that answer. His scowl intensified and his knuckles whitened. The guide's back straightened. Victor ignored them both. He watched Georg's reaction, first shock and anger that eventually became a smile and Victor knew he'd played it correctly.

'Okay,' she said, 'we'll do it your way.'

CHAPTER 6

Victor heard them a few seconds before he saw them. They entered fast, through the entrance on the wall next to the sink – five men full of intent, four with guns in hand. One shotgun. Three handguns. They didn't move or look like trained professionals but the way they held their weapons showed they were no strangers to violence.

The muscle reacted fast, turning and reaching for the Colt but a shout to stop and muzzles pointed his way made him think twice. The guide showed the palms of his hands while Georg kicked a crate in anger, or disgust or both.

Victor remained as he was. Aside from the elevator there was no exit close enough to risk moving to, and no way to get the shutter opened and closed before bullets started taking pieces out of him. Until he knew what was happening, there was nothing else he could do.

As he entered, the last of the intruders shouted, 'Ah, my dear Georg. Fancy finding you here.'

He was short, slight of build, dressed in a cheap suit. His hands were free of weapons but Victor paid him the most attention. The others moved closer and spread out, one covering Georg, the guide and Victor. Two at the muscle. The one with the shotgun pointed it at Victor. *Typical*.

Georg held her arms out questioningly. 'What are you doing here, Krausse?'

The man in the cheap suit stepped into the light. He was maybe forty years old. His thinning hair was black and short. Pockmarks covered the skin of his cheeks and forehead.

'I could ask you the same thing, Georg,' Krausse said, glancing around. 'But it looks to me like you're conducting some business, and without my prior knowledge.'

'Get out of here, Krausse,' Georg shouted, 'and take your clowns with you. What we're doing has nothing to do with you.'

'Oh, but it does,' Krausse laughed. 'We're business partners, remember?'

'We *were*,' Georg corrected.

Malice was in Krausse's smile. 'I'll be the judge of that.' He looked at Victor. 'Who's the suit?'

'What does it matter? He's no one.'

'It matters.' Krausse gestured Victor's way. 'Who are you?'

Victor stood casually. 'Like she said, no one.'

'You will be no one if you don't tell me what you're doing here.'

Victor glanced at each of Krausse's men. The three with handguns were twitchy – lots of little movements, swallowing. Light caught the sweat on their skin. The one with the shotgun was calmer, more focused, his small eyes barely blinking. The nostrils of his flat, misshapen nose flexed with relaxed, regular breaths.

After a moment Victor said, 'I'm making a buy.'

'And what are you buying?'

'Flowers for my mother.'

A couple of Krausse's men smiled.

Krausse exhaled. 'Funny fucker, aren't you?'

'I'm reading a joke book.'

Georg looked over a shoulder. 'Do us all a favour and stay quiet.'

'That's good advice,' Krausse said. 'We don't have to get unpleasant. I'm just here to take my rightful share of any transactions.'

'You mean you're here to steal,' Georg said.

Krausse smirked in response. 'If that's how you want to put it, my sweet, I'm not going to argue.' He turned to Victor. 'What are you buying? And think about your answer before you speak this time.'

Victor remained silent.

'He's buying explosives,' Georg said after a few seconds. 'A gun, stuff like that.'

'Interesting.' Krausse raised his eyebrows at Victor and nodded. 'Are they for your mother too?'

'She likes to stay active.'

Krausse laughed and his men joined him, guns lowering a few inches. Victor watched the guy with the shotgun turn to one of the others and shake his head in disbelief. The shotgun barrel angled down a fraction.

Krausse looked back to Georg. 'Where the hell did you find this guy?'

'He found me.'

'Figures. Just how much explosive is he buying?'

Georg shrugged. 'A reasonable amount.'

44

Krausse smiled at Victor. 'Then knowing Georg, you'll be paying an unreasonable amount for it.' He looked at one of his men. 'Take his cash.'

The man who approached Victor was about the same height – an inch or two over six feet – but bigger at the neck, shoulders and especially waistline. His face was hard, serious. He stank.

'You packing?' he asked as he came closer.

Victor said, 'Not unless you count my coffee.'

In the edge of his vision, Victor caught Georg glancing his way. Victor didn't glance back.

The gunman lowered his weapon as he approached. 'Just keep your hands where I can see them.'

He patted Victor down with his left hand. Not as thorough as Georg's muscle, but thorough enough. The man took the stack of money from Victor's hand and held it up for Krausse to see. He half-turned away from Victor to do so. Victor waited a second and took a small sidestep to the right.

Krausse didn't look happy. 'That's not a lot of money.'

Before anyone could respond, a cell phone rang. Victor approved of the ringtone: *Water Music* by Handel. Krausse struggled to pull it from the pocket of his suit trousers. He looked at the screen for a moment before denying the call.

'I hate these things. They rule your life,' he said, putting it back in the pocket. 'Now, you were about to tell me where the rest of the money is.'

Victor didn't say anything. He glanced at the other three of Krausse's men. They weren't as stiff as they had been when they first arrived. They looked in control, relaxing more as time ticked by. Comfortable.

'He was going to take me to it after he'd collected the stuff,' Georg explained.

'Now he can take me instead.' Krausse looked at the guy with the money. 'Count it.'

His back to Victor, the man put his gun into the left pocket of his jacket and started thumbing through the notes.

'Do I get to keep the goods I'm here for?' Victor asked.

Krausse said, 'I told you that you're funny.'

'What if I say please?'

Krausse laughed, turned to his men with a look of amused astonishment. They smiled or shrugged back at him, guns as close to their waists as shoulders. Victor took another small sidestep. The one counting the money now blocked his line of sight to the two with handguns to his left. And vice versa.

Victor spoke to Krausse without looking at him. 'Are you sure you won't reconsider?'

'Oh, I'm quite sure,' Krausse said.

'Then you leave me no choice.'

Victor squeezed the coffee cup in his left hand. The lid popped clear and he reached inside, drew out a black folding knife, extended the blade and drove it into the lower back of the man in front of him.

He stiffened and screamed, dropping the money. Victor let go of the knife, grabbed the gun from the man's pocket, and pointed it at Krausse's head before anyone could react.

The man with the knife in his back groaned and sank to his knees. For a moment no one else moved or spoke. Hundred-euro notes floated to the floor.

Victor's gaze flicked between the three other gunmen. Their guns were back up and they were anxious, looking from him to

Krausse and back again, waiting for orders. No one looked like he was stupid enough to shoot while Victor had a gun on their boss, but he couldn't be certain.

Krausse slowly clapped. 'Impressive performance.' He glared at Victor. 'Bravo.'

Victor glared back. 'You should see what I do for an encore.'

'Then let's not go there.'

'We don't have to,' Victor said. 'I just want what I came here for.'

The man with the knife in his back tipped forward and fell on to his side. He lay in a foetal position. Blood pooled on the floor around him. Victor had stabbed him between the spine and left kidney. A potentially mortal wound, but he could be saved if treated soon. Victor hadn't wanted to kill him outright in case it inspired one of the others into seeking some kind of foolish vengeance resulting in them both getting killed. These guys were likely friends and he wanted them more concerned about helping the wounded man than anything else.

Georg's own guys were out of Victor's field of view but he could see Georg in his peripheral vision; while predictably nervous with the change in circumstances, she was far from panicking. Victor hoped all three of them would have the intelligence to stay out of proceedings.

Having a gun pointed at his brains didn't seem to have much effect on Krausse. His smile was gone but he was calm, annoyed more than scared.

'So how are we going to do this?' he asked.

'Start by having your men drop their weapons.'

Krausse shook his head. 'I don't think so.'

'I won't tell you twice.'

47

Krausse nodded as though he had expected that exact answer. 'You're fast, my friend, but both you and I know you're not fast enough to shoot me and all my men before getting killed yourself. You're not the suicidal type, are you?'

'Not lately.'

'Good. And I know if I so much as try to tell my men to fire you'll kill me before I finish the sentence.'

'Before you finish the first word.'

'I believe you,' Krausse said. 'So it's a stalemate and we'll all keep our guns.'

Krausse wasn't the threat, his thugs were, but he was right, they were too spread out to risk shooting at. If they weren't, Victor would have shot them all already.

He said, 'I'm going to leave the money where it is and then I'm going to walk out of here. You're going to let me.'

'What about the other half of the money?'

'It's in a trashcan on the corner of the street where Ballindamm meets Alstertor.'

'Then we're done.'

'Not quite. Where's the equipment?' Victor asked Georg.

Georg was silent.

'Tell him,' Krausse ordered.

Georg's voice was quiet, defeated. 'It's in a van nearby. I'll take you to it.'

'No, no, no.' Krausse shook his head. 'You stay here. We haven't finished.'

'You're going to get all the money,' Georg said. 'Just go.'

'You double-crossed me, Georg. And this isn't even the first time. I know about that deal you did for those Munich fuckers without me. What kind of a man would I be if I let such disre-

48

spect go unpunished? That's the reason I came here, so we could *discuss* your betrayal,' Krausse explained. 'Tell him where the van is and give him the keys. You're not going to need them again.'

'No.'

'Tell him.'

Georg straightened, defiant. 'No.'

'Tell him, Georg, or I'll let my boys work off some of their frustration on you until you feel like cooperating.'

'*Fuck you.*'

Victor knew what was going to happen in the silence before Georg pulled a gun. When she did, Victor was already moving, gaining half a second head start over the others. He dived behind a nearby stack of crates a moment ahead of one of Krausse's men opening fire. The loud report from the handgun echoed around the warehouse.

Blood splashed as Georg took the bullet in the left shoulder before she could fully raise her small pistol. She stumbled, managed to fire at Krausse, but missed, the round blowing a hole in the wall behind him. Georg corrected her aim for a second shot.

A shotgun blast hit her in the stomach.

Georg collapsed backwards, falling on to the sheeting heaped near the elevator. Blood glistened on the plastic.

Georg's men panicked and drew their own guns. Victor watched as the muscle was first to go down, bullets hitting him simultaneously in the chest and back. The guide lived a little longer.

When the shooting had stopped, Victor heard the clinking of expended shells but, crouched down behind the crates, he couldn't see Krausse or his men. There were no groans or screams so he knew there was no one wounded. The man he'd stabbed was silent, unconscious. Victor didn't know what was going to happen next and standing up didn't seem like the best way to find out. If they planned on shooting him too, the crates would provide some protection, assuming there was anything inside. If not, at least they blocked line of sight.

'You can come out now,' Krausse said.

'I'm actually quite comfortable where I am.'

Krausse laughed. 'Tell me, my new best friend, how long are you planning on staying behind there?'

Victor checked the gun, a Glock 17. Aside from a few scratches it looked reasonably maintained. He released the magazine, saw that it was loaded with 9 mm FMJs and quietly pushed it back into place. He carefully moved the slide to look into the chamber. It seemed clean but he blew into it in case there was any dirt. Glocks were as reliable as the sunset; still, it didn't hurt to be sure. Victor loaded a round into the chamber, pulling the slide slowly to lessen the noise.

He said, 'Let's say until you leave.'

'I'm starting to like you,' Krausse said back. 'And I really mean that. But you know as well as I do that I can't let that happen.'

Victor thought quickly. He couldn't stay where he was for long. The more time he took to act, the more time they would have to surround him. He slipped off his suit jacket.

'What about our deal?'

'Our deal?' Krausse laughed again. 'You mean the deal we made while you had a gun pointing at my face? If that's the one you mean, your bargaining position has been severely weakened since then.'

Before the shooting had started, Krausse was at Victor's one o'clock, Shotgun at his two, and the two other men at ten and nine. Victor figured that if he moved fast and Krausse and Shotgun hadn't strayed too far, he could drop them both before they could return fire. The problem was the guys at nine and ten o'clock, and the fact that if Victor killed Krausse and Shotgun he would get bullets in the ribs from the other two in return. Alternatively, if he killed those two, shotgun pellets would shred him instead.

Victor heard whispering but couldn't decipher the words. He could guess the topic of conversation well enough however. Him, or more specifically, how best to kill him. They were unlikely to be students of military tactics, but it wasn't difficult to pull off a pincer movement when outnumbering the enemy four to one. And even Sun Tzu would find it hard to come up with a workable defence against such an attack. *Think*, Victor told himself.

Overhead, a strip light flickered.

He heard footsteps approaching from either flank. In moments they would attack from both sides at once. He'd be dead in seconds. No time left to formulate a plan.

He fired.

CHAPTER 7

The first strip light exploded in a shower of sparks and glass. Victor took out another three lights with his next three bullets, needing an extra shot to destroy the fifth. The last to go was the strip light directly above him and he used his left arm as a shield against the raining shards of glass that followed its destruction.

The floor plunged into darkness.

Victor threw himself to the floor on his right, head and arms now out of the cover of the crates. He couldn't see anyone but fired at where Shotgun had been standing a few seconds before. Two shots, a double tap, torso height.

The yelp and sound of stumbling told him he'd scored a hit but not a fatal one. The Glock's muzzle flash gave away his position and he immediately rolled clear before the returning fire blew holes through the wooden floor.

Victor was on his feet and moving fast, not caring about the noise he made, only concerned about putting some distance between him and his enemies. He knew there was a corridor of clear space through the stacks of crates and he blindly headed down it. He heard bullets strike crates behind him. Sparks flew as one struck a metal pillar.

He stopped moving after a few seconds, crouched, paused, evaluated. He was somewhere on the other side of the elevator. Though he couldn't see exactly where, he referred to the image of the layout in his head to get some bearings, reaching out a hand to guide himself into cover.

Victor could hear Shotgun grunting and cursing, Krausse trying to get him to shut up. The other two weren't speaking. Their careful footsteps were quiet but still audible. Glass crunched under shoes. Maybe thirty feet away.

Victor did a quick ammo count. The Glock held seventeen rounds in a full magazine. He'd used six bullets to take out the lights and two on Shotgun. Nine left. Krausse's men had all fired a few rounds and so far no one had reloaded. He expected they would only after they'd depleted their magazines. Most people did. When that happened Victor might gain a window of opportunity, but he knew it could be a long wait until that opportunity presented itself.

Shotgun's grunting ceased. Either he had taken control of his pain or someone had clasped a hand over his mouth. Victor had heard no sound of him collapsing to the ground so he was still on his feet, and if he was on his feet he was still dangerous. He didn't have to have a good shot to hit Victor with a spread of buckshot.

He looked around. The central area of the warehouse was in complete darkness. Visibility was so limited that Victor could barely make out the Glock in his hand. The tall windows on each wall allowed some artificial light from the streetlights outside into the area, but not enough to see by unless someone strayed close to the walls. The light penetrated no more than a couple of yards and Krausse and his men weren't so stupid as to go near those areas.

Victor untied his laces and slipped off his shoes. He took one into his left hand. With just socks on his feet, he made no sound when he moved. The glass from the exploded strip lights lay along the centre of the space, and Victor planned to go nowhere near there. He stayed low, his left hand outstretched to guard against any collisions, and crept over to the wall on his right. He was careful to move along the exact centre between the two areas of light shining through the windows.

He pressed his back against the wall and peered into the dark. If he couldn't see his enemies then at least he couldn't be seen either. It would take maybe fifteen minutes until his eyes adjusted to the lack of light, but he doubted he could remain hidden from four men for that length of time or sightlessly find his way to an exit undiscovered. His only option was to kill them before they killed him.

He concentrated on listening. He could hear tentative footsteps and the creaking of floorboards in several places. No more glass crunched, so Victor knew they were staying away from the centre space. He estimated the origins of the noise but he didn't have enough bullets to trust to sound only. That was why he had the shoe.

As soon as he had a good idea of the location of the closest gunmen, he threw the shoe lightly towards where he'd been previously crouching near to the elevator. When it landed, it didn't sound much like a person moving, but to guys high on adrenalin it was close enough.

Muzzle flashes broke the darkness.

Twin bullseyes.

Victor put two rounds in close proximity to where the nearest flash had appeared, switched his aim, fired another two at the second, and dropped to the floor.

A shotgun blast took a chunk from the wall a couple of feet to the right of his head and sprayed brick dust into his face. Before he could shoot back, the shotgun fired again, and again, blowing holes in the masonry above him. Small pieces of brickwork dropped down over him.

He kept low until the shooting had stopped. Brick dust and grit covered his head and shoulders, and was in his eyes and mouth. Apart from the pain and irritation, he wasn't concerned about his eyes. He couldn't see anyway. But he was fighting back coughing from the dust in his throat. He spat it out as quietly as he could.

Someone started wailing and thrashing about, agony overriding the need for stealth. Krausse wasn't trying to shut his man up this time. He didn't want to give himself away and end up in a similar situation. Victor didn't know if the other guy he'd shot at was dead or if he'd missed. He had to assume he was combatready. Shotgun had shown he could still shoot and Victor imagined Krausse now had a gun in his hands too. That made three enemies. The Glock had five rounds left. Not even enough for two shots at each. A slim margin for error, considering he was virtually blind.

Victor kept low and moved away from the wall, found some more cover. His eyes streamed water. He kept his left hand out before him to feel his way around obstacles so he could blink rapidly to try to flush the dirt from his eyes.

He changed position, proceeding slowly, conscious he was

heading towards the line of broken glass. With the shot guy's screams masking every other sound, Victor needed to be careful not to collide with one of Krausse's men. He didn't know if they were stationary or moving about. If the stairs were on Victor's side of the floor, he would have made a break for them, but the only exits were the far side of his enemies.

Whoever was shot continued to scream, though the volume of his cries gradually diminished as the life drained from him. Another few minutes and he'd be silent. Hurry up and die so I can hear again, Victor silently encouraged.

He managed to blink away the last of the grit from his eyes and could once more make out the Glock. The screams reduced to little more than a whimper until Victor could hear his own breathing. He held the Glock outstretched and waited for some indication of where Krausse and his men were located. He heard no movement, no panicked breaths, only the shot guy's moans. Victor changed positions, moving towards the far side of the elevator.

The floor creaked beneath his foot.

In response two shotgun blasts hit a nearby stack of crates. Splinters of wood flew off in all directions. He felt some snag his suit jacket. He dropped prone as two handguns opened fire an instant later. Bullets thudded into the crates shielding him, zipped over his head.

The firing didn't cease. They were shooting at the general area, trusting to firepower and hoping to score a lucky hit. The noise was deafening. For Victor it was either stay put or make a break for it. Moving into the line of fire was a bad tactic, but lying still and hoping not to be hit seemed like an even worse course of action.

Rounds continued to strike his position, hitting the floor, crates, and pillars. Shotgun pellets made a crater in the floorboards close enough for Victor to feel vibrations through the wooden planks. He knew he was running out of time.

There was a lull in the shooting. A handgun stopped firing. At first, he thought someone was reloading, but he heard another sound between the other gunshots. *Water Music* by Handel.

Victor didn't let the advantage escape. He made his move, quickly peering around the stack of crates. He saw nothing. He tried the other side, and a split second before the phone went silent, Victor saw the faint blue of the screen glowing through the thin fabric of Krausse's cheap suit trousers.

Victor angled the Glock and fired. Krausse screamed.

Victor was up on his feet and moving before Shotgun returned fire. The huge flash from the end of the barrel briefly illuminated him and Victor shot back with a double tap. Shotgun fell sideways into an area of light near one of the windows. Very dead.

The last gunman took a shot at Victor. The muzzle flashed on the far side of the warehouse, maybe sixty feet away. Victor fired, on the move, rushing closer. Too eager.

He knew he'd missed before the returning muzzle flash made it obvious. The bullet sparked off a metal pillar to Victor's left. He headed right, not risking firing back again at this range with only one bullet in the Glock.

Forty-five feet and the gunman fired at him again. He hadn't changed position, somewhere near the sink. The bullet didn't come close. He was shooting at noise only and Victor was a fast target. He headed back to the right, clipped a crate with

57

his leg and stumbled. The next round blew a hole through a windowpane.

Less than thirty feet. His enemy fired again, this time from a different position, behind a pillar. The bullet came close enough for Victor to hear the sonic snap. Fifteen feet. Another shot missed and Victor braced for the next one that he felt sure was going to hit.

No shot. Empty gun.

Victor heard the magazine clatter on the floor and the gunman frantically trying to reload. Victor closed the last few yards fast and the gunman came into view – a blurry shape of near black against the darkness. Victor heard a new magazine slammed into place and the shape moved, collapsing backwards, Victor's last bullet embedded in the gunman's chest.

Victor stopped, took a much-needed deep breath, and listened. He heard one man groaning somewhere in the dark. Everyone else was dead or dying silently. Victor dropped the empty Glock and prised the fully loaded one from his enemy's hand. He checked the corpse's pockets, finding a wallet and a lighter. He took both, glad there hadn't been any cigarettes as well to test his resolve.

He followed the map in his head to where his shoes lay, slipped them on, and then to where Georg had fallen, the groans growing louder the closer he got. Victor used the lighter to push back the darkness and saw Georg lying on her back, hands pressing down over the bloody mess of her abdomen. Blood pooled on the plastic sheeting beneath her and trickled on to the floor and drained through the gaps in the narrow boards. She stared up at Victor, her ghost-white face contorted by agony. Tears glinted on her cheeks.

'*Please . . .*'

Careful to avoid the blood, Victor checked Georg's pockets. 'Please what?'

'Help me.' Georg's voice was thin. 'I'll pay you . . . Anything you want.'

Victor held open Georg's empty wallet. 'What with?'

Georg didn't answer. Victor put back the wallet, ignored a cell phone, and pocketed a set of van keys.

'*Help me*,' Georg begged again.

'You're wearing body armour,' Victor explained, 'which is why you took a twelve-gauge to the gut and are still alive. But it's a concealable vest, so it has maybe nineteen layers of Kevlar. Enough to stop a nine mil travelling at twelve hundred feet per second, but not nine pellets of buckshot at the same speed. Maybe absorbed fifty per cent of the energy though, so none of those pellets reached your spine, but plenty of power left to shred your intestines. And that's without the slug in your shoulder. You'll be dead in fifteen minutes maximum. There's nothing I can do to stop that.'

'Phone . . . an ambulance.'

'And have my voice recorded by the emergency services? I don't think so.'

He found the guy he'd stabbed and pulled the knife free. Custom-made, all ceramic, with a kris edge and gladiator point. Far too good a weapon to waste in a corpse even without its sentimental value. Victor wiped the blade on the dead man's jacket before folding it away.

'I'm sorry . . . this . . . happened,' Georg said.

Her tone of voice really did sound sincere, but in Victor's experience excruciating pain had a habit of making people very apologetic. He stood.

'Help me . . . please,' she spluttered between grunts, 'or kill me . . . *it hurts* . . .'

Victor approached and stopped a few inches short of the blood pool. He angled the Glock.

Georg's gaze tracked the gun, but her eyes closed so she didn't have to watch. Not that there was enough time to register a muzzle flash and fear the ensuing bullet before impact, or enough time for the brain to recognise its own destruction. But Victor didn't fire.

Instead, he squatted down and reached into Georg's duffel coat. He withdrew the cell phone, dialled 112, switched it to speakerphone, and placed it in one of Georg's hands. Her eyes opened and stared at Victor, shocked.

'Remember to forget me,' Victor said before the line connected.

He headed to the elevator as the emergency operator politely asked which service Georg required.

CHAPTER 8

Central Intelligence Agency, Virginia, USA

Associate Deputy Director for the National Clandestine Service Roland Procter took a seat in one of the four black leather armchairs positioned in the corner of his office. The area was set to create an informal space for meetings and discussion, but Procter was usually happier to talk from behind his big desk. His current guest, however, warranted a more even playing field.

Enjoying the chair across from Procter was Clarke, who, though the same age, was at least eighty pounds lighter, several shades paler, and looking not too dissimilar to a French fry in a suit. But if Clarke was a French fry, Procter had to admit he was definitely the hamburger on their collective plate. Though Procter wasn't sure how much he weighed, it had to be north of two fifty. It wasn't genetics, it wasn't big bones, it was just that Procter liked to eat.

Clarke wasn't CIA and his credentials said Pentagon, but whatever his laminate proclaimed, Procter wasn't sure exactly who Clarke worked for these days. Clarke could have worked for none of the big agencies or all of them at once, or maybe one that was so secret Procter hadn't even heard of it. It didn't matter. What mattered was Clarke shared the same principles as Procter and the same balls to put those principles to good use.

'I've received word from my man,' Procter began. 'It seems there was a minor problem last week with the supplier in Hamburg.'

Clarke's eyebrows rose. 'What kind of a problem?'

'The fatal kind.' Procter gave a quick explanation of the facts as he knew them.

'Did Tesseract get away clean?'

'He claims so, and our people in Germany back up his story. The police have the killings down as a gangland incident. Georg, who is in fact a woman, was shot up pretty bad, but she's had three surgeries and is going to make it. I'm told she's conscious, and keeping her mouth closed. Not that it would make much difference either way. The cops over there aren't too concerned about a bunch of criminals blasting holes in each other. Privately, they're celebrating the destruction of two local gangs. They aren't looking for anyone, let alone our boy.'

'Good.'

'You sound almost disappointed,' Procter said.

Clarke ignored the barb. 'We have a real problem though. Regarding Bucharest.'

'Which is?'

'One of Kasakov's people heard Tesseract's shot. A Russian guy has spoken to someone inside Bucharest PD. They'd found the assassin's headless corpse by then. It was lying on a rooftop next to a sniper rifle, six hundred yards and a clear line of sight from the front door of the Grand Plaza where Vladimir Kasakov happened to be staying.'

'So what did Bucharest PD tell him?'

'What they knew about the shooter. Croatian freelancer, on Interpol's files. Guy was a real bastard, did mob hits for different people. And now Kasakov knows for sure someone tried to kill him. And he must know that someone intervened on his behalf. Maybe he knows who wants him dead or maybe he doesn't. But one thing's for certain: he's going to want to know who came to his aid and he's going to keep his head down.'

Procter shrugged. 'Doesn't bother me.'

'It bothers me.'

'It shouldn't. We'll just spin it to throw him off the scent. We'll make him think that the Croatian guy was killed for some other reason, and Kasakov's survival was nothing more than a lucky coincidence.'

Clarke had already thought of that, of course, Procter knew, which was why his returning point flowed so easily. 'True,' Clarke said, 'though it would have been better for him to carry on thinking he was beyond threat. Knowing how near he came to being bones in a box could complicate matters for us. Kasakov might change his plans, increase his security, reduce his profile. Hell, he could retire from arms dealing and take up politics.'

'It won't be a problem,' Procter assured.

'But if he was too spooked—'

'Then he'll calm down. Kasakov is well aware of the risks involved in the dubious way he conducts his life. Trafficking illicit heavy munitions to every dictator, warlord and death squad on the planet isn't something you stay in long term if you have trouble sleeping at night. Besides, do you really think no one's tried to take him out before? He's one tough son of a bitch. It'll take a hell of a lot more than a gunshot to scare the guy.'

'There's a difference between being scared and acting smart.'

'Trust me, that bastard's got balls of granite. Did you know that the French secret service tried to take him out back before he was a really big player? He screwed them on an Exocet sale. Came this close too.' Procter held his thumb and index finger an inch apart.

'I did not,' Clarke said evenly.

'Very few people do. It went down in Morocco, I believe. He was on vacation. A DGSE team went in shooting, took out most of Kasakov's retinue but only wounded him. Shot half his ear off. Did that stop him? No, it did not. He's even helped them sell some Mirage jets since then. And let's remember, the French came a lot closer in Morocco than our Croatian friend just did in Bucharest. I'm telling you, Peter, you don't need to be concerned about what old Vladdie boy will or will not do.'

Clarke's face hardened. 'It's not with Kasakov where my only concern lies.'

Procter sat forward. 'We've been through this before, and I do understand your reservations about my new employee.'

'I'm not sure you really do.'

'Listen, any risk he might potentially pose is more than offset by his value.'

'That value is still debatable at this stage.'

'I think you'll find his value has very recently been demonstrated.'

Clarke shrugged his narrow shoulders dismissively. 'So the prodigy passes the first real test, so what? That means he's useful, so are a lot of people. A lot more manageable people.'

'I think you're underestimating just how lucky we were to have him. In case you've forgotten, we found out someone was going to try to put a bullet in Kasakov all of forty-eight hours before it went down. Kasakov was off the grid and we had no way of warning him even if we knew where he was. All we had was one lousy intercepted phone call revealing where it was going to happen. We didn't know who was going to do it or how. We sent Tesseract in blind and he got the job done. This whole op of ours would have crumbled before we got to first base if Kasakov had been killed in Bucharest. So tell me, who else could we have sent, unofficially, to get us out of that potential disaster without also putting us in the spotlight? Me? *You?*'

Clarke straightened in his seat and put his right index finger to good use. 'Don't try to bait me, Roland. I have expressed reasonable doubts about who you've chosen to employ for this operation, none of which relate to Tesseract's abilities. May I remind you it's his loyalty, reliability, and accountability that I have issues with.'

'You did just remind me,' Procter said beneath arched eyebrows.

Clarke exhaled strongly. His normally pale face was flushed red.

'Peter, calm down before you give yourself an aneurysm. You came to me, remember? You asked me for help, not the other way around. Obviously, I'm glad you did, but we agreed at the beginning of our little scheme that you would allow me to run things on the ground as I saw fit. That includes whom I choose to put out there. Tesseract is extremely capable and utterly deniable. Anything about his history before he began working for us is irrelevant to me as long as he produces results.'

'As long as he does.'

'The point is,' Procter continued, lowering his tone, 'we needed him, we used him, and he pulled it off perfectly. We can't ask for any more.'

'But he is a risk to us, you can't deny that.'

'And I'm not. But his value outweighs the risk.'

'For now,' Clarke said. 'But remember, however much of a risk he poses at present, that risk only increases over time. And all the while our ability to manage it diminishes.'

'Then we'll act before we get into the red.'

'I hope so.'

'You worry too much.'

'You don't worry enough.'

Procter smiled. 'Which is why I have you,' he said. 'But let's get back on track, yeah? You'll be pleased to know Tesseract is in Berlin for the next phase of the operation.'

'Good. Let's see if your boy can keep us on a winning streak.'

'He will,' Procter said with the utmost confidence. 'And with Xavier Callo now in our custody too, things are progressing nicely.'

'What's the strategy with Callo?'

'I've left it up to the boys on the ground. I'm not going to play armchair interrogator from six thousand miles away. He's spent the last forty-eight hours in a car trunk with only a few sips of water so he'll to be pretty shaken by now. They'll get him on site by tomorrow, I expect, and then leave him to stew in an unlit cell for a few hours. Then they'll go in hard.'

'Sounds delightful,' Clarke said.

Procter leaned forward again. 'No less than he deserves.'

He heaved himself out of the chair and walked to the

window. Outside, early morning sunlight bathed the Virginia countryside. Procter loved this part of the country. If it were up to him, he'd move out of DC and get a nice rural house, maybe with a few acres for a horse. Patricia was too enamoured with city life though to give it up without one hell of a fight. Procter, a man who was always careful picking his battles, knew he wasn't going to win that one just yet.

'How sure are you he knows what we need?' Clarke asked.

'Oh, he knows all right. If there's a better link out there to Ariff's network then we'll never find it. That Egyptian scumbag has done a mighty fine job of staying under the radar for a very long time now.'

'Who's going to be asking the questions?' Clarke asked. 'Because whoever is in that room with Callo is going to learn a lot of information. Information that, when all this is over, could end up being used as leverage over us.'

'I think you're overestimating who I've got in mind. There'll be the British contractors you supplied and vouched for, of course, and they only know the barest of details. So no problems there. The guy overseeing it is Agency, and though he's an ambitious little prick, he's got balls of purest cookie dough. He won't breathe a word to anyone, ever.' Procter smiled. 'He's my own personal bitch. I've got enough shit on him I could ask him to cut a leg off for me and he'd say thank you for the privilege while he bled out. I keep him so strung out he doesn't know whether I'm Jesus Christ or the devil himself.'

The last part prised something resembling a smile from Clarke. Procter said, 'He'll do what we need done and within forty-eight hours we'll know enough to set up the next phase of the operation.'

Clarke seemed pleased for once. 'Then everything is going exactly as planned.'

'Exactly as planned,' Procter echoed. 'It's going to be beautiful.'

CHAPTER 9

Berlin, Germany

According to the dossier, Adorján Farkas would be arriving in Berlin the next day for a maximum stay of seven days. He would then return to his native Hungary, where, Victor presumed, either the Hungarian would be an exponentially harder target, or his killing would lose its value. A lifelong member of the Hungarian mob, Farkas was now fifty-two years old and making a name for himself outside the typical organised crime industries of drugs, extortion and prostitution, most notably in international people trafficking, and arms dealing.

The latter was why, the dossier stated, Farkas was to be removed from existence. In particular it was because Farkas was currently making a lot of money buying assault rifles from manufacturers in Eastern Europe and illegally selling them on to buyers in the Middle East. Farkas didn't seem like a particularly high-value target on the global scale of bad guys; there was probably more to it than just the arms sales.

The absence of a specific motive was further evidence of Victor's need-to-know status. Farkas was likely part of a chain Victor's handler wanted disrupting, and killing the Hungarian was either the simplest, or perhaps the only way of stopping the guns he traded killing Americans further along the line. Though, having had saved the life of one arms trafficker already, Victor knew that nothing was necessarily as obvious as it appeared.

Aside from an exact motive, the rest of the information on Farkas was particularly extensive – a lengthy biography, lists of associates, personal details and so on – but mostly useless. Recent photographs and Farkas's location were the most important, and sometimes only, information Victor needed. Precious few other facts were relevant to the completion of the job. And as those who compiled dossiers didn't operate in the field, what was relevant to them and relevant to Victor could be very different. Still, given the specifics for this particular job, it was better to have too much information than too little.

Farkas had to be blown up. No accident, no suicide, no gunshot wound, no slit throat. Farkas could only meet his end via high explosives. And only the explosives supplied by Georg would do.

Again, Victor hadn't been graced with an explanation, but, as with the motivation for Farkas's demise, he had a reasonable idea why this death had to be so particular. Blame. His employer wanted the spotlight for Farkas's murder to shine on some individual or faction, and whoever those people may be, the explosives Victor used would implicate them.

He examined the cyclotrimethylenetrinitramine he'd

acquired in Hamburg. Usually referred to as RDX, the compound was a common military- and industrial-use high explosive and one of the most destructive of all explosive materials. With the addition of some chemicals and motor oil, RDX formed plastic explosives like C-4, which Victor would have preferred to work with, but unfortunately he didn't have that luxury.

The fourteen pounds of RDX Victor had collected from Georg's van was packed in seven two-pound military-use blocks. Whereas plastic explosives were malleable, RDX was a hard white crystalline substance. With the blasting caps that accompanied the explosives, Victor constructed a compact bomb from a single block of RDX that had more than enough power to kill one man from several yards away. Using all fourteen pounds would have formed a devastatingly powerful device, but its larger size would render it problematic to transport, too difficult to plant secretly, and would make if difficult to fulfil one of the contract's requirements. Despite the obvious risks associated with using a bomb, Victor's employer had stated there must be no collateral damage. Not that Victor needed to be told. He wasn't in the habit of killing bystanders, but with explosives that was always a possibility, and the primary reason he didn't work with them.

Georg hadn't supplied any remote detonating equipment, so Victor needed to place the bomb somewhere only Farkas would trigger it. He could form an ad-hoc remote detonator by rigging a cellular phone to the blasting caps and using a second phone to trigger the bomb, but Victor wasn't keen on that idea unless he had no other choice. Such a bomb would require him to be in visual contact with the target at the time of detonation, which not only limited where the bomb could be placed, but also forced Victor to be in close proximity to the assassination. That and the fact that the one time Victor needed full service could very well be the exact moment when he had zero bars.

From the information supplied, however, Victor had a rough plan in mind.

For his stay in Berlin Farkas had rented out the penthouse in a block of luxury holiday apartments. He would have an entourage with him – anything between three and five of his mob subordinates – all of whom, based on Farkas's previous trips abroad, would stay in the penthouse too. There was no intelligence on whether or not they would be armed.

The weather was cold but sunny in Berlin when Victor passed the apartment building. It was a grand structure in the heart of Prenzlauer Berg, one of Berlin's most desirable districts. Four beautiful stone storeys rose from the street with one subterranean level beneath. Maybe two or three apartments per floor with a single penthouse.

Victor spent a while exploring Prenzlauer Berg, both routinely checking for surveillance and to get a feel for the area he would be operating within. It had escaped much of the devastation of the Second World War and so had been mercifully spared the post-war development the rest of the city had endured. What was built in the late nineteenth century as a working-class district was now a very affluent part of Berlin. There were many tasteful bars and restaurants, high-end fashion boutiques, delicatessens and cafés. Victor could see why a wealthy Hungarian gangster would choose to stay in this part of the city.

He took a seat outside a café bustling with people on their lunch hour. Clothes stores and eateries lined the leafy street. Opposite him was the metro station, particularly clean even by Berlin's high standards. He watched the people going about their days, especially the men in their early and mid thirties in their casual-but-stylish clothing.

After he'd finished his iced tea, Victor walked to a department store and perused the men's clothing section. A slim young guy asked if he could be of assistance.

Victor said, 'I'm going for casual, but stylish.'

He dismissed anything too bright or anything he would look too good in, much to the young man's confusion. He settled on two pairs of dark jeans, some patterned button-down shirts, a cream sweater, and a tan blazer, all loose fitting. He also picked up underwear, loafers, a leather shoulder bag, designer sunglasses and a pre-pay phone from different stores.

Victor's modest hotel was three stops along the line. He wanted to be close to where Farkas was staying, but far enough away that he would have the opportunity to conduct counter surveillance if he needed to take a direct route. In his single room, Victor changed into his new clothes. Suits were his preferred clothing for urban environments, but wearing one would make him stand out in Prenzlauer Berg, where men his age opted for more bohemian attire.

Earlier, he'd noted there were two possible locations from which to conduct surveillance – a chic coffee shop on the same side of the street as the apartment building, and a cocktail bar on the opposite side of the road. He entered the bar, bought a still lemonade with a slice of lime and sat outside.

The view wasn't a perfect one but he could see the entrance

to the building, and the bar justified his presence for what could potentially be many hours over several days. He took out a small notebook and pen and placed them on the table next to his drink. He made a record of anyone who entered or exited the building, and waited for someone who met his requirements. He was hoping to spot someone who looked like he or she wasn't a guest – a maid or janitor perhaps – but he saw no one who fitted the bill.

Eventually, he watched a man and a woman leave the building at the same time. They were in their late twenties, a good-looking couple who knew it and couldn't keep their eyes on where they were heading or their hands to themselves. As soon as they appeared, he could tell they were perfect for his requirements. In Victor's line of work, love could be an extremely useful emotion to exploit.

It was easy to follow them. Even if he hadn't been careful – which he always was – he doubted they would have seen him, let alone paid him any attention. They walked slowly, like most couples seemed to do, blissfully unaware of the amount of space on the sidewalk they took up. Annoyed singletons had no choice but to walk around them.

He followed them into a bar a few minutes after they'd entered. Inside, a lively audience of fans watched a Bundesliga game on several big screens. Victor spotted the couple at a table in one of the marginally quieter corners. He ordered a beer and stood where he could watch the couple while looking as if he was just another sports fan in for the game. The bar was warm and Victor watched the man take off his jacket and hang it over the chair. Like Victor, he had a beer, which he drank quickly. When the woman finished her white wine, the man stood up to get a second round. Placing his own beer down, Victor made his move, negotiating a path through the busy crowd while the man made his way to the bar.

Taking out his phone and pretending to write a text, he swayed a little as he squeezed past the table where the woman sat, brushing himself against the man's jacket hanging off the chair. Victor felt the weight of keys in one of the pockets, and faked a stumble, the phone falling from his fingers. He cursed under his breath as he leaned over to retrieve it with his left hand while his right slid into the man's jacket pocket to remove the keys. He stood up, shaking his head. In his peripheral vision, he saw the woman glance at him but there was no suspicion, just an amused smile, assuming he was a drunk sports fan.

At the bar, Victor took another mouthful of beer before leaving. He already knew where the closest locksmith was located and made his way there to get a copy cut. Returning to the bar, he handed over the keys to a barmaid, pretending he'd found them near to where the young couple sat.

The sports fans roared as the ball hit the back of the net.

It took a while to find a store that sold art supplies, where Victor bought paints, paper, brushes, pastels, and a bottle of pure graphite powder. At a cosmetics counter of a department store, he purchased a foldaway make-up brush with very soft bristles, blusher, and a bottle of perfume recommended to him by a friendly sales assistant when he asked for advice on buying for his girlfriend.

On his way back to his hotel he threw away his purchases save for the graphite powder and make-up brush. In his room, he changed into his suit and dipped the make-up brush into the graphite powder before folding it away and placing it in a pants pocket. He was running a little late for his appointment and walked slowly.

He found the realtor pacing outside the apartment building. She stood around five-seven, late twenties, smartly dressed in a navy trouser suit that gave her an air of pure business without hiding the very obvious facts she was an attractive and shapely woman. Her blonde hair was shoulder length and swept back from her face by the breeze. Predictably, her expression was one of annoyance and impatience. She checked her watch.

He was four feet away before she realised who he was. He gave her a polite smile. She didn't smile back.

'Miss Friedman, I take it,' Victor said in a Hamburg accent. 'I'm Mr Krausse. I'm sorry I'm late.' He offered no explanation.

Without sincerity she said, 'That's okay.'

He acted as though he didn't notice her tone.

'Thank you for taking the time to show me around.'

He offered his hand and she took it. There was hardly any grip.

She motioned towards the front door. 'Shall we?'

Friedman led him to the penthouse and unlocked and opened the door and stepped inside. Victor made sure to follow closely. The alarm system emitted a dull warning. There was a small box positioned in the far corner of the hallway where the walls met the ceiling. He couldn't tell just by looking at it what kind of alarm system it was, but given the exclusivity of the apartments, the security system would be more sophisticated than a

76

standard photo-sensor alarm. Probably a radar-based or more likely a passive infrared motion detector.

Radar-based motion detectors worked by emitting bursts of microwave radio energy, or ultrasonic sound waves, and reading the reflected pattern as those waves bounced back to the device. When an intruder entered the area and altered the pattern, the alarm sounded. With a passive infrared motion system, the device detected the increase in infrared energy caused by an intruder's body heat. It wouldn't be much fun trying to defeat either, but if human nature had its way, Victor wouldn't have to.

He positioned himself to watch as Friedman pressed buttons on the keypad. It would have been impossible to get close enough to see which numbers she pressed without alerting her, but he could see the movements of her hand and elbow as her finger hovered over the keypad. She pressed the first button, then he watched her elbow drop, then pause, then drop again; another pause, and then it moved back up to the top for the final number. Victor repeated the pattern in his head until he had it memorised. *Press, down, press, down, press, up, up, press.*

The realtor guided him through the apartment's lounge, kitchen, bathroom, and three bedrooms, the master of which had its own bathroom. Each room was lavishly decorated, leather sofas in the lounge, marble in the bathroom, stainless steel and granite in the kitchen. It had all the essentials of modern upscale living – dishwasher, huge wide-screen television, surround sound, latest games consoles and espresso machine. Everything a travelling mob boss could need.

He took his time walking around each room, examining

every fixture and piece of furniture. He saw the realtor in his peripheral vision checking her watch with increasing frequency. He pretended not to notice.

Eventually he dragged it out long enough that her phone rang and he wasn't surprised to see that she answered it without excusing herself. He nodded politely – a silent take-your-time signal – and she stepped into the kitchen to talk in private.

Victor hurried into the hallway. He removed the make-up brush from his pocket, unfolded it, and very gently swept the tips of the bristles against the alarm keypad. The fine graphite powder stuck to the oil left by Friedman's finger on four of the ten numbered buttons. One, two, five and eight.

He heard her call finish and he lightly wiped clean the keypad with his jacket sleeve. He dropped the make-up brush into his pocket a second before she appeared.

'Ready to go?'

As he walked towards the underground station, he put the one, two, five and eight together with the sequence he'd memorised – press, down, press, down, press, up, up, press. The code was therefore one or two, followed by five, eight and then either one or two again. There was no way of knowing which of the first and fifth numbers were one or two but it was a fifty-fifty chance. Alarms were constructed with mistakes in mind so he would be able to retype the code should he get it incorrect the first time.

Victor found that people whose jobs involved no danger were never as security conscious as they should be. For an apartment building with around a dozen properties, each with its own alarm system, to be completely secure each property would have its own code and that code should change for every new tenant. That was a lot for anyone to keep track of.

Maybe she would come back later to input a new code ready for Farkas's arrival. It would be the secure thing to do. But in the fight between security and laziness Victor would put his money on laziness every time.

CHAPTER 10

Warsaw Chopin Airport, Warsaw, Poland

Kevin Sykes stifled a jet-lag-induced yawn as he watched the blinking red and green wing lights of the incoming plane. The body of the descending Lear jet slowly appeared out of the night sky, the airport fog lights illuminating its underbelly. Unlike commercial planes, the Lear approached one of the airport's smaller and less used runways.

The noise of the approach was deafening, and Sykes pressed his palms over his ears. The plane's tyres screeched for an instant when they connected with the asphalt and gave off a grey puff of burnt rubber. The smoke dissipated in the cold air.

The white Lear taxied down the narrow runway and came to a stop fifty yards before two maintenance hangars. There were no airport workers in sight, as instructed. The plane's single door opened outward and the short staircase was lowered to the ground. It locked into position.

A man appeared in the doorway and descended the steps. He was strongly built, early fifties, wearing jeans and a thick sweater. He had thinning grey hair and a tanned, hard face. Behind him followed a similarly hard-faced man in his thirties. The wind whipped up the corners of his denim jacket and Sykes saw the handgun holstered to his belt.

He greeted the new arrivals at the bottom of the steps.

'Max Abbot,' the first man said in a working-class London accent, his voice deep and coarse.

Sykes tried not to wince as his hand was shaken. 'Pleasure to meet you, Max.'

Abbot gestured to his companion. 'That bastard is my associate, Mr Blout.'

Blout's face remained impassive. 'Hello.'

Sykes nodded in return, a little warily. His most recent experience of independent contractors hadn't been a good one, so he wasn't sure what he was going to make of these two Brits. He knew nothing about their backgrounds but assumed they were ex-military or intelligence, and were used to this kind of thing to have landed the gig.

'So,' Abbot said, rotating his head from side to side. 'This is Poland, is it? Looks no better on the ground than when you fly over it.' He rubbed his hands together. 'Let's make this quick, shall we? The sooner we get this done, the sooner we can get back to a country with some warmth. It's cold enough to turn a polar bear's dick into a facking icicle.'

'Agreed.'

Abbot turned in Blout's direction 'Bring him out.'

Blout ascended to the top of the steps and disappeared for a minute inside the Lear. When he appeared again, he pulled out another man. With his hands cuffed together and his ankles shackled, Xavier Callo stepped out of the doorway.

He was shorter than Sykes expected and looked like he weighed no more than a hundred and thirty pounds. Callo wore the kind of orange jumpsuit usually reserved for inmates and terrorists, which wasn't very subtle considering this rendition was as unauthorised as it got, but Sykes kept quiet. Callo wouldn't be out in the open long enough for it to matter. The jumpsuit was about three sizes too big as well, which only exaggerated his slightness. His head hung down so Sykes couldn't see his eyes. Each movement was slow, awkward. A chain linked his handcuffs to his ankle shackles. It all seemed a little over the top considering either Blout or Abbot could probably have carried Callo with one hand, but they obviously had their own way of doing things. Blout shoved Callo in the back and he began a careful descent of the steps.

Abbot noticed Sykes staring. 'He may look like something you'd scrape off your heel but he's as bad a mofo as I've ever had the misfortune of knowing. When the stuff we jabbed him with wore off he went ballistic, I mean like a crazy arsehole. Sunk his teeth in my thigh. Hurt like shit. That's why we've got him hog-tied.'

'How'd you get him?' Sykes asked.

Abbot smiled, full of pride. 'We were supposed to nab him at his villa. Had blueprints, a nice little plan we'd been dry running, but didn't need it. We watched him for three days, and all he did was chase snatch like some horny dog. And not just any birds either. Only went for tall 'uns. Taller they were, the harder Callo tried. So, we improvised. I got a working girl, the most stunning blonde you have ever seen, and tall as

82

me to boot. Told her a pack of bollocks about Callo being a fugitive and us being bounty hunters. Said he was a real bad lad, like a paedo or some shit. Anyway, we paid her to work her magic on him while he was drunk in a bar. Took her all of twenty-eight minutes to get him into a taxi. She even stuck him with the needle and blew me when I dropped her off, no extra charge.'

'Good work.'

'Cheers,' Abbot said, still smiling.

When Callo reached the ground, Abbot took him by the collar and pulled him forward. 'Come on, you slag, let the man take a look at ya.'

Slowly Callo raised his head. He was a mess, disorientated and completely exhausted. For the first time Sykes looked into his pale blue eyes and was pleased to see the fear they held.

'Good evening, Xavier,' Sykes said warmly. 'Welcome to hell.'

The room was simple, a cube, ten by ten by ten. The walls were unfinished concrete, as was the ceiling and floor. A single bare bulb hung in the ceiling but provided no illumination. A filthy mattress lay against one wall, but no bed. Callo sat in the middle of the mattress, hugging his knees against his chest and shivering. He was dressed in just his underpants and socks. The right sock had holes in the toes.

'I want to ask you some questions,' Sykes said from the open doorway, 'about Baraa Ariff.'

'I'm not saying anything,' Callo said defiantly, his breath condensing in the air. 'You can't do this to me. I'm an American. I have rights. I want my lawyer.'

Callo had been left on his own in the cold and dark for a little over three hours and looked suitably softened by the experience, if not completely broken. Sykes would have liked to have kept him holed up for at least a day, but he didn't have the luxury of time.

Folding his arms across his stomach, Sykes said, 'I hate to be the one to break this to you, but you're in what you might call a lawyer-free zone. Any rights you think you have do not apply here. You are in no country. You are in no time zone. No laws protect you here. This place quite simply does not exist. Now, tell me about Ariff and you can have your clothes back. Maybe some hot food. How does that sound? I know it's freezing in here. I know you're hungry.'

'No,' Callo said again, hugging his knees tighter. 'Fuck you.'

His voice was still defiant but tears glistened on his cheeks.

'Okay,' Sykes said with an exaggerated sigh. 'I did try being polite, but you're not leaving me any choice, are you?' He leaned back out of the doorway. 'Some help in here, please.'

Abbot and Blout charged into the cell and went straight for Callo. They dwarfed him. Their faces were full of aggression. Callo screamed the moment he saw them. Abbot grabbed his arms, Blout the legs. Callo thrashed, but didn't have close to the strength needed to match one, let alone two.

Sykes exited the room. Blout followed, one of Callo's ankles in each hand. Abbot did the same with his wrists. He fought all the way, crying and yelling, struggling as much as he could. They walked down a long, dark corridor. It was cold and damp, with the smell of faeces in the air. Their footsteps were loud. Other cries could be heard from elsewhere in the compound and Sykes noticed Callo ceased his own to listen.

'*No, please*,' Callo pleaded. 'You've made a mistake.'

Abbot looked down at him. 'Oh no, mate. You're the one who made the mistake. And this is where you pay for it.'

Blue light flashed up ahead and a piercing scream echoed down the corridor. Callo strained his neck to look as they passed an open doorway. A naked man was strapped to a chair in the centre of the room. His hair was soaking wet and his skin slick with water. Wires were attached to his genitals. Another man stood over him, and slapped him around the face. Then the door slammed shut and blue light flashed through the gap beneath. The screaming started yet again, and the aroma of roasted flesh filled the air. Callo gagged and pulled and kicked harder. The screams from behind the closed door drowned out Callo's own.

'Don't worry,' Abbot said, 'it's your turn now.'

Their destination had the same unfinished concrete walls as Callo's cell. There was a sink against one wall with a hose fixed to one tap. Against the opposite wall was a simple table with a portable electricity generator next to it. Two long cables were attached to the generator and resting in a pile on the table. The generator rumbled noisily. Exhaust fumes hung in the air. Abbot and Blout released Callo, who landed hard on his back, but quickly turned himself over and scrambled, on his hands and knees, for the door. Sykes stood in his way, and laughed as he easily blocked Callo's path.

Then Sykes shouted, '*Asshole just bit me.*'

'I warned ya,' Abbot said as he wrapped a thick arm around Callo's throat. 'This one's a facking lunatic.'

Sykes rubbed at his forearm and closed the heavy steel door

as Blout and Abbot dragged Callo backwards and forced him to sit on a cold metal chair. His arms were pulled behind his back and handcuffs locked his wrists in place. More handcuffs locked his ankles to the chair legs.

Abbot moved towards the sink and Blout towards the generator.

'*I'll tell you anything*,' Callo yelled.

Sykes nodded as he rubbed his forearm. 'We know that, everyone does. But that's the problem right there. You'll tell me anything. And anything is no good. Which is why we have to go through certain *procedures* to ensure what you do say is the truth.'

Callo spoke quickly. 'It will be, I promise.'

Sykes nodded again but didn't say anything. He looked at Abbot, who picked up the hose from the floor and aimed it at Callo. He turned on the tap and a jet of icy water struck Callo in the face. It was so cold Callo stiffened and exhaled sharply, face contorted, and head shaking from side to side, trying to get away from the painful blast. Abbot redirected the spray down over Callo's body until he was drenched with water. He bucked and screamed, kicking his legs out wildly. The chair, bolted to the floor, didn't move.

Sykes said, 'That's enough.'

Abbot turned off the tap. Callo sat shivering uncontrollably in the chair, teeth chattering, goose pimples covering his body, lips blue. He tried to speak, to beg for mercy, but he couldn't form any coherent words.

Abbot grabbed Callo's hair and wrenched his head to one side so he was looking at the table.

'You're going to want to watch this,' Abbot snarled.

He let go of Callo's hair and moved to the table. There was a brown paper bag lying on the tabletop into which Abbot reached. He removed two oranges, set them down so they were touching, and taped both to the table.

'Think of these as a representation of what's most valuable to you.'

Abbot took a black marker pen from a trouser pocket. He drew some little black lines on each orange. He laughed to himself. He then took the cables, which had crocodile clips at the ends, and clipped one to the skin of each orange.

'Ready then?' Abbot asked Callo, but didn't wait for a response. He gestured to Blout, who thumbed a switch on the generator.

The oranges started to glow and then vibrate. After a few seconds a warm citrus odour spread around the room. The vibrations intensified and the skin of one orange split open. Steam rose from the opening and juice bubbled through.

'Here we go,' Abbot said, slapping his hands together.

A split opened in the second orange. Other splits appeared and Callo watched with wide eyes as the oranges burst open and hot juice and pieces of flesh exploded outwards.

Abbot clapped his hands together again. '*Oh yeah*. That's the money shot.'

Blout flicked the generator switch. What was left of the oranges sat steaming on the table. Juice dripped from the edge. Chunks of orange flesh and skin lay scattered across the floor. A hot piece had landed on Callo's naked thigh, making him wince.

'Look,' Abbot said, laughing and pointing, 'bastard's pissed his pants.'

Callo's underpants were already soaking wet but the yellow colouring at the front was obvious.

Sykes took a step towards Callo. 'Get the point?'

Callo nodded. '*Yes, yes, I'll tell you the truth*.'

'Good,' Abbot said, 'because if you think this bad boy makes a mess of the oranges you wouldn't believe what it will do to a pair of bollocks.' He took the crocodile clips from the skin of the destroyed oranges. 'Whoa, these babies are hot.'

Blout opened out a folding knife and stepped towards Callo, who screamed at the sight of the blade. Blout used the knife to cut away Callo's underpants.

Abbot laughed. 'Guess that water is colder than I thought.'

Callo yelped as the crocodile clips bit into his scrotum.

Sykes walked forward. 'You see, Xavier, we're underfunded out here and we can't afford a polygraph. But you can see how we've improvised our own. Sure, it's not as sophisticated, but it works just as good. Better even.' Sykes gestured to Callo's groin. 'Would you like a more accurate demonstration of how our lie detector works?'

Callo shook his head as hard as he could. '*No, no, no . . .*'

'Okay,' Sykes continued, 'I can see you're convinced that it works, but we'll start off easy. Tell me, how's business?'

A confused look passed over Callo's face. 'Business?'

'Yeah,' Sykes said. 'Business. You know, the diamond trade. How is it? You making lots of money?'

'I . . . I guess. It could be better.'

Sykes laughed. 'Could be better?' He glanced at Abbot and Blout. 'You hear that guys? *Could be better*. I heard about your little trip to that Greek bar. You were throwing cash around like it was going out of style. And that villa overlooking the beach; bet a week's rent on that is a month's take home for me. So don't be modest. I don't know how you do it. Uncut diamonds look like shitty little rocks to me, but you've got the magic eye, don't you?'

'I guess.'

'What did I say about modesty?'

'Okay, I'm good at what I do.'

'Then just facking say so, prick,' Abbot spat.

'Excuse my friend here,' Sykes said. 'He's pissed because the coffee machine doesn't work. I'd offer you a water, but I guess you've had enough from the hose.'

Callo shook his head. He had been in a constant state of thirst for two days. 'No, some water would be good.'

'Okay,' Sykes said. 'Answer a few more questions and I'll have a cup brought in for you, how does that sound?'

'Thank you,' Callo said.

'Don't mention it.' Sykes put his hands in his trouser pockets. 'Tell me about your relationship with Baraa Ariff.'

Callo hesitated. 'What about him?'

'Just what I said. Tell me about your relationship with him. And don't forget about the lie detector.'

'I . . . I sell his diamonds for him.'

Sykes tilted his head to one side. 'You mean you fence his diamonds for him that he receives as payments for arm sales in Africa?'

'I don't know where they come from. I just—'

'You're a clever boy, Xavier, take a guess. What else would an arms dealer trade for diamonds?'

Abbot scooped out some flesh from one of the destroyed oranges and ate it. 'Hot orange ain't that bad.' Juice dribbled down his chin. 'Fancy a bit, mate?'

Callo shook his head. Blout threw some anyway. It hit Callo on the cheek.

'I'm waiting,' Sykes prompted.

Callo said, 'He gets the diamonds for arms.'

'That wasn't so hard,' Sykes said. 'I know you're afraid that word might reach Ariff that you ratted him out, but that problem only exists *if* you ever leave this place. Get the subtext? So make right now your priority and start answering my questions faster.' Sykes's eyes narrowed. 'Now, we've established that you fence Ariff's diamonds for him, so you profit from the illegal arms trade.'

'But I didn't know.'

'I don't give a shit whether you knew or not. I don't give a shit about who you are. I hate to be the one to break it to you, but you're not a very important individual. Does anyone even know you're gone? Would they care if they knew?'

Callo averted his eyes.

'That's what I thought,' Sykes said. 'Back to Ariff. What else do you know about him?'

'I'm not sure.'

Abbot gestured angrily. 'You're not sure what you know? What kind of bullshit answer is that?' His face was red. He looked at Sykes. 'We should cook his testicles right now. That will make him sure what he knows.'

'*No, no*,' Callo pleaded. 'I'll tell you anything you want to know.'

'Where is Ariff?' Sykes asked.

'I don't know. Why would I know?'

Abbot slapped Callo across the face. 'Because you were seen in Antwerp a week ago selling a large amount of uncut ice.'

'Which you got from Ariff,' Sykes added. 'So we know you've seen him recently. Are you really so dumb you do not get that some of the questions we ask you we already have the answers to? You tell me one more lie or try to be even the slightest bit evasive when answering and we're going to turn on the lie detector and go get your water. That's a two-minute round trip. Think what your nuts are going to look like after one hundred and twenty long seconds.'

Tears streamed down Callo's cheeks and he blinked to clear his eyes. 'Ariff's living in Lebanon now. He has a house in Beirut.'

'Where in Beirut?' Sykes asked.

'I don't know where exactly, I've never been. I last saw him in Cairo. It must be in the hills above Beirut because he said he had a great view of the city below and the sea. On the slopes of Mount Lebanon, because he said he had to get some cedar trees cut. They grow up there.'

Sykes turned down the corners of his mouth and nodded. 'That's pretty damn good deduction there. I'm impressed. Genuinely. Now, you sold his diamonds and you've got his cash and we know Ariff doesn't like to use banks. So how were you going to give it to him?'

When Callo hesitated, Sykes gestured to Blout. 'Flick the switch.'

Callo screamed, 'NO.'

'Then tell me.'

'It'll be somewhere in Europe or the Middle East. It always is. But I won't know until I get word. Then I'll go and hand over the cash. It's how it always works.'

'Will you meet Ariff himself?'

'Or his business partner,' Callo said. 'Gabir Yamout.'

'When will you get that message?'

'It'll be soon. Maybe this week.'

'Good boy,' Sykes said with a smile. 'You're doing great. Keep this up and you'll even get to see the sun again. Now, tell me how you'll receive the message.'

Sykes questioned Callo for a further hour before getting him his water as promised. It couldn't have gone better. Procter was going to be thrilled with the information Sykes had collected. It had been clear to Sykes just from reading about him that Callo would talk without the need for too much encouragement, or coercion as the CIA liked to call it. Sykes had read the torture bible of permissible interrogation techniques in the run-up to Callo's arrival, and knew what was allowed and what wasn't. Ball frying definitely fell into the latter category, but then this wasn't as it seemed.

The set-up Sykes had fixed for Callo had been perfect. They were in an abandoned Cold War bunker that served admirably as a CIA black site. Some rented locals had played the parts of prisoner and interrogators for the little vignette Callo had just happened to witness, with pork chops over a camping stove providing the smell of burnt testicles. The generator was real, though, the exploding oranges were real, but Sykes wasn't going to flick the switch. He just wanted Callo to believe he would.

Sykes's orders had been explicit. Callo was not to be harmed in any way, which was better than he deserved, but good because Sykes had some experience of violence and he knew he didn't have the stomach for real torture. Scaring Callo shitless was necessary, however, and a bit of roughing up was allowed so long as it left no marks. Callo was a career criminal and a fence with fingers in lots of illegal pies, so hurt or not, today's unpleasantness was a bit of karma for his long list of sins.

And, Sykes was surprised to admit to himself, it had been a lot of fun watching Callo squirm and beg.

CHAPTER 11

Berlin, Germany

The first of Farkas's entourage arrived alone. Victor spotted him easily enough, walking with a certain level of arrogance, expecting others to move out of his way, giving hard stares to anyone who didn't. The man looked about thirty with pale skin and dark hair that reached below his ears. He wore a poorly fitting suit and talked into a cell phone, shouting in Hungarian to someone Victor guessed was a wife or girl-friend.

Victor's grasp of the language was passable at best. He'd been refreshing his understanding of Hungarian since he'd first received the assignment, but there was still a long way to go. The Hungarian kept the phone wedged between his head and shoulder as he fumbled for his key to open the door. Sipping his orange juice outside the cocktail bar, Victor couldn't see whether the man was armed. He wrote a number one on a fresh page in his notebook and next to it listed the man's physical attributes and tactical awareness – *None*.

It was an hour before he made any more notes. The man left the building and returned thirty minutes later, this time laden with shopping bags and carrying a tray of five coffees. A supply run then, getting essentials in for the boss's arrival. Victor added the time the trip took and the brand of coffee purchased to his notes as well as writing *Unarmed*.

Farkas must be arriving soon, otherwise his coffee would get cold, so Victor finished his drink, gathered his things, and walked slowly along the street, a casual pace, just a local in no hurry to get to where he was going. He took out his phone, pretended to answer it, and engaged in small talk with the fictional person of reasonable wit.

The phone gave him a reason to loiter on the sidewalk outside the apartment building. He stayed a few yards away from the front steps. He wanted to be close when Farkas arrived but not close enough to smell his cologne, or lack thereof.

It didn't take long. A black Mercedes sedan pulled up outside the building and Farkas climbed out after one of his underlings held open the door for him. Farkas appeared fit and healthy, just shy of six feet and around one hundred and seventy-five pounds. The dossier listed him as both a couple of inches taller and some ten pounds heavier. Not too important intelligence to get wrong, but it didn't say much for Victor's sources. Unlike the other men who arrived with him, Farkas had a tan, probably fake. Too dark and too even. He wore an expensive-looking black suit with a red shirt and red tie. It was a stylish combination, or would have been without the chunky gold chain hanging above the shirt.

Victor continued his fake conversation and drew only a passing glance from one of Farkas's men. Three arrived with Farkas, one in his forties and the other two in their thirties, un-athletic physiques, all in suits, each with a suitcase, one with two, all armed. Handguns in underarm holsters by the way their jackets hung. They were relaxed but watchful. Victor detected no special training, military or otherwise.

The guy who'd arrived earlier appeared, looking flushed and apologetic. He hurried down the steps, pushing his hair back behind his ears. Victor figured the man was saying sorry for being late and that the penthouse was ready for Farkas's stay. Farkas looked at him with disdain but didn't say anything.

Victor waited a minute before leaving. He entered a boutique on a nearby street where he bought an entirely new set of clothes, dressed in them in the changing rooms and carried his old clothes out in a store-supplied shopping bag. He took a seat outside the coffee shop on the same side of the street as the apartment building and ordered a cappuccino and chicken salad panini. His position offered him a more restricted view of the street than the bar had, but he could still clearly see the sidewalk immediately outside the building.

The afternoon was sunny enough to justify wearing sunglasses and warm enough so that Victor draped his jacket over a chair. He took his time eating. The coffee shop had a selection of newspapers and he took one to pretend to read. He was hoping he wouldn't have to pretend for long as his instincts told him Farkas wasn't the kind of guy to stay cooped up inside on his first day. Either he would need to get down to business or more likely he would leave to get something to eat. Sooner rather than later.

By the time Victor was finishing his second coffee his wait was over. Farkas appeared with all of his four guys just after three p.m. They were laughing and joking, Farkas too, though far less enthusiastically. *Friendly, but not friends*, Victor noted. He watched as they passed, overhearing the one who'd arrived first mention something about a restaurant.

Victor waited until they were out of sight before leaving his chair. He used the set of copied keys to let himself inside and made his way up to the penthouse. He stood listening in front of the door for a moment to ensure no one was coming or going below him. The pick gun, though not loud, wasn't exactly silent either.

He removed the gun from his rucksack, inserted the long pick into the penthouse's lock, and squeezed the trigger. Immediately the pick vibrated rapidly and in seconds the lock was open. Victor hadn't used one for a while – lock picks could be disguised or hidden more easily – but he couldn't deny the pick gun's usefulness.

He opened the door and stepped inside. The alarm made its dull warning beep. Victor approached the keypad and entered one, five, eight, two. It didn't work so he tried two, five, eight, one. The warning beep stopped.

Victor entered the lounge and saw the Hungarians had already made themselves at home. The smell of tobacco hung in the air. There were mugs left on the floor next to the sofas and luggage sat on the coffee table. He scanned the area for anything he could use to his advantage but quickly dismissed the lounge as a strike point; then again, he'd never expected it to be.

The problem of how to place the bomb had been on Victor's mind since arriving in Berlin. It had to be somewhere where it was sure to be triggered, but only where Farkas alone could trigger it. With another four men sharing the penthouse with him, it meant that the answer hadn't come easily.

Remote detonation was out. The bomb could be planted on the street outside the building and detonated when Farkas passed. However, there were no convenient trashcans where Farkas was certain to pass. The device could be placed under a car parked outside, but it would be a risk planting it in the first place and the car could easily be driven off before Farkas walked by. And that was without the very real risk of civilian casualties.

The bomb had to be set inside the apartment. It could be placed under Farkas's bed and remote detonated when he climbed in, so long as he could be observed doing so. When the realtor had shown him around, Victor had looked through every window to see which buildings overlooked the master bedroom. There was one potential viewpoint, but if the bedroom drapes were closed it would render that position useless.

He toyed with the idea of placing the bomb on the underside of the mattress with a pressure sensor that would trigger the blast when Farkas lay down. The trouble was the bed was king-size and Victor had no way of knowing which side Farkas would sleep on. The sensor could only be set to trigger the bomb under considerable weight in case luggage or other items were placed on the bed. Someone else could trigger the bomb just by sitting or lying on that side of the bed; equally, if Farkas decided to sleep on the other side then the bomb would never go off.

The noise of the key in the lock registered instantly. Victor turned towards the bedroom door and gently pushed it closed. He listened as the front door opened and someone stepped inside; a lone man by the sound of the footsteps. One of Farkas's entourage. If it was Farkas himself returning, all of his men would likely accompany him.

Had the guy noticed that the alarm had been switched off? If so, Victor couldn't tell by his movements. He heard the man in the lounge, the sound of his shoes on the floorboards growing louder as he headed for the bedrooms. Maybe he was back because he'd forgotten something. Or maybe he was back because Farkas had forgotten something. Victor's gaze found the slim leather-bound notebook sitting on the bedside table. A schedule, maybe.

He squatted down to look under the bed. Finding it only a few inches in height, he stood back up, glanced at the wardrobe. It was full of hanging suits and suitcases. No room for him as well. The en suite bathroom was the best place to hide, except for the chance that the guy would decide to check his reflection before he left. If that happened there was only one way for Victor to deal with him and the job would fall apart.

The footsteps grew louder, closer.

The Hungarian with the long dark hair opened the bedroom door and stepped inside. The room was larger and nicer than the one he was sharing with two of the others. It smelled better too. He saw the black notebook and scooped it up into a hand. He slipped it into his inside jacket pocket for safekeeping.

He turned to leave, but on a whim of boredom opened the door to the adjoining bathroom.

Again, it was much nicer than the main bathroom that was quickly becoming a mess with the toiletries of four men competing for space. The shared toilet was already filthy with the bowl ringed by piss puddles. The Hungarian examined the expensive bottles that Farkas had lined the sink with and selected an intriguing tube of cream. He opened it, sniffed it, squeezed out a drop, and rubbed it into his hands. They felt soft afterwards. He replaced the tube exactly as he had found it. Farkas was a good boss most of the time but he was careful to maintain the hierarchy.

The Hungarian left the bathroom, reset the alarm and left the apartment. He didn't remember disabling it but he didn't think twice about it.

Victor heard the front door shut and remained as still as he could for exactly sixty seconds just to be sure before moving from his position. He pulled the curtain to one side and dropped down from the window sill where he'd been balancing with his legs contorted, his back pressed flat against the glass, arms stretched out for support. The sill hadn't been as deep as he would have liked, but the guy hadn't noticed the hang of the drapes wasn't quite as straight as they should have been.

The moment his shoes touched the carpet the alarm started to beep. Victor hurried to the panel and typed in the code.

Back in the bedroom, he took his bag from the wardrobe where he'd placed it with Farkas's luggage, set it on the bed, and took out the bomb. Confident in his decision, it took him less than four minutes to place the bomb and he was outside the building shortly after resetting the alarm. For Victor the job was effectively over.

Now it was all down to Farkas.

CHAPTER 12

Adorján Farkas was drunk. A couple of beers had preceded his steak and more beers and a few cocktails had followed the meal. His men had convinced him to make a night of it, and when five Hungarians did that the results were often messy. While in a country where no one knew Farkas, or how he made his money, he felt more relaxed than he often did at home, but he was in Germany on business and as such had to keep some level of control.

The members of his entourage had shown less restraint, downing copious amounts of German beer with their own meals before moving on to a range of spirits in the bar. They were well behaved, as he liked, and it was good to see his men having fun. Farkas encouraged such behaviour because socialising strengthened the bonds of loyalty. He had been a boss in the Hungarian mob long enough to know that he only maintained his position because his men allowed him to be in charge. They needed him to pay them and he needed them to carry out his orders and protect him against the hazards of the organised crime trade. Farkas knew that without his men to exert his will he was all but impotent.

There was a line though, a line between employer and employee that could not be crossed. His men needed to like him and respect him and in turn feel that he liked and respected them, but he could never be friends with them. There might be a time when a man in his service became a problem, either deliberately or unknowingly, and Farkas had found it was hard to torture and kill a friend. With no friends working for him, he was free to operate without interruption from that annoying little thing called guilt.

He walked behind his men as they made their way back to the apartment building. He was quiet while his men joked loudly with one another. Though collectively they had enough alcohol in their systems to kill a bull, he knew that they still had their wits about them. In Farkas's business one of the primary traits a man needed for success was to be able to handle his drink. A couple would probably spend most of tomorrow swallowing aspirin, but by the evening they would be ready to work.

On that day Farkas was due to meet some potential new suppliers. He was always looking to expand his burgeoning empire and he felt good about this trip's prospects. The suppliers came highly recommended and if things went well they would help round out Farkas's arms inventory. He shipped cheap Eastern European Kalashnikovs down to an Egyptian dealer, who in turn sold them throughout the Middle East and Africa. The money was okay and the risks minimal, but Farkas knew if he could get his hands on more sophisticated Western weaponry, he wouldn't have to deal with the Egyptian bastard – who Farkas knew ripped him off – he could go straight to the smaller dealers. He would cut out the middleman and massively increase his margins.

With luck, these German suppliers might be able to help him

do just that. He had his eye on some nice Heckler & Koch gear: MP5s, G36s, UMPs, the works. The market was there, ready and waiting. Farkas just needed to get his fingers on the goods. He also wanted a new pistol for himself. Something flashy that the other bosses back home didn't have.

In the penthouse, his men started raiding the kitchen for anything edible or drinkable. Farkas likened them to a pack of scavengers, already full and intoxicated but eager to gorge on whatever could be found. One of his men grabbed the TV remote and began flicking through the channels in search of porn and Farkas knew it was time to call it a night when he saw the genital-to-genital close-up on the screen.

His decision provoked some jeers but he waved his hand dismissively and headed to his bedroom. He turned on the main light and began undressing, throwing his dirty clothes in one corner. Then he unzipped his suitcase and rifled through until he found his pyjamas.

In the en suite, he brushed his teeth and washed his face before returning to the bedroom. He switched off the main light and climbed into bed. Taking the novel he'd brought along for the trip off the bedside table, he flicked on the lamp.

Farkas read a few pages before tiredness got the better of him. The book wasn't that good anyway – some thriller with too much talking and not enough killing. He folded over the corner of the page he'd reached and put the book down. He flicked the lamp off.

He lay in the dark for a few moments before switching the lamp back on and getting out of bed. He walked into the bathroom to relieve his bladder. Farkas pushed down the handle to flush the toilet. It didn't flush.

He pushed the handle down again, harder.

Inside the tank, the handle rose to open the flush valve. It drove the firing pin taped to the top of the lever into the detonator attached to the underside of the tank lid. The detonator blew and ignited the main charge of RDX packed into the empty tank.

The shock wave travelled outwards with an explosive velocity of more than eight thousand yards per second, obliterating the tank, and everything inside the room. The door blew off its hinges and smashed into the far wall of the adjoining bedroom, followed by flames and debris.

Chunks of Farkas dropped from the bathroom ceiling.

CHAPTER 13

Linz, Austria

Before he was due to, Victor found himself awake on his hard hotel-room bed. There was a racket coming from the corridor outside. Running, yelling, laughing, banging into things. It sounded like a couple of kids playing up to their parents, who in turn were louder still in trying to quiet their children down. That was the problem with being a light sleeper who primarily slept when others were awake. People were even less considerate than they were the rest of the time.

It was something he'd been forced to get used to, as he had no fixed sleeping routine. He slept when he could, for as long as he could. If it wasn't enough, he'd sleep another time. Those first few operations behind enemy lines had taught him the importance of getting rest whenever and wherever it was available, whatever the circumstances. It was a lesson he still put into practice. If he'd needed a comfortable bed and a good eight hours' uninterrupted sleep each day to be at the top of his game he would have died a long time ago.

Victor employed a controlled breathing technique to induce sleep quickly, which was one of the most important skills he'd trained himself in, though today it wasn't working. No amount of controlled breathing was going to defeat two screaming children and two yelling parents. Earplugs would have helped, but they'd also help anyone who might want to get into his room uninvited. Occasionally waking prematurely was preferable to never waking at all.

He'd slept fully dressed, as always, and back in the bedroom he stripped off his trousers and shirt. He did a workout and then ran a bath. The shower looked particularly appealing but he resisted its pull. With his head under the stream of pressurised water, it wouldn't take an expert to break into his room without him knowing about it. Only in the safety of his own house had he allowed himself the pleasure of a shower.

When the tub was almost full, he climbed in. The water was near scalding and just how he liked it. He lowered himself slowly until only his head and knees were protruding from the water. Unusually, the taps faced away from the door so he could bathe without stainless steel jabbing into him. He allowed himself half an hour, which wasn't tactically shrewd, but he needed the bath's help to relax his mind. The last ten days had been busy. Two contracts fulfilled with a gunfight in between. And people who worked nine-to-five claimed to have it tough.

He knew he had little justification to complain, however. No one had forced him into the life he led. He didn't like to think about the past, but he knew he'd taken all the steps towards who he was today willingly, even if at the time he didn't know in which direction those steps would eventually lead him. It was what he was good at, what he'd always been good at. From the fox to his first confirmed enemy kill to Farkas.

He closed his eyes and lowered his head under the water, but limited this luxury to no more than thirty divine seconds. He remembered something an associate had once told him: *If you don't like it, stop doing it.* A simple statement, but true all the same. He knew it would be easier if he liked it, a lot easier, but the problem was he didn't dislike it either. The fact the people he killed were even more execrable than himself made little difference.

He raised his head out of the water after twenty-three seconds. The relaxing effect of the bath disappeared. He felt agitated, restless. The price of thinking too much. Water splashed on the floor as he climbed out.

Later, he ate a high-protein, high-carbohydrate meal of trout and speckknödel dumplings at a nearby restaurant. He sat at a corner table, alone. The food was good but he cared more about the nutrients. The waiter, though probably no older than Victor, looked tired and old. Victor left him a considerable tip.

He had a couple of hours to kill and so explored central Linz. He visited the Lentos Museum of Art, the Castle Museum, and the seventeenth-century Church of Saint Ignatius with its bizarre choir stalls intricately carved with frightful, almost demonic figures. As the sun set, a pleasure boat ride along the Danube let him relax without constantly looking out for surveillance, before he disembarked and walked to the Hauptplatz at the heart of the old city. Tall baroque buildings surrounded the grand square, and Victor glided through the crowd to the Trinity Column at its centre.

Even if he hadn't known exactly where to meet her, he could have used the looks and stares of the men in the square to triangulate her position. She didn't see him approach, but few people ever did.

Victor took her wrist and she spun to face him, her surprise quickly replaced by a smile in turn quickly replaced by a kiss as she threw her arms around him.

It was dark in his hotel room. Victor lay naked on the bed. The sheets beneath him were crumpled, half on the floor. In front of the bed, a woman, bending over, retrieved her clothes from around the bed. Victor watched her, enjoying the spectacle created by her long, smooth legs and the thong that left her tanned ass cheeks exposed.

Adrianna was Swiss but born in England and spoke with the cultured accent of a British aristocrat. He knew her well enough to know she wasn't an assassin or a cop or an agent of some intelligence service. He could relax in her company – which was an impossibility with someone he'd only just met. Victor didn't trust anyone, but Adrianna was one of the very few people he didn't completely distrust.

'You shouldn't bend over like that,' he said. 'It puts strain on your lower lumbar muscles. Bend with your knees instead, you'll get a squat out of it too when you stand. Good for your thighs.'

'Emmanuel, you are *full* of useless information.' She looked back at him. 'Turn a light on, please. I can't see.'

'There's plenty of light.'

'For you maybe. But I hate carrots.'

He said, 'That's not the way it works,' and reached across the bed and switched on the second lamp. It had been repositioned so it wouldn't cast shadows over the window.

'Is that better?'

'Much better, thank you.' She found what she was looking for and stood up. 'Bet you've had those blinds closed all day, haven't you?' He didn't answer. 'No wonder you're so pale.'

He went to take a sip of his Scotch but found the glass empty. He watched Adrianna hook her bra and adjust her breasts so they sat correctly. She took a small brush from a snakeskin handbag and began running it through her hair. She could go from sex-messed to sophisticated businesswoman in under two minutes. She told Victor it was an art.

Adrianna always refused to tell him her age and when asked would simply answer, 'Old enough.' He didn't tell her he knew she had just turned thirty, had a master's degree in History from Cambridge, that both her parents were dead and her brother was living in America. He also knew that she worried about the fine lines at the corners of her eyes and that her hips were too big, but to Victor she was as close to perfect as anyone was ever likely to be. She never believed him when he told her she was beautiful.

She had an apartment in Geneva and one in London. He had been through every inch of both, though she had never invited him to either. The bugs he had planted were without invite as well. When they had first met in a Geneva bar he had shadowed her for a week before calling her number. He'd continued to shadow her on occasions in the following months. There had been nothing to be suspicious of. Which had surprised him. Eventually he had removed the bugs as an undisclosed courtesy. After all, he was a gentleman.

He poured himself a large measure of Chivas Regal. It was one of his preferred brands. A blend, but it trumped almost every other Scotch. Victor often found single malts to be overrated.

She laughed.

'What?' he asked.

'I can tell you missed me.'

'Why's that?'

She held up a cream silk blouse and cast him a sly smile. 'It's torn.'

'You look better without it.'

She made a face and said, 'Hmm.' She slipped the ripped blouse on and buttoned it up as far as it would go. She huffed, pushing her fingers through the holes so Victor could see the top three buttons were missing.

He shrugged. 'I'll find them and put them aside.'

'Throw them away, I don't sew.'

'Can't or won't?'

'Both.'

'Okay, I'll buy you a new one.'

'It's last season's,' she said, pouting. 'You won't be able to get it any more.'

He sat up straighter. 'Then I'll have to buy you two others from this season, won't I?'

She grinned.

'How about I take you for a late dinner?'

She zipped up her skirt and tucked the blouse in. 'I'd love to, but I really can't. Business to take care of.'

'You work too hard.'

'Need to pay the bills.' She sat on the end of the bed and bounced up and down a little, as much as the bed would allow. 'It's hard as concrete. You should complain.'

'I like it.'

'I'm amazed you get any sleep.' She put her shoes on, then was still for a moment, she spoke softly. 'Do you realise this is the first time I've seen you in over half a year?' She paused. 'I was afraid you were never going to call me again.'

He didn't look at her. 'I've been busy.'

She glanced back at him. 'Work?' When he nodded, she said, 'You work too hard.'

'Need to pay the bills.'

She smiled and then said, 'I always wonder what it is you do.'

'No shop talk, remember?'

Adrianna showed her palms. 'I know, Emmanuel, I know. I just get curious about you. That is allowed, isn't it? I have this fantasy where you're like a secret agent.'

'You think I'm a spy?'

She smiled shyly. 'Ridiculous, isn't it? It's because of your scars, I guess.'

'I was in the army,' he explained.

'I know. As I said, it's just a fantasy. I bet you do something really boring, like a banker or stockbroker.' She paused and smiled. 'I know, you're an accountant, aren't you?'

'Actually,' he said with a raised eyebrow, 'I'm a professional assassin.'

She burst out laughing. 'You can be so funny when you want to be.'

'No, I'm serious,' he said, sounding anything but. 'I just blew up a gangster with a bomb hidden in his toilet.'

Adrianna laughed harder. She put a hand to her chest. 'Stop it, please. You're going to kill me.'

'Only if you pay me a lot of money.'

He set his hands behind his head and Adrianna's laugh eventually became a smile as she took control of herself.

111

She examined him and said, 'You've put on a bit of weight. Muscle, I mean.'

He nodded. He'd always favoured speed over strength, but a recent and very painful encounter had convinced him that a little extra power could be useful.

'I've put some weight on too.' She pinched the skin of her stomach and grunted. 'But it's all blubber.'

'Don't worry about it,' he said. 'You look great, better even.'

'You are a liar, Emmanuel.'

'Why do you always say that?'

'Because I know you.' Her hand drifted to his outstretched leg and gently rubbed his calf. Her voice was quiet. 'You were different this time.'

'How do you mean?'

She shrugged and sighed. 'Not bad,' she assured. 'I don't know, just . . . different.'

'I've a lot on my mind.'

'Want to talk about it?'

'I thought you had to go.'

'I do. But you can call me later, you know, if you want.'

'Sure,' he said and took a large swallow of whisky.

Adrianna gave his leg a squeeze and with a big exhale pushed herself off the bed. She pulled down the hem of her skirt and combed her hair with her fingers in front of the sideboard mirror.

'On the side,' he stated. 'Under the newspaper.'

Adrianna turned to acknowledge him and slid the envelope out from under the paper. She placed it in her handbag.

He watched her. 'Aren't you going to count it?'

'I don't know why you always ask that. We both know I don't need to.'

'You're too trusting.'

She smiled a little. 'Why don't you ever ask me out? I mean on a proper date. Not like this.'

'You'd say no, and we have a good arrangement. Why complicate it?' He reached for his wallet. 'Let me give you something so you can get a couple of new blouses.'

'That's okay,' she sighed. 'It wasn't as expensive as it looks. And besides,' she took hold of her blouse's collar in both hands and opened it up, exposing her elbow-enhanced cleavage visible now there weren't enough buttons to cover it, 'I think it looks better like this anyway.'

After bathing and dressing in clean clothes Victor sat on the end of the bed, powered on his new laptop, checked his email to get the latest number, and used VoIP to call his nameless employer.

'Excellent work in Berlin,' were the first words Victor heard.

He didn't respond.

His employer said, 'Wasn't sure if you'd manage to pull it off without anyone else getting caught in the net, so to speak.'

'My instructions were to avoid collateral damage.'

'Don't think I don't get that it was a tall ask when using a bomb. So thank you.'

Victor remained silent. He stood and moved to the window. He used a finger to edge open the drapes a crack. He looked down on the street outside.

'Next dossier isn't ready for you just yet,' his employer explained. 'Details are still being verified, you know the sort of thing. Don't want to send you in without the full facts.'

'Perish the thought.'

'Exactly. So stand down while we're waiting. Unwind and have a little fun.'

'That's what I'm doing.'

'Good for you,' the voice responded, 'but don't go too wild. I need you ready to go at the drop of a hat.'

'I'm always ready.'

'Which is exactly what I want to hear. And anyway, you should be happy.'

'Why's that?' Victor asked.

'Because we're halfway there, my man. Two down, and only two to go. Then you're a free man again.'

After a pause, Victor asked, 'How long before you'll have the third contract ready?'

'Soon,' the voice replied. 'Very soon.'

CHAPTER 14

Beirut, Lebanon

The girl beneath Baraa Ariff was nineteen. Spanish. She had long wavy black hair that cascaded to her shoulders, flawless golden brown skin over a body that was slim yet curvaceous and just the way Ariff liked it. She also didn't talk too much, which was another attractive quality the Egyptian arms dealer was particularly fond of.

He couldn't stand women who tried to engage him in conversation or had the arrogance to dare ask him questions. If it wasn't so offensive, it would be almost laughable. Ariff considered few men his equal and no woman alive had yet earned his respect. They were either toys for his amusement or to carry and raise his children. Never both. A mother should be too busy looking after the offspring to have time to waste speaking to him and a vagina had no need of vocal cords.

Fortunately, he was wealthy enough not to have to deal with the opposite sex unless he wanted to. Since he lived with his family he had to spend more time in the company of his wife than he would have liked, but she had learned not to speak to him unless absolutely necessary. His daughters were different though; they were three heavenly creations not yet tainted by womanhood. If it were possible, Ariff would keep them that way forever.

The girl grunted. She couldn't speak Arabic and he didn't know a word of Spanish, so that all but eliminated the talking problem. A few cries when he used her body were thankfully as much communication as he had to endure on a typical visit. Today was even better than normal – the girl barely moaned as he moved himself on top of her.

As a result he was finished much sooner than usual and this pleased him immensely. For Ariff, the quicker any kind of gratification could be obtained, the better. He climbed off the girl, gave her a little slap on the thigh to show his appreciation of her body, and walked to the bathroom for a quick shower.

He let the warm water strike the top of his head and flow down over his body. He felt tired from the sex. He may have kept himself in shape but his days as a young man were long over. Ariff knew from his regular check-ups that he was fit and healthy for a sixty-eight-year-old. His blood pressure was considerably below the average even with the inherent stresses and dangers associated with his profession. He accepted that his business came with unavoidable risks and as such didn't spend too much time worrying about them. He paid other people to do that for him, and he paid them very well.

Five decades in the illicit arms trade had amassed Ariff a huge fortune, as it had his father before him. Ariff's father had smuggled weapons into Gaza from Egypt for almost thirty years until Israeli commandos killed him. Ariff had been little more than a boy then, but he had learned a lot from his father's death and always steered clear of moving merchandise himself, personally brokering only the most important deals.

The death of his father also taught him to be careful of those he dealt with. People who wanted weapons had enemies and by supplying those people, he would count their enemies as his own. This philosophy kept him away from dealing with anything chemical, biological or nuclear. The second he bought or sold such materials he would become the target of the West, particularly the United States. While he kept comparatively inconspicuous, he knew he was safe.

Ariff's main business was almost exclusively in the small arms trade. He bought handguns, sub-machine guns, assault rifles, man-portable machine guns, grenade launchers and missile launchers then sold them on. In addition to helping maintain a relatively low profile, he preferred to trade in small arms for a variety of reasons. They were easy to source, cheap to buy, and straightforward to conceal and transport across borders. Demand was also high. Because they were cheap, everyone wanted them.

Ariff had stopped trading in anything larger over twenty years ago, after he'd bought half a dozen T-72 tanks in Estonia that had been left behind by the Red Army. Despite the fact the tanks were perfectly maintained and in full working order, he could find no one who wanted to buy them. Governments didn't like to deal in such small numbers, and for the price of one tank a warlord could equip every man under his command with an assault rifle and ammunition. In the end, the Estonians had bought back the tanks for sixty per cent of what Ariff had paid for them. It had been a tough but important lesson for the arms dealer.

Despite primarily trading in illegal arms, Ariff conducted much of his business through legal channels. Weapons could be bought legally from supplier states, transported legally, but diverted for illicit use when they were thousands of miles from source. Half the time supplier states never realised their weapons hadn't ended up where they were supposed to, and the rest of the time they didn't even care. When big money was at stake, many suppliers would knowingly violate sanctions or embargoes so Ariff could ship their weapons straight to war zones to maximise their profits.

When business wasn't conducted legally, Ariff preferred to conduct it with as much legality as could be illegally purchased. He bribed officials to issue certified bills of lading and end-use certificates. When he couldn't bribe, he used expertly produced counterfeits. To keep on good terms with the border guards, airport officials and government cronies essential to his trafficking, Ariff made regular donations whether he was making a shipment or not. The more people were accustomed to bribery, the harder they found it to refuse. When making such bribes, it always helped if the receivers earned less in a month than Ariff would spend on a pair of shoes.

Those times when he wasn't operating under the flag of a particular state, Ariff smuggled weapons in every conceivable way, whether over land, sea or air. One of his favoured methods was to conceal weapons in humanitarian-aid cargoes. The Red Cross might be sending a plane full of grain to the Democratic Republic of Congo, but while the plane was being refuelled in

Egypt, a third of the sacks of grain would be emptied and refilled with guns.

Some arms dealers were more brazen in their illicit trade, openly exploiting the cracks in national and international arms trading. There were certainly enough cracks for Ariff to conduct a lot more trade, and hence earn a lot more money, but he didn't let greed pull him out of the shadows. No one who operated more openly than him had stayed alive and out of jail for as long as he.

When Ariff had dried and dressed himself, he entered the lounge to find the Spanish girl sitting awkwardly on a sofa. She was wearing a red silk dressing gown and nothing else. The way the fabric flowed over the curves of her body might have encouraged Ariff to stay longer, had he not seen the large Lebanese man sitting opposite her.

Gabir Yamout made the armchair look like it was made for a child. He wasn't so much tall as he was wide. There was an uncomfortable look on his face, but not because of the size disparity between himself and his seating apparatus.

Ariff smiled and said, 'Did you not enjoy the performance, Gabir?'

Yamout scowled but said nothing. Ariff walked to where an ornate mirror hung on one wall. He brushed the shoulders of his jacket with his palm and turned around. He reached into a pocket and drew out a folded handkerchief. He gave it to the Spanish girl and made a dismissing gesture. She promptly went into the bedroom and closed the door.

The pouch contained tiny diamonds – enough to make a fine ring or necklace. Sometimes African governments and warlords paid Ariff in precious stones, which in turn his jeweller sold on in Antwerp and Tel Aviv. The diamonds he gave to the girl were all flawed and not worth selling, but she would never know that.

'One of our suppliers is dead,' Yamout announced. 'The Hungarian, Farkas, was assassinated last week.'

'And why would I care?'

'His mob associates think we killed him because Farkas was planning to bypass us and go direct to our customers. I hear they will retaliate.'

Ariff laughed. 'Let them try. I'm more scared of my wife.' He faced Yamout. 'When are you getting my money?'

'I'll have the American bring it to Minsk,' Yamout explained. 'I can make the deal with the Belarusian and collect it afterwards.'

'Very efficient.' Ariff checked his reflection one last time and said, 'Come on, or we'll be late for Eshe's party. I don't want to keep my daughter waiting on her birthday. You did get her something nice, didn't you?'

Yamout rose from his seat and nodded. 'Of course, she's my goddaughter. I picked it up last week. This beautiful dress from Jordan. It's blue with gold, so pretty. I can't wait to see her face.'

Ariff's brow furrowed. 'You do realise Eshe is only eight?'

'Even eight-year-olds like pretty dresses.'

On the street outside Ariff climbed into the passenger seat of Yamout's Mercedes. There were two men sitting on the back seat, both with compact Ingram sub-machine guns resting in their laps. Ariff ignored them.

'What do we know about this Belarusian?'

'Not much,' Yamout said. 'But I have a solid recommendation and his prices seem very reasonable.'

'Take plenty of protection,' Ariff said as he sat back and closed his eyes. 'These former Soviets can never be trusted.'

Yamout put the Mercedes in gear and pulled away from the kerb.

Further down the road, a young man in a brown suede jacket started up his motorbike's engine and whispered something to someone who wasn't there.

CHAPTER 15

Linz, Austria

The target's dossier was waiting for Victor when he used an internet café to access his email account. As well as providing computer terminals, the store also rented out music and films. There were stacks of old DVD cases and video cassettes by the window, sleeves discoloured from too much sunlight exposure. The clientele were young – lots of teenagers and twenty-somethings. No one older than him. Multiple music tracks emanated from several different sets of headphones and mixed together to provide a disjointed soundtrack over the clatter of keyboards.

Sitting in a secluded corner, no one observed Victor opening the dossier and reading. Like the file on Farkas, it was an extensive piece of literature. Gabir Yamout was a forty-four-year-old Lebanese arms trafficker and a former officer in the Beirut police force. He was a Christian who had fought for the militias during the eighties civil war before going to work for an Egyptian named Baraa Ariff. Yamout lived in Beirut with his large family. He was Ariff's business partner, bodyguard and friend.

Victor examined the first photograph that accompanied the dossier. A covert head-and-shoulders shot of Yamout. He looked in his early thirties, at least ten years younger than the age listed in the dossier, which told Victor his target was good enough to keep himself off anyone's radar for a long time. Yamout was dressed in a casual shirt, wearing sunglasses. He had a neat moustache and beard. Short hair. He looked like an intelligent man, friendly. Nothing in his appearance gave away the dark way in which he made his money. In Victor's experience, it rarely did. Certainly not in his own case.

Back in Victor's hotel room, he connected to the VoIP call. His employer said, 'I've got some more work for you.'

'Gabir Yamout.'

'But there's a complication.'

'Isn't there always?'

'Yamout is hittable for one night only, two days from now. I know this is the second time I've asked you to do a rush job, but I can't help that. Time is of the essence here.'

'Of course it is,' Victor said. 'You're asking me to kill a major arms dealer with less than sixty hours' lead time.'

'I said I can't help that. It'll be different next time.'

'Like the Farkas contract?'

'Yeah,' the voice agreed.

'Like the Farkas contract that I had to rush because the rushed Bucharest job cut into my preparations?'

The voice didn't answer.

'This will be the third time in three contracts I've had to

123

operate with a limited time frame,' Victor said. 'Three for three is not a reassuring pattern.'

'I never claimed the work I needed doing was going to be easy. If it was, I wouldn't need you now, would I?'

This time Victor remained silent.

'As you can see from the dossier, Yamout is a pretty big fish,' the voice said, moving on. 'He's the business partner of Baraa Ariff and together they run an extensive organisation that ferries mainly small arms from source to smaller, localised buyers. Who in turn sell them on to the end users. Their client list is huge and predominantly based in the Middle East and Africa, and over three decades of trafficking we believe they've shipped close to a billion dollars' worth of guns to warlords, militias and terrorists.'

'They sound like a delightful pair.'

'Don't they just? So stubbing Yamout out under our heel is going to make the world a far nicer place. You should feel good about that.'

'I'm overjoyed.'

'You sound it.' His employer paused. 'Yamout is going to be in Minsk to meet a Belarusian gangster by the name of Danil Petrenko. Petrenko is a typical Eastern European crime boss, but he's happened upon a few crates of AKs he wants to unload. They're meeting at the Hotel Europe, where Petrenko has a suite booked for the occasion. We don't know how Yamout is getting to Minsk, or when he's leaving again afterwards, but according to my intel Yamout isn't likely to stay too long, either at the hotel or in Minsk, so you'll have to hit him as soon as the first chance presents itself.'

'Which means the hotel will be the only viable strike point.'

'I guess. But you know more about it than me, so I'll defer to your judgement.'

Victor said, 'I hope you understand how that will complicate matters.'

'How so?'

'Yamout is a career arms trafficker, a man who has survived and thrived in a ruthless, dangerous profession; a man smart enough to keep his face away from a camera for the last decade. He won't be meeting a foreign gangster on his own turf without substantial backup. And Petrenko won't be meeting a foreign arms dealer in his city without a show of strength. That's potentially a lot of guns pointing my way.'

'Are you saying you're scared?'

'I'm saying that without proper time for planning and surveillance I'm going to have to do this strong. I won't be able to stealth it.'

'Kill him in an elevator with an axe for all I care.'

'The chances of this going loud are extremely high.'

'I can live with that.'

'And a hotel is a very public space.'

'I'm sure you'll do everything in your power to keep civilians out of any crossfire.'

'Fine,' Victor said. 'I'm going to need some guns, and I'm going to need to pick them up in Minsk no later than tomorrow afternoon.'

'I can do that,' the voice said. 'What kind of guns are we talking about?'

'A lot of them.'

After finishing the call, Victor slept, setting the alarm in his head to wake him at eight p.m. He exercised and bathed, thinking about the upcoming Yamout contract the whole time, wondering what he hadn't been told, and whether that lack of information would get him killed. Accepting the position of an expendable asset came as part of an assassin's job description, but that didn't mean Victor had to like it.

Another arms dealer. A telling fact, and one his employer hadn't elaborated on. Like his current target, his previous had been part of that industry, and though his first kill had been a contract killer, he had died to save the life of yet another trafficker, Vladimir Kasakov. Three members of the arms trade in three contracts. Two to die; one to live. For what goal?

Victor pushed the speculation from his mind. It wasn't his place to know. He was just a triggerman. For years he had done everything in his power to not understand why the men he killed needed to die. But it was different this time. This time he wanted to know. He wanted to understand. He told himself it was for protection, because ignorance had almost cost him his life the previous year.

That justification didn't sit right, however. There was more to it than that, whatever it may be. The distrust he had for his employer was palpable. He knew any job could be a set-up in the making, or this theme of rushed contracts could result in him walking into a situation he couldn't walk back out of. If he had been working for some private client he wouldn't go through with the latest job. He would cease communication and never contact them again. But resigning wasn't an option. Private clients didn't have the power to give him up to police forces and intelligence agencies the world over, or have access to satellite imagining, facial-recognition software, or the ability to call on thousands of spies and assets.

And when it was finally over, would his employer honour their arrangement? Would Victor be allowed to walk away from the CIA's employ when he'd completed the last kill? Maybe the final job would come with a severance package of the two-in-the-head variety. But he had no choice but to see it through. If he ran, they would chase him, and they knew enough about him to succeed where others had previously failed.

Victor sighed. He wasn't in a position to walk away from his CIA employer, but it was time to start thinking about the steps he would need to implement if he was to do so and remain breathing. A new identity was the first and most important thing. A clean identity, one he hadn't used before. He didn't know how many of his old aliases had been compromised. He couldn't procure that now, however. But he would as soon as the opportunity presented itself.

He sat forward and typed another address into the browser window, bringing up a different email account he kept active as part of plying his trade. Among the hundreds of emails offering him cheap erectile dysfunction medication, the chance to make a fortune by simply handing over all his personal information to a friendly gentleman from Nigeria, and pills to increase the size of his penis, there was one of interest. He opened it up. It was a short message addressed to *my friend*, from a man named Alonso saying what a great time he'd had in Hong Kong but that he'd spent a lot of money there. He was on his way to Europe, only wasn't staying long. The email ended with, *how are you?*

Victor considered. The Hong Kong contract with its high purse and the European one that needed to be done fast would have come to him for first refusal, but if he didn't respond they would go to someone else. There were dozens, if not hundreds, of men around the world just like him. Victor had encountered enough of them to know he was far from unique, but that he had survived those encounters told him he was towards the top of the bell curve in his rarefied profession.

A month ago, he would have deleted the message without responding as per the terms of his employment. In light of the latest conversation with his control, things had changed. He needed to keep his options open. Victor composed a reply to Alonso, writing that it was good to have heard from him and that he would like to know more about his travels. He sent the message.

He logged off the terminal and sat for a moment, feeling calm but not wholly relaxed. If his employers wanted to play games, so be it. He could play games of his own.

Only Victor wouldn't be playing fair.

CHAPTER 16

Sixty miles south-west of Minsk, Belarus

It was cold in the back of the car. Xavier Callo sat with his shoulders hunched up and his arms tightly folded across his chest, hands buried beneath his armpits. It was Blout's fault; he smoked roll-ups as he drove, keeping his window down so the smoke drifted outside. The incoming draught flowed straight over Callo. His captors had supplied him with a coat, which he wore now, but it only did so much. Abbot and Blout were both built like they could play pro football and seemed content enough with the window open and the cold air blowing in.

A flat green land rushed by Callo's window. It was all empty fields, barely any signs of habitation, somehow dead. For a long time he didn't even know which country he was in, only realising he was heading towards Minsk when he started to see signs for the city. They were in both Belarusian and Russian, and Callo knew a little Russian thanks to his business. He was hungry but didn't say anything for fear of going back in the trunk.

When they had first started their journey Callo had spent a few hours in the back seat before Abbot had ordered him inside the trunk. Blout then held him down while Abbot taped his hands, feet and finally his mouth. He didn't say why, but stressed if Callo didn't keep quiet Abbot would rig up his own bollock-fryer and leave Callo to cook. He choked on gasoline fumes for about twenty minutes before he was let out, freed from his bonds and allowed on the back seat. No explanation was given, but Callo didn't need one.

It was clear he had been stuck in the trunk while they crossed a border. After being kidnapped in Athens, Callo didn't know where he had been taken. He had been on at least two planes and spent countless hours in car trunks. Based on the weather, he guessed he had been interrogated somewhere in Eastern Europe. Since he was now heading to Minsk, he must have been in one of Belarus's neighbouring countries, most likely Poland.

His body clock was completely skewed and he had no idea how long it had been since he had been kidnapped. He managed to get a look at the clock on the car's console, so he knew the time at least.

'Why are we going to Minsk?' he asked Abbot when he could no longer bear the silence or the not knowing.

Abbot had his arm resting on the window sill while he stared at the Belarus countryside. 'Yamout texted your mobile. He wants you to meet him there.'

'But I don't have the money.'

'You won't need it, mate,' Abbot assured him.

Callo tried to continue the conversation but Abbot didn't speak back. Blout had said nothing at all to Callo. The silence was distinctly unpleasant and left Callo's imagination too much time to work. He was scared of going to somewhere even more terrifying than where he had spent two hours hooked by the balls to a generator. Though, in truth, Callo couldn't imagine anything worse than having his testicles electrocuted. Maybe this time he wouldn't know the answers they wanted and they would actually flick the switch. He shivered and pushed his thighs together. He knew he was in over his head, but he also knew if these guys were going to kill him they could have easily done it already. There was no need to take him all the way to Minsk to do so.

He hadn't seen the suited guy since the interrogation. After Callo revealed everything he knew about Ariff and Yamout, he had been taken back to his cell and left there for maybe twenty-four hours. Then Abbot had awoken him, and he'd been allowed to take a hot shower, with no one watching him while he scrubbed and cleaned. New clothes were waiting for him and he received some decent food, as much as he wanted.

Callo had dared to hope his release had been pending, but instead they were going to Minsk. He hoped they weren't planning on using him as bait to kidnap Yamout. It wouldn't work. Callo didn't have the nerves to bluff his way through that kind of encounter. Plus, Abbot and Blout were sure to be outnumbered by Yamout's bodyguards. But they must have worked that out for themselves. So what did they have planned?

No one had shown him any credentials or said who they worked for, but the bastard who'd interrogated Callo stank of CIA. The Brits were either in on the kidnapping or just mercenaries doing the heavy lifting. Bizarrely, no one seemed to care that the majority of Callo's business was highly illegal, and in talking about Yamout and Ariff he had admitted his part in many crimes. He had fully expected to be charged with some smuggling beef at the least, but so far nothing. Maybe after he had done whatever it was that Abbot wanted doing in Minsk they would actually let him go. It wasn't as if Callo was going to go to Amnesty International and complain about being frightened by a pair of glowing oranges.

'Maybe another hour until we're in Minsk,' Blout said to Abbot.

'Hear that, mate?' Abbot cocked his head in Callo's direction. 'Not long now and this will all be over.'

Callo was happy to hear that.

CHAPTER 17

Minsk, Belarus

Victor had arrived in the city the night before after a relaxing flight from Austria to Minsk International Airport. He had no luggage with him except a carry-on bag holding a few effects that weren't essential, but he preferred to fly with at least some luggage. Airport security tended to watch out for people with none. A thankfully silent taxi ride from the airport had taken him into central Minsk, where he'd performed counter surveillance before arriving at his hotel, the Best Eastern.

As Yamout was expected to meet with Petrenko around or after nine p.m. at the Hotel Europe the next day, and because of the potentially short duration of his stay, Victor would need to kill him at some point shortly after this time.

He'd taken the Minsk metro across the city and hailed a taxi to take him back into the centre. A second cab immediately after the first took him around the city centre for half an hour. Victor then re-joined the metro for another thirty minutes, changing trains twice before exiting and performing counter surveillance on foot. Finally, a third taxi had taken him to Passazhyrski train station.

He bought himself a large cappuccino with caramel syrup from a stunning Belarusian brunette at a kiosk and drank his coffee leisurely while he circled the concourse. He saw no sign of any shadows. May in Minsk tended to stay in the low seventies so Victor was without an overcoat but kept the jacket of his charcoal suit buttoned up. The cappuccino was especially good, or maybe it was just the memory of the brunette that enhanced the flavour.

In the basement level of the train station he found the left-luggage facility and gave the false name provided by his employer.

An old guy then dragged two heavy Samsonite suitcases to where Victor waited and dabbed the sweat from his forehead with a handkerchief. 'What have you got in here, rocks?'

'Guns,' Victor replied.

The old guy laughed.

The tags on the suitcases showed they had travelled overnight from Moscow, but there was a good chance the contents had been switched somewhere along the way. By the weight of the suitcase in each hand, Victor knew exactly what they contained.

He took a cab back to the Best Eastern and entered his room. Victor wasn't sure how the hotel came by its name, as there was nothing best about it. His room was bland and uninviting, the bed soft and lumpy. He closed the drapes and laid the suitcases on top of the bed so he could check the contents. The interiors had been stripped out and replaced with thick foam rubber sheets, cut to fit several items.

Inside one half of the first Samsonite was a dismantled

Heckler & Koch PSG1A1 semi-automatic rifle and long sound suppressor. It was a very good weapon, perfect for urban use and easily one of the most precise semi-automatic rifles in the world, with an expected accuracy of sub-one minute of angle. Victor wasn't keen on one characteristic, however. The rifle ejected its spent cartridge casings a long way, which, at best, made sterilising the environment more difficult after shooting the weapon. At worst, it could give away his position. Victor assembled the gun and inserted one of the three detachable box magazines that were set into the foam rubber beneath it. Each magazine contained twenty match-grade 7.62×52 mm cartridges. Loaded, the rifle weighed almost eighteen pounds and was over forty-seven inches in length.

He set out the Garbini tripod on the bed and familiarised himself with its operation, adjusting elevation and rotating the PSG laterally. He set the fully adjustable butt stock and pistol grip to his requirements and peered down the Schmidt & Bender $3-12 \times 50$ scope. With a clear line of sight, he could kill Yamout from a thousand yards away.

Victor disassembled the rifle and placed each part back inside the case. In the lower half of the suitcase were a set of thermal-imaging goggles, a master keycard for the Hotel Europe where Yamout's meeting was taking place, a block of C-4 plastic explosives and accompanying remote and timed detonators. Victor took out each item and checked it.

Inside the second suitcase, not set into the protective sheeting, was a concealable Class IIIA armoured vest comprised of non-interwoven, thermally bonded Kevlar fibre. Victor tore away its plastic wrap and tried it on for size. It was a medium, which fit him snugly as he wanted, but did not reach down his abdomen as far as he would have liked. A large size would have, but would have been too bulky on his frame to allow him unhindered movement. Better to be fast and vunerable than protected and slow.

Set into the foam rubber of one half of the second suitcase were two suppressed handguns – a .45 calibre Heckler & Koch USP Compact Tactical and a .22 calibre Walther P22. Each gun had three fully loaded magazines packed with it. One by one, Victor took the guns out, checked and dry fired them a few times, then put them back in the case. He'd requested the handguns because both used ammunition that was naturally subsonic and therefore extremely quiet when used in conjunction with a suppressor. Both guns were also small and concealable, the USP 6.8 inches in length and the Walther just 6.3 inches. They had small capacities to go along with their small sizes, eight rounds for the HK and ten for the P22, but they were purely for backup.

If he couldn't use the PSG to snipe Yamout from a distance, Victor would be relying on the weapon in the second half of the suitcase to help him successfully fulfil the contract. The FN P90 was a strange-looking weapon even to Victor's eye. Made by Fabrique National of Herstal, Belgium, the P90 was a selective fire sub-machine gun constructed with a bull pup configuration enabling a long ten-inch barrel that didn't increase the weapon's overall length. This gave it quicker target acquisition as well as more accuracy than typical sub-machine guns.

Victor took the compact weapon out of the casing. Primarily composed of high-density impact-resistant polymer and lightweight alloys, when empty it weighed just shy of six pounds and was only 19.7 inches long. He wrapped his right hand around the pistol grip and thumb-hole and in his left hand took the enlarged trigger guard that doubled as the forward grip. Victor found the hand arrangement comfortable. It also helped control recoil, especially on automatic fire.

The selector switch was beneath the trigger guard and Victor thumbed it from safe to semi-automatic to automatic. He squeezed the trigger gently, feeling the weight necessary to fire a single round, and then depressed the trigger fully for automatic fire. It was a useful feature, giving him the option of firing either one shot or several without having to use the selector to change between fire modes. With a cyclic rate of nine hundred rounds per minute, the P90 could unload its fifty-round magazine in 3.3 seconds. The weapon fired a 5.7×28 mm cartridge extremely accurately, even on fully automatic. Dispersion was minimal, thanks to the round's low recoil impulse and the weapon's twin-operating recoil springs and guide rods.

Victor checked the four fully loaded translucent polycarbonate magazines that mounted horizontally along the top of the weapon. He could see that the magazines contained white-tipped SB193 subsonic ammunition. Each bullet was boat-tailed with a lead core and had a projectile weight of 55.0 grains with 2.0 grains of powder, producing a muzzle velocity of just under one thousand feet per second with an effective range of fifty yards. A supersonic round was comparable to a 9 mm JHP in stopping power, but the subsonic SB193, though heavier than a supersonic 5.7 mm, had less than half the velocity. Stopping power therefore wasn't going to be particularly high, but in Victor's experience, whatever a bullet's characteristics, two in the chest and one in the head stopped anyone.

He loaded a magazine and adopted a firing position. He looked down the P90's unmagnified optical reflex sight. The reticule displayed a pattern of two concentric circles. The largest was approximately one hundred and eighty minutes of arc for fast target acquisition at long range and a smaller circle of twenty MOA surrounding a tiny dot at the centre of the field. Victor moved to the room's wardrobe, opened it, and held the P90 in the shadows. The tritium cell low-light reticule appeared as two horizontal lines across the middle of the field with a single vertical line from the bottom of the field to the middle to create an open T-shape.

Victor removed the Gemtech SP-90 suppressor from the suitcase. He aligned it with the muzzle brake, pushed down and rotated ninety degrees clockwise to lock it in place. The unique mounting system enabled him to affix the attachment in less than two seconds, far faster than a traditional screw-on suppressor. The SP-90 added 7.25 inches in length and almost twenty ounces in weight to the P90. It also reduced the muzzle velocity of the SB193 round to 951 fps, but Victor found this had next to no negative impact on ballistics or accuracy in real-world situations. The plus side to the reduction in velocity was a suppressed P90 was even quieter than an MP5SD.

Victor put on the thermal imaging goggles, turned off the lights, and switched the goggles on. They detected the infared light omitted and the room became shades of black, grey and white. He released the P90's magazine and checked the front of the weapon where the infrared wavelength laser aiming module was located beneath the barrel. The laser designator was integrated into the receiver and didn't affect the P90's performance in any way. Victor flicked the adjustment switch from off to high intensity. There was a low intensity setting too, but Victor didn't plan on using the gun long enough for battery life to matter. He set the goggles so hot was displayed as black, cold as white.

A thin black beam, invisible to the naked eye, cut across the room and glowed where it struck the far wall. Victor swept the glow on to the television mounted on the wall. He squeezed the trigger, putting an imaginary burst into his reflection's head.

Plastic explosives, a sniper rifle, two handguns, and a sub-machine gun.

Yes, Victor thought, probably enough weapons.

CHAPTER 18

Washington, DC, USA

Nelson's Diner was a shiny sausage-shaped building a twenty-minute drive from Langley. Procter sat with a cup of coffee in a booth along the far wall from the entrance through which Clarke entered with his nose wrinkled at the smell of grease and frying meat. The place was almost full, lots of people like Procter who could do with losing a fair chunk of pounds. Clarke slid on to the vinyl-covered seat.

'You might want to try acting more like you belong here,' Procter said. 'You'll draw less attention that way.'

'Well, I don't belong, do I? Anyone can see that. Including you, I'm assuming. Which makes me ask, why here?'

Procter's gaze strayed off Clarke. 'Because this place makes the best steak sandwiches you've ever tasted. You should try one. It's worth coming to work just to have one at lunchtime.'

Clarke glanced over to a table where a couple of guys in overalls were eating hamburgers with fries and a few token lettuce leaves on the side. The buns looked flat and soggy and the fries were anorexic sticks of potato in thick oil coatings. Behind the counter a wide, sweating Latino was flipping burgers. Grill fat sizzled.

Clarke grimaced. 'I think I'd rather skip the stroke at seventy.'

'Cut the bourgeois prejudice for once, Peter.'

'So I'm prejudiced against plaque in my arteries. Sue me.'

A waitress appeared. She was tall, and young and pretty enough for Procter to quickly look her over, but too skinny around the bust and hips for him to look twice. Clarke paid her no attention.

Her smile was big and bright. 'Get you coffee?'

Clarke nodded.

'Another for me, please,' Procter said.

She filled Clarke's cup and poured Procter a fresh one. He added lots of cream and sugar. The diner did coffee thick, strong and exactly how Procter liked it. Just because it didn't have an Italian name, come in a waxed paper cup and cost three times as much, didn't make it inferior. Clarke took his black, as always.

'How's the coffee?' Procter asked.

'Like piss.'

'Well, I'm buying, so you'd better enjoy it.'

'We're not here to discuss the quality of caffeine-delivery systems.' Clarke put his cup back down. 'What's the situation?'

Procter said, 'Thanks to information we sucked out of Callo, we've been able to make a lot of headway in a very short time frame,' Procter began. 'It seems that Ariff's people have been negotiating with a Belarusian gangster named Danil Petrenko for some time now. Petrenko has access to big stockpiles of guns that Ariff wants to add to his collection. There's a face-to-face

141

going down in Minsk tomorrow night. Ariff is sending his top man to liaise with Petrenko. That top man is a Lebanese guy called Gabir Yamout. And yes, that's the same Yamout who we know has been at Ariff's side for years. Yamout is now Ariff's business partner, according to Callo. They're both Christians and are so close they're practically family. Which is why I'm sure you'll agree with me that Yamout makes the perfect target to take this thing of ours to the next level.

'We don't know how Yamout is travelling to Belarus, or where he's staying, but what we do know is that Petrenko has booked the top suite at the Hotel Europe in central Minsk for a single night. Tomorrow night. So Tesseract will strike at the hotel while Yamout is there.'

Clarke's long face was unimpressed. 'I really don't like the idea of a hit taking place at a hotel. Especially with such a short lead time. Could get messy.'

'Tesseract said the same thing. Look, is it ideal? No, it's not. But Yamout setting foot outside the Middle East is too good an opportunity to miss.'

'A hotel hit will get airtime.'

'I'm counting on it,' Procter said. 'It will be all over the news in Europe and therefore Ariff is going to hear about it very soon afterwards. And we want him to know with as little delay as possible.'

'Okay,' Clarke said, seemingly satisfied with the logic. 'Yamout isn't going to be travelling alone. Petrenko won't meet him by himself. Could be a lot of guys there for Tesseract to deal with. Might be too much, even for your MVP.'

Procter shrugged. 'I've got no reasons to doubt him. It's not like he has to go through every single one to get to Yamout.

Besides, if he can't pull this kind of job off then it's about time we found that out.'

'So we're gambling with his life now.'

'If you want to put it like that.'

'Tesseract is going to think we're playing him.'

'We are playing him.'

Clarke sat forward. 'He won't like it.'

'If he stamps his feet, we'll remind him who his daddy really is.'

'And he'll like that even less.'

Procter frowned, leaned forward. 'Do you seriously think I'm not already aware of everything you've just said?'

Clarke leaned forward too. 'Oh, I'm sure you've thought it through, Roland, but we're coming to polar opposite conclusions.'

'That's where you're wrong, my friend. We're coming to the same conclusions. But while they concern you, I'm happy with them.'

'You're happy with an angry assassin running around out there who may or may not do as he's told?'

Procter selected his words carefully. 'I'm content with it.'

'So tell me, what do we do if he's angrier than we thought?'

'Then we activate the contingency I've prepared.'

Clarke sighed. 'I think it's about time you revealed what that actually is.'

'I can't do that.'

Clarke's face flushed red. 'Why the hell not?'

'We may be in this together, but some things are best not shared, for mutual safety. As you are well aware.'

'I'm not sure this counts, Roland.'

'Okay, if we're going to put all our cards on the table, I want to know who is bankrolling this operation of ours.'

Clarke was silent for a moment. 'You know I can't say. We agreed on anonymity to protect all parties if something went wrong. I've told you all I'm at liberty to.'

'Spare me the speeches. Who are they?'

'I won't answer that,' Clarke said. 'So quit asking. And may I remind you that our sponsor doesn't know who you are.'

'Okay, don't tell me,' Procter said. 'But it works both ways.'

'It's not the same,' Clarke protested. 'Knowing what you plan to do with Tesseract, should he become a problem, is not going to compromise me.'

'Maybe not,' Procter admitted. 'But I don't want to ruin the surprise.'

Clarke was quiet for a moment. 'Why do I get the impression you're playing me as much as you are Tesseract?'

'Because you've been in this business too long, Peter. Like me. But we're on the same side here. We both want to take down these gun-running scumbags, and this is the way – the only way – to make that happen.'

Clarke seemed placated, at least for the time being.

Procter said, 'You haven't updated me on Kasakov yet. Is he still in the dark about Farkas?'

'So I'm led to believe,' Clarke began as he leaned back in his chair, 'but I expect he'll be emerging into the light any time now.'

CHAPTER 19

Moscow, Russia

The punch was a straight right that followed a stiff jab and caught Vladimir Kasakov a half-inch above his left temple. It wasn't a flush blow, but Kasakov didn't see it coming, and the ones that weren't seen always hurt the most. The Russian boxer who threw the punch was a solid two hundred and fifty pounds, a professional heavyweight, and known for his one-punch knockout power. The sixteen-ounce glove did little to cushion the blow that jolted the Ukrainian arms dealer's senses. He kept his guard high and tight as his opponent unleashed a flurry of hard left hooks and overhand rights.

Kasakov backed off and used his jab to keep the Russian at range. Kasakov's opponent was three inches taller – six-six – but they had the same armpit-to-fist reach, which meant Kasakov could employ his jab frequently and effectively. The Ukrainian's jab was his favourite punch; it was hard and accurate, and, though not a knockout shot, it set up other punches, and ten in the face each round took its toll on anyone and stopped them throwing back at the same time.

The Russian followed Kasakov as he backed off, flicking some jabs of his own but without the same conviction. He was just looking to throw the big punches, but Kasakov was using his better footwork and jab to stop the Russian setting his feet for power shots. The big man was good at cutting off the ring though, using lateral movement to slowly force Kasakov towards the ropes. That was where he definitely didn't want to end up. He stopped backing off and threw some straight right hands and hooks after jabbing, but had difficulty getting them through the Russian's textbook guard.

Kasakov wasn't used to backing down in the ring or outside of it and he stayed toe-to-toe, throwing punches and taking them. The adrenalin surge was huge. Some of his ringside underlings were shouting instructions, but the arms dealer ignored them. When it came to boxing, Kasakov ignored everyone.

He'd listened to his old amateur coach, but he was long dead and Kasakov had never felt the need to seek another. He had been boxing since he was six years old, and after forty years' worth of experience in the ring there was little anyone could tell him that he didn't already know. He'd had an extensive and successful amateur career, winning regional and national titles but missing out on the Olympics due to an elbow injury during trials.

That amateur career had been cut short when he was drafted into the Soviet army and sent to fight in Afghanistan. He was assigned to logistics, and by the time of the withdrawal had made the rank of major. When the empire fell apart Kasakov was in a perfect position to acquire and sell the redundant munitions he had helped transport and manage. The market in small arms was already too strong to compete with but Kasakov saw an opening for heavier armaments. His first customers were his old enemies in the Islamic State of Afghanistan. He made a killing selling off Red Army T-55 and T-62 tanks, and when the Taliban took over the country he continued delivering weapons to his old customers in what became the Northern Alliance. But recognising a good opportunity when he saw it, Kasakov began trading with the Taliban at the same time, selling them rockets to defeat the tanks, and then mortars to the Northern Alliance to defeat the anti-tank teams. When one faction was gaining the upper hand, he held off on resupplies, and cut his prices to the other to prolong the conflict and keep his business thriving.

He soon expanded into Africa, and using aircraft from the grounded Soviet Air Force flew in arms to nations under UN embargoes. Before long he had customers in south-east Asia and South America too and was coming to the attention of the international community. To stay operating he reduced his hands-on involvement in the trafficking business, employing others to take the biggest risks for him. He made sure his name was never on anyone's paperwork nor on any computer file. He wasn't sure how many companies he had, but it had to be close to a hundred registered in a dozen different countries. By the time any agency started to get a handle on what one was up to, Kasakov closed it down and moved its operations to one of his other companies in another nation. The web of ownership was so complicated even Kasakov had difficulty keeping track.

The day the Twin Towers fell he was smart enough to cut all ties with the Taliban and anyone connected to Islamic terrorists, but the damage had already been done and international pressure for his arrest was escalating, regardless of his preventative measures. Acutely aware of the growing momentum against him, Kasakov moved from his native Ukraine to Russia. Having made the Russian government billions by brokering arms sales he had no trouble gaining Russian citizenship. As Moscow never extradited nationals, he was safe.

That safety didn't extend into the ring, where the Russian giant found an opening in Kasakov's defences through which to send another hammer right hand. Kasakov saw it coming, but it still snapped his head back and momentarily buckled his knees. He'd never sparred the Russian giant before and now knew why his people had tried to keep them apart. The fight was tougher than expected. Much tougher. Kasakov wished he'd put in more time training in the preceding weeks, but with the assassination attempt in Bucharest and the slowdown in the business requiring his complete attention, he had drastically reduced his hours in the gym. He shook off the thought. So it wouldn't be a walkover today for a change.

Though training and fighting were now very much a solitary pursuit for Kasakov, he had, for many years, trained alongside his nephew, Illarion. Although the kid didn't have Kasakov's passion for the sport, he always trained and fought hard. As he matured out of adolescence they sparred together, and despite being far smaller than his uncle, Illarion's speed, youth and natural athleticism always made such bouts close enough that Kasakov did not have to fully pull his punches. He wondered what Illarion would say about how he was faring against the Russian. Kasakov was sure it wouldn't have been complimentary.

He managed to dodge away from the ropes and back to the centre of the ring to set about turning the fight around. The

Ukrainian kept no official scorecard for his fights, knowing that his underlings would score even the most one-sided beating against as a victory for their boss, but Kasakov scored the fight privately, for his own satisfaction. Neither man had landed anything significant in the opening round so he would have given that round even, but the last two had gone to the Russian, who had landed the bigger shots in both. Making it 30–28 against. Still three rounds to go. He would need to take them all to win the six-round contest. He might be able to jab his way to a draw, but Kasakov fought to win.

He attacked cautiously, throwing the jab, and landing flush, but doing little damage save for keeping the Russian giant at range. The giant's face shimmered with sweat, and the bridge of his nose was red from the jabs, but otherwise he was unmarked. Kasakov couldn't say the same about himself.

The Russian surprised Kasakov by jabbing back and Kasakov was happy to continue the jabbing contest, knowing he had the better technique. The arms dealer punched his opponent with four more to the face and one to the gut. Maybe this was going to be a walkover after all. The big overhand right that slammed into his left eye socket erased any thoughts of an easy fight in one humiliating instant. He'd been set up, tricked by a modicum of success, and timed to perfection. The punch hurt like hell and made the strength leave Kasakov's legs.

His vision blurred and he stumbled, but stayed standing and covered up while he tried to shake off the effects of the big punch. The Russian unloaded on him and every second that passed meant more and more stinging blows to Kasakov's arms, shoulders and head.

The Russian exploited Kasakov's high guard by throwing

some hard body shots that struck unprotected ribs. In response, Kasakov lurched forward, wrapping his arms around his opponent's, tying him up so he couldn't punch, trying to buy the time until his sight returned and his head cleared.

He leaned into the Russian so that his opponent had to support his weight as well as his own. Kasakov was extremely fit for his forty-seven years and was a master of pacing himself during a fight. He knew he should be fresher than this at the current stage of the fight, but the body shots had stolen his stamina. Wrestling with the Russian, who was the bigger man in the ring by twenty pounds, was wasting even more energy. This wasn't working, Kasakov told himself.

The crowd shouted their encouragement but their mirth was being beaten out of them as surely as the will to fight had been beaten out of Kasakov. The Russian wriggled his arms free and shoved Kasakov away. His head still swam from the big overhand right, and his legs had no strength. The next flush shot that landed would put him on the canvas. Even if he managed to get up again he wouldn't make up the additional lost point. His opponent pawed with a jab, and followed with another overhand right that Kasakov managed to deflect with his left glove. He doubted he would be so lucky next time. The arms dealer tilted his body to the right as he stepped forward and threw a short left uppercut.

The Russian groaned as the gloved fist hit him square in the crotch. Like Kasakov he wore a groin protector, but the metal cup and padding were never enough to stop the agony. The Russian sank down to one knee, face red and contorted. From outside the ring a chorus of cheers erupted and one of the underlings began shouted a count.

'*One . . . two . . . three . . . four . . . five . . .*'

Kasakov stood in a neutral corner, elbows up on the top rope, breathing hard. A thick film of sweat covered every inch of his skin. The Russian looked up at him and despite the pain in his face, Kasakov could see anger and disgust. He pretended not to notice.

'*Six . . . seven . . . eight . . . nine . . . TEN.*'

Kasakov raised a hand to the air to acknowledge the celebration of his underlings. He felt no joy at having won the fight by cheating, but neither was he ashamed. When faced with a greater enemy a smart man used whatever methods he could to even the field. The Russian was happy to accept the large payment for sparring with Kasakov so he would have to accept fighting by the Ukrainian's rules.

He climbed out of the ring and nodded and smiled to his underlings as they congratulated him on a great body shot. Some would not have noticed the blow had been illegal but plenty would have had an uninterrupted view. No one even hinted at it being even on the belt, let alone very low. The benefits of fear, Kasakov told himself. Illarion would not have placated him had he been there to bear witness, but he would have respected Kasakov's desire to win at any cost.

A head-on collision outside of Kiev had orphaned Illarion and killed Kasakov's only other living blood relative – his younger brother – as well as his brother's wife. Kasakov had done the noble thing and taken in the orphan. Children had once seemed irrelevant to Kasakov, but he enjoyed young Illarion's company far more than he would ever have imagined and soon, despite himself, thought of the boy as a son. Kasakov had no children of his own, and though he refused to have himself tested, was sure he was infertile. He and his wife never spoke of the situation, but it was the single stain on their otherwise perfect marriage and grew larger all the time.

One of the underlings unlaced his gloves and the arms dealer wiped the sweat from his bare torso, arms and face with a soft towel.

It was another minute before the Russian could stand back up.

After showering and changing, Kasakov left the locker room to see two well-dressed individuals – one man, one woman – standing expectantly nearby. Both were in their forties, the man was a fellow Ukrainian, the woman a Russian. Together they formed Kasakov's innermost circle. Each was supposed to be busy with other duties, so the presence of both indicated something important had arisen and their dour expressions told him this was not good news.

He imagined it was in regard to the recent attempt on his life in Bucharest. His people had been working hard to determine what had actually taken place and who had orchestrated it. No one had yet claimed responsibility for saving his life, so the arms dealer believed he had been saved merely as beneficial side effect of the morning's kill. Even so, he would like to know more.

The fact that he had nearly been killed convinced Kasakov to re-evaluate his travel and security arrangements, but did not unduly worry him. He had a long list of enemies, and had been the target for assassination more than once. Though this time had been the first in over a decade, the last being a French hit squad that had shot off half his left ear. Kasakov would have preferred a quieter life, but the billions of dollars he was personally worth easily made up for the risks of his chosen business.

Yuliya Eltsina was the first to speak. She was a former officer in the Russian security services and had been in Kasakov's employ for nearly eight years. Close to a foot shorter than Kasakov, slim, with age now marring her once obvious beauty, Eltsina still carried the air of hawkish knowledge and casual brutality that had propelled her through the ranks of the KGB and then SVR. Kasakov had no affection for Eltsina and often found her humourless company tiresome. The woman was, however, a genius at devising new strategies to keep Kasakov's arms trafficking empire flourishing beneath the noses of the international community. Her numerous contacts and friends in the intelligence agencies of Russia and the surrounding states enabled her to provide Kasakov with an assortment of otherwise inaccessible information on his business partners, rivals, suppliers and customers.

'We have a situation you need to be aware of.'

'Details,' Kasakov responded.

She handed Kasakov a dossier. 'In this file you'll find a police report pertaining to a bomb explosion that took place in Germany, last week. The bomb killed a Hungarian named Adorján Farkas, a high-ranking lieutenant in a leading Hungarian organised crime family. For the past two years Farkas had been supplying Baraa Ariff with cheap assault rifles. My people tell me that Ariff had Farkas killed because he was seeking to bypass Ariff and go direct to his customers.'

Ariff's business practices were of little interest to Kasakov so he waited patiently for the reason Eltsina was providing him with such information. Ariff's network didn't stray into

Kasakov's, or vice versa. Kasakov's attempts to move into the small arms trade had always been unsuccessful. Ariff's network was established long before Kasakov had even started in the business, and could not be competed with.

Kasakov's second advisor, Tomasz Burliuk, said, 'Also in the dossier is the chemical analysis completed by the BKA of the explosives used to kill Farkas. The reason this has come to our attention is that the analysis shows the compound that killed Farkas was RDX high explosive, Russian army issue. The RDX was unique in that it contained an experimental marker compound. There was an agreement between several countries to come up with a way of tracking explosives in an effort to combat terrorism. A few batches were made up, but the idea was abandoned. We bought the surplus marked RDX a few years back.'

Burliuk was one of Kasakov's childhood friends. He was tall, though not as tall as Kasakov, and had the easy confidence of a man who knew he was handsome and looking even better with age. He was immaculately groomed, hair perfect, beard expertly trimmed. He had been at Kasakov's side since the early days, for longer than Kasakov could even remember. A good man and a hard worker, Burliuk had started off by handling the accounting and number-crunching of the operation. Balancing the books wasn't something Kasakov was good at, but Burliuk was a master at managing money. These days, as well as the accounts, Burliuk handled most of the day-to-day decisions, leaving only the most important ones for Kasakov to make.

'That RDX was in turn shipped to Istanbul to be sold via an intermediary so it couldn't be traced back to us,' Burliuk added, then removed an inhaler from his inside jacket pocket, shook it briefly, and took a hit of asthma-relieving gas.

Eltsina continued for him. 'While in Istanbul it was hijacked by persons then unknown.'

Burliuk put away his asthma inhaler and delivered the climactic point. 'As you are aware, it was in this incident that your nephew, Illarion, was shot and killed.'

Kasakov had stopped reading the file the moment Istanbul had been mentioned. He felt pain worse than any punch flood through him. It made him feel weak, light-headed. He pictured Illarion's dead face and vivid bullet holes puncturing his corpse-white skin.

'How much of this is verified?' Kasakov said through clenched teeth.

Eltsina spoke again. 'The BKA forensic evaluation of the explosive is beyond question. Farkas was killed in Berlin at the end of last week by the marked RDX that was stolen in Istanbul four years ago when Illarion was killed. So far, there are no police suspects for the Farkas bombing. My contacts tell me that it was widely known in the Hungarian mob that Farkas was in Germany to buy new weaponry. He planned to set up his own network and cut out Ariff to increase his profits. Farkas's mob associates are convinced it was Ariff and want him dead. They don't know where he is, otherwise they would already be seeking retribution against him.'

Kasakov nodded, satisfied with the evidence he had been presented with. 'So if Ariff killed Farkas with my RDX then it was Ariff's people who stole it from me in the first place. And therefore it was Ariff who murdered Illarion.'

'But we need to exercise restraint,' Burliuk said quickly.

'Ariff's network is as strong as us, his reach is perhaps longer. We don't need a war with him while the North Koreans are watching us. Any hint of strife and they'll buy elsewhere. And we badly need that deal. They're already angry you couldn't make the meeting with their broker in Bucharest. Vladimir, please, you must listen to me. You must—'

But Kasakov wasn't listening. He handed back the file. 'Find and kill Ariff,' he said easily. 'This is our number one priority. Nothing else matters. Hire the absolute best. I don't care how much it costs. Torture and kill his family first. Make him watch.'

CHAPTER 20

Minsk, Belarus

From where Victor stood, the Hotel Europe looked like it deserved its five stars. It was seven storeys of early twentieth-century Modern-style architecture and occupied the north-west corner of a city block where Lenina Street met Internatsionalnaya. Bright white stone walls rose to sloped roofs of grey tiles. Lush trees lined the sidewalk. A young doorman stood outside with a military-straight back and a welcoming smile. Victor first walked past east along Internatsionalnaya, before circling around the block to walk north on Lenina. He grabbed a coffee and waited half an hour before walking south on Lenina and then west on Internatsionalnaya. An hour later, he reversed the routine. He wanted to take in as much information about the building and its immediate environs as possible and explored the surrounding nine-block area in detail.

The hotel stood in the cultural heart of Minsk. Places of worship seemed to be everywhere. Two blocks west, spires of the eighteenth-century Russian Orthodox cathedral rose above the nearby buildings, and further north on Lenina, Victor could see the St Maria Cathedral. Diagonally north-east across the intersection was Minsk City Hall, across Lenina stood the huge titled Main department store. Just walking around the locale, Victor passed the National Academic Yanka Kupala Theatre, the National Art Museum, the Belarusian State Academy of Music, and the mighty Palace of the Republic. Predictably, the area was a tourist hotspot and the streets were crowded.

The Belarusians and foreign tourists wore a mix of styles and fashions. Suited men were common enough for him to blend in easily with his chosen urban attire. The temperature was a pleasant seventy-two degrees and Victor kept his jacket open. The sun wasn't bright enough to demand sunglasses, but he didn't look out of place wearing them either.

The information supplied by his employer stated the meeting would take place in the hotel's Presidential Suite on the seventh floor. The suite had been booked for a single night by Petrenko's people, who were expected to number at least five, including Petrenko himself. Yamout was known to travel with up to five or six companions. So, maybe six or seven for Yamout's party, and three to five for Petrenko. Nine in total at the lowest estimate. Twelve at worst.

In a situation such as this, Victor would have expected a window of at least two weeks in which to plan and survey properly. He would spend that time working through every conceivable scenario, analysing each potential opportunity, working through a dozen possible approaches. He would operate using the most feasible plan at the best possible time. But that wasn't to be. He had just one night, just one opportunity to kill Yamout.

Doing it fast meant one of two options: from close quarters or from range. There were precious few potential sniping positions, and none that guaranteed a view of Yamout. Because the most up-to-date photo of Yamout the CIA had access to was a decade old, Victor was sure the Lebanese would employ preventative measures when travelling, such as entering the hotel through an entrance other than the main one and exiting via some other way. The hotel had several to choose from and Victor had no way of knowing which Yamout would use at a given time. Since sniping Yamout on his way in or out of the hotel wasn't viable, the only other option for a ranged kill would be to shoot Yamout through a window of the Presidential Suite. There were several buildings that offered angles on the seventh-floor windows of the suite, but at the moment all its drapes were drawn. If they stayed that way, Victor wouldn't get a shot. Even if Petrenko's people opened them all, unlikely as that was, there was no guarantee they wouldn't be closed again for the meeting, or that Yamout would helpfully stand in front of one.

That left close quarters. Which meant Victor would have to fight his way through the bodyguards to get to Yamout. If they had any tactical sense, there would be guys outside the door creating a first layer of defence and combined advance warning, probably two men, one of Yamout's and one of Petrenko's. Then more guys forming a second layer, maybe five guys strong, probably occupying the main lounge area, with the last layer – comprising Yamout, Petrenko and their most trusted guys – wherever the deal was to be negotiated, in the dining room or one of the bedrooms.

It was a tactical nightmare whichever way he looked at it. To get to Yamout required going through close to a dozen enemies, all carrying guns, all no doubt willing to use them. Petrenko's men were unlikely to throw themselves to Yamout's defence, but in the chaos of battle they would assume the threat was to them as well and fight back accordingly.

Even if Yamout and Petrenko stayed out of proceedings, Victor could be up against ten gunmen. Close quarters as well. The dossier stated that Yamout employed only top-class body-guards, ex-military, probably guys that cost a small fortune to hire but kept their cool in a firefight. The intelligence on Petrenko suggested his men would be of a lesser calibre, but as members of the Belarusian mob, they would know how to un-safety a pistol. And it didn't require much skill to hit a man-sized target in an enclosed environment where the average range would probably be no greater than seven or eight feet. All anyone would need to do was point and squeeze.

The only way he was going to pull it off was to do it fast, with maximum surprise. Hit them hard when they weren't expecting it.

And not miss.

Victor had been supplied with blueprints of the hotel, but a two-dimensional representation of three-dimensional space was only so much good. The suite was occupied until check-out time and then the maid would take over and clean before Petrenko's arrival. Victor didn't know what time that would be, but there was a chance he would be able to do a walk-around of the strike point beforehand. But if Petrenko arrived too early, then Victor wouldn't get that opportunity. Presidential Suite aside, he still wanted some first-hand experience of the hotel before the time to attack came around.

The doorman gave Victor a big smile and opened the door for him. Victor nodded and walked into the lobby. It was a vast and impressive atrium, illuminated by natural light that shone through the hotel's elegant glass cupola over one hundred feet above. Internal ringed balconies for each floor overlooked the central open space and two glass-fronted elevators that stood in the middle of the lobby. Luxurious sofas and chairs were clustered in various locations. A lobby bar occupied the wall to Victor's left, the long reception desk directly opposite. Perpendicular to the elevators, a gigantic Florentine mosaic panel-painting rose almost to the ceiling high above Victor's head.

He didn't slow down as he entered to avoid risking being mistaken for a new arrival and catching the eye of one of the two receptionists. He walked at a casual pace, his eyes moving constantly, matching what he was seeing to what the blueprints had showed or hadn't showed. The lobby was busy but not crowded. A steady flow of people moved about, entering or exiting the restaurant or bars, walking towards or away from the elevators. Others waited, sitting at the lobby bar or on one of the tastefully upholstered sofas. The high price of the rooms ensured the hotel had a wealthy patronage. The less-obviously affluent, Victor took to be tourists whose currency went further in Belarus than at home.

Killing Yamout in the lobby had seemed a possible option before, but it was too big, too open, and as Victor didn't know how Yamout would enter, it would be impossible to set up properly. Yamout and his people were likely to use the elevators, but it wasn't guaranteed. Besides, there was another problem.

There were several blips on his threat radar caused by patrolling security. They had the competent look of well-trained rent-a-cops who wouldn't necessarily go out of their way to enter a gun battle, but probably wouldn't flee from one either.

In addition to the security, Victor noticed a single man sitting on an armchair near the elevators, holding a folded newspaper but not reading it. He seemed uncommonly interested in who walked in and out of the elevators. He wore a brown suede jacket and dark trousers. His complexion and hair were both too dark for a Belarusian. A tourist then, except a tourist wouldn't have been pretending to read a Belarusian newspaper. Interesting. One of Yamout's men, Victor presumed. Maybe he was here to scout the hotel before Yamout arrived.

The watcher paid Victor no attention as he walked past but Victor would have to be careful. Even though the watcher probably had orders to observe only what Petrenko's people were doing, if he saw Victor enough times he might realise he was someone to watch.

In his pocket Victor carried the hotel master keycard, which gave him easy access throughout the hotel. Though watchful of security cameras, he had been in enough hotels throughout the world to know their most likely positions, and therefore kept his face angled away from them as best he could. It didn't always work perfectly, but better they recorded him now if it meant he could avoid them when it mattered most.

There were no guest rooms on the ground level. Instead, the floor was occupied by the hotel's many facilities. The sixty-seven-room Europe offered all the normal services of a high-end hotel, plus a hairdresser's, beauty parlour, five bars, a night club and Turkish bath. The amenities were of little interest to Victor, and he planned to kill Yamout in the Presidential Suite, but he had been in the assassination business long enough to know that even the most thoroughly planned job could go awry. The ability to improvise was an important attribute in the contract killer's skill set. And if he did have to improvise, he wanted to have a good understanding of his surroundings. Victor took his time here, checking where all the exits were and how usable they would be in a range of circumstances pertaining to his escape. He didn't see the job going down any other way except one that would require him to leave in an extreme hurry. Even with suppressed weapons he couldn't kill twelve men silently.

Eventually things were going to get noisy and once that happened he would have only minutes before the police arrived. The nearest metro station was a ten-minute stroll, a five-minute hustle or a two-minute run. The closest bus stop was far nearer but he would need to get off the streets as quickly as possible and waiting for a bus wouldn't help him do that. His best bet was to grab a taxi and get out of the city centre before the police presence escalated and blocked him in. But he had to rely on a taxi passing by, and he hated leaving something so necessary to his escape to chance.

He could steal a car, but if the police were on the lookout for it he could inadvertently bring them to him even sooner. Until he had a clean identity sorted, he didn't want to create the paper trail by using a rental. Plus, he didn't know Minsk's streets well enough to escape easily by car and there was no time to learn them before tonight. Better to start on foot and have the option to use either metro, bus or taxi as required.

Victor took the elevator to the seventh floor. He strolled around the corridor, pausing to peer over the railing to his right and down to the lobby below. He looked up at the glass cupola ceiling. The sky beyond it was a deep blue. Enough natural light spilled down that few other light fixtures were needed. He pictured the cupola's effect at night and then counted the steps to the Presidential door and from the door to the stairwell.

It was a little after ten-thirty a.m. There was a maid's cart near the Presidential. He could hear a vacuum cleaner. Victor didn't know how long the maid would have left to clean the room, but he planned to wait nearby until she had finished. It took ten minutes before she left the suite and pushed her cart away. He waited until she had gone before using the internet option on his phone to log into the hotel's network with a password provided by his employer. He checked the booking register. He didn't want to take a tour of the Presidential only to be joined by Petrenko and his men two minutes later. Unlikely, given that official check-in wasn't for another hour and a half, but he didn't know if Petrenko had preferential treatment being a frequent guest and local crime lord. The register showed nothing, but Victor didn't move.

An elevator reached the seventh floor and its doors opened. A man stepped out. He was around six feet tall, mid twenties, with closely cropped red hair, dressed in jeans, sneakers and sports jacket. He had a lean but hard fighter's physique and gave Victor the universal tough guy stare as he sauntered in the direction of the Presidential. He definitely wasn't a hotel employee and though Victor had nothing to tell him what Petrenko looked like, this guy was unlikely to be him. Too young and too obviously stupid.

Victor didn't wait to confirm the tough guy was going to enter the suite; he took the stairs down to the floor below and moved along the balcony corridor until he was in a position to turn around and look upwards. The second glass-fronted elevator was ascending. The glare on the glass stopped him from initially making out any details but he could see two or three figures. As the elevator rose past him, the glare disappeared to reveal three men – two more tough guys in jeans and sportswear and one older, better dressed man who held himself with the unmistakable air of a natural leader. They exited the elevator and headed to the Presidential.

So Petrenko was allowed to check-in early, whether by having an arrangement with the hotel or from just slipping the receptionist some cash for the privilege. Victor used the stairs to reach the lobby and took a seat in the bar while he waited.

The man in the brown suede jacket was still in his chair, still pretending to read his newspaper.

An hour went by before Victor was given the opportunity he was waiting for. The man he took to be Petrenko exited an elevator along with the young tough guy and the two in sports coats. They walked through the lobby and left the hotel via the main entrance. At which point the watcher in the brown jacket stood up from his chair, dropped his newspaper down where he'd been sitting, and followed.

If the three men Victor had seen were the sum total of Petrenko's entourage then the suite would now be empty. There was always the chance another man had joined Petrenko while Victor had been in the bar, but there was only one way to find out.

He waited for a few minutes before taking the elevator up to the fifth floor and used the stairs for the last two. He gave a

165

polite knock on the Presidential's door and waited with an equally polite smile. Whether or not someone answered would also tell him more about the accuracy of the intelligence he'd been supplied with. The dossier had stated Petrenko's party would be at least five strong.

It took a second knock and a minute wait but the door was opened. One point to the CIA and any chance of Victor getting time by himself in the suite vanished. Another thug stood before Victor, dressed in a T-shirt and jeans. The T-shirt was emblazoned with the fiery logo of a German rock band.

'Yes?'

The man spoke in Russian. If he'd answered in Belarusian Victor would have struggled to make the next part work – as he didn't speak the language – but only a small percentage of Belarusians used their native tongue before Russian.

'Hotel management,' Victor said. 'Just wanted to make sure everything is fine with the suite.'

'Uh, yeah.'

The man looked flustered. His face was flushed, the front of his T-shirt tucked into the waistband of his boxers, and the zipper of his jeans was undone. The man's face reddened as he noticed this a second after Victor had.

Understanding he'd interrupted a session in front of the hotel porn channel gave Victor an idea. The man in front of him was clearly embarrassed and caught in the awkward fight-or-flight reflex of laughing it off or shying away. His tactical awareness couldn't be lower.

'I need to take a look around the suite, sir,' Victor said.

No request, no chance of being denied.

'Uh, yeah, sure.'

Jerkov stepped aside and allowed Victor to pass. He heard the noise of a zipper being hastily tugged up.

The Presidential represented the pinnacle of luxury in a very luxurious establishment. Victor stepped into the spacious lounge. The carpet was thick and immaculately clean. The walls were an off-white panelled effect. Oil paintings hung at various locations. Immediately to his left was a white, L-shaped leather sofa, and white armchair, set around a small white coffee table. To his right was an interior wall with a dresser stood before it. A telephone sat on top.

The lounge opened up past the sofa to his left and into a dining area with a table and four chairs. The suite did the same to the right where the space contained a desk, chair, and another sofa. Set before the sofa was a large television, switched off. A box of tissues sat on the sofa.

'Is everything to your satisfaction?' Victor asked.

The man avoided eye contact as he replied, 'I guess.'

Victor walked through the dining area and into the master bedroom. It was large, with mirrored built-in wardrobes and a king-size bed. A door by the wardrobes led to the en suite bathroom. The second bedroom was at the opposite end of the suite.

There was a briefcase on the dining table but there was nothing else Victor could see that belonged to Petrenko or his men. They were clearly here for business only. A single negotiation with Yamout and that would be it. The meeting might last only an hour, or perhaps go on for several, but Victor planned to act as soon as Yamout arrived. It would help him to wait, to let everyone get past the adrenalin that would accompany the initial face-to-face with dangerous associates. But he didn't know the specifics of what Yamout and Petrenko were doing, and if he waited too long the negotiations might finish and everyone could be gone before he burst in through the door.

By entering early he would still have surprise on his side. Both groups would be so busy watching each other for signs of betrayal they wouldn't be prepared for an attack by a third party. It was still risky with so many enemies in such a close space. He would need to be at his best. One miss, one mistake, one surprise would be enough.

He noticed Jerkov starting to shake off his embarrassment so Victor wished him a good stay and left.

Yamout was due to arrive at the hotel for nine p.m. Victor checked his watch. Eight and a half hours until show time.

CHAPTER 21

'Who was that guy?'

The speaker was short and muscular. His T-shirt was tight across his chest, shoulders and arms. The drapes were pulled across the windows of the suite and the light from the laptop monitor in front of him cast a pale glow over his tanned face. He looked to his right at the man sitting next to him. He was taller, slimmer, more senior.

'I don't know,' the slim man said. 'But he didn't look like hotel management to me.'

'Me either.'

The slim man turned over to a fresh page of his notebook and wrote a new log: *11.17, tall man (suit, dark hair) enters suite. He claims to be from hotel management. Looks around for a minute. Leaves. Don't believe he's management.*

The laptop monitor was subdivided into five video feeds. One occupied the upper-left quarter of the screen and one the lower-left quarter. The right-hand side of the monitor showed the other feeds in three eighth-sized windows with another window showing controls for image and sound adjustments.

Each video feed was wirelessly linked to a tiny camera hidden inside the Presidential Suite and displayed a continuous live stream. In the upper-left monitor window the view was from an air vent high on a wall and showed the edge of the dining table at the bottom of the window, the door to the master bedroom on the right side, the main door in the top-right corner and the TV area at the top of the screen. The lower-left window showed the suite from the opposite angle. The other three feeds showed the master bedroom, second bedroom and a view from the television set.

None of the angles were perfect, but given the short amount of time they'd had to install them, the men were happy with their work. What wasn't picked up by the camera's fisheye lenses was recorded by the powerful microphones that accompanied them.

So far the cameras had recorded Petrenko and his first three men arriving and them sitting around talking, mostly about sports, gambling and women, nothing about business. Then the fifth man turned up and was chastised for being late and ordered to stay put while Petrenko and the other three left to get food. The late arrival had wasted no time locating a box of tissues and finding the adult pay-per-view, only to be interrupted by the man in the suit.

There was a knock-knock at the door. Both men looked up. When a third, harder knock sounded, the slim man stood, looked briefly through the spyhole for confirmation, and opened the door.

'Number Three looked right at me,' the new guy said. He was younger than the other two. 'Cover is still good, but had to break off. No drama. They're just going for waffles.' He

170

hung his brown suede jacket over a chair. 'What's been happening?'

The slim man said, 'Someone claiming to be management had a look around.'

'Show me.'

The video operator clicked on the upper-left window and rolled the mouse wheel down to rewind the footage for a few seconds. He let it play.

'No way is that guy hotel management,' the young man said.

The slim man asked, 'How can you be so sure?'

'I saw him enter the hotel a couple of hours back. Walked right through the lobby. Never said anything to any staff and no staff said anything to him. There wasn't even any acknowledgement between them. If he was management, someone would have at least said hi.'

'You get a good look at him?' the slim man asked.

'Sure. Six-two, one eighty, dark hair, dark eyes, nice suit.'

The video operator grinned. 'You checking him out?'

'Screw you, I notice everyone.'

'Ignore the resident child,' the slim man said. 'What did you make of him?'

'Nothing,' the young man answered. 'He was just a guy. No reason to look at him twice.'

The slim man thought for a moment. 'I really don't like him. If he's not with the hotel, why was he in the suite?' The other two men shook their heads. 'Whatever he wants, it can't be good. He shows up again, I want to know straight away. If he's a risk, we take him out. Got it?'

CHAPTER 22

Yamout and his people arrived at the Hotel Europe with as little fanfare as an arms trafficker and six bodyguards could manage. They passed through the lobby with one guy working point from about ten feet ahead of Yamout. Another four surrounded him – two a little in front, two just behind – with the sixth man following at the back, approximately five feet away. It was an effective formation and Victor was glad he didn't have to make the attempt here in the lobby. The group drew glances from most of the other occupants in the lobby but the steely gazes of the bodyguards ensured that few stared long except for the watchful rent-a-cops.

Apart from Yamout and the point man, none were Arabs. They were all pale-skinned, probably either Belarusians or Russians or from other neighbouring former Soviet states, hired for this gig because they were local and knew the language. Each man was alert, clearly knowing his job, and had the strong but not overly muscled build of bodyguards paid to do more than simply look mean. The point man was probably one of Yamout's personal staff. He seemed at least as competent as the rest.

Yamout was no more than six feet but well over two hundred pounds. He was in reasonable shape though – the legacy of a naturally strong build and a physical youth, but an increasingly less active maturity. The whole group wore suits, Yamout in navy, the bodyguards in charcoal or black. Their pace was brisk but not hurried, demeanour all business but with a touch of arrogance. There was no luggage.

The way their jackets hung told Victor the bodyguards were armed. The five white guys all had belt holsters on their right hips. Not as concealable as carried underarm, but better for quick draws. Victor couldn't see a weapon on the Arab working point, but he didn't doubt he was still armed. There was no sign of a gun on Yamout either, but he hardly needed one with so much protection.

Victor was sat in the lobby bar with a lemonade. He was noticed by the bodyguards but, like everyone else in the area, quickly dismissed as a possible problem. He was just an unremarkable man in a suit, sitting alone in a bar. No threat to anyone. It was something he worked very hard on – appearing harmless when he was anything but.

The point man reached the elevator and hit the call button. The doors were opening just as Yamout reached them. The point man went in alone and rode it up to the seventh floor. Yamout and the others waited in front of the elevator for a minute before answering a phone call. The point man letting him know it was safe to go up, presumably. Yamout gestured to one of the bodyguards, who promptly hit the call button. The second elevator opened and Yamout and his men stepped inside. Victor watched them ascend.

There was no sign of the watcher, and there hadn't been for

hours. Victor didn't like not knowing where he was, but there were only so many things he could control. He checked the time, picked up his bag, stood, and left the lobby. Using the hotel master keycard he accessed a door to the staff area, followed the memorised layout he'd taken from the blueprints, and, after making sure no one was nearby, entered the appropriate room.

It was dark and warm. Tiny lights glowed and flickered in the darkness. The hum of machinery filled Victor's ears. He closed the door behind him and flicked the light switches. Strip lights illuminated the hotel's electrical room and its large array of equipment. Along two walls were electric switchboards, circuit breakers, transformers, distribution boards and other electrical equipment. Vast amounts of insulated wiring and cables ran along the walls and ceiling.

Victor placed his bag on the floor and took out a pair of thick rubber gloves. When they were protecting his hands, he opened the switchboard panels. Inside were banks of copper busbars connected to the switchgear. Victor removed a zip-lock plastic bag containing six golf ball-sized spheres of C-4. He placed these carefully throughout the switchboards, making sure he kept away from the bare busbars and the huge charge that flowed through them. When the C-4 balls were in place, he pushed a slapper detonator into each one. The detonators were connected to a simple digital timer.

Victor set the timer to three minutes, grabbed his bag, and left the room.

Gabir Yamout stepped out of the elevator behind two of his bodyguards. Elkhouri, Yamout's point man and chief bodyguard, had ridden up to the seventh floor separately. He had both announced Yamout's imminent arrival to Petrenko and checked out the lay of the land. The serious-faced Arab was Yamout's most trusted hireling, having been at his side for over ten years. He was both a bodyguard and an advisor, and always had Yamout's safety and best interests at the forefront of his mind.

In the early days, Yamout had been like Elkhouri and had been simply a bodyguard to Ariff. As Yamout became more trusted, he had garnered more responsibilities, and now was a business partner and friend first, bodyguard second. Elkhouri had taken over as head of Ariff's security and if Elkhouri had told Yamout it wasn't a good idea to continue with the meeting, without question Yamout would have taken the man's advice and left. From the call Yamout had received minutes before, Elkhouri was happy with what awaited them, or as happy as he could be when meeting ruthless gangsters on their own territory.

Elkhouri was waiting outside the suite's door alongside two large Belarusians. They wore designer jeans and labelled sportswear and couldn't look any more like ivory-coloured savages if they tried. Both visibly tensed when they saw just how many men Yamout had brought with him. That was good. Yamout always showed up in force when meeting with a new contact, especially in unfamiliar surroundings.

One of the savages hurried back inside the suite, obviously to report to Petrenko about Yamout's numbers. How Petrenko reacted to this news would tell Yamout everything about the man he could ever need to know. Elkhouri gave Yamout a small nod.

He approached the lone thug left holding open the door, who stepped aside to allow Yamout past. Four of the bodyguards went in first, followed by Elkhouri and then Yamout. The final bodyguard stayed outside the door with Petrenko's man.

Yamout was no stranger to luxurious hotel rooms but even he was quietly impressed by the Presidential Suite.

Petrenko stood in the centre of the lounge area, smiling as though he was pleased to see Yamout. He didn't smile back. They were strangers meeting to do business, not friends meeting socially. Behind Petrenko was the primate from the door with two other similarly attired gangsters. Petrenko was dressed more stylishly than his men, in linen trousers, loafers and a white button-down shirt hanging loose and with the sleeves rolled up to the elbows. He looked around fifty and seemed almost civilised compared to his employees. None of Petrenko's men had any guns out and Yamout gave Petrenko some credit for this. Though outnumbered he wasn't intimidated. Or if he was, he was doing an excellent job of disguising the fact.

'Mr Yamout, it's nice to finally meet you,' Petrenko said in Russian.

He held out a hand.

Yamout took the hand loosely and they shook. 'Thank you for inviting me to your city.'

'It's beautiful, isn't it?'

Yamout nodded. If it was, he hadn't noticed.

They released hands.

'Come,' Petrenko said. 'Let's sit down.' He glanced around at Yamout's men. 'I don't think we're going to have enough chairs.'

Yamout didn't respond. There were plenty of places to sit throughout the suite if not in the immediate vicinity. Petrenko was fishing for an explanation as to why Yamout had brought along so many guards. He wasn't going to get one.

Petrenko led Yamout through to an area of the suite where a large television was set in front of a leather sofa and armchairs, immediately settling himself in one of the chairs without first allowing Yamout to sit. The arms dealer wasn't sure whether this was typical of Belarusian manners or a petty response to his own failure to justify his number of bodyguards. Either way, it didn't improve Yamout's opinion of the man.

Yamout took a chair for himself. Elkhouri and one of Petrenko's men shared the sofa. Petrenko's man, red-haired and square-faced, took off his sports jacket to reveal a vest underneath. He was sweating. The others waited in the lounge area.

'Drink?' Petrenko offered.

'No, thank you.'

'Or maybe something to eat? The food here is excellent and room service very brisk. You won't have long to wait.'

'No, thank you,' Yamout said again.

'As you wish,' Petrenko said. 'I take it you want to get straight to business.'

Yamout nodded. 'I didn't fly two thousand miles to fill my stomach.'

Petrenko smiled, but in a different way. His demeanour changed, hardened. The friendly host act had gone. 'Good,' he said. 'I hate wasting time when we can be making money.' He crossed his legs and slouched in the armchair. The leather creaked. 'As I'm sure you have already been told, I have a large stockpile of small arms, both former Soviet and modern Russia army munitions. Assault rifles, machine guns, even rocket-propelled grenades. Everything.'

He took a briefcase from the coffee table and opened it. He removed a sheet of white paper and handed it to Yamout. 'As you can see, my prices are very reasonable.'

Yamout spent a minute reading through the long list of weaponry and the accompanying prices. Then he spent another minute pretending to read while a scowl deepened on his face. He passed the document to Elkhouri, who performed a similar routine.

'These figures are not what I had been expecting,' Yamout said.

Petrenko adjusted his seating. 'In what way?'

'Your pricing structure is too high and doesn't make a lot of sense.'

Petrenko's calm persona vanished and Yamout glimpsed the hot-tempered man it was hiding. '*Doesn't make a lot of sense.* What the fuck does that mean?'

'It means—'

The lights went out.

Elkhouri was up from the sofa immediately. There was a commotion in the adjoining part of the suite, anxious body-guards made more anxious by not being able to see.

Petrenko exhaled heavily. 'The hotel will have the power restored momentarily, I'm sure.' He raised his voice to be heard throughout the suite. 'Everyone stay where you are and keep calm. No one do anything stupid. It's just a blown fuse.'

'Maybe we should go,' Elkhouri suggested in Arabic. He seemed uncommonly agitated.

'When this idiot is selling guns for a third less than what Ariff would pay,' Yamout said back, 'we can afford to sit here for a few minutes.'

'Everything okay?' Petrenko asked.

'My friend is afraid of the dark,' Yamout replied drily.

'He shouldn't worry,' Petrenko assured. 'We're perfectly safe here.'

CHAPTER 23

Victor had been waiting in the stairwell when the power went. With no windows, the space became almost completely black. He already had the thermal imaging goggles in hand and he fixed them in place and switched them on. Through the goggles, everything appeared as shades of pale grey. The cool walls were almost white. The hot light bulbs were black. Victor slipped off his shoes and removed the P90 from his shoulder bag.

He released the gun's safety, left the bag on the floor next to his shoes and jacket, and pulled open the stairwell door, using his foot to stop it swinging back shut. Victor raised the gun in both hands and pushed the stock against where his chest met his shoulder. He set the P90's laser designator to high and the needle-thin beam glowed across the space, flaring where it hit the far wall. He stepped through the door.

Artificial light from sources outside the hotel glowed through the glass cupola. Maybe enough illumination to spot him at five feet, but no further. The seventh floor's open-sided corridor was long and narrow and formed an almost complete circle around the central space. The door to the Presidential

180

Suite was twenty-two feet away. Two men stood outside it. One of Petrenko's guys in jeans and sports, one of Yamout's bodyguards wearing a suit. Their clothing appeared as dark grey through the goggles, with the cooler wall and door significantly lighter. Their heads and hands were black. They had handguns drawn, heads moving from side to side, unsure what to do, blind in the darkness. It had been six seconds since the lights had blown.

The end of the infrared beam glowed on the closest guy's chest. Two 5.7 millimetre bullets hit him in the sternum. A third struck between the eyes.

The noise of the P90's gunshots were barely audible *clicks*. The sound of the bullet's penetrating flesh was louder. The P90 ejected the spent cartridge cases straight down and they clinked together on the carpet. Victor fully depressed the trigger and drilled a burst into the furthest man's torso as he turned in reaction to the first dropping. He stumbled but stayed on his feet, his brain slow to catch up with what had happened to his body. Victor took a step laterally left to get the angle, squeezed the trigger halfway, and put another bullet through his forehead before he had a chance to cry out in surprise or pain. He fell on top of the other corpse. A neat pile.

Victor hurried to the suite's door, working on the assumption that someone on the other side had heard the two guards go down and was preparing for him to breach. Unlikely, and even if they had, it was more unlikely still that they would have shaken off their shock in time to think about defending the door, but Victor had only stayed alive this long by preparing for the worst at all times.

He stood directly before the door, aimed the P90 slightly

downwards for typical torso height and fanned a long burst through the door to spread the bullets over a wide arc across the room beyond. The chance of scoring a hit was minimal, but his aim was to distract and panic whoever was on the other side long enough for him to get through the door without taking a bullet. Victor put a second burst through where the handle and lock were located.

He angled the P90 back up, kicked open the door and charged in two steps, dropped to a crouch, looking immediately left, shooting the first man he saw in the chest. He fell on to the dining table, knocking over chairs.

Victor tracked right, saw another dark shape at the far side of the room, fired, watched the shape collapse into a dresser. Glass smashed.

A step forward and Victor glimpsed the top of something or someone crouched behind a sofa in the TV area. He put a burst through the cushions, heard a scream, and fired off another. No more screams. His gaze swept over the room a second time. No one.

The suite was large, absent of light but shades of pale grey through his goggles. Thick drapes shaded all of the windows along the far wall, which had prevented him using the rifle, but helped him now. Only the smallest trace of light from Minsk outside filtered through, and wouldn't enable anyone to see further than a couple of inches. Glancing down, Victor saw that the fifty-round magazine still had maybe ten rounds left, but he released it anyway.

He was reaching for another when a door burst open to his left and a man rushed out. He wore suit trousers and a vest, his bare arms black like his face. The middle of the vest was dark with sweat. He was armed, a big pistol clutched in both hands, moving erratically, his head doing the same, eyes searching the darkness, failing to see Victor crouched no more than ten feet before him.

Victor drew the holstered USP into his left hand and shot the man with a double-tap to the head. The bullets blew out the back of his skull and left brain matter glowing black on the wall behind. Victor re-holstered the HK and fitted a second magazine into the P90.

He stepped over the most recent corpse, through the dining area, and quickly into the suite's master bedroom. It was less dark here, a two-inch-wide gap in the drapes letting in more light from the city outside. Empty. Victor stopped at the door to the adjoining bathroom, spread a burst through it, opened it fast, moved in faster. No one hiding in the shower cubicle or bathtub.

Two guys outside the suite, four guys inside. Six down. Five left: Yamout, Petrenko and three bodyguards. He checked his watch. Twenty seconds since the first shot fired. It seemed much longer. It always did.

He heard a noise – something clattering – from behind him, coming from the opposite end of the suite. He turned around, exited the bathroom and the master bedroom, stepping back out into the lounge. Without shoes his footsteps were silent on the thick carpet. He hurried into the TV area, hearing a whisper he couldn't decipher from the second bedroom, an answer he likewise couldn't understand. Victor stood to the left of the door, depressed the trigger completely for full auto, firing a waist-high burst through the door at a ten-degree angle, sending the bullets along the wall directly to the door's right, then switched positions and shot another burst from the opposite side.

There was a groan, a clatter of metal on wood. In these kind of situations, people always stood or crouched to the side of doors.

He shot through the handle and lock before dropping to his stomach. He shuffled forward until he was lying with his left shoulder against the skirting board, body parallel to the wall, head in line with the doorframe. He pushed the door open a fraction with the muzzle of the SP-90. The door creaked faintly.

In response, sternum-high holes exploded directly through the door panels. Bullets embedded themselves in the wall at the far side of the suite, some at head height, others higher still. Two shooters then, one very low – prone or kneeling – the other in a tactical crouch.

Victor, still on his stomach, kicked a dining chair and it fell over, thudding on the carpet. The shooting paused at that, and he added a wheezing groan to the ploy as he crawled forward in front of the door, elbowed it open and immediately saw the first shooter – the one he'd shot through the door – sitting on the floor, back against the room's bed, legs splayed out before him in a pool of black blood. The man saw Victor a split second before 5.7 mm bullets punctured his heart, lungs and spine.

Victor quickly rose into a crouch, acquired the second man crouched down on the far side of the bed, using it as cover, his face contorting in an instant of surprise as Victor appeared seemingly out of nowhere before him. Victor shot him twice in the forehead, stood, swept through the room, but saw no one else. That left the adjoining bathroom. Where the second dead guy fell, he'd brought down one of the drapes and the artificial night light of the city flowed into the room.

The bathroom door was closed. Three guys left, now

crowded into the bathroom for safety. Trapped. Victor checked the magazine, saw it still had around thirty per cent capacity. More than enough.

He walked forward but stopped when he heard the crunch of an expended shell casing somewhere behind him – from the lounge. He turned around fast, moving into the doorway, expecting to see a bewildered guest or rent-a-cop investigating. Instead, he saw the dark grey silhouette of a slim man in the middle of the lounge, another by his side, shorter and muscular, both with arms out in front, holding pale grey handguns in their black hands. They'd already seen him in the faint gloom provided by the uncovered window, and fired first.

Their suppressed gunshots clacked in the quiet air, muzzle flashes tiny black bursts through the infrared. They fired almost in unison, the first bullet catching Victor on the right triceps, the second hitting him three inches below his sternum and dropping him before he could shoot back.

The impact knocked the air from his lungs and despite the shock and pain he lay still, hearing their footsteps rushing closer. He breathed as shallowly as he could, eyes shut so they didn't catch the light, right fist still closed round the P90's grip. His stomach ached from the subsonic bullet but the pain was only like getting punched, thanks to the Kevlar vest. The arm wound hurt, but he fought to keep it from his face.

He figured they were more associates of Yamout, probably responding to a panicked cell phone call. They had to have been close to have got here so quickly; on the same floor, in another suite, but must have arrived earlier since Victor had not seen them. He thought of the watcher from the lobby, cursed himself for thinking the watcher was alone.

185

Their footsteps slowed as they came closer. In the darkness they wouldn't be able to see he was wearing body armour. The floorboards beneath the carpet creaked as a heavy foot stepped close to Victor's right leg. A shoe nudged him in the hip. A useless check, but one people with too much adrenalin in them tended to make.

Another voice shouted from the bathroom of the master bedroom. It was in Russian – presumably Petrenko – a desperate plea for help. A second cry sounded in Arabic, presumably from Yamout. There was no response from the two men near Victor.

The foot near to his leg moved and Victor sensed the man standing next to his right arm. A second man moved to his left, then past him. The man to his right stepped over his arm and Victor waited until he'd taken three steps forward before opening his eyes. He rolled his head back, saw the grey shapes of the two men ahead of him, upside down, stepping into the bedroom, slowly, despite the cries for help.

Victor clutched the P90's forward grip in his left hand, raised the sub-machine gun over his head, took aim on the first man's back and squeezed the trigger.

A jagged line of bullet holes tore along the man's spine. The recoil of firing upside down and without proper support made the P90 dance in Victor's hands and waste rounds. He shifted his aim and watched the second man shot in the hip, back, arm and head. Both men hit the carpet, dead.

The pain began to intensify in his arm. He checked the wound. It was bleeding but not badly. The bullet hadn't gone in, but had dug a shallow groove through the skin and muscle. Not serious but he wouldn't be doing any push-ups for a while. He rose into a crouch.

A bullet ripped a chunk out of the carpet and floorboard next to Victor.

He felt another cut the air above. There was a third party-crasher firing from the lounge, having difficulty making out exactly where Victor was, so low to the ground. Victor quickly brought up the P90 to return fire but he didn't have time to fully acquire the target and missed. The suppressing fire did its job, however, and the gunman ducked into cover, but the P90 clicked empty.

There was no time to reload – the gunman could reappear at any moment – so Victor dropped the sub-machine gun, drew the USP, adopted a two-handed grip, held his breath, and waited for his attacker to show himself.

He did. Victor fired.

There was no cry but he heard the distinctive wet *thunk* of a .45 calibre slug punching through flesh.

If there were three men he hadn't known about there could easily be more, so Victor stayed still for five seconds, waiting, USP trained on the space in the centre of the lounge where anyone else entering would appear. When they didn't, he stood. Thanks to the open lobby, the noise of his attack would have carried far, suppressed weapons or not. Hotel security could be on the way. The police may have already been called.

He knew he should abort, extract immediately, but his target was less than twenty feet away.

He rushed back into the second bedroom, careful with his footfalls to avoid tripping on the corpses in the doorway. He could hear the sound of traffic as he approached the en suite door, understanding what that meant before he felt the draught. He kicked open the door.

Light through the smashed-out window provided enough illumination for him to see the bathroom was empty even without thermal imaging goggles. The window was small but big enough for even a large man to squeeze through if his life depended on it. Victor stepped into the tub, stretched upwards to peer through the gap. There was blood and strips of clothing on the fragments of glass that hadn't been cleared. He saw the exterior of the hotel. No three men, but a ledge wide enough to shimmy along. He heard sirens.

Victor dashed back through the suite, realising by the groaning from the lounge that the last guy he'd shot wasn't dead, just incapacitated. Victor ignored him, exited on to the balcony corridor in time to see an elevator descending, already two floors below him, the hint of grey and black from those inside. The elevators, unlike every other electrically operated device in the hotel, wouldn't have been rendered useless when Victor blew the power. Most systems had auxiliary power for just such emergencies.

He fired and a cobweb of cracks appeared in the elevator's glass front a second before he lost the angle. He shot anyway, firing at the roof, squeezing the trigger until the gun was empty, knowing a .45 calibre ACP had little chance of penetrating the steel machinery that sat atop the elevator, but he wasn't going to beat it to the lobby, and however he got there it was going to be too late to intercept Yamout, especially with armed hotel security about. He reloaded and emptied a second magazine in less than four seconds. Useless, but there was no time to do anything else. The elevator was one hundred feet below him.

Gone.

The job was over. He'd failed. Now all that mattered was escape. Any problems his failure would create would have to wait.

He headed to the stairwell, noticing pale green light emanated through an open doorway further along the balcony corridor, leading to the suite next to the Presidential. The source of the light had to be something on battery power, a laptop monitor probably. Victor thought back to the three guys who had charged into the Presidential barely a minute after him. They had to have been stationed in the next suite along to have arrived so fast, but they hadn't responded to the cries for help from Petrenko and Yamout. Not friends of either, so who were they?

He didn't have long to get an answer but he'd been forced to kill three more men than he'd been paid for. Those men had tried to kill him and stopped him fulfilling his contract, a fact that could have fatal consequences. He needed an explanation.

'Don't move,' a voice said in Russian from behind Victor. The voice carried the confidence gained from the possession of a firearm. A firearm Victor presumed was aimed directly at his back.

He stopped. Two feet from the doorway.

'Drop the gun.'

There was nothing to tell him exactly where the speaker stood, so if Victor tried anything he would be trusting to speed only, relying on the fact he could turn around, raise his gun, acquire the target, and score a fatal hit before the speaker had time to apply a few pounds of pressure on his weapon's trigger.

Victor let the USP fall from his fingers and thud quietly on the carpet.

'Now lose the goggles.'

Victor lowered them to the floor.

'Turn around.'

Victor did.

A man stood in front of him, no more than ten feet away, equidistant between Victor and the stairwell. The cupola provided enough light to illuminate the suppressed pistol in the man's hands and the sheen of sweat on his face. He looked out of breath, having probably sprinted up several flights of stairs. He had a long face, stubble. Victor recognised him even without the brown suede jacket. The watcher.

'Who the hell are you?' the watcher asked.

The words were in Russian but it wasn't the speaker's native language. Victor couldn't place the accent. He didn't answer. He wanted to ask the same question.

'Kick away the gun,' the watcher ordered.

Victor complied, but only hard enough for it to skid a few feet.

The watcher stepped nearer. He moved at a cautious speed, glanced at the two dead bodyguards outside the door of the Presidential.

'Cops will be here soon,' Victor said.

The watcher ignored him and gestured with his pistol. 'Lose your backup too.'

Victor reached around to the back of his waist where the P22 was holstered.

'Do it very slowly,' the watcher prompted.

Victor drew out the Walther and brought it round to the front.

'This time don't drop it, toss it away.'

Victor did – but he threw it forward – at the watcher. Not to inflict injury, just to distract. The watcher's eyes instinctively glanced at the gun sailing towards him and he flinched to move out of the way. By the time he recovered, Victor was through the open doorway.

He flung the door shut behind him and saw that the source of green light was a laptop monitor, as he'd expected. It was divided into six windows, five displaying a different image from what had to be hidden night-vision cameras next door in the Presidential Suite.

He didn't think any more about it. All his thoughts were centred on the man on the other side of the door, the man who had a gun while he had nothing.

CHAPTER 24

Victor crouched in the darkness, balancing on the balls of his feet. The air in the room was warm and stale. He could smell cologne and sweat. His right arm throbbed. The only light entered through thin gaps between the drapes, but there was enough to see the lounge area of the suite around him. It was different from the Presidential in both size and layout, smaller and less opulent. There were two interior doors leading off from the lounge that he guessed led to bedrooms. The bedrooms probably had their own bathrooms, but otherwise there was nowhere else to go. He could steal Yamout's trick and go through one of the windows and on to the exterior ledge, but that strategy relied on his enemy standing idle and letting him.

Victor didn't move. He waited. If the watcher wanted him, he would have to come and get him. The lounge was the largest open space and the easiest to defend himself within. He could see the silhouettes of a large sofa, sideboards along two walls, a coffee table, the desk where the computer sat and two chairs before it. All obstacles for an attacker and potential weapons to be used against one.

He heard quiet footsteps outside the main door, a few moments before suppressed gunshots sounded and six holes blew through it. Two high, two low, two in between. But all in straight lines. Victor was far enough out of trajectory not to be concerned.

For a second he thought the watcher might not have a keycard, but the latch clicked and Victor felt the faint pull of a draught as the door opened. There were four *clack* sounds as the watcher spread rounds across the lounge. Again, Victor didn't need to move.

The watcher stepped into the room, slow and controlled because he knew his enemy was unarmed. As expected, the watcher wore the discarded thermal imaging goggles. The dark lounge would appear to him as shades of light grey with Victor as a distinct dark grey shape with a black head and hands. The watcher didn't see him.

But Victor saw the watcher.

The single infrared gathering optic on the goggles protruded several inches from the eyes, greatly limiting peripheral vision at very close range. Victor, standing to one side of the door and no more than twelve inches from the watcher's flank, was in his blind spot.

Victor made his move, going for the outstretched gun, but the watcher must have realised the problem with his peripheral vision because he whipped the gun away before Victor could grab it.

Instead, Victor adjusted his footing and collided with the man, knocking him backwards and into the door hard enough for him to grunt with the impact. Before he could recover, Victor slammed an elbow at his face, coming from below, aiming under the goggles, and felt it connect with cheekbone and drag across the side of the face while his left hand grabbed the watcher's right wrist and kept it, and the gun, locked against the wall.

Victor took a fist to his abdomen in response, a short punch, not enough leverage to really damage him but enough power to still hurt. The Kevlar took something out of the blow, but not much. It was followed by several more left hooks. Victor grimaced and responded with elbows that didn't hit squarely. The watcher's head was an elusive target, deftly rocking from side to side.

Victor changed tactic, took a half-step back, let go of the wrist, grabbed the man by the shoulders with both hands, and swung his knee upwards. The watcher moved in time and the knee caught him just above the groin, making him wince but not striking enough nerve endings to take him out of the fight.

The goggles collided with the side of Victor's head, delivered on the end of a solid butt. He saw stars and lurched backwards, recovering enough to grab the gun and holding hand before it was in line to fire. The watcher powered forward while Victor was still dazed, throwing his bodyweight at him, forcing him backwards, off balance.

He stumbled a few steps before his hips found the back of the sofa and his attacker pushed him over. Victor let go of the gun, tumbled backwards over the sofa and on to the floor, landing on his feet, took two fast steps away into the darkness, dodging to the side before the watcher could squeeze off a hasty shot.

Victor leapt straight at the watcher, going low, taking the man's legs out from under him with a takedown that sent them both crashing to the floor.

The watcher took the brunt of the fall and Victor heard the

gun bounce across the carpet. He ignored it, used his weight to pin his enemy down while he tried to get his left arm hooked around the guy's neck. The watcher fought back, hammering fists and elbows into Victor's sides and lower back. They were well placed, striking his kidneys and vulnerable ribs. Victor grimaced against the pain but kept on working his left hand under the watcher's head.

He forced it around and under the back of the neck so that the crook of his elbow was wedged behind it. He then grabbed his left hand with his right, gripped hard with both, lurched to the right, rolling off the watcher, landing with his back on the floor, side by side with his opponent, Victor's arms following the movements so that the edge of his right forearm ended up over the watcher's throat.

Victor squeezed.

The pressure immediately closed off both of the watcher's carotid arteries, stopping blood reaching his brain and depriving it of oxygen. He thrashed wildly in response, throwing elbows into Victor's tensed stomach, tried to claw at his eyes, but didn't go for Victor's arm because the watcher knew he couldn't escape it in the ten seconds he had before he lost consciousness. His only chance was to force Victor to let go.

But that wasn't going to happen.

Victor maintained the choke for sixty seconds after the watcher went limp to ensure he passed from unconsciousness into brain death.

He climbed to his feet and stepped away from the corpse, toeing the dropped gun where it lay on the floor. Had he known it was that close, he might have gone for it and saved himself some hassle. Still, good to get a workout. His abdomen and lower back stung from the repeated elbows but there was no real damage. He might have some bruises in the morning but that would be the most of it. His head hurt worse. His wounded arm continued to throb. The fight hadn't done it any favours, but it hadn't been significantly worsened.

He pulled open a curtain so he could see more clearly. There wasn't time to search the room, but he checked the watcher's pockets, and took his wallet, the suite keycard, and a spare magazine for the watcher's gun. The weapon was a SIG Sauer P226. The watcher had fired eleven rounds so Victor knew the magazine had four left. Victor released it and loaded the fresh one.

For a second he thought about taking the computer with him but it was too big to conceal and would tie him directly to the crime. He put fifteen 9 mms through it to make sure the recordings on its hard drive could never be recovered, and threw the SIG down next to the dead watcher.

Victor exited the suite, figuring he had two minutes to get out before the first police responders arrived, and hurried back into the Presidential. He tore down a drape for light and saw a slim figure writhing on the floor, a bullet hole beneath his right collarbone. It was bleeding profusely. Blood soaked his clothes. His handgun was on the ground, only a few feet away, but out of the wounded man's reach. Victor took it. Another SIG.

He grabbed the man by his shirt, looked him in the eye and asked in Russian, 'Who are you?'

No answer, but Victor saw he'd been understood.

He pressed his free palm over the man's mouth and hooked his thumb under the man's jaw to clamp it shut. With his right hand still gripping the SIG, Victor pushed his spare thumb into the bullet hole.

His left hand stifled the screaming enough for Victor to twist his thumb around inside the wound. The man beneath him thrashed as agony wracked his body. Victor stopped in time to avoid the man fainting and wiped the bloody thumb on the guy's jacket, keeping the palm pressed hard over the man's mouth until he'd taken control of himself.

'Who are you?' Victor said again.

The man spoke, each word punctuated by heavy breaths. 'Just. Kill. Me.'

'Who do you work for?'

He didn't answer, but managed to form a something resembling a smile.

Victor held the guy's mouth shut and pushed his thumb back into the bullet hole. He twisted and jerked it around.

Muffled screams followed, louder. The man bucked, eyes wide, veins prominent under the skin of his forehead and temples. Victor counted to seven before removing his thumb. It was another five seconds before the man had calmed down enough for Victor to take away his hand.

'Who?

'*Kill . . . me.*'

The guy was deteriorating fast, his breathing shallow, voice even quieter, the time between words longer.

Victor leaned closer. 'Who sent you?'

The man's head lolled back, eyes closing. Victor checked the pulse. It was barely there, the heart on its last few hundred beats. He rifled through the dying man's pockets. A wallet with fake ID inside, but maybe it would still help, some cash, and a set of car keys but no key fob. It had been four minutes since it went loud. If Minsk PD weren't here already, they would be by the time Victor left. He stripped off the tactical harness, Kevlar vest and holster straps. He hid the gun in the back of his waistband and wiped the sweat from his face with his sleeve and headed for the stairwell.

He didn't know who the four guys with SIGs were, but he knew he had inadvertently stepped into someone's operation and killed the surveillance team. But these guys were more than just watchers. They knew how to shoot, and how to fight. Someone had sent them. Someone would want to know who had killed them.

Victor put his shoes back on and descended hurriedly, the pain in his arm worsening as the adrenalin in his system faded. He joined a group of frightened guests on the fourth floor and acted similarly distressed as they rushed down to the lobby. It was packed with people, all scared by the gunshots from high above, security trying to keep control but smart enough not to risk their lives for the company if they didn't have to. Hotel staff had lit candles to provide some illumination and the light helped Victor quickly find his way out through one of the side entrances.

Police cars were pulling up outside as he walked away.

CHAPTER 25

'Not long now,' Abbot said.

Xavier Callo was in a small apartment in a tower block somewhere in Minsk. He'd arrived with Abbot and Blout several hours before and had spent most of the following time lounging on the sofa watching US sitcoms dubbed into Russian. He had plenty to eat and drink, mostly junk food and soda, but Blout had fetched the groceries and good eating obviously wasn't something the inexpressive ape understood. Still, food was food and despite being thin Callo had a big appetite. Empty bags of potato chips and candy bar wrappers lay on the floor around his bare feet. He wasn't allowed to wear shoes.

Abbot stood by the window and Blout was elsewhere in the apartment. At least one of the two was with Callo at all times. They'd only let him use the john with the door open and Blout standing just outside. Callo had given the prick something to listen to.

They were waiting for something to happen, that much was as clear as polished diamond. Callo had no idea what his captors were waiting for. He hadn't been told or given any indication and he wasn't about to ask.

He was tired. There were no clocks in the apartment but Callo knew the time and the date by checking the news channel on the TV when no one was looking. He did so several times and felt very proud of his cunning. The apartment consisted of two bedrooms, one bathroom, lounge and dining area, kitchen and hallway. It was neat and clean but the whole thing, furnishings included, probably cost less than Callo's last trip to Athens. Whoever was running this operation, CIA or otherwise, was obviously a cheapskate. If the powers that be had splashed out for a nicer pad maybe the two ogres guarding him would be able to relax a little. Callo's eyelids were heavy.

'Can I go to bed?' he asked, when he could no longer fight the tiredness.

'You're having a giraffe,' Abbot said without looking at him.

'Then I'm just going to fall asleep right here.'

'Suit yourself,' Abbot said. 'I'll wake you when we need you.'

Immediately Callo felt less tired. What did they need him for? Blout entered the lounge and gestured for Abbot, who followed Blout back into a bedroom, leaving Callo alone for the first time. He contemplated dashing for the door, but the idea was short-lived. He'd be caught before he had it open, and would no doubt get a serious beat down for his actions. Better to just sit tight. They couldn't keep him indefinitely, after all.

Callo muted the TV and edged along the sofa so he was closer to where Abbot had disappeared and heard voices speaking Russian, maybe from a radio. They were too quiet for Callo to understand what was being said.

Abbot re-entered suddenly and Callo leapt back to the middle of the sofa. If Abbot had seen him move, he didn't show it. Abbot thrust a cell phone into Callo's hands and then took a piece of paper from a pocket of his jeans. He held it in front of Callo.

'This is what you're going to do,' Abbot said, expression intense, a hard edge to his British accent. 'You're going to phone Gabir Yamout. You're going to tell whoever answers what's on that piece of paper. You speak Arabic, right? You can paraphrase it, put it in your own words, but you'd better say it all.'

Callo took the paper and quickly read what was written. 'Yes, I speak it. But I don't understand. This doesn't make any sense.'

'You don't have to understand it,' Abbot said. 'You just have to say it.'

'But I—'

Before he could finish, Abbot slapped Callo hard across the face. The phone fell at Callo's feet. His cheek stung badly. He looked up at Abbot, suddenly afraid. He noticed Blout was back in the room.

'Phone Yamout,' Abbot repeated coldly, 'and say what's on the facking piece of paper.'

Callo picked up the phone and dialled the number.

'Please,' Callo said. 'But no one will answer. It'll go to voicemail. Then I'll get a call back.'

Abbot shrugged. 'Just make sure you act scared.'

Callo didn't get it, but he sat listening to the phone ring for about ten seconds it went to voicemail.

Callo repeated what he saw on the paper. It was just a few short sentences – an outright lie – and Callo didn't have to act scared.

Before he'd finished the last line, Abbot snatched the phone from him and hung up. 'That was good, Xavier.'

He seemed genuinely happy and Callo managed a weak smile in return, despite his face still stinging. Blout went back into the other room.

Callo looked at the piece of paper again. 'Oh no,' he said. 'I missed out the part about the hotel. I'm sorry.'

Abbot gave a big shrug. 'That don't matter. The exact details aren't the important bit, it's the delivery that sells it. And yours was top notch. Very convincing.'

'Really? Thank you.'

Blout returned with a rucksack that he set down on the dining table. He opened it and took out a wallet. He threw it to Abbot, who emptied the contents. Callo watched his credit cards, receipts, cash and other litter from his wallet rain down on to the carpet. Abbot then tossed the wallet away and used his foot to spread the pile around on the floor.

'What are you doing?' Callo asked. 'That's my stuff.'

Abbot didn't answer. Callo looked to Blout, who was rooting around inside the bag.

'Is that all you wanted me to do?' Callo found the courage to ask.

Abbot rolled up his shirtsleeves. 'That was half of it, and you did great. You did a good job. Like I said, very convincing. Which is what we needed you to be. But now we need you to be convincing for the second part.'

Callo nodded, eager to please. 'I can do that.'

Abbot gave a strange smile. 'I'm sure you'll do fine.'

Blout put on a pair of latex gloves. He gave a second pair to Abbot.

'When do I make the next phone call?' Callo asked.

Abbot shook his head and stretched the gloves over his big hands. 'No more phone calls. What we need you to do now is convince your A-rab friends that you were attacked like you told them.'

Callo's gaze flicked back and forth between Abbot and Blout. 'But I said I'd escaped my attackers.'

'Ah,' Abbot said with a nod, interlacing his fingers to push the latex into place, 'but they found you again.'

Blout stepped menacingly closer. Callo stared up at Abbot, finally understanding, his eyes filling with water, head shaking weakly from side to side.

Abbot stood over Callo and pulled his right elbow back and made a fist.

'Sorry, mate,' Abbot began, 'but you really should have seen this coming.'

CHAPTER 26

Victor arrived back at the Best Eastern half an hour after leaving the Europe, which was quicker than how he would prefer to do things, but proper counter surveillance wasn't an option with an injured arm. Two hours making sure he wasn't followed was fine in theory but not if the wound got infected as a result or was spotted by a vigilant police officer.

In his room, he stripped off his clothes and ran a bath. While the bath was running he examined his wound in the mirror. Blood stained his entire arm. The wound itself was about four inches in length, maybe an eighth of an inch in depth, and it was bleeding far worse than when he'd first been shot. He fitted the plug in the sink and turned on the hot water tap. The hotel room came with a kettle, mugs, teabags and sachets of instant coffee and sugar. Victor dropped two teabags into a mug and poured in just enough cold water to wet them. He took a clean T-shirt from his luggage and ripped it into strips. The resulting pain made him grimace.

He lowered his injured triceps into the sink and in seconds the water had turned a pale red. With gritted teeth, he washed the wound to get rid of any traces of clothing or other debris. He patted dry his arm with a towel, took the damp teabags from the mug and pressed them over the wound. He kept his elbow and shoulder horizontally aligned to balance the teabags while he wrapped a strip of T-shirt around his arm. He bound the wound firmly, but not too tight, to give the teabags the best chance at working. The haemostatic tannins found naturally in tea would help stop the bleeding, reduce the chance of infection, and aid the healing process. Victor checked the teabags after five minutes, finding them soaked with blood. He replaced them with two more and bound the wound with slightly more pressure. When he checked after another five minutes the bleeding had stopped.

Victor tore open a sachet of granulated sugar and carefully poured it into the wound channel. He didn't know if the wound was infected, but the sugar's antimicrobial action would ensure that it wouldn't become so. And if it was infected the sugar would hopefully kill the bacteria, or at least slow its spread. He then rebound his arm with another strip of T-shirt, downed two miniature bottles of vodka from the mini bar and lowered himself into the bath, keeping his right arm clear of the water.

Now his wound was clean and had stopped bleeding it could begin healing properly. He was going to have another scar, but when he already had so many one more wouldn't make too much difference. He wasn't in the habit of taking off his shirt in public, but if the scar turned out to be too prominent yet more of his money would end up in the pocket of plastic surgeons. Aside from rich women, assassins were probably their best customers.

Good as teabags and sugar were at patching up injuries, it would have been better to use proper first-aid equipment. He hadn't been able to risk trying to find an all-night pharmacy so soon after the attack as the police would be at their most watchful. Victor doubted they would know they were only looking for one man, at least so far, but if he was out on the streets he could be stopped at random. They would probably be smart enough to put hospitals and drug stores under surveillance.

The police presence would be huge all night, with the hope of catching the culprits as they fled. Running was the expected course of action. It was what criminals did in such situations. And Victor considered it a fine tactic in a crisis. If a location was compromised, withdraw. Once out of the initial danger area stop, regroup, formulate a plan. But a hasty withdrawal in this case was too risky with his wound. At night there were few people on the streets to disappear among and less means with which to escape with speed. While so fresh, the injury would be hard to disguise and would hinder him if he was spotted.

He felt tired. The adrenalin hangover was at its peak and he had to fight to keep his eyes open. Images of the attack flashed through his mind. It couldn't have gone worse: Yamout had escaped, Victor had been forced to kill someone's surveillance team, and he'd been wounded in the process.

He didn't know much about the team, but he knew they had been there to record the meeting between Yamout and Petrenko, yet had no affiliation with either despite their intervention when Victor had started massacring everyone. If they had been associates of Yamout or Petrenko they would have responded to the cries for help. They weren't Belarusian security services either.

The watcher's Russian hadn't been good enough for a local, and cops or domestic spies would have identified themselves as such, and tried to arrest Victor instead of shooting at him.

He pushed the thoughts out of his mind for the time being. He wasn't going to work anything out lying in the tub, and it was all moot if he didn't get out of Minsk.

The taps pressed uncomfortably into his shoulders but it was necessary to face the bathroom door. He had it open so he could see into the bedroom and the small mirror positioned on the floor and angled so he could watch in it the reflection of the hotel room door. He didn't expect anyone would be coming through it, but precautions only paid off if they were taken every time.

He spent twenty minutes in the bath enjoying the heat and the alcohol in his bloodstream. His tolerance was high enough that the intoxicating effect was minimal. A jolt of adrenalin would easily override it if it came to it, but the effect was just enough to help him unwind. He kept the watcher's SIG in his left hand at all times.

When he was dry, Victor tidied and cleaned the bedroom and bathroom. Where blood had been, he wiped with a strip of T-shirt dampened with more vodka from the mini bar. The bloody towel and evidence of his ad-hoc first aid went into his attaché case. He set out a clean set of clothes and ordered room service, then got dressed while he waited for his food to arrive. After he'd refuelled and ensured all of his effects were packed and he was ready to flee at a second's notice, he tucked the SIG into the front of his waistband and lay down atop the bedclothes.

If his employer at the CIA hadn't already found out what had happened, he would soon. Maybe the voice would be more forgiving if he knew that only the intervention of a third party had prevented the contract's fulfilment. Or maybe killing those men would prove to be costly and put his paymaster under too much pressure.

And make Victor a liability he could do without.

CHAPTER 27

Danil Petrenko was as angry as he was scared. It enraged him that someone would dare try to take him out in the middle of his own city, and it terrified him that they had very nearly succeeded. As a precaution Petrenko clutched a .50 calibre Desert Eagle as he paced about his apartment, barking orders or just venting his frustration and anxiety. His lieutenants had called every man under his control and had them rush to his residence to provide protection. If whoever had attacked before tried again, they'd have a small army to get through.

He had men outside the building, in the lobby, and guarding the elevators and his front door. Six of Petrenko's biggest, meanest gangsters were with him in the apartment itself. All were armed. Every window was locked closed, all blinds or drapes shut, every light was switched on and candles had been set and lit in every room in case the power was cut like last time. Like Petrenko himself, his men were on edge, aware that mere hours before three of their own had been killed in a merciless assault.

Aside from his men now acting as guards, there were more

out on the streets banging on doors and snapping fingers, all trying to find out who was behind the attack and why. Every other criminal he knew or cop he paid off was doing their part, some out of fear, others because they were scared of losing income if Petrenko was killed. Motives were irrelevant to Petrenko. All he cared about were results.

The Lebanese bastard hadn't been behind it. That was pretty obvious to Petrenko. He had seen the look in Yamout's eyes as they had climbed through the bathroom window and on to the precarious ledge. No one could fake that kind of terror.

It had been about three hours since he'd fled the Europe with his only surviving man. His apartment was the penthouse of a ten-storey block in one of Minsk's most expensive and desirable neighbourhoods. He lived with his glamour-model girlfriend, who had locked herself in the guest bedroom to keep out of the way of Petrenko and his men.

One of his men came out of another room. He had a shotgun in one hand and a cell phone in the other, held with the speaker against his chest.

'I've just had a call from downstairs,' the man said. 'He's here.'

'Okay,' Petrenko said, nodding. 'Send him up. But make sure him and his men have no weapons. And don't take your eyes off them for a second. Got it? Not for a second.'

While his man gave the go-ahead to the guards in the lobby, Petrenko splashed some water on his face, swiped his sweaty hair back from his forehead, had another fat line of Bolivia's finest. He wiped the white residue from his nostrils, took a deep breath and waited in the lounge for his guest's arrival.

A minute later, there was a knock on the door and Petrenko heard his men taking guns and ushering the guest through to where he sat. He stood up the moment Tomasz Burliuk entered. The tall, handsome, immaculately groomed Ukrainian, Vladimir Kasakov's closest advisor, was followed by two bodyguards.

'Danil,' Burliuk began and took out his asthma inhaler. 'What's with the lack of manners?'

'I'm sorry, Tomasz, but I can't be too careful. You don't know what it's been like for me. I almost died tonight. I almost *died*.'

Burliuk put the inhaler to his lips and breathed in as he depressed the mechanism. 'Tell me what happened.'

Petrenko flopped back on to a chair. He shrugged and gestured as he assembled his thoughts. 'We were just beginning negotiations when all the damn lights went out. I thought it was nothing. A fuse maybe. But no more than thirty seconds later my men started dying. Damn it, Tomasz, someone tried to kill me. In my own city. I had to climb through a window just to get away. Look –' he gestured to his wrists, which were lightly scabbed where the broken glass had grazed him '– I almost killed myself in the process.'

Burliuk slipped the inhaler back into a pocket and took a seat in an armchair opposite Petrenko. 'What about Yamout?'

'What about him?'

Burliuk stroked his beard. 'Did he escape as well?'

'He got away. None of his bodyguards did. He brought six men with him. Can you believe that? At the time I was enraged by such disrespect, but now I should thank him. Maybe if he hadn't brought so much muscle, I wouldn't be here.'

'Where is Yamout now?'

Petrenko scoffed. 'How would I know, and why would I care? The second we left the elevator we went our separate ways. We didn't hang around to discuss travel arrangements. He's probably back in the desert by now.'

'Was he injured?'

Petrenko frowned. 'Who gives a fuck? For all I know, it's his fault I nearly died . . . Wait a second. Maybe they weren't after me, but Yamout.'

'You can't know that for sure,' Burliuk said. 'You have enemies, don't you?'

Petrenko nodded, but his thoughts were becoming clearer. He sat forward and said, 'I have more enemies than God. Every criminal in this city wants my blood. But they are all rightly afraid of Danil Petrenko and what I can do to them and their families.' He stabbed himself in the chest with a thumb. 'I am the king of Minsk. Any attack against my throne is akin to treason. And anyone crazy enough to attempt to usurp me would at least have the sanity to strike when I'm at my most vulnerable, not when I'm surrounded by guards and with Yamout and all his men present.'

'If you say so, King Danil.' Burliuk gave a little bow of his head.

'I'm glad you agree, Tomasz, because I hold you responsible.'

'What?'

'You brokered the introduction between Yamout and myself. I would never have dealt with the man had you not first vouched for him.'

Burliuk said nothing.

Petrenko said, 'I'm glad I sent for you, because now you need to make amends.'

Burliuk laughed briefly. 'You don't send for me, little king. You request my presence, and by my grace I decide whether to grant you that favour.'

Anger reddened Petrenko's face. He stepped towards Burliuk, the cocaine in his blood making him feel powerful over these unarmed foreigners.

Burliuk's bodyguards immediately came to life, blocking his way. Petrenko smirked at them and brandished his Desert Eagle. If he wanted to, he could execute the two impudent weaponless thugs at any moment he—

In the time it took to blink, one of the bodyguards drew a pistol and pushed the muzzle against Petrenko's cheek.

'You need to educate your thugs on how to properly frisk a man,' Burliuk said emotionlessly.

Petrenko gulped and dropped his gun. None of his own men were close enough to see what was happening.

Burliuk whispered to his bodyguards and they backed off.

He said, 'There is no need for such unpleasantness, Danil. Let us resolve this amicably.'

Petrenko nodded. 'Fine.'

'What would you like me to do?'

'I want whoever came after me dead.'

'Why, when the target was Yamout, not you?'

Petrenko scoffed. 'The target is irrelevant. What matters is they attacked me, in my suite, in my city, and killed my men. I've told you that there are many who would like nothing more than to see my kingdom topple. I am stronger than any one rival, but not strong enough to fight them all. And now, after this humiliation, they'll believe me weak. I need to show my strength and I need to show it fast. You can help me do so.'

'Danil, I don't think—'

'Don't you dare say no to me, Tomasz. I've been a good friend to you and Kasakov. How many shipments have passed through my land safely and without incident? I came across these guns myself and I offered them to Kasakov first, out of courtesy, but you weren't interested. So I line up my own buyers, but then you come along and ask me to deal with Yamout instead, as a favour to you, and one which I am willing to do as a mark of respect. You don't tell me why and I don't ask, I just do. But that was before I had good men murdered because of that favour. And now I ask myself, why were you so keen to have me sell those guns to Yamout? You'll be happy to know that I haven't yet worked out the answer, but I'm sure whatever arrangement you had with Yamout was outside Kasakov's knowledge. I wonder what he would say if I told him his right-hand man was up to something behind his back.'

Burliuk didn't answer for a long moment. Then he said, 'You would forfeit your life so needlessly?'

'I don't think you are in a position to threaten me.'

'You misunderstand me. I'm merely pointing out that if you bring this news to Kasakov he will kill you as surely as he will kill me.'

'Nice try. But I'm a little harder to trick than that. Kasakov does not compete with Yamout, I know that much. He won't give a shit that I have dealt with him. He'll care that you have, though.'

Burliuk laughed. 'Then you are a fool. Kasakov would visit horrors upon you that are indescribable. My arrangement with Yamout is without Kasakov's knowledge, you are correct about that. Yamout did me a favour, and in return I introduced him to you. This wasn't a problem until recently. But now, Kasakov has discovered Yamout's organisation is responsible for the death of his beloved nephew and he wants revenge. If he learns I have dealt with his sworn enemy I will suffer the same fate. As will you.'

'I don't believe you.'

Burliuk took out his cell phone. 'Then call Vladimir now and roll the dice with your life.'

Petrenko thought for a minute and waved his hands. He said, 'Okay, you win, Tomasz. Put your damn phone away. Well played, as always. I do hope for your sake you can play Yamout as well.'

'I have no need to play him. Yamout does not know who I am and Kasakov will have him killed soon enough.'

'I'm delighted that you have nothing to worry about,' Petrenko sneered. 'So let's turn our attentions back to my concerns. I still have my rivals to consider. I need to show there is a price to be paid for striking against me.'

'Then tell me, what have you learned so far about your attackers?'

Petrenko shrugged. 'Nothing as yet.'

'This happened over three hours ago.'

Petrenko shrugged again. 'My people are doing everything they can. Every thug in this city is being smacked around to see what he knows.'

'So you know who you are looking for?'

'No, but . . .'

'Did you see any of the gunmen?'

'No.'

Burliuk paced the room. 'Did you hear anything? Anything at all? Voices, maybe?'

215

'No,' Petrenko said again.

'Did anything happen before Yamout arrived?'

'Before? Why?'

'Because they didn't just turn up and start shooting. They must have staked out the hotel first. They were there before Yamout arrived, maybe even before you arrived. They must have been watching for him. Did you see anyone?'

Petrenko shook his head. 'No.'

'And your man who escaped?'

'I don't know.'

'Then find out.'

Petrenko shouted for his man, who entered the room. He looked nervous.

'Today,' Burliuk said immediately, 'did you see anyone who didn't fit in at the hotel. Foreigners, perhaps. They might have dressed differently. Did anyone seem to be watching you, however casual that watching might have been? Perhaps someone looked at you for more than a second . . .'

The man shook his head. 'I didn't see anyone suspicious or foreign. The only person I even remember seeing at all was from the hotel management.'

'When was that?' Burliuk asked.

Petrenko added, 'Yeah, when?'

'While you were out for food. Just a few minutes after you had gone.'

Burliuk said, 'What did he want?'

'I don't really know. He just checked the suite.'

'What was his name?' Petrenko asked. 'The management know not to interfere with my dealings there.'

'He didn't give it.'

'Describe him,' Burliuk said.

'He was my height, but skinnier. Same sort of age. Short dark hair.'

Petrenko's eyes narrowed. 'You idiot. No one who works at the hotel looks like that. He was one of them. I should have your eyes for this.'

'Tell me you got a good look at him,' Burliuk said quietly.

'Yes,' Petrenko's man was quick to assure.

'Good,' Petrenko said, pointing. 'You just saved your life.'

Burliuk said, 'Picture him in your head. Think of the shape of his nose, the colour of his eyes, how far apart they were. Everything, every little detail.' He turned to Petrenko. 'You have cops on your payroll?'

'Of course.'

'Call them and get a sketch artist over here immediately. When the picture is ready, every one of your men needs a copy. Have them check hotels and guesthouses, ask every receptionist and maid if they have seen him. Put people in the airport and train stations. Speak to taxi drivers, bartenders, everyone. Spread money around, offer a reward for information. Give the picture to men you can trust. Saturate the city. Someone will have seen him, or will see him. With luck, he and his friends are still here. If not, there will be a trail to follow to those who sent them.'

Petrenko was quiet for a moment while he decided how best to make his point. 'But what if we do find them?' he asked eventually. 'What then? Last time they wiped out both mine and Yamout's bodyguards in seconds. They are ruthless killers. My men are thieves and thugs. They are not soldiers.'

Burliuk waved a hand dismissively. 'I will help you on this

matter, and in return you will forget the part I played in your deal with Yamout. Agreed?' Petrenko nodded. 'I'll make a call and bring in some professionals. They will handle it. All you have to do is find him.'

CHAPTER 28

Dark clouds hung in the sky over Minsk. Victor walked on the left side of the street, along the kerb so that inconsiderate or clumsy pedestrians couldn't brush or bang into his wounded arm. It throbbed continuously. In the morning, he'd visited several pharmacies to buy first-aid supplies, cleaned and dressed the wound before resting and sleeping through the rest of the day. He was waiting until rush hour before getting out of the city. It was the best time for making an exit. Maximum people. Maximum cover.

After the killings of the previous night Victor had plenty of enemies to concern himself with. He doubted Yamout would still be in the city, let alone hunting for him with all his bodyguards dead, but that left Petrenko's people, whoever the surveillance team worked for, and the authorities.

The police wouldn't be on to him without an eye witness, but they would be hunting for anyone suspicious. With cameras covering the Presidential Suite, the surveillance team would have captured his face when he surveyed the suite earlier in the day before his attack. He'd destroyed the computer, but if recordings had been backed up elsewhere he had a real problem. As for Petrenko, one of his men had survived, along with Petrenko himself, but in the frenzy of combat Victor couldn't be sure which one. If that man happened to be Jerkov, whom Victor had briefly conversed with, they might have worked out the significance of that particular visit and would also know what he looked like.

Victor wore cheap shoes, cheap jeans and a cheap jacket, all purchased from a thrift store. A similarly cheap ball cap was pulled down tight over his head. He walked with a slight stoop to disguise his height. He was a block away from the Europe, keeping pace with a group of Russian tourists, walking a step behind as though he was one of them, occasionally nodding and smiling like he was part of their conversation while he looked for the car that matched the keys he'd taken from one of the surveillance team.

They had been smart operators. Aside from their Belarusian IDs carried in case they encountered the authorities, they'd been operating sterile. They wouldn't have parked their car in the spaces opposite the hotel, or anywhere else too close. They would have parked a tactical distance away where they wouldn't have been noticed by Petrenko or Yamout, but close enough to be practical.

From his previous reconnaissance Victor knew all the likely parking spaces in the vicinity, and mentally narrowed the list down to two: either at a small parking lot to the north-east behind a row of stores, or the long line of parking spaces that ran along the west side of Oktyabrskaya Square. The first lot was the more discreet of the two, but was harder to get to, and hence slower to leave with haste. Smart operators wouldn't have boxed themselves in if another option was available. He'd checked it anyway, because he was thorough, but hadn't found the car.

Victor was now at the second option, walking south. To his left, at the centre of the huge square, stood the Palace of the Republic. The rectangular building had sharp Stalinist columns set along every wall, a plate-glass façade, and was used for political ceremonies, concerts, summits, and exhibitions. The nearby parking was predictably busy and anonymous, and connected to two main thoroughfares. Had their roles been reversed, Victor would have parked here.

He saw fifty-one vehicles parked in a long row along the square's west side. If the keys had included a radio fob, Victor could have just pressed it until the indicators flashed. There was no maker's badge on the key ring either. Both had likely been removed by the team as a security precaution. Smart operators.

As they had numbered four, their car would have to be big enough to carry them all, so it would be a four-door sedan or SUV. Discounting the small sedans and coupes left thirty-six potentials. An SUV would stand out too much during mobile surveillance, so he dismissed those to bring the pool down another three. The team's sedan would be a mid-range vehicle, again for anonymity's sake, so Victor ignored those that were more than ten years old and those less than two, as well as the odd luxury BMW or Merc. Sixteen cars remained. The colour would be a muted tone, something that wouldn't catch the eye. No red, white or black. Seven remaining. As the team were not native to Belarus and Minsk their car would most likely be a rental with a company sticker and Belarusian plates. Three left. As it had been parked since at least the previous evening, it would have picked up a parking ticket. Two left. Finally, smart operators always reverse-parked to facilitate a faster exit.

One left.

It was a dark grey Saab, four years old, with a Europcar sticker on the windshield. Victor folded the parking ticket into a pocket and inserted the key into the driver's door. It unlocked, and he climbed inside. The door closed with a reassuring thunk. The interior was clean and unremarkable and Victor sat for a moment with his hands resting on the steering wheel, listening to the sound of traffic passing, and people walking by. Thunder rumbled in the distance.

The glove box contained nothing apart from the smell of greasy food, no doubt from the remains of a takeout stashed inside. He found a packet of soft mints in the driver's door pocket and chewed one while he turned the ignition. The Saab's inbuilt satnav powered on and Victor navigated to the most recent entries. He wasn't surprised to find the log empty. The rental company would have wiped it after the previous client had dropped it off, and the surveillance team had been cautious enough not to use it and risk leaving an electronic map of their movements.

He thumbed the trunk release and climbed out. A young woman with long blonde hair tied into a ponytail stood on the other side of the flowerbeds that lay between the parking spaces and October Square. She used a small camera to take shots of the Palace of the Republic before she looked his way and smiled in the polite way polite people did to strangers they took to also be polite. Rude people tended to be remembered more acutely than those who were polite, so Victor smiled back.

He sensed she wanted to engage with him, perhaps to chat

about the architecture of the Palace of the Republic, maybe to share some of the facts she'd learned from a tourist brochure. He looked away, as if he was too distracted to talk, and she went back to her photographs. He waited until she had walked away before opening the Saab's trunk.

Two large black sports bags lay inside. One was empty except for a few electronic cables. The second contained tiny cameras and microphones, likely identical to the ones hidden throughout the Presidential Suite of the Hotel Europe. They were battery-powered with wireless transmitters, very small, very concealable, and very high tech. There were more cables, tools and other surveillance paraphernalia.

Victor took the bag and climbed back into the driver's seat. The odometer read 91,000 kilometres travelled. Beneath the odometer, the trip meter read 49 kilometres. If the rental company had reset the satnav's trip log, it would have reset the trip meter too. Europcar rented vehicles out from Minsk National Airport, which was approximately 41 kilometres from central Minsk. That left about 8 kilometres unaccounted for. Either they had got significantly lost on their way into the city, which Victor doubted, or they had been somewhere beyond the hotel.

It was unlikely they had all travelled together on the same flight to avoid attracting undue attention. As there were four, he expected two might have flown in, and the other two arrived in Minsk by some other form of transport, probably train as they would have had to bring the surveillance equipment, which wouldn't get through airport security without difficult questions being asked. The two who had flown in had arrived second, otherwise the Saab's trip meter would have read at least 82 kilometres. The suite next to the Presidential had two double beds, so only two would have checked in, again to keep a low profile. The other two team members had to sleep somewhere.

So, 8 spare kilometres, assuming they'd made no mistakes on the drive. If they'd only completed one journey between the hotel and the safe house, that was a radius of 4 kilometres in a straight line. In a city, where there were few straight routes, that reduced down to maybe a 2.5 kilometre radius, or a circular area of 18 square kilometres. The centre of Minsk. Somewhere in that area was another hotel or even safe house used by the two team members who hadn't stayed at the Europe. Such a distance could have been covered on foot or on public transport, but with the surveillance equipment to move, a car had been necessary. Plus maybe they'd intended to follow Yamout or Petrenko after the deal was completed and they went their separate ways.

Victor circled the Saab, examining the bodywork. It was mostly clean – recently waxed by the rental company – but on the windshield, outside the swathe of clear glass from the wipers, was a thin layer of pale grime. Victor ran a finger over it. The substance on his fingertip was slightly moist. He rubbed it dry with his thumb until he was left with a fine grey powder the consistency of talc. He re-examined the bodywork, finding no evidence of the powder except for a few thin pale streaks on the front bumper and residue in the grooves on the bonnet and grille.

Victor took the bag of surveillance equipment, but left the car. If the police weren't looking for it yet, they would be soon. At an internet café he compiled a list of hotels in central Minsk within a 2.5 kilometre radius of October Square, then used a payphone to dial each one, asking for the names he had from the Belarusian driver's licences he'd procured from the team, but no hotel he called had any guests matching those names. He checked hotels further out but with no result.

If they hadn't stayed at a hotel they must have used some other kind of establishment. That wouldn't be a hostel, as they would have required more privacy, but it could be a private residence.

He thought about the grey powder. Had time allowed, Victor would have set off on foot, but with an 18-square kilometre area to cover he couldn't hope to complete the task before he needed to leave. He had to find the location before the cops did, if they hadn't yet. He hailed a taxi.

The driver was a plump Belarusian woman with glasses and the biggest smile he'd seen in a long time.

In Russian, pretending not to speak the language well, he asked her, 'Do you know where the, uh . . . *build* site is near here, on . . .' He trailed off, as though he couldn't remember or pronounce the name of the street.

'Kirova . . . Nemiga?' she offered slowly, helpful and smiling.

'Kirova,' he said, with a smile of his own.

She dropped him off at the east end of the street and he walked west, quickly realising that she'd misunderstood him, or he hadn't made himself clear. Roadworks were taking place. It looked like they were fixing a water main. He hailed another taxi.

'Nemiga,' he said to the driver.

As they turned into the street, Victor saw scaffolding framing a building halfway down the block. He had the driver pull over.

Nemiga was in a rundown neighbourhood approximately half a mile from October Square. The street was lined with narrow-fronted townhouses painted in pastel shades. Victor approached the building with the scaffolding. He heard the sounds of busy work emanating from the property – shouting, banging, and the rumble and whine of power tools. A cement mixer was set on the sidewalk outside.

The Saab didn't have to be parked near the mixer to get cement dust on its windshield, depending on the wind that day. Not that where the car was parked helped him much. The team would have taken a spot wherever it was available, if the space outside whatever building they'd used wasn't free. There were maybe twenty houses on each side of the street, forty in total, thirty-nine potentials after discounting the house being worked on. He could knock on every door, and further reduce the potentials by crossing off any house where someone answered, but even then he could be left with twenty-five or more properties to break into. But there was a simpler way of narrowing down his selection.

He looked at the sky. The clouds were dark and had been all morning. The ambient light was limited. Victor walked along the sidewalk until he found the only house with all of its drapes closed.

It had a good deadbolt, but Victor had been picking locks for fifteen years. He closed the front door behind him and dropped the lock picks back into a pocket. He stood in the hallway and listened. There was no alarm, but Victor hadn't expected to find one. If someone broke in the team hadn't wanted the police to show up and start asking questions they didn't want to answer.

In the days when Victor had his own house he'd gone with the same philosophy.

He didn't know if this was a safe house owned by whoever they worked for or somewhere that had been rented just for this job. It was dark. The hallway was narrow with a threadbare carpet and flaking paint on the walls. The ceiling light had no shade. A set of stairs led up. A door stood in the wall to his right. The hallway opened up into a kitchen ahead of him. He opened the door first, finding himself in a small lounge with a two-seater sofa, armchair, TV and little else to suggest it was anyone's home. A camp bed was set up in one corner with a small suitcase opened out next to it. The bed hadn't been made. The suitcase contained clothes and toiletries and nothing else. A side pocket was open, but empty.

Victor tried the kitchen next. The fridge was a quarter full with milk, cheese, sliced meats, some vegetables and orange juice. The cupboards were mostly empty, except one contained bread and canned goods. Plastic knives, forks and spoons were mixed together loose in a drawer. The kitchen led to a bathroom. Several damp towels competed for space on the rail.

Upstairs there were two bedrooms. The first was small, with a single bed against one wall and another camp bed against the other. Each had been recently slept in. That made three. The suite back at the Europe must have been used purely for surveillance then, with the team commuting from here, probably operating in some kind of shift arrangement, travelling back and forth to rack up the trip meter. Victor searched through the suitcase he found next to each bed. Like the one downstairs they had clothes and toiletries and nothing to tell him who these guys

227

were. As with the one downstairs, they had open but empty pockets, one on the front of the case, the other on the inside lid.

The last bedroom was larger than the first, with a slept-in double bed where the fourth team member had rested, most likely the leader. When Victor stepped inside the room his heart rate increased by several beats per minute. Not because there was an open suitcase sat on the bed, with clothes scattered around it on the bedclothes. Not because there was nothing else inside it of use to him. His heart rate quickened because on the opposite wall to the double bed was a fifth recently used camp bed.

But no suitcase.

CHAPTER 29

Zürich, Switzerland

In a dark room two men who were not Swiss stood before an antique wooden desk. The first man was in his early thirties and wore jeans and a windcheater. The second was old, very short, wearing a suit. He stood slightly hunched over. Before them a laptop computer sat on the desk. Video footage filled the laptop's screen. The footage had been recorded with state-of-the-art infrared cameras, of a hotel suite. The recording showed three men, acting shocked and confused. The laptop's speakers played strange sounds.

'He's shooting through the door,' the man in the windcheater explained.

The older man nodded and watched as one of the three men jumped down behind a sofa a second before the suite door burst open and a man with a sub-machine gun and night-vision goggles charged in and opened fire, mercilessly gunning down the two standing men, and then the third through the sofa. There was no sound of gunfire, only the results of it.

The man in the windcheater said, 'Silenced FN P90. He's using subsonic ammo. That's why we can't hear it.'

The video footage cut to another camera as the man with the P90 continued his assault, shooting through a bedroom door and lying down next to it, before opening the door and killing those in the room beyond.

The man in the windcheater rubbed his tired face and said, 'My team is next.'

The gunman was then shot by two men arriving behind him, and played dead until they had passed him, then killed them also. He exchanged fire with a final man, before shooting him and leaving. The video jumped forward in time, and the man had returned to squat down next to the last man he'd shot, who wasn't dead. He stayed squatted down for almost half a minute.

'Is he questioning him?' the old man in the suit asked.

'I expect so. The microphones didn't pick it up. He wouldn't have told him anything.'

'How else are we exposed?'

The man in the windcheater answered. 'The authorities will have found the surveillance equipment, of course, but I retrieved and disposed of the plane tickets and passports of the others. Our computer was destroyed – I believe by the assassin as a pre-caution. Not that it helped him, as we had the footage continuously backed up to the safe-house server, otherwise we wouldn't have anything of him.'

'Show me the other part.'

The younger man tapped some keys on the laptop and used the track pad. The infrared footage was replaced with colour footage of the hotel suite. Two men were visible, conversing in Russian.

'Which is the one who killed my boys?' the old man in the suit asked, leaning closer.

'The guy on the left is a member of Petrenko's entourage. The man on the right claims to be from hotel management, but he doesn't work there and does nothing except look around the suite. Reconnaissance, of course.'

'So we have his voice, and his face.'

'And nothing else. I'm so sorry, Father.'

'But that's enough,' the old man in the suit said as he reached for his phone.

CHAPTER 30

Mount Lebanon, Lebanon

'This is Xavier Callo,' a scared voice said. 'I'm in Minsk.' There was a pause, the sound of heavy breathing. 'Tell Yamout it's a trap. Vladimir Kasakov is going to kill him.' Another pause, longer, more breathing. 'He tried to kill me already but I got away. Tell Yamout—'

'That's it,' Yamout said. 'That was Callo's message. He made the call shortly before he was beaten to death.'

Baraa Ariff nodded, not quite believing what he was hearing. He sat in an eighteenth-century Turkish armchair carved ornately from ebony. Before him a mobile phone set to speaker sat on a coffee table. Yamout sat opposite Ariff, perched on a hand-stitched silk couch.

'Play it again,' Ariff said.

They listened to Callo's words another time. Ariff shook his head before the recording had finished.

The two arms dealers sat in silence for a moment. They were in the combined lounge and bar of Ariff's private wing on the second floor of his mountain villa. It was cool and quiet in the room. Ceiling fans thrummed softly overhead. Set within the north-east corner wing he also had an office, kitchen, bathroom, bedroom and balcony for his exclusive use. The area was inaccessible to his wife and daughters due to an electronically sealed door that only he and Yamout knew the code to.

Ariff sat back in the armchair. 'What time was the call made?'

'The voicemail log says nine-thirty, last night.'

'Nine-thirty,' Ariff said thoughtfully. 'Shortly after you were attacked.'

Yamout nodded.

'So Kasakov went after Callo and you simultaneously. A coordinated strike against us. But Callo's death matters nothing to me except I have now lost the money he owed us, and we need the services of a new diamond merchant. Both of which are trivial. What is important to me is that you, my dear friend, were cunning enough to escape Kasakov's foul assassins.'

Yamout made a face. 'Yet I came within a hair's breadth of losing my life. His men were but a room away from killing me. I employed no cunning in my escape, only terror. I am lucky to be alive. It is nothing short of a miracle.'

Ariff gave a mocking smile. 'Don't be ridiculous. God would no sooner save you than he would me. Miracles are reserved for the pure and the good. We are neither. Men like us must make our own miracles.' Ariff stood. 'Come.'

Yamout followed him through the door into the rest of the villa. The décor changed markedly. Ariff liked his private rooms to be simply decorated – animal-skin rugs on the floor, comfortable furniture, nothing that did not serve a practical purpose. The gold-painted armchairs, bronze statues, Persian rugs, crystal chandeliers, exotic house plants and original oil paintings in the rest of the villa were the doing of Ariff's wife. She had extravagant tastes and had the interior of the house set like the palace of an opulent prince.

They descended the huge marble staircase. When Ariff reached the bottom his youngest daughter appeared, seemingly out of nowhere, and sprinted straight up to him. He caught Eshe under the armpits and hoisted her off her feet. He blew raspberries on her belly. She laughed hysterically. Yamout watched and smiled.

The nanny came rushing after Eshe. 'I'm sorry, sir,' she said to Ariff. 'Eshe, come here, don't bother your father.'

Ariff lowered Eshe and stroked her hair. 'Do as you're told, my dear.'

The nanny took Eshe's hand and pulled her away.

Ariff was still smiling when they entered the massive garden that lay behind the villa. It stretched into the distance, seeming to meet the mountainside that rose high behind the villa. There were no clouds and the sun was hot. A guard patrolled on the far side of the crescent-shaped swimming pool. He was armed with an assault rifle – not one of the cheap AKs that were Ariff's main product – but an American-made Armalite. The villa was set within forty thousand square feet of land patrolled continuously by six mercenaries. Two more were stationed inside the house itself while another two monitored the twenty security cameras and dozen motion sensors that ceaselessly watched over Ariff's home. Ariff only employed the best to watch over himself and his family.

'If he came after me,' Yamout said. 'He'll come after you too.'

He walked the thirty feet to where a large pergola stood near to the swimming pool. Beneath its tiled roof were couches and chairs. Ariff took a bottle of Sabil mineral water from a free-standing refrigerator. He offered one to Yamout, who shook his head. Both men sat down in the cool of the shade.

'And we will be ready for his assassins when he does,' Ariff said.

'You don't seem particularly concerned.'

'Don't think that means I am naive. Remember, they could not get to you when you were so far away from home.' He gestured at the guard. 'Do you think they will be more successful where we are strongest?' Ariff relaxed in his chair. 'Ever since I was a boy my life has been in danger. Now my hair is grey and my face is lined yet I still breathe. Will Kasakov survive as long as I?' He shook his head again. 'But for caution's sake move yourself and your family here with me until this thing is over. I have six bedrooms standing idle. It will be good to finally make use of them.' He smiled. 'You will not be in the way and your own men can be added to those already here. We will be invincible.'

'Thank you, I would feel better with my family behind your walls.'

'Don't mention it. Your family is my family.' Ariff held his arms out. 'This will be our castle. I welcome his killers to try and strike at us here. We will show that fool just how foolish he really is. Let Kasakov send his killers into our domain and we shall send them back to Russia in little pieces.'

Yamout exhaled and stood. 'But why attack us now, after all these years? We do not fight for the same business.'

Ariff sipped some water and said, 'He should have no reason

for wanting you or I dead, agreed. We have made no move against him, nor has there been any strife between our traffickers. And if there were some unknown personal grievance there would be no need to kill Callo. But remember, Kasakov has been trapped in Russia for some years now. The UN pressure to apprehend him is considerable. This could be affecting his ability to deal in heavy armaments.'

Ariff set his water down and stepped out from under the pergola. He unhooked his cufflinks and folded up his shirtsleeves. He walked to the edge of the stone patio, slipped off his sandals, and walked barefoot on the grass. It was cool and moist beneath his feet. Yamout walked with him.

Ariff said, 'Vladimir does not have the infrastructure to flourish in the small arms trade. His giant cargo planes that are so good for delivering tanks to warlords are not subtle enough to sneak assault rifles and rocket-propelled grenade launchers into a war zone. He knows he can't compete with us, which is why he has never made more than token efforts in the past. But he must believe if he can wipe us out he can fill the void that is left.' Ariff shook his head but smiled. 'He must be insane to think that, and to have come after us like this, so blatantly, so arrogantly. That he failed to kill you, which of course I am glad of, is proof enough that his intelligence is second to his ambition. He will suffer for his lack of foresight.' Ariff stopped to face Yamout. 'We are now at war, Gabir.'

Yamout exhaled and squinted against the sun. 'Yet how are we going to strike back? Russia is a long way for us to reach.'

Ariff nodded. 'Do not forget that Kasakov's empire overlaps with our own. We deal with many of the same parts of the world, with the same clients. Our paths cross frequently. If he thought he could sweep us away without leaving himself exposed he is very much mistaken. We need not stretch our arm all the way to Russia when Kasakov is already so close. We will attack his network. We will destroy his shipments. We will kill his traffickers. We will slice off his fingers one by one and leave his empire crippled.'

Ariff smiled and set his hands on Yamout's shoulders. 'Then, when he has no strength left to resist us, we will deliver the killing blow.'

CHAPTER 31

Minsk, Belarus

Victor climbed out of the taxi and into the cold, wind and rain immediately darkening his overcoat. His gaze swept over the small group of taxi drivers standing together under a bus shelter, laughing and joking, smoking cigarettes. No one else nearby was stationary. Pedestrians hurried on their way, faces down, shoulders up. The weather was too bad to be outside without the strongest of need. Even watchers would want to stay warm and dry. If the train station was under surveillance it would be from inside not out. That suited Victor just fine.

Minsk Central was a huge station built in the Stalinist style that managed to remain grand and imposing despite the freezing downpour. Crossing the road, Victor could see a couple of armed police officers patrolling the square. Both looked alert. Not unusual. He showed nothing on his face, displayed nothing in his actions – just another anonymous businessman on his way home.

There was a tight feeling in the pit of his stomach, but he

ignored it. He moved around a Belarusian family who seemed happy enough to wait in a position where they blocked the better part of the main entrance.

Air travel was the quickest way of creating distance, but also the most watched, the most regulated, the most restricting, and by far the best way of getting apprehended. A car offered the most freedom, but, whether he stole one and gambled with the watchfulness of the police, or hired one and added exposure to one of his aliases, was not without its negatives. A train, though not perfect, was usually the best option. He could pay cash without being noted, needed no identification, and created no paper trail outside of a ticket that would be destroyed once its use was spent.

As a boy he'd loved trains, and had spent endless hours watching them from his dorm window that overlooked a station. Back then he'd longed to drive them. Instead he killed people, and now his fondness for trains extended only to their benefits in extraction.

Inside the station the concourse was noisy and crowded with commuters. Victor glided among them. His eyes, partially shielded behind a pair of non-prescription glasses, flicked back and forth between the faces of those standing along the walls or sitting down, where he would position himself if he were watching people enter. He was searching for recognition, some action or movement that would give away surveillance, but he saw no indication that he was being observed. He didn't relax. Just because he saw no one watching him, it didn't mean that no one was. If Petrenko's network was large enough and they were smart enough, his description, maybe even a picture, could have been passed around. Train stations and airports could be watched.

He circled the concourse several times. He bought a cup of

coffee, a newspaper, browsed books, acting casually, trying to cut down as many lines of sight as possible in the hope of drawing out watchers. Professional shadows could be working in multi-sex couples or disguised as station employees. He doubted Petrenko's network would be that proficient, but he had no doubts that whoever the surveillance team worked for were. He noticed an athletic and alert young woman with a buggy but no child in his peripheral vision twice. The child might be with the father or there might be no child at all. Passing windows, he watched her reflection to see if she was watching him, but at no time did she look his way.

Victor headed to the men's room and spent five minutes waiting in a stall before coming out to find the woman was nowhere to be seen. He checked the departure boards, found an appropriate train, and joined the queue for the ticket counters. He behaved like any other Belarusian, not worthy of attention, but he caught a short man look his way. It was only one time and maybe it meant nothing but maybe it meant everything. The man had a round face, bald, about twenty pounds overweight, wearing a train company uniform. Victor looked at his watch for a few seconds and stepped out of line. He entered a pharmacist and perused the shampoos before looking up in the direction of the bald guy. He wasn't there.

'Hrodna,' Victor said in Russian when he reached the ticket counter. 'The next available train.'

'Seats are only available in first class.'

'That's fine.'

He waited until three minutes before the train to Hrodna was due to depart before walking to the platform. He watched every man or woman that came on to the platform after him. If he had

240

a shadow, they would be forced to wait too so as not to risk getting on the train to find he wasn't following. No one hung around, or otherwise made him suspicious. Victor waited until just one minute before the departure time before boarding. No one followed.

He found his seat in the first class carriage at the front of the train. It was on the aisle, set facing forward, with a table. Victor sat down. A man was sitting opposite.

'Boy do I hate trains,' the man said in American-accented English, talking loudly. 'All the waiting around. I mean, let's go already. Know what I'm saying?'

Victor looked at him, but didn't answer.

'Walt Fisher,' the man said, offering his hand across the table. 'I figure you're not a Ruskie.'

Fisher looked mid-forties, dressed in a striped shirt, top button undone, tie loose, suit jacket draped over the seat next to him. His cheeks were flushed and fine droplets of sweat lined his hairline.

'You mean Belarusian,' Victor said, deciding it wasn't worth pretending not to speak English. He shook the hand. It was warm and moist.

'Whatever. Belarusian, Russian, is there a difference?'

Victor shrugged.

Fisher nodded. '*Exactly*.'

'How did you know I'm neither?' Victor asked, genuinely intrigued.

'They don't travel first.'

'Ah,' Victor said, not commenting on the various Russian-language conversations going on nearby.

Fisher allowed himself a smug grin. 'You have a name, son?'

'Peter.'

'You're a lime— you're a Brit, ain't you?'

'Very perceptive,' Victor said, adding a more stereotypical British emphasis on the mid-Atlantic accent he'd been using.

'I hope so, friend. That's nigh on ninety per cent of my job.'

Fisher stank of bourbon and, aside from the volume of his voice, seemed harmless enough. Some people just liked to talk.

'Just been brokering a big-ass deal with the Reds,' he explained, before adding, 'Is it still okay to say that?'

'No more or less so than "limey".'

He let out a booming laugh. 'Yeah, sorry about that. Habit.'

'No offence taken.'

'In mergers and acquisitions,' Fisher announced. 'What about you?'

'I'm a consultant.'

'What field?' Fisher clicked his fingers before Victor could respond. 'No, don't tell me.' He bit his lip and pointed. 'Human resources.'

'Is it that obvious?'

Fisher clapped his hands together, pleased, proud. Other passengers looked over in response at the sudden noise. 'Soon as you stepped onboard I said to myself: here's the man who does the hiring and firing.'

'Mostly firing.'

'Sounds cutthroat.'

Victor raised an eyebrow. 'You have no idea.'

Three minutes after the departure time the train hadn't started moving. No announcement had been made. Victor liked punctuality, even more so when he had enemies in the same city.

He stood up to take a better look out of the window. Fisher watched him. Victor couldn't see anything to explain the delay. Nothing to worry about then. Probably.

'So anyway,' Fisher said. 'On the way here . . .'

Victor sat without talking as Fisher recounted a story about his supposedly hilarious journey from his hotel to the train station. Fisher was drunk and talkative and by exchanging pleasantries Victor had given his new best friend licence to talk for the entire trip. Another time Victor might have enjoyed playing the part of Peter the human resources consultant to pass the time, but Fisher was too inebriated to control the volume of his voice, and he was drawing too much attention. That attention was naturally focused on Fisher, but those passengers might also remember who Fisher was so loudly talking to.

When the train hadn't moved after another four minutes, other passengers were becoming disgruntled. There were lots of heads turning to look out of windows and mumbled annoyance. A stewardess with a trolley was making her way along the aisle offering drinks. When she reached Victor he asked for a mineral water. Fisher requested a bourbon.

'Still or sparkling?' she asked Victor.

'Sparkling, please.'

She looked through the bottles on her trolley for a moment before turning back to Victor. She frowned.

'I'm sorry, sir, it appears I only have still today. ' She seemed genuinely apologetic.

'Don't worry about it, still is fine.'

'Are you sure? I can go and look for some.'

'You'd better not,' Victor said. 'If you don't serve these people some alcohol first you might not make it back alive.'

She smiled while she served Fisher his bourbon. The smile was inviting, pinks lips glistening. 'I think I'll brave it. Be right back.'

As soon as she was out of earshot Fisher slapped the table with the flat of his palm. People looked again. 'You lucky son of a gun, you're in there.'

Victor remained silent.

The stewardess brought Victor his sparkling mineral water and placed it on the table with a clear plastic cup of ice.

'Thank you so much,' Victor said, giving her his best smile. 'You're an angel.'

She smiled again. Maybe Fisher was right, maybe he was in there.

'Honestly,' she said. 'It's quite all right.'

Her tone told him he had breached her professional wall. It hadn't been hard. First-class passengers rarely had the inclination even for eye contact. One who was polite, offered praise, and made her smile probably became an instant confidant.

'Could you tell me what's with the delay? Victor asked.

Her brow creased in deliberation and she quickly looked from side to side before leaning closer to him.

'I'm not supposed to say,' she confessed. 'But we're holding the train.'

'What's the reason?'

'The company haven't told us.' She leaned even closer and he felt her breath on his cheek. 'But if you ask me there's someone on this train who shouldn't be, if you know what I mean. I think they're sending some people over as we speak.'

Victor didn't have to pretend to be concerned. He waited until she was serving someone else before standing. He walked down the aisle, into the vestibule, and entered a toilet. He waited ten seconds and flushed the bowl, using the noise to screen the clatter of broken glass as he smashed the mirror above the sink with an elbow.

From the basin, he selected a piece of glass about six inches in length, roughly triangular in shape, long sides and a short base. He slipped it, point up, between his suit jacket and shirt-sleeve on his left arm. He folded the cuff of his shirt back to act as a stopper and shook his arm to make sure it was secure.

He left the toilet and moved to the near exit. The door was already open. Cold air blew in from the platform. On the other side, six feet away, were three men. The first man was tall and lean with a hard angular face, dressed in a suit and overcoat. The other two were shorter, wearing dark trousers and casual jackets, the first with a patchy beard, the second wearing rimless glasses. They weren't cops, and they looked different from both Petrenko's men and the surveillance team members. They hesitated, surprised to see him, unsure what to do. Not that experienced then.

He stepped off the train and walked straight at them.

They halted, confused by his actions, nervous because of the sudden change in the hierarchy of predators and prey. The one with glasses gripped the pistol at his belt.

'What are you going to do,' Victor asked him as he neared, 'shoot me here with thirty people watching?'

The man's eyes were narrow behind his glasses. He didn't respond but the hand moved a little away from the gun.

Victor stopped three feet away. 'Shall we take this elsewhere?'

Both shorter guys immediately glanced at the tall man but he didn't look back, didn't see them. He stared straight into

Victor's eyes, unblinking. His angular face showed nothing, but Victor could feel his thought process, weighing up the many pros of taking Victor somewhere a little more private as opposed to the many cons of shooting him in front of a train full of witnesses.

'No reason why we can't be civilised about this,' Victor added.

'Yes,' the tall man said with a little smile, 'let us be civilised.'

CHAPTER 32

There were no other travellers on the platform, but the bald guy in a train company uniform was staring in Victor's direction. The tall man backed away a step, his gaze never leaving Victor, and motioned with his hand for him to walk forward.

Victor did and the two shorter guys immediately moved to his flanks. They were both muscular, serious expressions, confident enough in Victor's passivity not to grab hold of him or to keep hands close to weapons. The bald guy continued to stare.

Victor remained stationary while the shorter guy with the patchy beard patted him down on his thighs and hips, and around his waist and under his arms. It was done quickly to avoid attracting attention. Which was smart. But the frisk didn't go anywhere near Victor's left wrist. Which wasn't smart.

The searcher found the SIG in the back of Victor's waistband and slipped it into one of his own pockets. 'He's good now,' the guy said.

The tall man motioned with his head.

With the guy wearing glasses in front and the other two men behind him, Victor was led along the platform, but away from the concourse, towards the bald guy in the uniform, who opened a worn-looking metal door. He then hurried away, doing his best to avoid eye contact with Victor.

The tall guy nudged Victor in the back. 'Eyes forward, my friend.'

He followed the first man into the corridor beyond the metal door. It was dark and cool with bare brick walls, dimly lit. The door closed behind Victor and he heard the muted sound of the train to Hrodna pulling away from the platform. He hoped Walt Fisher found someone else to talk to.

They took a left turn and he was led down a series of long featureless corridors until the only sounds were those of their shoes on the floor. Victor kept his head fixed forward, but his eyes moved continuously, taking in everything about the location, memorising the route and looking for advantages. All the corridors were the same: bare brick, plain doors, sprinkler nozzles in the ceiling. Nothing to tip the odds in his favour.

They turned another corner and the lead guy opened a door. He gestured for Victor to enter the dark room beyond. He walked in first and the light was switched on to reveal a small room, ten feet square. Cardboard boxes were stacked against one wall and a simple table with plastic chairs against the other. A mop and metal bucket stood in a corner. The air smelled stale and dusty.

'Sit,' the tall man said.

Victor turned around. 'I prefer to stand.'

The tall man took a step closer. 'It was an order, not an offer.'

'All the same,' Victor said. 'I think I'll stand.'

The tall man's eyes narrowed a fraction. 'Sit. Down.'

Victor remained standing.

The tall man made a gesture and the patchy-beard guy rushed forward. He had short, blond hair and dark circles beneath his eyes. He was maybe five inches shorter than Victor, but far more heavily built, jacket straining against the strength in his shoulders and arms. In return, Victor knew the guy saw only weakness. Which was how he always preferred it. He offered no resistance as he was flung backwards against the wall. He grunted, but didn't need to.

Maintaining eye contact with him the whole time, Victor straightened down his jacket and took a step towards his assailant. It was a long step, bringing him well inside the blond guy's personal space. An unmistakable challenge that was greeted with a smile.

The punch itself was fast but clumsy – they were too close together, no room for the man to get all his power into it, his posture awkward, lacking in balance. Victor tensed his abdominals but didn't try to stop it. The punch hit square in the gut. He dropped to one knee, coughing.

All three of his captors laughed and Victor continued to cough and splutter far longer than he needed to. The guy who'd punched him stepped back to where the other two stood closer to the door.

'Perhaps you are ready to sit down now,' the tall man said.

Victor slowly stood and pulled out one of the plastic chairs. He sat down in his own time.

'What happens next?' he asked, a pained and broken edge to his voice.

They gave no response. The tall man took a cell phone from

his hip pocket and hit a speed-dial number. He held it to his ear while it rang.

'We have him,' was all he said when it connected.

There was a pause, the person on the other end talking.

'Yes, at the station,' the tall man answered. 'No, he is still alive. Do not be concerned, we have him out of the way. Your source can show you where.' Another pause. The tall man stared at Victor, who sat sheepishly. 'No, we can take care of it. He has been no trouble at all.'

So far, Victor silently added.

He noticed the two shorter men weren't watching him particularly intently. All their attention was on their boss and the phone call. They weren't worried about Victor – he'd already shown them he could be easily subdued. Good. But all three were clustered together by the door on the far side of the room. Not so good.

The tall man mumbled something and slipped the phone away.

'Not long, my friend,' he said to Victor, 'and then this is all over.'

'Suits me,' Victor said back. 'I hate waiting.'

The tall man smiled and took a step towards the table. Victor could smell cigarette smoke on the man's clothes.

'I hope you do not mind me saying, but you are being surprisingly calm about this.'

'I'm always calm,' Victor admitted.

The man nodded thoughtfully. 'I suppose men of our profession must learn to be in control of our nerves.' He sat down opposite. 'Did you ever believe that this would be how it all ended?'

'Can't say I did.'

The tall man stroked his chin for a moment. 'How long you been in this business?'

Victor acted as if he had to think. 'A long time,' he said eventually.

The tall man nodded. 'That is what I deduced. Myself, I am relatively inexperienced. But I am a fast learner.' He smiled, revealing sharp, irregular teeth. 'Before, I was a police officer. Not as generous a wage, but it taught me a lot about how not to get caught doing this more profitable work.'

'Prefer this?'

'Absolutely, my friend. Not only is it far better paid . . .' He flashed another smile. 'It is a lot more satisfying.'

'A man should take pleasure from his work.'

'Indeed.' He shuffled his seat forward. 'Though no means of employment is without negatives, of course.'

'Very true.'

'Since you are more experienced than I, have you any advice to share with me?'

'Don't get killed.'

He smirked. 'You know, my friend, you really should have listened to your own advice.'

Victor stared at him. 'I'm not dead yet.'

'Yet,' the tall man echoed. He stroked his chin again. 'I liked what you said before, about being civilised. I think I will use that myself sometime. You do not mind if I steal your line, do you?'

'Not if I can get a cigarette while we wait.'

The tall man reached into his pocket. 'Always happy to grant a dying man his last request.' He smiled at Victor, man to man.

251

'My wife keeps telling me to quit. *Yap, yap, yap* in my ear all day long.'

He took out a lighter and packet of cigarettes and put them on the table. He slid them towards Victor.

'I stopped myself,' Victor said. 'About six months ago.'

'And do you miss it?'

Victor slid the packet closer and toyed with the lighter. 'Every day.'

The tall man looked at him with a degree of understanding. 'Is that why you quit, for a woman?'

'Something like that.'

'Well, she will not see you now,' the tall man said. He checked his watch 'You have five minutes. Smoke all you wish.'

'Actually,' Victor said after he'd edged the cigarette packet a couple of inches closer, 'I've changed my mind.' He set the lighter on top of the packet. 'Thanks anyway.'

The tall man shrugged. 'Suit yourself, my friend. Now there is more for me to enjoy.'

He sat forward, reaching across the table. His fingers closed around the cigarette packet.

Victor grabbed the outstretched wrist in his left hand, pulled the piece of broken mirror from his sleeve, reversed his grip and drove the point through the tall man's hand and into the table below it.

He screamed. Blood poured out from around the glass.

The other two guys hesitated an instant – pure shock. Victor leapt up from the chair, grabbed it, hurled it their way. The guy in glasses reacted in time to dodge, but the one with the patchy beard and blond hair was too slow. The chair struck him in the chest and sent him to the floor.

By the time the guy in glasses regained his balance, Victor had already crossed the room and shoulder-barged him into the wall. He grunted against the hard brick, arms flailing, torso exposed. Victor punched him – a short uppercut to the solar plexus. The man gasped, breathless, face screwed up in pain, sagging against the wall.

Victor turned to face the guy on the floor as he scrambled on to his back, drawing a handgun out from under his jacket – a big .45 calibre suppressed Smith & Wesson automatic. Victor took a quick step forward, kicked the gun from the guy's hand as it angled up, kicked him again in the side of the head and stamped down on his face. Bone and cartilage crushed under his heel. Blood cascaded over the man's cheeks.

Victor spun back around to see the gasping man against the wall fumbling for his own gun in its underarm holster. With the suppressor already screwed on, the weapon was too long to draw with speed. An amateur mistake. Victor grabbed the hand on the weapon before it could be withdrawn and elbowed him twice in the face, smashing his glasses and fracturing a cheekbone. Victor felt the strength go in the hand, tore the gun away, pushed the suppressor against his enemy's stomach and fired twice, turned around again in time to see the man with the smashed nose retrieving the .45 and swinging it in his direction.

Victor shot him three times in the chest.

The tall man screamed – no words – just an incoherent mix of fear, desperation and pleading.

'No one can hear,' Victor said. 'That's why you brought me all the way to this room, remember?'

The guy shot in the stomach slid down the wall, not dead but dying fast, his broken glasses hanging from one ear. Blood soaked his jacket. A smeared trail of exit-wound gore glistened on the wall behind him. He groaned quietly.

Victor stepped over the corpse on the floor so he could face the tall man. His angular features were warped – half pain, half terror. The skin of his face was white and sweaty with shock. The hand pinned to the table was pure red. Blood pooled around it and dripped from the closest table edge. His other hand, the left, was beneath his overcoat, struggling to get at the gun holstered under his left armpit. Not an easy thing to do at the best of times.

Victor pointed the .45 at the guy's face and he stopped what he was doing. With his spare hand, Victor reached over and took the gun out for him. He saw it was a Smith & Wesson like the one he already had and tossed it away.

'*What do you want to know?*' the tall man yelled. '*I will tell you anything.*'

Victor picked up the chair from the other side of the room and placed it next to the table. He brushed off the seat and sat down perpendicular to the tall man.

'I know you will,' Victor agreed. 'You can start by telling me who you were speaking to on the phone. Who's coming?'

'A Belarusian. My client. Danil Petrenko.'

'Will he come alone?'

'There will be men with him.'

'How many?'

Victor rested a finger on the top of the glass shard. He didn't have to move it. The threat was enough.

'There are four more of us,' the tall man blurted out. He was frantic, eyes wide and staring at the six-inch glass shard impaled through his hand.

'Are you part of Petrenko's crew?'

'No, we are freelancers. Hired killers.' He paused a moment, thinking. 'But we were not going to kill you, my friend,' he added, quickly. 'Petrenko just wanted to talk to you.'

'Try again.'

A desperate look passed over his face. 'Okay,' he said after a pause. 'But I promise it was just business, nothing personal.'

'It never is.'

'You understand, I was merely following my orders, doing my job. You know how it is. You are just like me.'

'I don't see the similarity.'

'Petrenko is the one you want, not me.'

'So I don't need you then.'

White showed all around the tall man's irises. 'Please do not kill me.'

'How many targets said that to you?'

'I . . . I do not know.'

'I'm guessing a lot. But how many of those times did you spare them?'

There was a brief pause before he said, 'Sometimes.'

'Then you're not very good at what you do.'

'Please,' the tall man begged. 'I have told you everything I know.'

'You have,' Victor agreed, 'but I said nothing about letting you go if you did.'

'Please.'

Victor stood. 'You really should have listened to my advice.'

'Okay, my friend,' the tall man said, hurriedly, desperately, 'I have never spared anyone. I am an evil man. But you said it yourself, you are not like me. So do not be like me now. Do not become what I am.'

Victor stared down at him and said, 'For the things I have done I know the devil saves a place for me in hell. So when I am to burn, what does one more sin matter?'

He angled the .45.

'NO . . .'

CHAPTER 33

Victor had the Smith & Wesson reloaded and tucked into his waistband. Two spare mags rested in one jacket pocket and the three dead men's cell phones in the other. Pulling open the room's door, he saw a young guy in the corridor beyond. He was in his early twenties, with long hair poking out from underneath a dirty cap, wearing overalls, a tool belt hanging from his hips, bobbing his head and mouthing lyrics as headphones blared out metal Victor hadn't heard with the door closed. He was four feet away and already facing Victor, eyes widening and mouth falling opening at the sight of three dead and bloodied bodies in the room beyond the open door.

In less than a second the Smith & Wesson was out of Victor's waistband and drawing a bead between the young guy's eyes.

'Do you want me to kill you?' Victor asked.

The kid managed to shake his head.

'Then throw me your wallet.'

His gaze never leaving Victor, he did as instructed. Victor opened it up and took out a driver's licence. He held it up for the young guy to see, before slipping it into a pocket.

'I'll forget you. You forget me. Deal?'

He nodded, and Victor threw back the wallet. The kid didn't even try to catch it. It bounced off his chest and fell at his feet.

Victor said, 'You want to wait there for fifteen minutes before getting help, don't you?'

Another petrified nod.

Victor stepped around him and used the map in his mind to make his way back along the maze of empty corridors. After a minute, he heard the sounds of the train station. Soon afterwards, he saw the metal door. The tall man had said they had five minutes before Petrenko arrived. That was three minutes ago.

The platform was crowded with commuters boarding the next train out. There had to be at least thirty men walking briskly along the platform in Victor's general direction. None looked like the man Victor had seen ascend and then descend in the elevators at the Hotel Europe yesterday. He couldn't see four hired killers either or the bald guy in the uniform.

He closed the metal door and moved further along the platform, using the commuters and a pillar to conceal him while he watched the door. He hoped Petrenko didn't bring all of the shooters with him otherwise it was going to get very messy in that room.

A couple of minutes passed and Victor didn't see anyone go near the door. It was possible that there was another way to get to the room where he'd been taken, but he didn't believe this team had carte blanche access to the whole train station. More likely the bald train company employee had unlocked this one door for their use and told them the best place to do their business. Victor planned to thank him for that just as soon as the chance presented itself.

The people started to thin out on the platform as the train's departure time grew closer, enabling Victor to see clearly along to where the platform joined the concourse. Still no sign of Petrenko, a group of assassins, and their guide.

The last of the passengers boarded the train and the doors locked, leaving just two stewards and Victor behind. He looked at his watch and stood as though he was waiting for the next departure, but using the pillar to hide him from view should they show.

The train rolled away and the stewards walked off to do whatever they did in the time between departures. As the train left the platform Victor was able to see across to the platform on the other side of the tracks, and the bald train company employee standing among the crowd of waiting commuters, answering some enquiry as he performed his day job, stress free, even smiling.

The guy looked up and noticed Victor before he could make a move, and realisation immediately took over surprise. He tugged a cell phone from his trouser pocket and brought it to his ear. Tempting as it was to just draw the .45 and put two into his chest cavity, there were more than a fifty people waiting for their train around him, all probably with phones. Fifteen seconds after killing him the call could be through to the police switchboard. Thirty seconds later every cop in the area would be after Victor.

Instead, he hurried towards the concourse. A fast walk, not running. At a train station, running would attract less attention than elsewhere, but once the bodies had been found and security footage reviewed he didn't want witnesses adding his description to police reports. The bald guy understood what he was doing and did the same. Absolute physical fitness was part of Victor's job description but he couldn't make it pay off without getting noticed, and the bald guy had half the distance to cover. He reached the concourse first and disappeared into the sea of commuters.

Victor was five seconds behind, but having a few inches on the average height helped him out in situations like this. He spotted a flash of scalp moving away quickly and veered towards it, dodging around stationary men and women anxiously staring at the departure board. He turned side-on to squeeze through a group of tightly packed commuters and lost sight of his quarry.

Victor kept moving, heading in the same direction, alert, eyes sweeping back and forth in case Petrenko appeared, saw the bald guy emerging from the far side of the crowd, moving fast, stumbling. He looked back, made eye contact with Victor and powered on, heading for the main exit.

When Victor broke free of the crowd he sprinted after him, closing with every stride. He couldn't grab him without being noticed, but there was little Victor could do about that. Emerging out on the small square in front of the station, he saw the bald guy gesture wildly in Victor's direction as he approached a group of five men heading towards the station. One of whom Victor recognised from the elevator at the Europe: Petrenko.

Victor slowed but they'd already made him. Petrenko hesitated, terror spreading across his face, but the others hurried forward, hands going under jackets or into pockets. They didn't draw any guns because Victor was reaching for the Smith & Wesson in his waistband so they knew he was armed. They kept coming. They out-gunned him four to one, fifteen yards between them, clear lines of sight. No reason for them to be concerned. He'd bet he had the quicker reflexes but at best he'd get three shots off before two came back at him. Only one of them would need to hit. Victor wasn't going to draw his gun because it was suicide. They knew that. But if any of them drew, so would he, and whoever tried to pull their gun first would be riddled with 9 mm holes before the others killed him. They knew that too.

The bald guy kept running, going straight past Petrenko and to the taxi rank. Victor continued to walk backwards, now inside the train station, trying to get into the safety of the crowds. They came forward faster than he could back off but he didn't dare turn his back on them. Without any words spoken, two of the shooters broke off from the main group, going left and right respectively, moving to the flanks while Petrenko and the other two maintained their relentless approach. Within seconds, the two flankers were at the extremes, and then out of, Victor's peripheral vision. He turned his head quickly, left then right, trying to keep track of them, but couldn't do so and keep watch on the others.

A group of elderly men and women passed in front of him from right to left, moving slowly, checking brochures of some kind. A tour group, probably. They blocked the line of sight between Victor and his pursuers. Victor turned, ran.

He dodged through the crowd, seeing the two flankers doing the same, closing in from either side, limiting his options. All they had to do was to get close enough to slow him down and let the rest pile in. He headed for a set of escalators, leaping up two steps at a time, pushing past other travellers. The first of Petrenko's men reached the escalators and Victor hit the emergency stop button when he was three steps from the top. The man at the bottom fell forward, momentum working against him. The other passengers groaned and cursed.

The ruse bought Victor a thirty-second head start. Not enough time to outrun them, but maybe enough time to hide or pick his battlefield. At the top of the escalators was a small shopping mall, two levels of maybe a dozen outlets each. He glanced around, saw stores selling clothes, sporting goods, lingerie, greetings cards, cosmetics. Nowhere that met his criteria.

He rushed on, rounding a corner, slowing down so people didn't look at him and signpost his path. He passed kiosks selling freshly made fruit smoothies and remote-control toy helicopters. He entered the mall's food corner. Around him were cafés, restaurants and bars. One bar looked good. Lots of people inside.

The bar was open-fronted and he entered briskly, the prosaic mall music replaced by the sound of dozens of conversations competing against each other and the eighties music blasting out of wall-mounted speakers. He acted casually, just a businessman after a drink while he waited for his train. No one paid him any attention. He straightened his appearance and approached the bar.

A young guy who looked too smart in both appearance and mind to be a bartender caught his eye and Victor asked for a vodka lemonade. While he waited for his drink, he stood behind some of the other patrons, positioned so he was mostly obscured from the view of anyone passing outside, but at the same time letting him to see out. No sign of Petrenko's men so far.

Aside from the escalator he'd ascended, there must be another way back on to the concourse. Hopefully, his enemies knew the station better and had already rushed off in the wrong direction to block him off. Either that or they would have more than twenty stores to check. If they were smart, they'd block off the exits first to trap him. The mall wasn't that big, so he doubted there was more than one other means of getting back to the concourse. If they had a man watching that and the escalator, that left two to search the mall if Petrenko wasn't actively involved, and he'd looked too scared upon seeing Victor to start hunting him down now. If the two searching the mall split up they could cover the ground faster, but if they did encounter him it would be one on one, and as it wasn't hard to work out what had happened to the tall man and his two helpers, Victor doubted any one of the new four wanted to tangle with him alone.

The bar was large, its many customers spread throughout the space, sitting in booths that lined the wall, tables, or at the bar itself. They were mostly travellers and business professionals, many on their own, no one he guessed would constitute a regular. He blended in well, but Petrenko's men were looking for him. Only him. A single man. No reason why Victor should make it easy for them.

He spotted a good mark straight away. She sat at the far end of the bar, perched elegantly on the high stool, alone, head tilted his way, eating green olives off a cocktail stick. Her glass was empty enough to warrant another drink. She didn't look too much like the other business types and her manner was too relaxed for a traveller. He looked her way until she saw him and they made eye contact. She held it for a few seconds and he gave her a smile. Nothing too strong, but with unmistakable meaning attached. She looked away, then back for a second more.

The bartender returned with his drink and he took it over to the woman.

'Buy you another?' he asked in Russian, talking loudly over a blast of synthesiser.

He sat down on the stool next to her, sitting to her right so she shielded him from the opening to the mall.

Her eyes slowly examined him from heels to hair before she finally answered, 'Sure.'

'Walt Fisher,' Victor said.

'I'm Carolin.' She pulled an olive off the cocktail stick with polished white teeth. 'Nice to meet you, Walt. You're American?'

Victor nodded.

'Good,' she said, switching to English. 'I like Americans.'

She had a cultured Russian accent and a strong face that would have been striking in her youth. Up close, he could see she looked like she was pushing a decade older than he was, but probably thanks only to her surgeon. She was slim, long limbed, her straight auburn hair cut short. A hint of grey at the roots. She wore a pencil skirt, lots of jewellery and a white blouse complete with plunging neckline.

He motioned to the bartender. 'What'll you have?'

'Dry martini. And some more olives. Lots of olives.'

264

Victor reiterated to the bartender.

'Plenty of women in here,' Carolin said, 'so why sit down next to me?'

'Because you're not here for the same reason as them.'

'How do you mean?'

'Everyone here is passing through on the way to somewhere else. You're not.'

'That obvious?'

'No, but being perceptive is nigh on ninety per cent of my work.'

She nodded, smiled. 'I'm here because my husband is a fat workaholic who only gets hard for his assistant, I'm in Minsk so he doesn't see what I get up to, and I'm in this bar because I like a certain kind of man. How's that for a reason?'

'That's a pretty good reason.' He leaned closer. 'And if I may be so bold as to say so, your husband clearly doesn't know what he's missing.'

Not the smoothest of lines, but he needed a quick result or to move on.

She regarded him with an amused smile. 'Not very subtle, are you, Walt?'

'Not very,' he replied and he shuffled his stool closer.

'Good,' she said with a wry smile. 'I like honesty.'

'Here you go.'

The bartender placed the martini before Carolin. Victor paid.

'What shall we drink to?' he asked, raising his drink.

Carolin touched her glass to his. 'To honesty.' She took a long sip and her eyes widened in approval. 'Delicious.'

Over her shoulder, Victor saw three men outside the bar. Petrenko's freelancers. The two flankers plus one other. They wouldn't have had time to search through the other stores that fast, so they'd figured out he wouldn't hide somewhere like that. They entered the bar and looked around. Carolin noticed his distraction but didn't acknowledge it. The single remaining freelancer was elsewhere, guarding an exit or at Petrenko's side.

'So what brings you to Minsk?' she asked.

Victor took a sip of his vodka lemonade. 'Work.'

'Closing a deal?'

'Something like that.'

He lost sight of them for a moment. He didn't want to adjust his position for a better view in case his movements caught their eyes.

'Are you okay?' Carolin asked.

'I'm a little tired. Long journey.'

The men reappeared in his view. They were straining their necks, looking around the bar, but looking for a single man, not one half of a couple.

Carolin looked at him meaningfully. 'You should try and unwind then.'

He nodded. One of Petrenko's men gestured in the direction of the men's room, but the other shook his head, not believing Victor would trap himself there. Which was true.

'My hotel's across the street,' Carolin said. 'There's a mini bar in my room. We can empty it and my husband will pick up the tab.'

The two flankers gave up and moved on to search elsewhere.

Carolin said, 'Don't be scared. I'm only inviting you for a drink.'

Victor stood. 'Another time perhaps.'

'You don't have to run off,' Carolin said.

Victor didn't respond. He felt bad for the rejection she must be feeling, but there wasn't a lot he could do about it. He checked his watch. Nine minutes before the kid with the tool belt raised the alarm. Not long, but Petrenko was still nearby.

CHAPTER 34

Victor checked the kill team leader's cell phone as he walked among the consumers and travellers. It had the marks of a well-used personal phone, not a sterile item purchased for a specific job. That confirmed what he already knew – these guys weren't elite operators. But there were still four of them and a bullet that found its mark still killed regardless of the shooter's qualifications. Victor opened up the call history on the tall man's cell and dialled the most recent number.

A man he took to be Petrenko answered in Russian after the second ring. In a cautious tone he said, 'Yes?'

Victor didn't speak. He listened to the background noise. He could hear Petrenko's breathing, the echoing sound of a public address system, the hustle of commuters. There was no public address system currently sounding in the mall area but he could just about make one out as it drifted through the air from the main concourse. Victor headed towards the escalators. He kept his eyes moving, checking ahead, his flanks, reflections, anyone looking his way.

'It's you,' Petrenko said.

He sounded surprised but controlled. Intrigued and scared at the same time. His voice carried the accent of a well-spoken Minsk resident, an educated man, wealthy. Victor heard the click of fingers close to Petrenko's phone. He pictured the Belarusian gesturing and mouthing to the freelancer not in the mall. In the background the public address system continued to broadcast its message. Someone had parked their car in the wrong place and it needed moving. Victor heard the clatter of cutlery or coffee cups – he guessed from someone clearing a table near to Petrenko.

'That's right,' Victor said back.

He walked briskly, always looking for signs of his enemies but seeing no one.

'How did you get this number?' Petrenko asked.

'How do you think?'

A pause, then, 'What do you want?'

'To ask you some questions.'

'Go ahead.'

'Face to face.'

Petrenko laughed briefly. 'I'm sure you do. Why don't you meet me in the parking lot? We can go for a drive and talk in my car, about whatever you'd like.'

Victor reached the escalators. He gazed down at the concourse to where a number of cafés and eateries were clustered together. Dozens of people sat at tables drinking, dozens more walked past in an ever-moving mass. No sign of Petrenko.

Victor held the phone at arm's length in the direction of the concourse for the count of five. At four, the announcement through the public address system stopped its broadcast. He heard Petrenko click his fingers again, this time faster, more urgently. Victor turned away from the escalators and followed the sign for the stairs.

'I'd prefer somewhere a little further away,' Victor said into the phone.

'Why?'

Behind Petrenko's voice Victor heard the dull clank of something metal. Then a few seconds later he heard the exact same sound again. Victor began descending the stairs. He wrapped his fingers around the phone's microphone to muffle his voice and disguise the echo of the stairwell.

'Because,' he answered, 'in the last ten minutes I've killed three of your men and it won't be long before someone notices.'

Victor heard another clank.

'Okay,' Petrenko said, sounding more confident. 'I understand what you're saying. I don't want the police involved either.'

Victor reached the bottom of the stairs and walked out on to the concourse, alert for signs of a shooter watching, but as expected there was no one there. He kept his fingers over the microphone. He looked up to the various station signs jutting from the walls or hanging from the roof. He saw what he was looking for and changed direction.

'What do you want from me?' Petrenko asked.

'I want to get to know you.' Victor walked quickly through the crowd, passing a bank of ATMs and a winding queue of people eager for money.

Petrenko chuckled. 'Anything else?'

'And to convince you not to kill me.'

'You'll have to give me a very good reason not to.'

Victor pictured Petrenko smiling. He walked faster, avoiding a group of young guys standing in a small circle, eating burgers and slurping milkshakes.

'I know just the thing to give you.'

Petrenko laughed. 'And what would that be?'

'Your life,' Victor said, but not into the phone.

Petrenko stiffened. He didn't speak or move. Victor stood behind him. To the left was a public toilet. An elderly man inserted coins and pushed through the metal stile. It clanked as he did so.

'I'm sure I don't need to tell you not to turn around,' Victor said.

Petrenko swallowed. 'My men are close by.'

'No they're not,' Victor said. 'Three are in the mall and while you were talking to me you sent the fourth towards the escalators. He'll realise in a moment I didn't come down that way, but a moment is all I need.'

Petrenko took his phone away from his ear. 'What do you want?'

'Start walking,' Victor dropped the phones into a trashcan. 'Head towards the exit.'

Petrenko started walking. He didn't hurry. Victor walked behind him, keeping Petrenko in his peripheral vision while he watched out for his other two guys.

'Walk faster if you want to keep your knees.'

Petrenko increased his pace. 'Don't kill me. I'm begging.'

'Whether I do or not depends on you.'

'I'll scream for help,' he said, voice cracking.

'Then I'll shoot out your spine and be gone before anyone even thinks about coming to your aid.'

They left the train station. Now the rain had stopped it was marginally warmer outside than when Victor had arrived.

'Which way?' Petrenko asked.

'Which way would you like to go?'

271

'Left.'

'Then we'll go right.'

He kept close to Petrenko, but not too close. Friends or colleagues would keep a respectable distance. They walked for a few minutes, Victor telling Petrenko when to turn left or right and when to cross roads. They stopped in an alleyway.

Victor asked, 'How did you know what I look like?'

'I don't suppose it's worth lying,' Petrenko said, looking over his shoulder.

'Keep your gaze ahead,' Victor ordered, 'and lie if you think I'll believe you. But I'll take a finger for every time I don't.'

'One of my men saw you in the hotel suite beforehand.' The breath caught in Petrenko's throat. He swallowed, and continued. 'I used my contacts with the cops to get a sketch artist's drawing composed and circulated. I can give you money,' Petrenko said, stalling, 'drugs, women. Whatever you want.'

'I don't want money. Or drugs or women. You must have worked out by now that my target was Gabir Yamout, not yourself, but you came after me anyway. I killed your people, I attacked you in your own city, you couldn't let that go unpunished and expect to keep your reputation. I understand that. But like you, I can't ignore such actions.'

'Well, get on with it,' Petrenko spat. 'You found me, big fucking deal. Just kill me and be done. You won't get any sport from me.'

'I'm not here for sport.'

'Then what?' If you were going to kill me you would have done so already.'

'Very good,' Victor said. 'I don't want you dead. I want you alive.'

272

'Why?'

'My target was Yamout, not you. That you found yourself in the crossfire was an unavoidable coincidence. For which I'm sorry.'

'Apology accepted,' Petrenko said flatly.

Victor said, 'Forget about me.'

'What?'

'Withdraw the picture. Tell your people I'm dead, if it helps you save face. Tell them I was killed in a gun battle with your hired thugs.'

'Why?'

'Because I'm telling you to,' Victor answered without emotion. 'Because I'll kill you if you don't. Go back to your life and I'll go back to mine.'

'It would never work. No one will believe it without your body.'

'There are three bodies in a back room at the station. So make it work. And if it doesn't work, I will come back. If I could get to you now, I can get to you again.'

Petrenko stiffened. 'I believe you,' he said, swallowing, 'I do. You win. I'll do what you want.'

'We have a deal then?'

'Yes,' Petrenko agreed. 'We have a deal. But answer me this: why are you letting me live? Why not just kill me?'

'I only kill if it serves a purpose,' Victor explained. 'And killing you would not stop my picture being out there. That's all I care about. If I killed you now, to ensure it never surfaces, I would need to wipe out your entire organisation. And I just don't have the time.'

'Just who the hell are you?'

273

'Who I am is not important. What is important is I'm letting you live, and if you want to stay alive you'll never ask that question again.' Victor circled around Petrenko to face him and said, 'Hold very still if you like your life.'

Petrenko, his face glimmering in sweat, watched with horror as Victor reached into the breast pocket of Petrenko's shirt. When Victor withdrew his fingers something was left behind.

He took a step backwards. 'In your pocket I've placed a little parting gift. It's a container of trinitrooxypropane. You'll know it better by its more common name: nitroglycerin. It's only a small amount, but if you make any sudden movements, or even breathe too heavily, it will blow a hole the size of a fist through your chest.'

'*Oh my God.*'

'Careful,' Victor said and brought a finger to his lips. 'I wouldn't speak louder than a whisper, if I were you.' He stepped away, walking around Petrenko until he was out of the Belarusian's line of sight. 'If I ever hear that someone from Belarus is asking about me I'll come back, but you won't know that until I'm standing over your bed.' He stepped away. 'And remember, whatever you do now, make sure you move very, very slowly.'

It took an agonising six minutes for the team hired by Burliuk to find Petrenko. He hadn't dared move so he had phoned, and was drenched in sweat by the time he heard his name being shouted. Two idiots appeared, red-faced and out of breath. They were as unfit as they were dumb.

Very slowly and quietly, he explained the situation. The two men looked at him blankly.

274

'One of you,' Petrenko said through gritted teeth. 'Take it out.'

Neither said anything.

'Someone had better do it right now.'

The bigger of the two nudged the smaller and he meekly stepped forward.

'Just hold still,' he said as he approached.

'Shut up and get on with it.'

When the man was close enough for Petrenko to smell the tobacco smoke on his clothes, he reached towards the shirt pocket.

'Do it slower than that, you imbecile,' Petrenko whispered. 'It's nitroglycerin. Highly unstable. If you don't do it slowly you'll kill us both.'

The man's hand was shaking. He was more terrified than Petrenko. The guy extended his index and middle finger and lowered them slowly into the shirt pocket. He gasped as his fingers touched the bomb.

'Careful,' Petrenko whispered.

After a deep breath to compose himself, the man withdrew his fingers. Petrenko couldn't see what they held.

'That's it,' he said. 'Nice and slow.'

'It looks like a cigarette lighter.'

'And it's full of nitroglycerin,' Petrenko whispered. 'So be careful with it.'

Petrenko took a step away. His underling held it at arm's length.

'Put it on the floor,' Petrenko said, stepping further away.

The man's face was flushed and sweaty. He squatted down an inch at a time until he could lower the lighter until it touched the concrete. He gently laid it flat. He released a huge breath when his fingers were free of it.

Petrenko stepped around the lighter and backed off. His man followed.

'What now?' he asked.

'Detonate it,' Petrenko said.

'With what?'

'You're armed, aren't you?'

The hireling sighed and drew his silenced pistol. 'Are we out of range?'

'Of course we are,' Petrenko spat. 'Now shoot it.'

The aimed, took a breath, and fired. The lighter disintegrated, spraying out liquid, but there was no explosion.

Petrenko waited expectantly. Still no explosion. 'What the hell?'

He pushed past the shooter, knelt down, and tentatively touched a finger to the small puddle of liquid. He smelled it. Just lighter fluid.

'*Bastard*,' Petrenko yelled, then laughed.

CHAPTER 35

Moscow, Russia

Tomasz Burliuk disconnected the call from Petrenko and slipped his cell phone away. The Belarusian gangster had informed him that the freelancers Burliuk had hired were successful in giving Petrenko his show of strength, though three had died in the process. Burliuk cared nothing for dead hitmen. All he cared about was that Petrenko would keep the arrangement with Yamout a secret, and Kasakov would never find out Burliuk had made a deal with his best friend's mortal enemies.

Burliuk took a composing breath and checked his reflection in the closest wall mirror for signs of stress and seeing none used his palm to brush the shoulders of his suit jacket. He flattened a wayward strand of hair, turned and returned to the far side of the dining room where Kasakov sat with Eltsina and two prospective clients. They were North Koreans, both serious men in their fifties, representatives of Pyongyang.

The club was one of Moscow's finest and Kasakov's personal favourite, which meant it was Burliuk's favourite too. Burliuk frequently accompanied his friend when dining, but it was rare to see Eltsina at the same table. Whereas Kasakov and Burliuk were friends as well as colleagues, neither had any affection for the Russian. She was a humourless woman who rarely smiled and never seemed to have any fun. Jokes that had Kasakov crying with laughter would often garner no reaction from Eltsina. For this particular meal, however, her expertise was needed.

Doing business with North Korea was practically guaranteed to raise Kasakov's profile if any aspect was not conducted with the utmost discretion and careful strategy to limit exposure. Despite the huge sums of money to be made selling arms to the communist regime, as well as selling on weapons of their own manufacture, traditionally Kasakov only brokered with Pyongyang when the timing was just right, and the risks minimal. Now, however, times had changed and the need for a large deal with the communists was imperative to the organisation.

'Gentlemen,' Kasakov was saying, 'I trust you enjoyed your meal and are ready to talk merchandise. As you're aware, I'm offering you the unique opportunity of adding the Mikoyan MiG-31 to your nation's air force. This is the very rare and extremely sophisticated BM multirole version of the interceptor model, which has significant upgrades to the original design. These include, but are not limited to, the ability to carry air-to-ground missiles, HOTAS controls, advanced avionics, digital data-link capability and Zalson-M passive electronically scanned phased array radar. That PESA has a detection range of

four hundred kilometres and enables your pilots to simultaneously attack both ground and air targets. Your catalogue has the
full list of the extensive improvements.'

Kasakov smiled before continuing. 'Now, NATO has seen fit
to designate this aircraft the Foxhound, which I think you will
agree is a very apt name. The planes of Seoul and Washington
will be like foxes to these merciless dogs.'

The North Koreans sat without expression.

Burliuk took his seat next to Kasakov and whispered, 'I'm
very sorry about that.'

Kasakov nodded, but Burliuk knew him well enough to
feel his displeasure. No one else at the table acknowledged
him.

'The MiG-31BM is a very rare fighter,' Kasakov added.
'With these mighty jets in your air force you will join a powerful and elite cadre of nations. Aggressors to your country's
sovereignty, America included, will be terrified to send their
planes into your airspace or their ships into your waters. Your
strength will be unmatched, and your ambition realised. I have
twenty for sale for the very reasonable sum of seventy million
dollars each. This price is non-negotiable and includes delivery
of the planes to the location of your choice at the time of your
choosing.'

One of the North Koreans spoke. He was tall, deathly thin,
his jet-black hair cut short. 'The Indians will sell us upgraded
MiG-29s for forty million each.'

Eltsina gave a small shrug. 'Of course they will. Especially
when they are worth no more than fifteen million, upgraded or
not. And those upgraded MiGs will have been modified in India.
We are offering genuine Russian-manufactured hardware,

surplus to requirements, but that has never been used operationally. They are in perfect working order. Moreover, when you buy from us, you know with one hundred per cent certainty that you will receive one hundred per cent of your order.' She smiled and raised her eyebrows. 'You won't have a repeat of that unfortunate Kazakhstan/Azerbaijan affair.'

The North Koreans began conferring among themselves in their own language. It sounded to Burliuk like an alien tongue. He shook his inhaler and used it to ease his breathing.

Kasakov turned to Burliuk and gestured for him to move closer. As he did, Kasakov whispered, 'Kindly tell me what was so urgent that you had to leave the table in the middle of a deal that you said yourself we desperately need.'

Kasakov's voice was quiet, tone calm and controlled, but Burliuk could feel the malice.

'Forgive me, Vladimir, but I assure you it was necessary. I heard a rumour yesterday, from an associate of mine in Minsk, that an assassin would be travelling through the city on his way to Russia to make an attempt on your life. I sent some people to check the validity of the rumour. It turned out to be true. My men intercepted the assassin. Unfortunately, when they tried to detain him there was a gunfight and the assassin was killed before he could be questioned.'

Kasakov looked surprised, buying the lie perfectly, and then even smiled a little. 'Then you're forgiven, my friend.' He looked at Eltsina. 'I thought you were in charge of my security, Yuliya. Maybe I should give your pay cheques to Tomasz from now on.' Eltsina smirked but she didn't respond. Kasakov smiled and reached for his wine. He took a large swallow. 'Oh,

280

and on this matter, if either of you would be so gracious as to discover who is so keen to have me killed, I would rather appreciate it.'

Across the table, the North Koreans were still conferring.

'I heard something about a mass killing at a hotel in Minsk,' Eltsina said to Burliuk. 'Is this the incident you are referring too?'

Burliuk sipped his mineral water and avoided looking at her. 'I'm afraid I haven't yet got all the details.'

'When you have,' Eltsina said, her tone gentle and understanding, 'I would very much like to hear them.'

Burliuk nodded.

'More importantly,' Kasakov said, 'what is happening regarding the bastard who killed my nephew? Have you found out where he is hiding yet, and commissioned someone to extinguish his miserable existence?'

Eltsina said, 'We're following leads, but Ariff never stays in one place for more than a year or two and takes many precautions to avoid being found. Therefore it's taking some time. But I promise we will locate him. An American team looks to be the best option to send once we know where Ariff is. They come very highly recommended by my associates in the SVR. The team's track record is excellent. The only problem is, they are asking for a lot of money.'

Controlled anger passed over Kasakov's face. 'When I said money is no object, what did you not understand?'

Eltsina frowned. 'I do not sign the cheques. It was Tomasz's idea to negotiate their price down.'

Kasakov looked at Burliuk. This time the anger was not controlled.

'They're asking for a ridiculously huge fee, Vladimir,' Burliuk countered quickly, feeling his lungs tighten. 'You expect me to manage your finances, and that is what I am doing. For the money they are asking we could employ an army. I'm not exaggerating.'

Kasakov leaned closer to Burliuk. 'If they are as good as Yuliya says they are then cease negotiations immediately, and pay them whatever – and I mean *whatever* – they want. Each second Ariff breathes and Illarion does not is unacceptable. If they bring me the Egyptian's intact head so I can mount it on my wall, I shall pay them triple. Is that clear enough?' Burliuk nodded. 'Just make sure that worthless dog and his family are dead. Quickly.'

The North Koreans stopped talking and looked back across the table.

'So, gentlemen,' Kasakov began, anger gone, back to business. 'Have you made up your minds?'

The thin North Korean interlaced his fingers. 'What about armaments? Tell us what you intend to deliver with the planes.'

Burliuk used his inhaler a second time and fought not to smile. Everyone, governments included, wanted something for nothing.

'A hound without teeth is no good to any man,' Kasakov said, 'but sharp fangs cost money. You'll be pleased to know I have near enough unlimited access to air-to-air missiles such as the R-33 and the newer R-77, as well as air-to-surface, including the X-55 anti-ship missile. Please, my dear friends, check your catalogue for a full list of prices. However, as a sign of our enduring friendship, if you would be so very kind as to buy all twenty jets then I will supply each with a full armament of your choice of missiles. No extra charge.' He paused. 'So, do we have a deal?'

The thin North Korean nodded. 'But we want assurances of quality.'

'Of course,' Kasakov said with another smile. 'You can have a money-back guarantee.'

CHAPTER 36

Washington, DC, USA

Procter met Clarke in the Smithsonian National Zoological Park. He was waiting next to the Great Cats enclosure, watching a couple of Sumatran tigers lying on the ground, doing nothing. It was a warm day, which meant it was hot for a guy of Procter's size. He stood next to Clarke and watched the tigers. They continued to do nothing.

'They look bored,' Procter said after a moment.

Clarke didn't turn his way. 'What animal built so perfectly to kill merely wants to be fed?'

Procter nodded. Few other visitors were near but Procter spoke quietly regardless. 'I know what you are going to say, so don't, all right? Things didn't go exactly as planned last week in Minsk.'

Clarke didn't say anything. One of the tigers yawned.

'Yamout made it out of the country alive, true, but Yamout is just the bishop, we're going after the king here. The important thing is that we struck Ariff's network right where he's going to really feel it. Forget the fact that Yamout survived, what matters is that Ariff is going to be furious his best pal almost ended up a corpse. He's still going to do the two things we wanted: he's going to be on guard against further attacks and he's going to want to deliver a nice big fat dollop of payback to the culprit. And courtesy of Callo, both Ariff and Yamout are going to believe that Kasakov was behind it. So that's score number one.

'As for number two, Kasakov now knows the RDX that killed Farkas came out of the batch stolen from him when his nephew was killed. If he hasn't already begun moving against Ariff, he will very soon. But now Ariff knows Kasakov is gunning for him he's going to be that much harder to hit, so Vlad won't just be able to wipe him off the face of the Earth like he might have if Ariff didn't take steps to protect himself. Kasakov is already hard to hit.' Procter paused for a second. 'The result is exactly what we want: the world's two most prolific arms dealers thirsting for each other's blood and entrenched in a war for hopefully years to come. The flow of illicit arms will be damaged so badly it might never recover. We'll save countless lives.'

Clarke huffed. 'I'm well aware of the strategy, Roland.'

'I know you are,' Procter agreed, 'but it doesn't hurt to be reminded of it when things become a little less clean than we would have liked.'

Clarke was still watching the tigers, one of which was now sleeping.

'Roland,' he began, still without looking Procter's way. 'I hate to be the one to break this to you, but it couldn't have been much dirtier. Your boy managed to gun down, what was it, twelve people? And if the initial reports are correct, four people who had been staying in the next suite along are among the dead.'

'And I'm deeply unhappy about those civilian deaths,' Procter assured. 'But Tesseract didn't have a lot of choice with the strike point. It would have been great if Yamout and Petrenko had met in a cabin in the middle of nowhere, but they didn't. Civilian casualties are always a possibility with these things, and we need to wait to hear from Tesseract before passing judgement.'

Clarke scoffed. 'Your MVP failed to kill Yamout and took out four civilians in the process and you want to hear from him before passing judgement? Roland, please. You need to accept the facts: Tesseract is not as good as you hoped he would be, and he's an even greater liability than I feared. He managed to kill one civilian casualty for every two bad guys. We might as well have shelled the building. At least then we would have taken out Yamout as well.'

'Being from the military,' Procter commented, 'you should be more accepting of collateral damage.'

Clarke's eyes narrowed.

'Speaking of collateral damage,' Procter said, 'there's something you need to know. Regarding Callo. Those Brit contractors we used contacted me after making the call to Yamout's people. Callo tried to escape. Abbott and Blout had no choice but to neutralise him before they were compromised. I'm pissed off about it, but I'm not going to lose any sleep, and neither should you. Callo was a disgusting excuse for a human being. You know that as well as I do.'

Clarke sighed and shook his head. 'I vouched for Abbot and Blout, so I take responsibility for what happened with Callo. But, like you said, I won't lose sleep over him. I wish I could say the same about Tesseract.'

Procter rested his palms against the fence. 'There is a lot we don't know, Peter, so let's not jump the gun and condemn him without all the facts. When he reports in, we can have a proper debriefing. Our primary objective was achieved, even with Yamout alive. That's what I call a success in this game.'

Clarke said, 'I think it's time we re-evaluated our relationship with this assassin.'

The second tiger joined the first and closed its eyes. They lay side by side.

Procter shook his head. 'I'm having a hard time understanding why you are so quick to write him off. Need I remind you that he completed his first two assignments perfectly? If he hadn't saved Kasakov in Bucharest we would never have been in a position to get our little war. We are only this far into our plans and able to discuss how we continue because of the work he has done. Kasakov is going after Ariff, and Ariff will be going after Kasakov. All thanks to Tesseract.'

'Exactly,' Clarke said. 'We have set things into motion so now we can start thinking about tying off loose ends.'

'Hang on a minute, Peter. Things are in motion, that's true, but we are still going to need Tesseract at least once more, don't forget.'

'If we even get to that stage. Which we won't if Tesseract failed to get away cleanly. I'm sure the Belarusians won't be too concerned with a bunch of dead gangsters and mercenaries, but what about those four civilians? They'll want to know why they died and who killed them. That's another spotlight on us. We could have a huge problem walking around out there. We can't allow that.'

Procter sighed. 'I very much doubt he's left his fingerprints all over the damn hotel. Until he has made himself into a genuine problem then I don't want to hear another word about loose ends.'

'I find this protectiveness for your new pet quite touching, Roland. But if he has or will become a liability then I expect swift and decisive action.'

Procter nodded and said, 'Of course. You have my word.'

CHAPTER 37

Hindu Kush Mountains, Afghanistan

The huge aircraft was one hundred and ninety feet long with a wingspan of over two hundred feet, and a height of more than forty. It was a Soviet-made Antonov An-22, a cargo plane, one of the largest in the world, with a payload of up to 180,000 pounds. That capacity had been reached with two partially disassembled MiG-31B jet fighters and accompanying missiles and spare parts filling the aircraft's cargo hold.

The Antonov was flying at an altitude of twenty-two thousand feet above sea level and its shadow passed over the snowy peaks of the Hindu Kush mountain range in northeastern Afghanistan. The sky was blue and cloudless, the air thin and free of turbulence. The Antonov had begun its long journey at an airport outside of Novosibirsk, Russia, and since leaving the country had flown south over Kazakhstan, Kyrgyzstan, and Tajikistan before entering Afghan airspace. The circuitous route would also take it over Pakistan, then India, Thailand and several bodies of water before it reached its destination of North Korea. North Korea and Russia shared a border, but the international community paid far too much attention to it to risk flying over directly with illegally traded arms.

Each member of the crew was highly experienced in the extra-long flights necessary to deliver weapons to Kasakov's customers around the globe. They numbered five: pilot, co-pilot, navigator, and two flight engineers. All Russians, except the Ukrainian pilot. He had flown An-22s in the Soviet air force and made almost a hundred times more money now working for Vladimir Kasakov than he had for the communists. The other four crew members were too young to have flown for the Soviet Union and had been poached from the private sector. What they flew for the arms dealer, and to whom, never bothered them. All that mattered was their generous salaries.

The plane cruised near to its maximum ceiling but the mountain peaks and ridgelines were only a few thousand feet below. The shaking of the fuselage and monstrous whine of the Antonov's four massive engines prevented the flight from being peaceful, but the view of the snowy peaks glowing from unfiltered sunlight was a beautiful one.

The pilot was grey-haired, perpetually unshaven and forever chewing an unlit cigar. He'd flown Antonovs into Afghanistan during the Soviet invasion and all this time later the country was no different. It was a cursed place, destined to be a battlefield for the rest of time. Why the Soviet Union had ever wanted to add it to the empire was beyond him. Soon the West would finally be driven out and the land could revert back to its natural barbarism.

He glanced casually at his flight instruments for a quick check, but he rarely paid too much real attention to them. For him, flying was more about instincts than dials and levels. It was, and always had been, his life, and he did his job with a confidence born from long familiarity. In his experience, worse things happened on firm ground than in thin air.

He popped open a can of his favourite German beer and took a long swig. Wiping foam from his chin, he offered the two other men in the cockpit a can each from the six-pack. The co-pilot grabbed one and had a similarly long drink. The navigator, boring as always, turned down the offer.

Both drinkers belched happily.

Ten thousand feet below, two Afghan men with binoculars stood on a mountainside. Despite the hot sun it was cold twelve thousand feet above sea level and they wore Pakol hats and long coats to stay warm. Their binoculars were American-made and donated by the military to be used by the then-Northern Alliance. The Taliban had long been overthrown, but the Afghans had kept their useful gifts. A donkey stood nearby, chewing dry grass.

'That's it,' one said and lowered his binoculars. 'Heading this way.'

The other Afghan nodded. 'Right on schedule.'

The Stinger was already set up and waiting, carefully leaning against a nearby boulder. The older Afghan handled it easily and hoisted the weapon on to his shoulder. It was just under five feet in length and weighed thirty-three pounds. The Afghan's proudest moment was when he had last used a Stinger to shoot down a Soviet Hind helicopter gunship during the late eighties. This feat was still talked about today, and the young were awed whenever he told the increasingly exaggerated tale. Of the hundreds of Stingers supplied to the Mujahideen during the conflict with the Soviets, around sixty per cent had been purchased back by the US as part of a fifty-five-million-dollar programme. This Stinger was part of the forty per cent unaccounted for.

The Afghan inserted a battery coolant unit into the hand guard and pressed a button. Nothing happened. Cursing, but not surprised, the Afghan released the battery and was handed another by the second man, who had spare batteries ready and waiting. Again, nothing happened when he pushed the button. The Stinger and its launcher were decades old and all of the original battery coolant units had ceased working after a few years. These units had been recently supplied, but were still far from brand new. The Afghan inserted a third battery into the hand guard and this time it worked correctly, spraying argon gas into the launcher tube to cool the missile's seeker head, making it sensitive enough to infrared to stay on target.

The Antonov grew larger in the sky as it neared the two Afghans.

It took a few seconds for the gyro spin-up to complete and electronics to activate, during which time the Afghan removed the protective lens cap from the end of the launcher and set his eye to the sighting scope. The field of view was narrow and he searched the sky to locate the plane.

'To your right,' the second Afghan said to help, 'and up.'

The older Afghan adjusted the launcher as directed. 'I've got him.'

A second later, he heard the distinctive tone telling him the seeker had locked on to the target.

The Afghan could taste sweat on his lips as he super-elevated the weapon by aiming it almost vertical. This ensured the launched missile would gain sufficient altitude before the main motor fired. If it didn't, the back blast could take off the user's face. The Afghan had seen it happen.

He depressed the trigger and 1.7 seconds later the launch rocket propelled the missile out of the tube. The launch engine fell away from the ascending missile and the forward control fins and fixed tailfins extended. At a height of twenty feet, the solid-fuelled main motor ignited.

A huge roar and plume of vapour emanated from the missile and within two seconds the Stinger missile had accelerated to over twice the speed of sound.

'*What the hell is that?*'

The co-pilot's voice snapped the Ukrainian pilot from his thoughts of home and his wife's ample bottom. He had been lounging in his seat, one hand on the controls, and dropped his can as he straightened up to look where the co-pilot was pointing. German beer sloshed across the cockpit's floor. The pilot's eyes widened in disbelief at the fiery speck in the distance, trailing smoke and vapour that arched down towards the mountains.

Behind the pilot, the navigator was on his feet. 'Is that—'

'*Yes*,' the pilot snapped in answer as he grabbed hold of the controls and heaved them back towards him. 'That's exactly what it is, and it's heading right for us.'

'How long until it hits?' the navigator frantically said as the fiery speck quickly grew larger.

The pilot didn't answer. He concentrated on pulling on the controls to make the Antonov climb.

The navigator screamed, '*Turn us around.*'

Again the pilot didn't respond. The plane's maximum speed was four hundred and sixty miles per hour but they were cruising at around three hundred. He watched the speedometer slowly turn clockwise, the acceleration tempered by the climb, knowing that even if the Antonov was already at maximum speed there was no way he was going to outrun a missile travelling at more than double that speed.

'*Turn us around,*' the navigator screamed again. 'Why aren't you turning us around?'

'Shut up and sit down,' the pilot yelled back. 'I'm trying to save your life.'

From his time in the Soviet air force the pilot knew that ground-to-air missiles had limited ranges and a comparatively low maximum ceiling. His only hope was to get the Antonov to an altitude where the missile, for all its speed, wouldn't be able to reach.

The two Afghans watched the ever-lengthening trail of white vapour shoot across the sky. The trail was a jagged curve of straight lines as the Stinger's guidance system used proportional navigation to make adjustments to its flight path, plotting a course to where the Antonov was heading so that it could intercept it.

'Why is the plane doing that?' the younger Afghan asked as they saw the Antonov climb steeply.

The older Afghan wasn't sure, but he didn't want to look ignorant in front of the youngster and so answered, 'They're scared.'

'Will it still hit?

The older man said, 'I don't miss.'

They watched as the missile sped towards the Antonov, its passive infrared seeker locked on to the heat from the aircraft's engines. In less than three seconds it had closed the distance.

The Stinger hit the Antonov's starboard wing between the two engines and its three-kilogram warhead detonated. The wing was ripped in half by the explosion and the detached section tumbled earthward.

The pilot wrestled with the controls. His clenched teeth bit through the unlit cigar and it fell into his lap. The whole plane shook violently and he fought to keep it level. The altimeter needle turned counterclockwise.

'*We've lost engine number three,*' the co-pilot yelled. '*Engine number two is on fire.*'

'Deactivate it,' the pilot said.

The co-pilot operated the controls to shut down the burning engine.

'Shit,' the pilot said as he watched the altimeter swinging ever more rapidly counterclockwise.

The ropey muscles in the pilot's arms were hard, his knuckles white, tendons straining beneath the skin. The co-pilot was similarly fighting with his own set of controls.

'We're not going to make it,' he said, and looked to the pilot for a counterargument. He didn't get one.

When the altimeter hit fifteen thousand feet the pilot said, 'We're going to crash. Prepare for emergency landing.'

Below them the mountains of the Hindu Kush were huge, imposing and very close. Fifteen thousand feet above sea level

295

was only five thousand feet clear of the mountains. The pilot desperately tried to guide the Antonov towards a valley where he might just be able to put it down safely. But the plane wasn't responding.

'*Fourteen thousand feet,*' the co-pilot yelled.

The Ukrainian pilot blinked sweat away from his eyes. Behind him the navigator was screaming, but the pilot ignored him. All his focus was on making it over the next ridgeline. Maybe on the other side there would be somewhere to crash-land. Maybe.

'Thirteen thousand.'

The mountain seemed to shoot up before them. The pilot pulled on the controls with all his strength. He felt something tearing in his arm but refused to give up the fight despite the pain.

'Twelve thousand feet.'

The mountain filled the view from the cockpit.

'*WE'RE NOT GOING TO MAKE IT.*'

The pilot closed his eyes.

The Afghans watched through their binoculars as the Antonov's underbelly clipped the ridgeline, crumpled, and spectacularly tore apart. An instant later its aviation fuel caught light and the ensuing monstrous explosion tossed the wreckage across the sky.

The two Afghans clapped and cheered as burning chunks of fuselage rained down over the mountainside.

CHAPTER 38

Lavarone, Italy

The Alps were a good place to lay low. Mountains always were. By definition they were remote and light on people. There were countless places to hide. With his mountaineering, climbing and survival skills, Victor could exploit the terrain and climate, turning them to his advantage and against any enemies. He liked the scenery too, the peacefulness, the sense of isolation. Adrianna would have loved the area, and had Victor not being lying low, he might have invited her to join him.

The Lavarone plateau was located in the north-east of the country. It was a lush, rural area of several small towns and villages. There were a little over one thousand residents spread across eleven square miles of woods and pastures. Tourists and passers through were common enough for Victor to blend in. Three international borders lay within one hundred miles.

He had a room at the Albergo Antico in the centre of town. It was the perfect kind of establishment to hide out in for a few days; big enough to have some anonymity, but not so big as to lose track of who else was staying; modern enough for decent amenities, but not so modern as to have security cameras everywhere. The lobby was strictly functional, not the kind of open space where people could just hang around. The location was good too. From his window, he could see the street outside and the main highway passed straight by. Again, not the kind of place where people would loiter without a reason. The proximity to the highway would also aid him in a fast exit if it was needed. The modest rates meant the bribes he paid to the desk clerks were particularly reasonable. Separately, he asked them to let him know if anyone enquired about him, directly or otherwise. The food also happened to be excellent, which always helped make laying low a little easier.

Victor had been in Italy for two days and in Lavarone for one, which he'd primarily spent in a paddleboat on the lake and then visiting the huge Belevedere-Gschwent. He'd read about the fortress before and he rarely gave up the chance to see a part of military history if the opportunity presented itself. The Belevedere-Gschwent and its museum also made a good place for drawing out shadows, but he'd seen no one suspicious since arriving in the country.

Victor didn't know what to expect, but expecting the worst came both easily and naturally. Hoping for the best was a privilege reserved for regular citizens and dead assassins. There was an even keener edge to his counter surveillance and precautionary measures than usual. The failure of the Yamout contract was never far from his thoughts, in particular the fact his failure was due to the intervention of a third party. A third party that he had been forced to kill four of and who had shot him in return. He rubbed his arm. Still sore. The injury wasn't too

298

much of a problem, but what the surveillance team's employers might do in response was far more serious.

He'd destroyed their laptop on which they had recorded him via hidden cameras in the Presidential Suite, but there would be backups of those recordings, he was sure. They had been too skilled in combat to be poor at surveillance. Whoever they worked for would have Victor's face, his voice, and could at this very moment be tracking him down. The encounter with Petrenko's men at the train station would give any pursuers even more intelligence on him.

Petrenko wouldn't be a problem. Victor had left the Belarusian far too scared to risk retribution. That took care of one potential enemy at least.

Which left his employer.

There was no internet café in Lavarone so Victor caught a bus to one of the larger, neighbouring towns. There he spent two hours performing counter surveillance before entering the lone establishment and sitting down in front of a computer. It was the first time he'd checked his CIA-supplied email account since before attempting the Yamout contract. As expected, there was a request to make contact for a post-action report regarding Minsk. He'd missed the prearranged call, but this wasn't commented on. The tone of the email was neutral, nothing to give away just how angry his paymaster was at Yamout's survival. The voice wouldn't be happy about it, that went without saying.

Victor rubbed his right triceps before typing a response, stating a time he would call. A few days without strenuous activity had done his wound some good and it was healing well. There had been no infection and the pain was gradually subsiding. He took no painkillers for it. Pain, despite its inherent negatives, was the best indicator he had of how the injury was healing.

He spent the rest of the afternoon exploring the towns and villages of the Lavarone plateau, taking buses and walking, occasionally chatting with the friendly locals about their beautiful region, but never truly relaxing.

Victor returned to his hotel after dark, a newly purchased compact laptop hidden in a backpack. In his room, he powered on the computer, connected to the hotel's internet, downloaded and installed the required software, and called his paymaster.

'What happened?' the voice demanded.

'No attempt at small talk today then?'

'No, not today, my man. Not when last week you failed. Not when you got four civilians killed in the process.'

'When you give me such a limited time frame in which to kill an arms dealer shielded by ten armed men, in a restricted location, you should recognise such a contract has a limited chance of success.'

'Don't expect the second half of your fee,' his employer countered, 'and don't think you only have the one job left for me after this debacle. I thought you were better than that, I really did.'

'Given the unforeseen circumstances I encountered, if you had anyone else capable of pulling off that job, you really should have used them instead.'

A pause, before, 'What circumstances?'

'I don't know where you're getting your information from,' Victor said, 'but it couldn't be less accurate. Those four civilians I killed were not civilians.'

'So who were they?'

'I don't know,' Victor answered. 'I spotted one of them when I first arrived. At the time I thought he was one of Yamout's people. But they weren't allied with either Yamout or Petrenko. They were a surveillance team, though I use that term lightly. They didn't shoot or fight like your typical pavement artists. They had Petrenko's suite rigged with cameras linked to a computer in the suite next door. When I went after Yamout, they intervened, which is the only reason they died and Yamout lived.'

His employer processed the revelation for a long moment before saying, 'If they intervened, then they—'

'No,' Victor interrupted, 'when Yamout called for help they did nothing. If they had any association, they would at least have answered. They ignored Petrenko's call for help too.'

'Did you speak to any of them?'

'Briefly. They told me nothing useful, but they spoke in Russian, though I don't believe they're Russians. Or Belarusians. The only one I saw in the daylight had tanned skin and dark hair. I guessed he was Middle Eastern, working on the assumption he was with Yamout, but he could have easily been South American or Mediterranean. Or just had some of that heritage.'

'That's pretty broad.'

'Did I say it wasn't?'

'I don't suppose they had ID on them, did they?'

'Belarusian driving licences.'

'Genuine?'

'Expert fakes.'

'So they've got resources.'

'Plus training, experience, financing, and accurate intel –

301

unless Yamout and Petrenko advertised their meeting in *Arms Dealers Weekly*.'

'So you're saying some intelligence agency was running an op on Yamout or Petrenko and we've stepped right in the middle of it?'

'Is the most likely case,' Victor agreed. 'Or they're private operatives working for some other organisation or individual.'

'You said they had rigged Petrenko's suite up with cameras, right?'

'Yes.'

'So logic would dictate they were watching Petrenko, else they would have spied on Yamout back in his own country, wouldn't they? Could have been cops or domestic agents looking to bust Petrenko for one of his many crimes.'

'None of them tried to arrest or apprehend me,' Victor explained, 'which they would have done had they been from the Belarusian security services. My guess is they were interested in what Yamout and Petrenko were discussing, as opposed to them as individuals.'

'Either way, we've been compromised. How exposed are you?'

Victor had been waiting for that question. He knew his employer would be paying very careful attention to his answer.

'Minimally,' Victor said. 'I'm a careful kind of guy, and the four team members are all dead. I put a magazine full of nine mils through their computer's hard drive. No one's going to be able to recover the recordings.'

'Good,' his control replied through a sigh of relief that should have been better disguised, considering the implications had Victor's answer been different. 'And what about the next day?

302

I heard there was a significant number of deaths at some train station. That wouldn't be your doing, would it?'

'I extracted by car,' Victor answered. 'Anything that happened the day after is likely to be Petrenko striking out against enemies he suspects came after him.'

'I suppose so.'

From the tone, Victor couldn't be sure whether he'd been believed, but there was nothing his employer could do to prove the incident at Minsk Central had been Victor's doing. Any security-camera footage would be inconclusive at best.

'Right,' the voice said after a moment, 'if there's no exposure there's nothing to worry about. I'll let you know if that changes, but until then we carry on as normal. I won't need you right away, but stay in Europe. You'll be back to work soon enough.'

After the call had disconnected, Victor sat still in the darkness with only his thoughts for company. He examined one of the wallets he'd taken from the surveillance team, as he had done several times already. Aside from the Belarusian driver's licence and some cash, it was empty. There would be fingerprints, of course, and if those they belonged to were on anyone's database no doubt the CIA could identify that person, but Victor didn't want his employer to know anything about his attackers before he himself did. If Victor's suspicions proved to be correct, then it could put him in a very precarious position with the CIA.

He thought about the events at the Hotel Europe. There were some grey areas where he couldn't recall every detail, but that was always the same after combat. Certain events remained vivid for years, whereas others – not necessarily of less significance – disappeared from memory within minutes. Victor didn't understand the physiological or psychological reasons behind it, and he didn't want to either.

Checking his other email accounts, he found a reply from Alonso, dated last week. The email explained that Alonso was in Europe for just one more day and if they were going to meet up it had to be very soon. That had been several days ago, so Alonso's European contract would have gone to an alternate professional. The email also went on to say that, in retrospect, Hong Kong hadn't been that much fun and Alonso wouldn't recommend going. Victor deleted the message. He could have used the money the Hong Kong job would have given him, but it had been withdrawn for some reason. Maybe the client had got cold feet or the target had been hit by a train.

Victor found he'd missed out on another job from a different broker too. A Kazak working out of Moscow, who Victor hadn't done a job for in years, had an unspecified but very dangerous contract worth a potentially huge fee. He wanted to pitch Victor for it. When Victor replied to the email asking for more information, the message was bounced back. The recipient account was no longer active, so like the Hong Kong job it might have been withdrawn, or perhaps it had already gone to another killer or killers. His other accounts were full of spam and nothing else. No one was offering work. He had been out of the market for over six months, so it was hardly surprising brokers were going elsewhere.

He didn't believe his employer was going to be a problem, at least not yet. But the voice on the other side of the world would want to know whose surveillance team Victor had killed just as much as Victor did, and Victor wanted to find out first. It would have helped his cause to have kept his findings to himself, but it wouldn't have been long before his employer had discovered that those additional bodies hadn't belonged to civilians. Being found to have withheld information wouldn't improve his precarious position with the CIA.

Another day of healing and he would move south to Bologna. If Victor was going to identify the men he had killed in Minsk before his employer did, he was going to need some help.

CHAPTER 39

Moscow, Russia

Despite the smiles, anecdotes, kind words and handshakes, Vladimir Kasakov was bored, frustrated and wishing he was anywhere else. The party was typical fare for the Moscow elite. There were politicians and oligarchs and celebrities all rubbing shoulders, acting friendly and laughing while secretly hating each other. The oligarchs hated the power the politicians wielded, while in turn the politicians hated the wealth of the oligarchs, and both hated the popularity of the celebrities, who hated the politicians and oligarchs simply for not being celebrities too. Kasakov was unique in that he hated them all.

He threw some champagne down his throat. He stood alone, only caring about when the next tray of canapés would pass his way. Despite doing his best to give off leave-me-alone signals, plenty of people wanted a piece of him, and it took an enormous act of self-restraint not to start throwing hooks and uppercuts. Normally he was able to mingle deftly, converse affably, and tell a mean joke. For all that he loathed such parties and their odious partakers, it was essential that he attend to maintain the acquaintances, contacts and friendships necessary to remain a free man. Even though Russia never extradited nationals, there was always the chance some politician might turn against him, whether to take over his business, gain favour with the international community, or perhaps, unlikeliest of all, out of moral decency. So long as the Ukrainian had the backing of the rest of Moscow's aristocracy, he could sleep easily. Tonight, however, Kasakov couldn't put on his party face. All his thoughts were consumed with Illarion, Ariff and the vengeance he so urgently needed.

The only person at the party he had any time for was on the opposite side of the room, hanging on the words of some handsome Russian actor. Izolda wasn't alone. There had to be a dozen wives similarly enraptured, and a dozen husbands jealously trying not to let it show. The difference between Izolda and the other wives was that the handsome actor was obviously as taken with her as she was with him. It wasn't surprising. Kasakov's wife looked simply gorgeous, as always. Tall, slim and graceful, she outshone every woman in the room. Her backless evening gown managed to be both unashamedly sexy yet undeniably elegant. Some of the less classy wives showed off their inflated chests with necklines that almost reached their navels, and could neither frown nor smile thanks to their stretched and frozen faces. Izolda's black hair was tied up – how Kasakov preferred it – and the style elongated her already enviable neck. The diamond earrings that had been a birthday gift from her husband danced and glittered as she laughed.

The actor made another joke, and by the strength of the

mirth it generated from the coven of wives he had to be something of a comedian. Kasakov had watched him in a couple of Russian films and knew the man had to be a better comic than actor. The man leaned close to Izolda and whispered into her ear, at which she smiled, wide and carefree. For once Kasakov could not detect the pain she hid so well from others, if not from him. They had been married for a little over fifteen years, and though Izolda was in her late thirties now, she was still without a child. It killed Kasakov to know her unhappiness was his fault.

Izolda laughed again and her hand moved to the actor's arm. He was no more than thirty and no doubt as fertile as he was handsome. Kasakov imagined Izolda was fantasising about sleeping with the actor at this very moment. From the way he looked at her, the actor's own thoughts were certainly no different. If she succumbed to his charms, Kasakov couldn't blame her. It was his infertility that caused her to cry into her pillow in the middle of the night when she thought he was asleep. He pictured the scene, a month from now, when she came to him to announce the miracle they'd been waiting for. He would hold her, and they would both cry and he would never comment that their child looked nothing like him, else kill her for the betrayal.

Izolda glanced his way and saw him watching. Guilt and fear began stripping the smile from her face, but Kasakov hid his thoughts, smiled and waved back as if he was ignorant of the scene unfolding before him. She was convinced by him, or convinced enough, to regain her own smile. Maybe it wouldn't be the actor now, but if not it would be someone else eventually. Kasakov could feel it in the pit of his stomach.

'Have another drink,' a familiar voice said. 'You look like you could use it.'

Kasakov turned to see another annoyingly good-looking face. Tomasz Burliuk was holding two champagne flutes. He handed one to Kasakov.

'I didn't think you were coming.'

Burliuk sipped some champagne. 'I thought you could use the company.'

Kasakov gestured. 'I take it you've seen my wife.'

Burliuk stared at Izolda for a long time before saying, 'It's hard not to.'

'Every woman hates her,' Kasakov remarked. 'Every man desires her.'

Burliuk took a big swallow of champagne. 'And yet she's yours and yours alone.'

Kasakov nodded and pretended he didn't notice how his best friend gazed upon his wife.

'So,' Burliuk said, finally tearing his eyes away. 'Who is our gracious host tonight?'

'Some oligarch who bribed and threatened his way into buying up formerly state-owned gas reserves,' Kasakov explained. 'He now controls most of the supply piped to Europe. He's a complete prick.'

'You say that about everyone.'

'With this guy, it's an understatement. He spends money like it's meaningless. I heard he has fifty cars. *Fifty*. Can you believe that? And three private jets. He makes me look like a peasant.'

'We were peasants once.'

'Which is why we appreciate what we have.' Kasakov lightly backhanded Burliuk on the chest for emphasis. Then he sighed and said, 'And tell me, my oldest friend, what is the point of any of it?'

Burliuk looked confused. 'I don't understand.'

'I'm tired, Tomasz. I'm tired of living like this, only sneaking out of the country for business, not able to risk going back to my homeland. I'm tired of carrying the weight of an empire on my shoulders. Some days I honestly do think that—' Kasakov's phone vibrated and interrupted him. He checked it. 'Eltsina,' he explained. 'She's outside. She says it's important, so I'd better go and find out what the bitch wants.'

'Shall I come too?'

Kasakov shook his head. 'Stay here and keep an eye on Izolda.'

Burliuk looked confused. 'What do you mean?'

'I don't know . . . just keep an eye on her.'

Kasakov found Eltsina standing on the oligarch's driveway. The petite Russian was not on the guest list and so security hadn't let her inside the dacha. Kasakov could have got his charmless advisor an invite, but he would sooner give up boxing for embroidery. Eltsina was clearly troubled. The breeze played with the strands of hair that had come loose from her ponytail.

'What?' Kasakov asked.

It took Eltsina a few seconds to find her words. 'Vladimir, I'm sorry. We've lost the North Korean shipment.'

'What are you talking about? How could we have lost it?'

'The plane carrying the first two MiGs never made it out of Afghan airspace. It crashed in the mountains earlier today.'

Kasakov grabbed Eltsina by her blouse. If he wanted, he could lift the tiny woman off the ground with one hand, but instead he pulled her closer.

'*Crashed?*'

She swallowed and nodded.

Kasakov released her and let out a cry of exasperation. His huge hands were tight fists, the tendons in his neck pushing out against the skin. He growled through gritted teeth.

Eltsina straightened her blouse and jacket. 'I don't know what to say.'

He shoved Eltsina in the shoulder. She winced and stumbled backwards. 'You can start by telling me just how we lost two hundred million dollars' worth of assets, and my most experienced crew.' He shoved Eltsina again, harder. She stumbled further backwards, only just managing to avoid falling. 'And when you've done that, you can tell me how I'm going to tell the North Koreans that they won't be getting their first two fighters as guaranteed.'

'I . . .'

Kasakov glanced back to the dacha. The security guys were watching but knew not to get involved. He pushed his fingers through his hair, thinking. 'Something is going on here. This is the third time in the space of a week we've had a major setback. First we lost that convoy of anti-aircraft guns in Ethiopia to a UN inspector who just happened to check our trucks for the first time in eight years. Yesterday our representatives in Syria missed their handover.'

'They were found two hours ago in a ditch outside Damascus,' Eltsina explained. 'All dead. Throats slit.'

He glared at Eltsina. 'They say once is happenstance. Twice is coincidence. Three times is enemy action. *So who the fuck is doing this to us?*'

Eltsina shook her head.

'Don't you dare,' Kasakov spat. 'Don't you dare tell me you

311

don't know anything when I'm paying you a fortune to know everything.'

'There's no evidence,' she began. 'Obviously the UN wouldn't kill our people or shoot down a plane. But whoever did those things could also tip off the UN to our convoy.'

'Who?' Kasakov demanded.

'Only someone with a considerable knowledge of our business would be able to strike like this.'

'Who?' Kasakov demanded again.

'Baraa Ariff. He would know enough about us to make these attacks possible.'

'And how would he know?'

'Warlords who buy our tanks and heavy munitions also buy his guns and bullets. We bribe the same officials. Mercenaries who protect our trucks protect his as well. Our people cross paths with his own almost on a daily basis.'

'I don't believe it. Ariff is a snivelling, pathetic Egyptian pig. He would never dare start a war with me. *You* have more balls than he.' Kasakov undid the buttons of his tuxedo in an effort to cool down. He pointed at Eltsina. 'Besides, what's his rationale? Has he learned I want him dead?'

'All but impossible,' Eltsina assured. 'I sought killers only via respected brokers and my contacts in the SVR and FSB.'

'Then why is he doing this?'

Eltsina said, 'There can only be one explanation: he seeks your business. He must have sent that sniper to Bucharest, thinking without your leadership he could sell to our clients unopposed. By chance, some enemy of the sniper intervenes. Then Ariff sends another, only for Tomasz to find out and for him to send his men to intercept the assassin in Minsk. So Ariff abandons his ambition to have you dead and instead attacks our network, seeking to leave us crippled and turn our clients against us.'

'After all these years of coexisting he finally grows a backbone. Had our roles been reversed and it had been me whose business had existed long before he came to prominence, I would not have waited so long to crush my potential competition. I wish it was not about business. I wish he knew I wanted him dead. I wish he was acting in self-preservation. I want him to live in fear. I want him to look at his family and imagine them screaming.'

Eltsina remained silent.

Kasakov said, 'I'm sure this new revelation will serve as additional motivation to track him down.'

She straightened up. 'Motivation cannot be higher, Vladimir. He will suffer for the death of your nephew. All my contacts have been petitioned for intelligence. Our most trusted people are gathering information. No effort or expense is being spared. Ariff has remained hidden for years, but he will be found eventually, I promise you.'

'But how much damage will he have caused us before then?'

Eltsina didn't answer.

'What is the situation with the American team?'

'Burliuk has agreed to their demands and we have them on a retainer so we won't lose them to some other job. But until we locate Ariff, they are just waiting.'

'If what you say is correct, and Ariff knows how to hit us because our businesses frequently overlap . . .' Eltsina nodded. 'Then we must know as much about his organisation as he does ours. So let's return the favour. Have anyone with even the slightest connection to Ariff killed. And triple my security. Ensure everyone who works for me knows what's going on. Everyone needs to be on guard. That piece of shit could hit us again at any time.'

'You need to be aware that a war with Ariff will make our people fearful and damage morale, which has already suffered with the decrease in business these past few years.'

'*I DON'T CARE*,' Kasakov roared, saliva striking Eltsina's face. 'Let them be scared. I've made them rich. A little fear will remind them to be grateful.'

She nodded, not daring to wipe the spittle from her cheek and lip.

'I want Ariff dead,' Kasakov whispered coldly. 'And while I wait, I'll watch his empire burn to the ground around him.'

CHAPTER 40

Bologna, Italy

It was always a pleasure visiting Bologna. It was a city of beauty and history in a country steeped in both. The city's centre fascinated Victor with its architecture, monuments, porticos and eight-hundred-year-old fortifications. He gazed out from the top of the leaning, three hundred and thirty feet tall Torre degli Asinelli. It was the taller of Bologna's famous Two Towers, and the expansive cityscape below him was all red rooftops and ochre walls except where grey medieval towers jutted above the rest of Bologna's low-rise skyline.

Nearby Florence drew the tourists, keeping Bologna more authentic and unspoiled, and Victor hoped it would always remain that way. The comparatively few visitors meant there were less foreigners for Victor to hide among, but the city was all the more pleasant to walk around for the lack of camera-equipped sightseers.

The weather was hot and dry. Victor wore a white linen shirt and loose cotton chinos and kept cool walking through the shaded maze of the city's famous portico arcades. In all there were twenty-five miles of covered walkways: perfect for drawing out and losing any surveillance. He saw none and continued his walk to the Via Rizzoli, where he perused the many quaint book and antique stores in between using the plate-glass storefronts of fashion boutiques to further check for shadows. No one registered on his threat radar, but he remained cautious while eating lunch and he continued to perform counter surveillance while seeking out the city's Renaissance palaces when the majority of stores closed between one and three p.m.

Victor had no enemies in Italy, which was one of the reasons he liked to visit when he could, but after the run-in with the surveillance team in Minsk he had to be especially careful. Whoever they worked for could be tracking him down right now, which was why it was so imperative to find out who they were.

When he was content he had done all he could to avoid being shadowed, Victor walked into a low-ceilinged *osteria* and surveyed the crowd of strange faces that turned in his direction. He was still within the city centre but the neighbourhood was poorer, shabbier and less welcoming. He made eye contact with those who looked his way to show he wasn't an easy target, but didn't stare long enough to invite a challenge. Conversations began again and he ordered a Coke from the skinny barmaid and sat down on a stool, shifting his weight a few times to get comfortable on the hard seat. An old man two stools along asked if he had a light. Victor shook his head.

He sipped his drink and waited. He had his back to the rest

of the bar, but the corner tables were all occupied and a huge mirror behind the bar let him keep an eye on his flanks.

It took a few minutes before someone took a stool next to him. The man was short, slightly overweight, with thick arms and a dark, unkempt beard. He was somewhere in his fourth decade and judging by the deep yellow nicotine stains on his hands and teeth Victor didn't give him more than a couple more.

'I hear you're looking for Giordano,' the man said, without looking at Victor.

'He's a hard man to track down. Do you know where I can find him?'

'I know so many things I fear my brain is not large enough to hold them all.'

'Where might I find him?'

'It pains me to say that you cannot. But I am a helpful soul and will fetch him for you. He is terribly shy of strangers, you understand.'

Victor didn't believe what he was being told for a second. If the bearded man told Victor where to find Giordano, his own usefulness would have been cut short. By keeping Victor in the dark he kept himself as middleman and maintained his profit margins.

Victor opened his wallet and thumbed through the hundred-euro notes inside. He took out one and laid it on the bar, but kept a finger on it.

'Tell me where I can find Giordano.'

The man reached for the money, but Victor slid it away from his eager fingers.

'Where?' Victor asked.

The man grunted. 'That's not how these things progress. Let me unburden you of that ugly piece of paper and I can introduce you to him.'

'Very well.' Victor slid the note from the bar and placed it back inside his wallet. 'When can you arrange such an introduction?'

'How does tomorrow sound to you?'

'Too late,' Victor said, understanding the game.

'Alas, these arrangements take time,' the man said.

'And money?' Victor placed two hundred-euro notes on the bar. 'How about you take me to him now?'

The bearded man said, 'That sounds perfectly amicable.'

They walked through the Piazza Maggiore. Locals and tourists sat around the grand square, enjoying the sun and Bologna's friendly atmosphere while pigeons jostled for crumbs and flapped out of the path of charging children. The piazza was fronted on all sides by buildings dating back to the Middle Ages. To the south, Victor could see the Basilica di San Petronio dominating the square. Its huge façade was composed of elegantly constructed blocks of white and red stone with elaborate carvings and archways at the bottom. Above, however, it was merely topped by crude bare bricks. The result was bizarre to most, horrible to some, but Victor found it strangely appealing – the mix of the beautiful and the ugly.

The bearded man maintained a slow walking pace and smoked cigarettes the whole way, lighting a fresh one while the dying embers of the previous still glowed in the gutter. Victor tried to stay away from the smoke as much as he could because it was the sweetest aroma he'd smelled in a long time and one that tested his resolve. The city streets were narrow and notably absent of trees – the one mark he gave against Bologna's beauty. The bearded man led him through several of the meandering porticos and Victor realised the route they were taking was just as meandering. He was happy to play along and enjoy viewing the array of old terracotta buildings they passed. Modern architecture was rare in Bologna and the city felt as though time had stood still within its walls while the world changed around it.

Eventually they passed beyond what remained of the medieval walls surrounding the historic centre. The streets became more crowded, the traffic louder, the lights brighter. The bearded man led Victor for another fifteen minutes before they veered off into an alleyway that ran along the back of a row of restaurants.

'This is where we part ways,' the bearded man said, taking the cigarette from his lips. 'It's been a pleasure. Now, just walk up there and round the corner.'

He pointed and held out his hand.

'Giordano?'

'That would be far too easy, would it not? You'll find a newspaper under a wooden box. Find the puzzle page. In the crossword is a time and a place. Farewell.'

The air was warm. Music from a nearby bar drifted over him. Victor walked slowly, gaze sweeping over the area, but there was nothing to concern him. He found the box and the paper and folded the puzzle page into his pocket.

The low sun made Victor reach for his shades as he walked back into central Bologna. He passed through the crowds, unnoticed, unremembered. When he had been young he'd wanted everyone to look at him. Now, if anyone did, they were his enemy until proved otherwise.

He used the city's punctual buses to get around. For some reason, taxis didn't seem to stop when hailed. Victor spent an hour swapping between buses, before heading to the train station where he sat on a platform bench, thumbing through a classic car magazine. When the eighteen-fifty train to Rome arrived he waited until eighteen-forty-eight before boarding. A few people boarded after him.

On the train, he stood in the vestibule, his hand on the door, counting each passing second. Through the window, he watched for the attendant on the platform give the train driver the all-clear, then he flung the door open and jumped out. He slammed it shut behind him and heard it lock a moment later.

Out of the corner of his eye he saw the attendant shake his head. Victor ignored him, looked back and forth along the platform.

No one else had disembarked.

The café was small, elegant, with round white tables and stools instead of chairs. The walls were smooth and white with lots of mirrors. Victor liked that. For once he could sit anywhere he chose and with mere flicks of his eyes see the entrance, counter, restroom doors, even the long, perfectly toned legs of the blonde sitting to his right. Though the distraction the latter caused was certainly more of a hindrance than a benefit.

The scent of freshly ground coffee perfumed the air. The establishment was spacious but full, vibrant and noisy. Victor sat with a newspaper spread out before him and a tall glass of orange juice sitting next to it. Condensation beads hung from the glass. The hands on the clock above the counter said that it was nine p.m. He would give it another ten minutes, enough time to explain some bad traffic. If he hadn't shown by that time then it would be too bad.

He came through the door as Victor was finishing off the last of the orange juice. He looked the same as he always had – slim, tanned, blond, flawlessly groomed, perpetually young, unshakably confident, impossibly good looking.

He smiled at Victor as he approached and said, 'Vernon, my favourite shark, come all the way to Bologna to see me. This whole city is honoured by your presence.'

'A shark?'

The blond man sat down opposite. 'It seems to me the metaphor fits quite aptly. I was thinking about it on the way here.' He leaned closer and whispered, 'You swim undetected through the ocean, strike without warning and then disappear back into the depths, unseen but always feared.'

'Nice imagery,' Victor said, without inflection.

'I know, right?'

'You're late, Alberto.'

Alberto Giordano shrugged, didn't say anything, the action itself the explanation for his tardiness.

'I almost left,' Victor continued.

'And not see me? Preposterous. People always wait for me.' Giordano's smile suddenly disappeared as he noticed Victor's right hand was under the table. 'What's that about, Vernon?'

'What do you think?'

Giordano made a face. 'Such bad manners. I thought we were

past all that nonsense. If I'm so threatening, why did you even want to meet?'

'I'm lonely.'

He gestured to Victor's unseen hand. 'When you treat people like that, I can't say I'm too surprised.'

'Says the man who sent me halfway around the city today.'

Giordano grinned. 'A little adventure never hurt anyone. Don't pretend you didn't enjoy it. Besides, you always told me I needed to be more careful. A multi-faceted defence, and all that silly stuff. This is me being more careful. If people want to see the great Giordano himself they can dance to his tune so he can first see their true rhythm. And it works, too. Can't have this handsome face marked by some uncouth ruffian now, can we? And don't try to act offended – you put a friend of mine on a train to Rome. He got caught without a ticket. Do you know how much the fines are in this country? I swear the fascists are still in power.'

'I don't like being followed.'

A waitress approached, her elegant uniform stretched tight over her curves. Her eyes lit up when she saw Giordano and she gave him a wide smile. If she noticed Victor, she didn't show it. Giordano ordered an espresso for himself and another orange juice for Victor.

'I assume, despite the obvious pleasure of my company, you'll be requiring the usual product,' Giordano said.

'Yes.'

'What nationality?'

'I'm thinking Italian this time.'

Giordano smiled. 'Vernon, please, I'm not sure you're beautiful enough to be one of us.'

322

'I'm beautiful on the inside.'

Giordano laughed and they made small talk until the waitress reappeared and placed their drinks down. She spent a few minutes flirting with Giordano, leaning over the table so the fact the top buttons of her blouse were undone was obvious. The temperature must have spiked in the interval since she took their order, Victor thought. He sipped his orange juice and tried not to get in the way. Eventually, she took Giordano's number and went back to her work.

'It can be a curse, being me,' Giordano said wistfully after she'd gone. 'When you look like this, every woman wants to talk with you. I can't not, otherwise they'll think I'm rude. And before you say anything presumptuous, I even talk with the hideous ones. I just don't call them.'

Victor didn't respond. He said, 'The identity has to be genuine. And completely clean.'

'For you, Mr Shark, nothing less. You have a photo, I take it?'

Victor took a passport-sized photograph from a pocket and handed it to Giordano. 'There's something else I could use your help with.'

'I can *try* and teach you how to talk to women if you like,' Giordano said with a wide grin. 'But I can't promise they'll want to talk to you.'

'I do get by, Alberto.'

'Don't think I don't know what that means, my friend. My sister, though no beauty, is a pleasant enough woman. I think you'd get on. She's quiet, like you.'

'You'd let your sister see someone like me?'

'What a person does for a living does not define him. We all need money, do we not? How we elect to acquire it is not a reflection of our hearts but our society. Am I a forger or am I Alberto Raphael Giordano, friend, lover, artist, son? Besides, you are a good man, Vernon, even if you don't want to believe it.'

'I appreciate the offer, but a date is not exactly what I had in mind.'

Victor withdrew his hand from under the table and placed one of the wireless cameras he'd procured in Minsk on to the tabletop. Giordano stared at the empty hand for a moment, smiled, and shook his head.

'Now why would you be so mean as to make me believe you were holding a gun? I'm hurt.'

'I'm sure the waitress will help you feel better.'

Giordano smiled again and picked up the camera. 'Nice,' he said, examining it carefully. 'Better than nice.'

'What can you tell me about it?'

'It's US made. Wireless range of up to fifty metres in an urban environment, up to a hundred outside. Both full colour and infrared, high-resolution images. Lasts a week on a nine-volt battery. This is brand new tech. Government use only. Vernon, I had no idea your tastes were so refined.'

'How would you go about getting one of these?'

'With enormous difficulty, and more money than I would spend to win the heart of Venus herself.'

'But it would be possible if you weren't an American government agency?'

'Anything is possible.'

'Could you get hold of a dozen of these if you needed to?'

Giordano held up his hands. 'I appreciate the vote of

confidence, Vernon, but I wouldn't even try. I'm sure I could get one, maybe even three, but I have no wish to have CIA beasts kicking down my door to ask me why I have restricted materials.'

Victor nodded, and tried to keep his thoughts from his face. He asked, 'Could you trace the camera's serial number to find out who bought it?'

'For you I will happily try.'

'See what you can do,' Victor said. 'But be discreet. Don't take even the slightest risk for this. Please. Whatever the outcome, you can keep the camera.'

Giordano glanced in the waitress's direction. 'I might test it out later.'

Victor shook his head. 'How long until I can collect the passport?'

'A few days,' Giordano said.

'Call me the second it's ready.'

'I detect an urgency that is most unlike you.'

Victor didn't respond.

'In some trouble, Vernon?'

'You could say that.'

'Then why not leave that trouble far behind you and retire while you're still young and *relatively* good looking? Live, don't just exist.'

Victor took a sip of orange juice and said, 'When I was first starting out I used to think about what I'd do when I'd put away enough money to retire. I worked out a figure and promised myself I wouldn't do this for a day longer than I needed.'

'Sensible and commendable. How long until you reach this number?'

'I reached it a long time ago.'

'Retire then. Enjoy your life.' He smiled and sat back. 'Like me.'

Victor shook his head. 'If only it was that simple, Alberto. I've been doing this too long. I've made too many enemies. If I retire, I'll get soft, I'll get slow. I won't see them coming when they finally track me down.' The smile left Giordano's face. 'You were right – what you said before. I am a shark. As soon as I stop swimming, I'll drown.'

CHAPTER 41

Zürich, Switzerland

The man who met Zahm had a low centre of gravity. He was squat and overweight, with a face that was kind, while the soul beneath was anything but. Deep lines bisected his forehead and spread out from the corners of his eyes. He stood with a slight stoop brought on by the early stages of a kyphosis hump. His eyes were red and watery. Liver spots dotted the thin, wrinkled skin of his hands and forearms. He wore a loose linen shirt, slacks and sandals, and held a canvas shopping bag in his left hand. He stood a full foot shorter than the six-four Zahm and greeted him with his head tilted way back so he could look the taller man in the eye. Zahm wore sunglasses. The air was warm and dry. No clouds spoiled the perfect sky.

'Hello, my son,' the shorter man said with a smile that showed his small, perfectly white teeth. 'It's wonderful to see you again.'

'And you, Father,' Zahm said back with an imitation of a smile. 'You're looking well.'

Father cast his old eyes over Zahm's muscular frame. 'Not as well as you, of course.'

Despite the smiles and friendly words there was no genuine warmth between them. Zahm played along because the pretence was important to Father. They shook hands, with Zahm careful not to squeeze too hard. If he didn't think about it first he tended to hurt whoever's hand he shook with what he considered a modest grip. And this was no man to hurt, physically or otherwise. They released hands and out of habit Zahm looked around for watchers.

Zahm was well aware that his size made him easy to follow, so he had to pay extra attention to remaining unobserved. He stood with Father in the grounds of the University of Zürich. Students sat on the nearby lawns, reading books, making notes, or just enjoying the sunshine. A typical scene, peaceful, except Zahm detected surveillance. A young woman sat on a bench close by, eating an ice cream. On the surface she looked just like the other students – the same casual clothes, the same earbuds, the same well-worn bag. Her demeanour was all student too, enjoying the sun and being young, head bobbing gently to her music. It was her forearms that gave her away. They were slim but Zahm could see the ridges of strong muscles not gained from a conventional workout or from playing sports. Those muscles were honed from endless classes in self-defence and unarmed combat. The same classes that Zahm had so excelled in.

He gave no indication he had made her. It would be impolite. She was not a threat, merely a precaution. Father liked to have people close by. He had survived three assassination attempts and was always on guard against the fourth.

'Shall we take a walk?' Father suggested.

Father took short steps, partly due to his age and size, but mostly because he never liked to rush. Zahm's long legs made it difficult for him to match the old man's slow pace, and he had to concentrate so as to not stride ahead. After a minute he looked over his shoulder and saw the young woman had started walking too.

'Thank you for meeting me,' Father said. 'I'm so very sorry I had to disturb you on your downtime. Well earned, as always.'

Zahm said, 'No problem.'

'Especially fine work your team did last month.' Father patted him on the arm. 'I'm very proud of you.'

In Zahm's mind the work was no finer or less fine than any of the other assignments his unit had performed.

'Thank you,' he said, to be courteous.

After a few more steps Father said, 'I'm afraid that I may have to ask you to go away once again.'

'So soon?'

Father nodded. 'Something has very recently arisen that I cannot trust to anyone else.'

Zahm's professional curiosity had been hooked but instead of further information he was led in silence for a minute longer. Father never liked to rush. When they were in a quiet corner of the campus, Father stopped walking and turned to face him. The young woman was out of sight but Zahm was sure she was nearby.

'Last week I lost four of my boys,' Father explained, sadness in his voice. 'They were on a surveillance operation, in Minsk, watching a buy between a Belarusian criminal and a Lebanese arms dealer by the name of Gabir Yamout.'

Zahm had heard the name Yamout before. He knew who he was, what he did, and who he did it for. Zahm frowned at the wasted opportunity.

Father smiled sadly. 'I can see your thought process, my son. Your operational skills may be exceptional but we really must work on your poker face.'

Zahm looked away.

'Yes,' Father said, 'we knew Yamout was in Minsk, and no, I did not send anyone to kill him. That would have been terrible manners, considering Yamout works for me.'

Father began walking again. Zahm followed, waiting patiently for Father to provide additional details. This time when Father stopped he elected to sit on the grass of one of the University's lawns. He removed his socks and sandals, and let out a satisfied groan as he made fists with his bare toes. Zahm squatted on his haunches, his shoulders to the sun. The young woman was back, this time in a light jacket, wearing sunglasses, no earbuds or ice cream, and with her hair tied back in a ponytail. To a casual observer she would look like a different person, but not to Zahm's trained gaze.

'Yamout works for me,' Father said again. 'But without his knowledge, of course.' Father gave another little smile and his white teeth shone in the sun. 'We've had people watching him and his business partner Baraa Ariff for over a decade. At their homes, where they go out for dinner, when they take their children to the zoo, and especially when they meet with their clients. The logic is very simple: our enemies will always desire weapons, and if it is not Ariff and Yamout who supply them, others will. Arms dealers are middlemen. Eliminating them solves nothing.' Father paused. 'But with Ariff and Yamout

330

alive, we can watch them and their people and find out who they supply, and in doing so identify our enemies long before they put those weapons to use.'

Zahm nodded, understanding the strategy and feeling annoyed with himself for being so quick to anger before he knew the facts.

Father said, 'There's that poker face again.'

'What happened to the surveillance team?' Zahm asked.

Father waited while two male students walked nearby, talking loudly and gesticulating in the way only those under twenty found acceptable. When they were out of earshot he continued. 'Yamout was in Minsk to buy weapons, not to sell them, though we did not know that in advance. While he was meeting his supplier, an assassin attempted to kill him. My boys, passionate and selfless as they were, did not hesitate in intervening to preserve our link to Ariff's network. We've protected both Yamout and Ariff in times past, always without their understanding, and in this instance my boys acted most courageously, but four out of the five were viciously murdered by the assassin.'

Father took a moment to compose himself and wipe his eyes with a patterned handkerchief. He said, 'Yamout survived the attack, so my brave boys succeeded in protecting one of our most valuable sources. But their sacrifice is no less tragic for that.'

'Who were the shooters?'

Father shook his head. 'Singular. We have him on film. He worked alone. I've never seen so much death so quickly.'

He reached into his shopping bag and produced a file folder. He handed it to Zahm, who looked through stills of the incident.

'At this time we don't know who the assassin represents, but as he went after Yamout once, he could again. Or others might in his place. Perhaps Ariff will be targeted too. If they die, one of their many lieutenants would likely take over, and it might take us months to adapt to the new leadership, all the while losing opportunities to track our enemies. An even worse outcome would be that some unaffiliated arms dealer or dealers steps into the void left behind and we would know nothing of them. We can't allow that to happen.'

Zahm nodded.

Father said, 'But there is more for us to consider than the need to protect the operation. I have lost four of my heroic children. And in dying they saved a life of the very worst kind.' He paused, revulsion and anger taking the place of grief in his sagging face. 'That fact sickens me to my stomach. What would their families think if they knew who their loved ones had died to protect?' He paused again to compose himself. 'My son, I want your unit to avenge them.'

'Of course,' Zahm said without hesitation.

'I appreciate your enthusiasm, but don't be so hasty to commit yourself and your people to this mission. Who knows how many others were involved in this, or how long it could take to find them all. And don't forget, the assassin himself is a dangerous target. Like yourself, he is an exceptional killer.'

Zahm gave a placatory nod. 'Regardless, I still accept. My team is the best I've ever worked with. One man, however dangerous, is still one man. Our people deserve vengeance, and I can promise you my team will share these sentiments. We will be honoured to kill this killer and those who sent him.'

Father took Zahm's hands in his own. 'I knew I could count on you, my son.'

'Do we know who this assassin is, or where he is?'

'No to both,' Father answered. He reached into his canvas shopping bag again and handed Zahm a file containing another series of photographs. 'But these were taken at Minsk Central train station the day after the attack. As you can see, there are two men walking together, one a little way behind the first. We do not see the face of the second man, but I believe him to be the assassin we seek. The first man has been identified as Danil Petrenko, the Belarusian crime boss Yamout went to Minsk to meet with.'

Zahm examined the photographs. 'He looks like a captive to me.'

Father nodded. 'Yet he flew out of Belarus later that day with his girlfriend on a flight to Barcelona. I think it might be worth you having a quiet word with Mr Petrenko.'

CHAPTER 42

Bologna, Italy

Victor had a room at the Villa Relais Valfiore, a charming hotel about six miles south-east of Bologna. While he waited for Giordano to complete his work Victor had explored the acres of vineyards near the hotel and the rolling countryside beyond. He walked and lay in the sun, giving his wound as much time to heal as possible and the sun a chance to stain his skin. It had been a week since the bullet had grazed his arm and the thick scab was coming away at the edges and the muscle only hurt if he pushed against it. Yesterday, he had begun running to maintain his fitness, though he avoided his usual bodyweight exercises so as not to hinder his arm's recovery.

His room offered a view of the hotel's large swimming pool, but he resisted its pull. The weather had been hot and dry and perfect for swimming but he couldn't risk the stares his wound and collection of scars would draw. In clothes, he was forgettable. Out of them, no one forgot. The evening was no good either. The pool was well lit and even if onlookers didn't notice his scars his musculature would draw its own looks. Surviving meant going unnoticed at all times.

The *contessa* who ran the hotel was especially friendly and Victor was forced to engage in small talk like all the other guests did, else stand out and be memorable. The guests were mostly older Italian tourists and foreign couples. Everyone was frustratingly sociable and he found himself drawn into frequent conversations. He was the only single male, as far as he could tell, and made sure to be personable but boring, claiming to be an accountant who had recently divorced. No one tried to chat with him twice.

The bus to Bologna arrived on time and he disembarked with a '*Grazie mille*', to the driver.

At Le Stanze del Tennete he had a lunch of garbanzo soup followed by prosciutto-filled tortellini with a glass of crisp local Pinot Grigio. The restaurant was located inside the sixteenth-century Palazzo Bentivoglio Pepoli and he took his time over his meal, enjoying the five-hundred-year-old frescoes on the wall as much as the food itself. After lunch, Victor strolled through the russet arcades and porticoes, passing students and rollerblading teenagers, pausing to watch a heated game of dominoes between two elderly Bolognese gentlemen with too much red wine inside them. He applauded the winner as did the rest of the small crowd that had gathered around them, and departed as the dominoes were mixed up ready for the rematch that was sure to be just as heated.

He saw no sign of surveillance, but performed his usual countermeasures during the walk to the Orto Botanico in the north-east corner of Bologna's centre. The botanical garden was one of the oldest in the world, dating back to 1568, and framed on two sides by the medieval walls that surrounded central Bologna. Victor was an hour early, and he spent the time walking through the grounds like any other visitor, examining the huge array of trees, plants and flowers on display, and the various habitats created within the gardens.

Giordano was waiting for him at the pond wetland habitat, watching dragonflies buzz around water lilies and aquatic beetles swimming across the glassy surface of the water. Today he was on time. He smiled as he saw Victor approach. No one else was nearby.

'Vernon, you do look better with a little colour in your face.'

Victor returned the smile. 'How's your new waitress friend?'

Giordano blew out some air and said, 'Exhausting.'

'I trust the last two days haven't been all pleasure.'

'Of course not. I have been hard at work when I haven't been hard at work.' He winked and reached into an outside pocket of his jacket. He produced a padded envelope. 'My best, as promised.'

He handed it to Victor, who opened the envelope and removed the Italian passport it contained. Victor thumbed through it, unsurprised to find it every bit as genuine as Giordano promised, except that it now had Victor's photograph instead of the original owner's.

'Tolento Lombardi,' Victor read aloud.

'He's a construction worker,' Giordano explained. 'A construction worker who borrowed money off the wrong people. He sold them his passport to help clear his debt, and they were

336

then kind enough to sell it on to me. Mr Lombardi is a most clean citizen. Not even a parking ticket, and he's never been out of the country. He's painfully boring, and therefore perfect for your purposes.'

Victor nodded and ran a fingertip over the image of his face. 'This is even better than the last one I bought from you. How do you switch the photograph without leaving marks?'

Giordano grinned. 'Well, that's my secret, is it not? Else everyone could do what I do. But, as I like you, Vernon, I will tell you I have refined my techniques, so I'm glad you noticed the improvement. Passports are getting harder to modify all the time. It's almost as if they want to stop people like me. Fascists. But my method of using solvent fumes to strip wafer-thin layers of laminate away, one at a time, is quite ingenious.'

'Modest to a fault.'

Giordano bowed his head briefly. 'Once the laminate has been stripped it's child's play to insert your photo and re-laminate. Result: no trace of modification. Sounds simple, does it not? Yet no one else can do it like I can.'

Victor pocketed the passport. 'Which is why you charge such a competitive rate.'

Giordano laughed. 'And I'm worth every cent, as I've no doubt you too are value for money. When you use this passport, I'd like you to carry your new self in the appropriate manner. Remember, Vernon, people are going to think you are Italian. I don't want you letting the side down.'

Victor would have smiled, only he knew Giordano wasn't joking.

A family of four were drawing near so Victor and Giordano walked to the tropical hothouses. Inside was an expansive collection of orchids and bromeliads. The air was very hot and very humid.

Victor asked, 'Did you find anything out about the camera?'

'I did what I could, which wasn't as much as I would have liked, but I only know so much. That kind of tech is closely watched, as I told you before, but anything sold is traceable. In this instance there isn't much to tell, but maybe it will help you anyway. I managed to track the serial number from source in America to the United Kingdom, but that's where the trail stops. Officially, at least.'

'Who bought it?'

'A company called Lancet Incorporated purchased that camera and twenty-nine like it about eight months ago. They were one of the very first to.'

'Who are they?'

Giordano's face shone with perspiration from the heat and humidity. 'I figured you'd say that so I asked some associates to check them out. They're registered in Switzerland, own some property in a few different countries, some stock in other companies. Seems like they aren't being run too well as they've been making a loss for the last few years.'

'So they're a front.'

Giordano shrugged. 'I'm just passing on what I was told. It's up to you what you make of it.'

Victor nodded and handed the Italian a padded envelope. Giordano thumbed through the cash inside.

He said, 'Overpaid again, I see. Generous to a fault.'

They exited the hothouse and left the botanical gardens.

On the street outside, Victor said, 'Thank you for your work and your assistance, Alberto.' He held out his hand. 'Much appreciated.'

Giordano shook it. 'A pleasure, as always. Don't leave it so long next time.'

'I won't.'

They walked their separate ways. After a moment Victor heard Giordano call him and he turned in response.

Giordano looked serious for once. 'Vernon, don't stop swimming.'

Later, Victor sipped brandy in his hotel room while the voice on the other side of the world said, 'The suite next to the Presidential was rented out by a couple of men with Belarusian IDs, but unsurprisingly those identities have turned out to be bogus. As for who they are, I haven't got enough intel to even hazard a guess. What I can tell you is they are not Belarusians and aren't from this side of the Atlantic. When I know more, you will. What about you, my man?'

'What about me?' Victor asked, as if he didn't understand.

'That's a nice try, pal, but do you expect me to believe you've been sitting on your behind this last week? Because if you do, then you're either seriously underestimating me or seriously overestimating your ability for BS. You kill a four-man surveillance team, you're going to want to know who they work for. Or have you survived this long by burying your head in the sand?'

'I've followed some leads,' Victor admitted.

'There we go,' the control replied in a pleased tone, 'honesty and trust and all that. So, why don't you share those leads with me and we'll see if we can't get an answer to this?'

The sound of air and saliva being sucked through teeth followed.

'Excuse me,' the voice said, 'Steak sandwich for lunch. Happens every day.'

Victor took a breath. He wasn't used to sharing intelligence. He wasn't used to sharing full stop. Especially with an employer that could prove to be his worst enemy. But all he had was the name of a front company and he wasn't going to find out more without a large investment in time. And the longer he was in the dark about who sent the surveillance team, the longer he was exposed. If they were who Victor thought they were he couldn't afford to waste time on ignorance.

He said, 'I've got a name.'

'Which is?'

'Lancet Incorporated. They're based in Switzerland, and shipped some of the surveillance equipment from the US to the UK. They're a front for someone. That's all I know.'

'*That's all?* There's no need for false modesty.'

Victor sipped some brandy.

'I've never heard of them,' the control said, 'but pretty soon I'll know how they take their coffee.'

CHAPTER 43

Beirut, Lebanon

Ariff sighed as he left the Spanish girl's apartment, unsatisfied and frustrated. Her Arabic vocabulary was expanding and with it she had become increasingly vocal during his recent visits. Today had reached new heights of annoyance. He would give her one last try before seeking out a new creature to take his pleasure from. If only he knew a mute.

The apartment was owned by Ariff and located on Al Hamra Street, in one of Beirut's most cosmopolitan districts. The Egyptian arms dealer had lived in many cities across the Middle East but he was particularly fond of Beirut for the unique warmth and almost coziness of its tree-lined streets and distinct neighbourhoods. There was so much concrete in the city that on an overcast day Beirut could look dull and lifeless, but when the sun was out, which was thankfully more often than not, the city was bright and vibrant.

Ariff ignored two of his people standing as sentries on the street outside and climbed into the passenger seat of the waiting

BMW. Yamout was in the driver's seat, two more bodyguards in the back. Ever safety-conscious, Ariff had increased his security considerably after Kasakov's attempt on Yamout's life and the subsequent attacks across the network over the two weeks since.

The two sentries climbed into a black Range Rover parked in front of the BMW. The driver signalled to Yamout and then pulled away from the kerb. Yamout followed. Ariff closed his eyes. It was a long drive through Beirut from the Spanish girl's apartment to his villa on Mount Lebanon.

'Baraa,' Yamout said.

'I don't want to talk, my friend,' Ariff replied, 'until we get back to my villa.'

Ariff could tell that Yamout wasn't going to be satisfied with that, but the Lebanese waited a few seconds before speaking again. 'I'm sorry to disturb you, but—'

'If you're sorry, why disturb?'

'I have news.'

Ariff sighed. 'That cannot wait an hour?'

When Yamout didn't answer, Ariff opened his eyes. Yamout was sitting very still, face pensive.

'I thought you'd want to know straight away,' Yamout explained. 'The shipment of weapons for the Sudanese has been ambushed by rebels. The president is furious that his five thousand rifles are now in the hands of his enemies.'

Ariff sighed and said nothing.

'He'll never buy from us again now. Not ever. Kasakov must have tipped off the rebels. Baraa, we can't go on like this.'

'Wars are always costly.'

'Is that all you are going to say? First Farkas is blown up and the blame is cast on us, then they come after me in Minsk, and now we lose our biggest customer in the whole of Africa. Not to mention the people who've disappeared, been openly butchered, or who've fled for their own safety. This war will cripple us before long. We must seek peace with Kasakov.'

Ariff laughed. 'If we go begging for mercy from that Ukrainian devil, do you think he'll call off his dogs? Don't be stupid. He'll smell our weakness and crush us. And I would sooner put a gun in my mouth than parley like a woman.'

'News of our war with Kasakov has spread like a plague. No one is going to be crazy enough to deal with us and put themselves in that maniac's crosshairs. Every day we bleed from his strikes.'

'We will outlast him. We have numbers he does not. We have loyalty he cannot match.'

'Yet he has wealth we can't compete with. Wealth that can buy numbers and loyalty.'

'But Kasakov rots as a prisoner in Russia while the whole world wants to see him in chains. I can walk where he can only dream of. I can whisper in ears that cannot hear his loudest screams. Have faith, my friend. As the sands trickle through the hourglass his resolve will surely crack. So let us maintain our own. He with the strongest will shall emerge victorious from this.'

'What good is victory if we have no customers left? Even the ones we can safely supply are deserting us.'

'Kasakov, using his influence,' Ariff explained. 'It was to be expected, my friend. He will try to weaken us in any way he can.'

'It's working.'

'But not for ever,' Ariff assured. 'Our clients won't stop

343

wanting guns just because of Kasakov's bribes or his threats not to sell them heavy armaments. In this century, wars will be fought with guerrillas, not battalions. Kasakov has more to lose than us. Our customers need rifles and bullets more than they need tanks. They will come back to us.' Ariff looked at Yamout. 'Be patient.'

They drove for a while. Ariff enjoyed the warm sun on his face but he couldn't relax enough to sleep. Whatever the calm he expressed to Yamout, the conflict with Kasakov was a real concern. Yamout was stiff in his seat as he drove, his hands clamped on to the steering wheel.

Ariff yawned. 'Since you've done such a superb job of destroying any chance I might have of sleeping, you may as well tell me what our people have achieved recently. Tell me of our victories against Kasakov.'

'The plane our friends shot down in Afghanistan turned out to be an Antonov An-22. We don't know what it was carrying, but the plane alone was highly valuable. Kasakov has only three of them.'

'Now two,' Ariff said with a laugh. 'You see, Gabir, Kasakov bleeds more than us. He uses those Antonovs to transport tanks and other planes. Whatever the cargo was, it will have been worth tens and tens of millions. And do you think he will risk sending another of his cargos over Afghanistan? I think not.'

Blocky seven-storey buildings overshadowed the road, which was jammed with slow-moving one-way traffic. Brightly coloured signs promoted stores lining the sidewalks. A brave guy on a scooter was defying the system by driving the wrong way between the two lanes of cars and received a chorus of horns in response.

Yamout said, 'I've told you about all the attacks in Syria and Tripoli, haven't I?' Ariff nodded. 'Since then we've managed to sabotage a deal and kill some more of his traffickers. In Tunisia this time. From what they admitted before they died, they were important members of Kasakov's organisation.'

Ariff grinned. 'Excellent, Gabir. Truly excellent. That Ukrainian bastard will be enraged at himself for ever believing he could move against us. Regardless of how or why this war began, it is us, not him, who are winning. Take comfort in our victories.'

Yamout nodded, sufficiently convinced by Ariff's assurances to relax for the moment. He turned on the radio, and Arabic pop music thumped through the BMW's speakers. Yamout tapped his fingers on the steering wheel. Ariff smiled to himself. The big man had absolutely no rhythm.

The highway took them across the city. The traffic was fast moving; experience and quick reflexes were required to keep up with the flow safely. Palm trees lined the central reservation. Ahead was a giant billboard advertising McDonald's, complete with a huge yellow arrow pointing out which turning to take. With the world's finest cuisine available in Lebanon, Ariff couldn't understand why anyone would ever opt for a simple burger, but sheep always followed the shepherd.

The BMW drove Ariff through one of Beirut's older districts and down a narrow street overlooked by grand sandstone buildings. Shining SUVs and sedans were parked along both kerbs. The space between was barely wide enough for two cars to pass each other.

The traffic stalled at the intersection some ten cars ahead. Horns were sounded. The BMW stopped behind the bodyguards' Range Rover. Neither Ariff nor Yamout could see the cause of the hold-up, but Yamout added his own horn to the chorus.

Pedestrians used the pause in the flow of traffic to dash across the street. A small old man squeezed between Ariff's BMW and a Toyota SUV behind while two big women covered in burkhas and veils stepped off the far kerb two cars ahead and made their way over the road. They walked slowly, awkwardly, and disappeared out of sight. Ariff shook his head. No matter how many times he witnessed such oppression, he knew he would never get used to it.

'What a religion,' he said to Yamout, who nodded.

The explosion was deafening.

The concussion shook Ariff's whole body and he let out a cry of pure surprise. Yamout was just as shocked. Smoke rose from the bodyguard's Range Rover directly in front. Ariff and Yamout looked at each other, disbelieving, confused. Scared. People on the sidewalk near the Range Rover were writhing on the ground. A woman screamed.

Gunshots.

Both men flinched at the sound. Automatic fire roaring, high cyclic rate, close by. Ariff was frozen in his seat. He didn't know what to do. He glimpsed muzzle flashes coming from the far side of the Range Rover and realised someone was shooting at his men. He heard dull *thunks* as bullets slammed into the Range Rover's armoured bodywork. Sparks flew from its sides. Stray rounds cracked the bulletproof windshield in front of Ariff's face.

Yamout already had the transmission in reverse before Ariff could yell, '*Get us out of here.*'

The two bodyguards behind Ariff had their Ingrams cocked and ready. The BMW travelled just a couple of feet before it struck the Toyota behind. Yamout repeatedly punched the horn but the SUV didn't offer any more room. The thunder of automatic weapons didn't relent. Blood splashed against the inside of the lead Range Rover's rear window.

Ariff's eyes went wide. 'Yamout . . .'

A gunman appeared, moving along the centre of the road. A balaclava covered his head. In both hands he clutched an Armalite assault rifle with under-slung grenade launcher. A black burkha was draped over his shoulder like a cape. He gestured at Yamout with his weapon before firing off a burst into the air. People on the street outside were screaming and running away. Drivers and passengers fled their cars.

Yamout tried to execute a turn to get out of the line of traffic and on to the sidewalk but there was no room. The front bumper crumpled against the Range Rover. Bullets smashed against the windshield before Yamout's head, but didn't penetrate. He shouted an order to the two bodyguards in the back of the BMW.

The bodyguard behind Yamout flung open his door and jumped out into the road. Immediately the masked gunman opened fire. Bullets pinged off the metal and were stopped by the armoured glass.

The bodyguard fired the Ingram from the gap between the door and car. The sub-machine gun was small and boxy, seemingly unsophisticated, but its cyclic rate was twelve hundred rounds per minute. The bodyguard let off a panicked burst that emptied the magazine in a matter of seconds. Thirty bullets hit the road, Range Rover, neighbouring cars but not the gunman, who dropped to a crouch and reloaded his assault rifle.

'*NOW, NOW*,' Yamout screamed. '*GET HIM NOW.*'

The second bodyguard was out of his own door fast. He rushed past Ariff's window, jumped up on to the hood of the BMW to drill the gunman before he could finish reloading. Instead the bodyguard contorted and flailed, his bullet-riddled body striking the hood and bouncing off on to the sidewalk. Blood sluiced down the BMW's windshield.

'*There's another one.*'

Ariff saw a second burkha-draped gunman on the other side of the Range Rover. He was kneeling down on the sidewalk, also armed with an assault rifle. The only bodyguard left alive hurriedly reloaded his Ingram. Yamout reached past Ariff and opened the glove box. He grabbed a handgun from inside.

'*Get in the back, Baraa,*' he yelled. '*Close the door.*'

Ariff struggled to get from the passenger seat and into the back. His heart beat frantically inside his chest. He flopped down on the back seat and stretched to grab and close the door. The bodyguard to his side squeezed off some controlled bursts. Return fire struck the BMW around him.

Ariff kept low on the back seat, breathing heavily, not daring to stick his head up too far. His ears stung from the gunfire.

'We can't stay here,' Yamout said. He was crouched down in his seat, gun in one hand, the other fumbling for his cell phone.

Ariff didn't respond. They couldn't stay but they couldn't leave either.

The bodyguard fired another burst before the Ingram was empty. He quickly released the spent magazine and slammed in another. No one shot at him. Ariff couldn't see why. Maybe he had killed them both. *Please, make it be true.*

The bodyguard cocked the weapon, but before he could fire again, a man appeared behind him – suddenly, terrifyingly. Another masked gunman. He stabbed a knife into the bodyguard's throat and disarmed him of the Ingram in one fluid move. A geyser of blood sprayed from the huge hole in the bodyguard's neck and he fell gurgling to the ground.

Yamout tried to turn but flames spat from the Ingram's muzzle and holes exploded through the back of the driver's seat. Yamout contorted and flailed.

The shooting stopped and Yamout's head hung limply forward. Bloody bullet wounds were spread across his back and arms.

Ariff screamed. He screamed louder when a grenade sailed through the open doorway. He watched it fall out of sight, landing somewhere in the foot well on the passenger's side.

It exploded with a monstrous bang and blinding flash of light. Ariff saw nothing but white, heard nothing except a piercing whine. He was too disorientated to move or even cry out. Hands grabbed his ankles and dragged him over the back seat. He fell into a crumpled heap on the road, on top of his blood-drenched and dying bodyguard.

More hands grabbed Ariff and pulled him upright. He had no strength to fight. The toes of his shoes scraped along the ground. His hearing began to return first. He heard screaming and yelling but it was quiet and muted. Ariff's vision came back slower, but a still image of the car interior – the last thing he'd seen before the explosion – overlaid everything else. He could just make out one of his attackers rushing ahead, yelling and shoving scared pedestrians out of the way. The other two had Ariff between them, holding him up with their arms under his.

They rounded a corner. He saw a van parked up ahead. The lead captor opened the vehicle's back doors, and Ariff was shoved inside, the gunmen either side of him following.

Ariff shouted for help but a rifle butt slamming into his face broke his nose and he lost consciousness.

CHAPTER 44

Colonial Beach, Virginia, USA

Seagulls squawked overhead. Procter stood on the end of the narrow pier, wearing sunglasses, gazing eastward across the Potomac. The temperature was mild, the sky blue and cloudy. Windy. Procter's kind of day. The beach wasn't busy – an old guy threw sticks for his Labrador, a couple of people jogged, but the river had its fair share of water sports enthusiasts. There were fleets of sailboats and paddleboats as far as Procter could see. Procter didn't much like being out on the water, but he liked looking at it.

He heard the tap of footsteps on the pier boards behind him.

'Beautiful day,' Clarke said as he stopped alongside Procter. His tone was happily normal, no stress, no anxiety.

'No,' Procter disagreed, 'it's not. Ariff's missing.'

Clarke stammered, 'In what sense?'

'In the sense that there was a shootout two days ago on a

street in downtown Beirut. In broad daylight, if you can believe it. Masked gunmen disguised in burkhas ambushed Ariff's motorcade. Used a grenade launcher to blow out the armoured glass of the bodyguards' SUV and filled the vehicle with close to sixty rounds. Gabir Yamout and six of Ariff's bodyguards were killed. The whole thing was over in under a minute, start to finish. Ariff was not among the dead, but a man fitting his description was seen being dragged away by the attackers.'

Clarke looked paler than usual. 'Jesus Christ. But eye witnesses are notoriously unreliable. We can't know for sure Ariff isn't—'

'That's not all,' Procter said, turning to face Clarke. 'Soon after Ariff was snatched, his villa was attacked. Several more bodyguards were killed. The wife and son of Gabir Yamout were shot dead. Ariff's own wife and his three daughters were kidnapped. A nanny hiding in a closet heard everything. Neither they nor Ariff have been heard from since.'

'*Jesus*,' Clarke said again.

'How the hell did Kasakov get to Ariff so damn fast?'

Clarke didn't attempt an answer.

'I just don't get how he could have found Ariff in a matter of weeks. I mean, even the Agency didn't know where Ariff was hiding out. It took us months to establish Callo as a solid link to Ariff's organisation. Then we had to kidnap and interrogate the prick to find out what city Ariff was in. And even then we had to put bodies on the ground to establish where in Beirut Ariff actually lived. Yet Kasakov gets the same intelligence in a tenth of the time.' He sighed, shaking his head. 'That man is something else.'

They stared across the water for a moment. A college-age kid thrashed past on a jet ski.

'I'm as surprised as you are,' Clarke hesitantly began. 'But our plan relied on the fact that Kasakov and Ariff knew enough about one another to inflict damage.'

'To their networks,' Procter corrected. 'There's no reason why Kasakov would know where Ariff, who has been under the radar for twenty years, was living. They've crossed paths with their businesses, but never personally. Ariff's exact whereabouts was the one thing that Kasakov would certainly not have known before this began. But he found it out.' Procter clicked his fingers. 'Just like that. He may well be the devil himself.'

'He's just a man.'

'Ariff will be dead by now, or wishing he was. I don't even want to think what happened to his wife and kids.'

'That's not our fault,' Clarke stated as he poked Procter in the chest. 'Ariff put them in danger by living his life the way he did. He signed their death warrants with every rifle he sold, with every bullet fired at the innocent, with every IED that killed and maimed with explosives he supplied. He did this to them, not us.'

Procter nodded. He pushed a palm against his forehead. 'I know, Peter. You're right, as always. But our war is over a mere month after it began. All our work, all that careful planning to ensure Kasakov and Ariff tore each other's empires apart, it's all been wasted.'

Clarke looked away. 'We haven't yet got an accurate figure on the damage Ariff caused Kasakov's network. But when we know, I'm sure we'll find that it has been substantial. And remember, Ariff and Yamout are dead. Their network is leader-less and will be in disarray from the war with Kasakov. The flow of small arms has been effectively cut off.'

'Until more dealers take over.'

'Yes,' Clarke agreed. 'But even if we've only hampered the flow of weapons for a few months, we might have saved dozens of lives. Maybe more. And it's not just Americans who will be saved. Think of all the death squads and terrorists across the world who won't be getting guns, ammunition and explosives.'

Procter let out a growling sigh. 'But this thing should have lasted months, maybe even years. Ariff and Kasakov should have pummelled each other down until there was nothing left of either of them.'

'There was always the chance this would end sooner than we wanted, even if we didn't believe it could be this early. No plan ever works perfectly.' Clarke patted Procter on the shoulder. 'Take comfort that it hasn't blown up in our faces. And we've done so much good, Roland. We really have.'

Procter smirked. 'You say that like you're trying to convince yourself more than me.'

Clarke stared at Procter. 'None of us can change the world, Roland. But we have made it a little more palatable. If only for a time.'

'I'll send Tesseract to get rid of Kasakov to bring things to a close. With luck, his lieutenants will fight for control over the empire and leave it fractured and weaker. And talking of Tesseract, we have another problem you need to be aware of.'

'Yes?' Clarke asked, warily.

Procter said, 'Regarding the four civilians Tesseract killed in Minsk who turned out to be someone's surveillance team. Well, he came up with a name: Lancet Incorporated. I did some digging, and it turns out that they're a Swiss company that specialise in shipping goods that have been traded via under-the-table deals.'

'For who?'

'Us,' Procter answered. 'You and me. Not specifically the CIA or the Pentagon, but for the good old US of A.'

Clarke said nothing.

'Lancet ship all kinds of things from the Eastern Seaboard across the Atlantic. Things like state-of-the-art surveillance cameras. Things like Hellfire missiles.'

'To who?' Clarke asked, eyes widening.

'The kind of people who worship on a Saturday.'

It took Clarke a second to process Procter's words. 'The Israelis?'

Procter nodded.

Clarke said, 'If Lancet are a stepping stones between America and Israel, then that surveillance team must have been—'

'There's no "must have been" about it. That's exactly who they were. Tesseract only tangled with four, but in total there were five Mossad agents running a surveillance op on Yamout. They were part of an ongoing initiative to keep tabs on Ariff's organisation. It's simple, but very smart. They find out who Ariff and Yamout supply with guns, and if those customers turn out to be enemies of Israel then they receive a nice little visit from a team of Kidon assassins or one of the aforementioned Hellfires. These watchers also act as babysitters to make sure Ariff and Yamout stay vertical. The Israelis see it as a case of "better the devil you know". Whoever kidnapped Ariff must be really slick to do so under Mossad's nose.'

Clarke exhaled. 'How long has this op been going on for?'

'A long time. Like ten years, maybe longer.'

Clarke shook his head and closed his eyes. He pinched the skin at the top of his nose. 'How do you know all this?'

'I'll come to that in a minute. Fortunately, Mossad don't know a great deal about what happened in Minsk when their people got killed.'

'Sounds like there's a "but" coming.'

'But,' Procter continued, 'they're looking for the man who killed their team.'

Clarke picked up the significance of the wording instantly, just as Procter knew he would. 'Not men?'

Procter shook his head.

'If they know it was just one man, then they must have spotted Tesseract.'

Procter nodded but didn't respond. He looked away.

'If they're looking for Tesseract,' Clarke said, 'they'll want to know who sent him. And he knows your face if not your name. And even if he doesn't know you're CIA, he's smart enough to guess.'

Procter slowly nodded.

'But Europe is a big place and, as you keep saying, Tesseract is a special kind of guy. They're not going to be able to find him, right?'

Procter didn't answer. He toyed with the change in his pocket.

'What aren't you telling me, Roland?'

Procter looked Clarke in the eye and said, 'You need to see something.'

Procter withdrew his smartphone and thumbed a few buttons. He passed it to Clarke, who examined the screen.

The phone's screen was filled with an image of a room with a white carpet, white walls, expensively decorated and furnished. Standing in the room were two men. A large man stood in the background, side-on to the camera. The second man was the focus of the image. He was tall, wearing a suit, face to the camera, well lit, perfectly identifiable.

'Holy crap,' Clarke said. 'That's him.'

Procter nodded. 'Just slide to see more. Not that you really need to, as that one says it all. There's video footage too, with audio. In Russian, granted, but it's still his voice.'

'How the hell did you get hold of this?'

'Mossad has passed to us everything they have on the incident.'

Clarke stared at Procter for a long time before saying, 'They've asked for the CIA's help finding him.'

'And it's been granted,' Procter said. 'Satellite, facial recognition, HUMMIT – everything. The Director wants to demonstrate our commitment to one of our closest allies.'

'This is bad, Roland,' Clarke said. 'This is really bad. Are you going to be involved?'

Procter shook his head. 'Chambers is overseeing it. We've been helping for about a week so far. I'll get *some* updates, but I won't be able to influence.'

Clarke looked as scared as Procter had ever seen him. 'What are we going to do?'

'We send Tesseract after Kasakov, as already discussed, and we tell him to disappear straight after.'

Clarke raised his eyebrows. 'Or?'

'Don't even think it, Peter. It's not Tesseract's fault Mossad were watching Yamout. He couldn't have predicted that. Hell, we didn't. I brought him into this operation, and I'm not going to turn on him as soon as we get a little heat.'

'*A little heat?* Roland, are you joking? This is about as hot as it can get. They have his face, they have his voice. They know where he was and when. You think that isn't enough to establish a trail? This is Mossad we're talking about here. They don't play by the rules. They'll do whatever it takes to find him. They'll send a Kidon team, and eventually they'll track him down, you know they will. That's what they do. They'll make him talk. You'll be identified, then me. Best-case scenario: this operation blows up in our face and we find ourselves facing an oversight committee. That's if we're lucky. Israelis like their revenge served ice-cold, don't forget. You think they'll forgive us for killing their people because we're allies?' Clarke shook his head. 'It's over. Have him kill Kasakov, and then we cut our losses.'

After a minute of silence Procter said, 'He can keep a low profile. This will blow over eventually. These things always do. When there are no leads after a month, resources will be reassigned. The Israelis won't find him on their own. I have faith in his abilities.'

Clarke pointed an accusatory finger. 'You found him once, remember.'

'That was an entirely different set of circumstances. He was on his own. This time I can help him.'

'You want to take the risk?'

Procter didn't answer. He heard laughter and looked down the beach to where a little girl was flying a kite, guided by her father. Procter couldn't help but smile. He looked back at Clarke.

'If anything goes wrong killing Kasakov, or Mossad get too close to him, I'll activate the contingency. Happy?'

Clarke didn't answer.

CHAPTER 45

Ljubljiana, Slovenia

Slovenia's capital was spread before Victor. His hotel room was on the fourteenth floor, high enough so that it wasn't over-looked by other buildings, letting him enjoy the rare pleasure of open drapes. The city beyond his hotel-room window was muted beneath grey clouds, but the dawn rising over the snow-covered peaks of the Kamnik Alps in the distance made it a view to savour.

His employer, sounding not unlike how Victor imagined a father might to his son, said, 'We need to talk.'

Victor took a seat at the room's meagre desk on top of which sat a laptop. He drank Sicilian lemonade from a frosted glass bottle.

The voice sounded through the computer's speakers again. 'There is a serious problem you need to be aware of. Regarding Lancet.'

'I take it this problem is the fact the team I killed in Minsk were Israeli Mossad.'

'How did you—'

'I asked myself who would have the motivation, means and guile to run a surveillance op on Gabir Yamout, and who the United States would sell restricted technology to. There was only ever going to be one answer.'

'I take it you understand the seriousness of the situation.'

'Of course,' Victor said. 'Your tone so far has been quite evocative.'

'This is no time for jokes. The Israelis recorded you real good, my man, when you took that recon of the suite. I have to say I was very surprised you did that. I thought you were more careful. The surveillance team's cameras got your front, back and everything in between. I've seen the stills. They're crystal clear.'

Victor nodded to himself. He'd assumed the video feed had been backed up elsewhere, but at times like this it wasn't much fun being right. His enemies had his face, his voice – albeit in Russian – and would be able to work out his height and weight. It would give Mossad as good a profile on him as anyone. Anonymity was always his best form of defence and without it he was vulnerable.

'Given the limited time frame I had to operate within,' Victor said, 'that reconnaissance could not have been avoided.' He paused, then added, 'And I take it Mossad have requested CIA assistance to look for me, which is why you've seen the stills.'

'I'm sorry to say they're getting the best-bud package on this one. The full power of US intelligence is, in effect, being loaned to Israel.'

'They must want me pretty bad.'

'That they do, my man, that they do. Mossad are easily the

361

most vengeful intelligence organisation on the planet, and that's without the fact the head of their operational arm has taken a particular interest in this incident. He's as old as Israel herself, and takes attacks against his people very personally, like they're all one big extended family. They call him Father, if you can believe it.'

'Do you want me to disappear?'

'No, no, you absolutely can't do that,' the control quickly answered. 'I still need you to be available. I've got another job for you, which we'll come to in a minute. We're going to need to work together to ensure the Israelis don't catch up with you, okay? Neither of us want them to find you. I'm going to do everything possible to help you out, but that's going to be limited to intelligence updates only. I need to keep a low profile and maintain my distance from this as much as I can. If I draw suspicion my way, it's only making it easier for them to get to us both. You're going to be on your own for the most part.'

Victor had expected as much, and he was used to surviving and operating alone with enemies after him. At least this time he had the advantage of being aware of the situation beforehand as well as knowing who he was up against. And if his employer kept his word and gave him updates it would make staying out of Israeli crosshairs somewhat easier.

'They've already dispatched the Kidon team,' the voice said, 'who I believe are currently in Minsk scouring for clues. I take it you don't need me to tell you about Kidons?'

'They're assassination and kidnapping teams. Operate with a large degree of independence from Mossad, conducting their own research and surveillance. A fully operational unit consists of at least four men and women to perform the kill itself, with more providing surveillance, backup, clean-up and logistical support.'

'And they're good,' the control added, needlessly. 'They're really good.'

'I'm well aware of their capabilities.'

'Then let's hope you don't get a first-hand demonstration.'

'I'll keep my eyes open for guys wearing tennis gear in my hotel elevator.'

'Cute, but don't forget Kidon are the reason why every bad guy in the Middle East checks under his bed before he goes to sleep.'

'I won't forget.'

'Good man. Eventually, regardless of the CIA's desire to help our Jewish cousins, resources will be diverted elsewhere. No offence, my man, but there are bigger fish to fry than you. And when we turn our focus elsewhere the Israelis will be stumped. On their own, Mossad don't have the manpower or the technology to find you unless you do something stupid and help them out. Which I know you won't be doing. Call me if you notice anything suspicious and I'll pass on all information about the Kidon's progress that comes my way.'

'Of course,' Victor said. 'Because if they do find me they're going to take me somewhere for a private chat. And we both know the result of those kinds of conversations. They'll extract everything I know about you, which isn't a lot, but it will be enough to point them in the right direction. You'll help me as much as you can because you don't want to be next.'

'No I most certainly do not. You're very right about that. All of our necks are on the line.'

'*All* of our necks?'

'The two of us are not the only ones involved in this operation.'

'So it's an operation now? Not simply unconnected targets?'

'I never said they were unconnected.'

'You never said they were connected either.'

'You didn't need to know,' the control said. 'Just keep your head down and this will blow over before you know it.'

Victor wasn't sure if he believed that, but certainly the first month would be the most dangerous. If the Kidon team hadn't found him by then, Victor would be able to relax a little, though never fully. Israelis had long memories.

He hadn't shaved in the three weeks since Minsk and now had a short beard to help disguise him. His hair hadn't been cut since Romania, but it hadn't grown long enough to change his look significantly. He could cut it shorter than it had been in Minsk, but with more length he had more options to change style. He would need to buy himself some non-prescription eye-glasses and coloured contacts. The tan he'd gained recently would also help. The disguise wouldn't get him past facial recognition software but might help him avoid being ID'd by a watcher.

'Now we're on the same page with the Israelis,' the control said, 'we can move on to your next assignment. I'm sending you through the dossier.'

When the new email arrived in his operational inbox, Victor opened the message and downloaded the attached doc-ument. It opened to show a square-faced man with Slavic features and short black hair, somewhere in his late forties. Victor would have recognised the face even without the distinctive scarred ear. It was the face that had looked at him with such intensity in the Grand Plaza Hotel in Bucharest over a month before, the face of the man who had offered to buy Victor a new suit, the face of the man whose life Victor had saved. The man he now had to kill.

'You'll recognise him from Bucharest, of course,' the voice said through the speakers. 'His name is Vladimir Kasakov, a Ukrainian arms dealer. If there really is an antichrist, this guy could be him.'

'I know who he is,' Victor said through a tight mouth.

'Then you know you'll be doing the world a huge favour by putting Kasakov in the ground.'

Surprises were high on Victor's list of personal and professional dislikes, but that the man he'd recently saved from assassination was the man he now had to assassinate was perhaps the height of both. Such a job felt somehow wrong to his doctrine as a professional. In the many years he'd been a hired killer he'd never once been tasked with a similar contract.

'Are you there?' the control asked.

Victor remained silent.

'You want to know why we had you save Kasakov five weeks ago only to have you kill him now,' the control said, as if reading Victor's thoughts. When Victor didn't respond, he continued: 'I can understand that. I'd want to know if I were you. Circumstances have changed. It's complicated, not something you need to know inside out, but in short we needed Kasakov alive then but now we need him dead. I trust you don't have a problem with that.'

Victor shouldn't. It was a job like any other of the many he had performed, too numerous to count – though he knew if he tried he would be able to remember every name, every face. And it wasn't as if this target was some heroic individual whose death would be objectionable. Vladimir Kasakov helped make war and genocide possible. There should be no issue with killing such a man.

But Victor had talked to him, shared a personal connection with his target, however brief that connection had been. He had looked Kasakov in the eye long before he had been told to kill him. More than that, he had saved the man's life. It shouldn't matter. But it did.

'Well,' the control said. 'Do you have a problem with this?'

'No,' Victor said carefully.

'Good.'

'What I do have a problem with is that Kasakov and his bodyguards have seen my face. I walked straight past them and they noticed me. They knew a shot had been fired so they were checking out everyone. Had I known that Kasakov would be – or even just might be – a target, I would have made sure that didn't happen. Now I won't be able to risk getting close to Kasakov in case I'm recognised. That limits my options. And less options makes the job considerably more difficult and more dangerous.'

'Ah, I see,' the control said. 'I'm sorry about that.'

'Sorry isn't good enough.'

'Listen, my man, this is not a partnership. I'm your boss. You're an employee. If I say sorry you should feel immensely fucking privileged.'

'I told you before not to curse in my presence.'

'My mistake. But you're making a mistake if you think I care about your prudishness for bad language. I've apologised for the Kasakov situation, so you had better accept it, and move on. You've got a target to familiarise yourself with, so do it.'

'This time the dossier had better contain everything I need to know, not just what you think I need to know. If I find out that this isn't the case, or if there are any more of these kind of surprises, then I will not be happy.'

The control's voice dropped a few decibels. 'I don't take too kindly to threats.'

'I don't make threats. It's a statement of fact. Whether you take kindly to it is not my concern.'

The sound of heavy breathing lasted for some seconds. Victor waited for the control to say something.

'Let's both of us just calm down,' the voice eventually said. 'Okay?'

'I'm always calm.'

'Well, I'm not,' the control added. 'But I'm big enough and ugly enough to admit when I get it wrong. I've said I'm sorry already. I should have told you before Bucharest that Kasakov could be a target further down the line.'

Victor said, 'I've done three contracts so far for you: in Bucharest, Berlin and Minsk, and each one has been rushed, or I've gone in without the full facts. Now I have Mossad after me, and you're asking me to kill a man who knows my face. And once this job is out of the way you expect me to fulfil yet another contract for you, one that is in addition to our original agreement.'

'Are you refusing to do this?' his control asked. 'Because for a man who has so many enemies that probably isn't the smartest move.'

367

'I'm not refusing the contract, I'm telling you that once Kasakov is dead our arrangement is over. This is my final job.'

Silence. Victor stared out of the hotel-room window. The rising sun cleared the mountains.

Eventually, the voice said, 'Fine, you win. Kasakov is your last hit. After that, you're a free man. You can go sell flower baskets on the streets of Bangkok for all I care. But you don't go back to being a freelance shooter. No way. You take contracts from me or you retire and stay retired. If there is so much as a hint that you're involved in a kill then I'll do everything I can to bring you down. Do we understand each other?'

'I understand you. I hope you understand me.'

'So,' his control said, 'can we get back to the Kasakov assignment?'

'That depends,' Victor answered, 'on one final condition. If I'm going to kill him, it has to be how I choose.'

'You can do it any way you like. In a couple of weeks' time he's taking a vacation at his dacha on the Black Sea coast. He'll be guarded, but he should be easier to get to than when he's at home in Moscow. I'll have more details on the location soon, but you have enough to be going on with for now. He'll be there for two weeks, so you've got all the lead time you could want.'

'Good,' Victor said, and finished his lemonade.

'And this time,' the voice assured, 'I guarantee there won't be any surprises.'

CHAPTER 46

Heathrow Airport, United Kingdom

The flight from Dulles had been long. Clarke had spent the first four hours working – reading reports, signing documents, compiling his own reports – and the rest of the time sleeping. He woke up to the gentle tones of a stewardess telling him they were approaching Heathrow and he needed to fasten his safety belt. The sky outside the plane's window was blue and mostly clear. There wasn't a rain cloud in sight. So much for the stereotype.

As soon as the plane had touched down, Clarke was switching on his phone and checking his messages and emails. He had a couple of dozen – which was about average for the time period – but he paid attention to only one. It told him he wasn't wasting his time crossing the Atlantic. Which was good because Clarke didn't much like the English or British or whatever the hell the correct term for the self-righteous population was. The Scots weren't too bad if they could be understood, and Clarke had never met anyone from Wales, but the rest of the UK he didn't have a whole lot of time for.

The official reasons for his visit encompassed a trip to the Ministry of Defence, SIS headquarters and GCHQ. He was representing the Pentagon, at his own request, and if anyone ever decided to look particularly closely they might conclude that Clarke never really had to go to Britain himself. Intelligence could be shared through other means and there was no need to put a friendly smile on anything. There was never any need to encourage or coerce cooperation. Whatever his personal dislikes, Clarke respected Britain's loyalty to her allies.

Heathrow was predictably horribly busy. Clarke walked through the terminal at a relaxed yet focused pace. He had an overnight bag but no other luggage to collect, as he would only be staying the night if absolutely necessary.

Clarke passed a store that sold soft drinks, confectionary, newspapers and books. He made for the books and spent a few minutes perusing the covers of the bestsellers. In the hardcovers were lots of biographies of British celebrities, most of whom looked too young to have a life story worth telling. He sidestepped to the paperbacks, which were mostly fiction. Clarke was an avid reader but he rarely had time for novels. History and politics were his subjects. He saw a few books he recognised from the shelves in the States and selected a paperback with a cover he liked the look of. He noted that novels in the UK tended to have much more arty jackets than their US counterparts. He skimmed the book's blurb. Something about terrorists and a plot to destroy America.

A woman to the right of Clarke said, 'I've heard that one is very good.'

'I'm going to take a wild guess and say the good guys manage to stop the terrorists at the end and save the day,' Clarke replied without looking at her.

The woman chuckled. 'Not your genre?'

Clarke shook his head and put the book back on the shelf. 'I prefer fact over fiction.'

'A cerebral man then.'

'I have my moments,' Clarke said.

He turned and faced the speaker, who smiled and inclined her head in a brief nod. She was smartly dressed in a business suit, somewhere in her forties and attractive. She was short and slender but held herself with an obvious inner strength. Her eyes were small and intelligent and cold. She took another book from the shelf and handed it to Clarke.

'Maybe this would be more to your liking.'

Clarke accepted the book without looking at it. 'Thanks, I'll give it a try.'

The woman seemed pleased. 'I think you will not guess how it ends quite so easily.'

Clarke spent a minute reading the back and flicking through pages without interest, before saying, 'I'm not sure meeting here was such a good idea.'

'It is a perfect place to talk,' the woman replied. 'This is the busiest airport in the world. Look around you. Do you know how many people pass through it each day? I read nearly two hundred thousand. This is a liquid city. We are all but invisible.'

'Unless British intelligence knows you're here.'

'Impossible. Few outside of Russia know I even exist, even less know how I am employed. To the British, Yuliya Eltsina is

371

but a simple, albeit successful, businesswoman. She is in London to see clients. Besides, I am a very cautious lady. I take many precautions.' She made a floating gesture. 'I am but a ghost gliding among the living.'

Clarke thumbed through the book to maintain the act. 'I'd like an explanation regarding Beirut.'

'What about Beirut?' Eltsina asked, infuriatingly calm and composed.

Clarke frowned. 'Kindly stop the charade. Playing the fool isn't your forte.'

She said, 'My astute powers of telepathy inform me you are talking about the attack on Baraa Ariff.'

'Of course I am. Do you think I'd fly halfway around the world to discuss anything else?'

Eltsina shook her head, but said nothing.

'I'm waiting.'

'For what?'

'An explanation.'

'And what, dear Peter, would you like me to say?'

'We had an understanding. We had a deal. Long before I told you where to find Ariff we specifically agreed Kasakov was not to move against him until I gave the all clear. We agreed this war would last months, not weeks.'

Eltsina raised her small hands. 'You have to understand the position I was in. I had no choice. In the past few weeks Ariff has killed eight of our people. Important people. He also destroyed four major shipments, at a loss of almost half a *billion* dollars.'

'And? Attacks were inevitable. We discussed Ariff's ability to hurt you a hundred times, so don't plead ignorance now.'

'These were not the minor attacks I anticipated. The level of damage being done to the organisation was far, far too severe. Another two months of such incidents would have left Kasakov's empire as but a broken kingdom.'

Clarke sighed. 'I would have helped you rebuild. You knew that.'

Eltsina sighed too. 'It was Kasakov himself who forced the matter. He was going crazy with the desire for vengeance against Ariff, even before the attacks against us started. As his intelligence officer, that anger was directed at me. I was failing him too greatly. If I hadn't delivered Ariff when I did then I would not need fear growing any older.'

Clarke scoffed. 'Don't be so overly dramatic.'

She stared at Clarke. 'My dear Peter, you do not know Kasakov like I do. I have been at his side for many years and I have borne witness to his rage innumerable times. Never have I known a man so vindictive, so without conscience. But nothing I have ever seen compares to what he has become.' Eltsina spoke in hushed tones. 'You must trust me when I say that you do not want me to tell you of his capacity for brutality.'

Clarke broke eye contact. 'Then feel free to keep it to yourself.'

'I am desperately sorry for acting unilaterally in this, but I had to make a decision under impossible circumstances. Is it cowardly for wanting to live? If so, then I am a coward. And don't forget: with me dead, your plans would have been forfeit. This way we can still achieve our objectives.'

'I've been put in a very difficult situation, Yuliya. The person whose help I enlisted to make our objectives achievable does not share our goal. It was for his sake that this war needed to

373

continue for some time. You should have told me you were moving against Ariff so soon. You should have warned me.'

'Life flows like a river, and we must adapt to its ever-changing course.'

'What kind of bullshit is that? I don't like changes being made to a very carefully constructed plan. My associate is a smart man. If he suspects what I've been doing . . .'

Eltsina leaned closer and delicately rested a palm on Clarke's chest. 'You are a creative and intelligent man. Maybe the smartest man I've ever known. You will placate this associate of yours.'

The angry tone had gone from Clarke's voice when he asked, 'Who did you use to snatch Ariff?'

'An American team. They were outrageously expensive, but came with numerous recommendations and an impressive track record. All of which I believe, as they were flawless in apprehending both Ariff and his family.'

Clarke said, 'And there is no danger of Kasakov discovering the RDX from the batch stolen in Istanbul was not taken by Ariff?'

'None whatsoever. Vladimir does not like me but he has absolute faith in my abilities. I have told him the BKA analysis of the bomb that killed Farkas matches that of the stolen RDX and he believes it. I am his chief intelligence and security officer. There is no one else in his organisation with my sources, and Kasakov has no reason to look into the matter further.'

'And Kasakov will still vacation at his Black Sea dacha?'

Eltsina nodded.

'Good,' Clarke said. 'Then you need to be in a position to seize power very soon.'

'As I told you, the network has been struck very hard. Morale among our people is the lowest it has ever been. They have lost money from this war and will continue to lose money from its repercussions. They know Kasakov has risked their lives for personal motivations. They resent him, and I have whispered enough poison to ensure that resentment is aimed at Burliuk too. They are ready for new leadership, and will accept anyone who can repair the damage done, even a woman. When Kasakov is dead, I will have enough support to resist Burliuk's natural ascension.'

'And this new leader had better not forget who helped give her the throne.'

'I will not forget. You really need to have a little more faith in your friends. I shall be your puppet princess of arms, dealing only with factions that you have approved. And with Ariff out of the way, I will incorporate his business into mine so that the world's supply of small arms and heavy munitions is controlled by me alone. Then America's enemies will find their flow of weapons has run dry. We both win. And together we are about to turn over a new page in this world's history.'

Clarke left the book aisle and waited for Eltsina to join him outside the store.

She appeared with a candy bar and took a bite. 'Brits sure know how to make this stuff.'

Clarke said, 'What do I need to know about Kasakov's vacation plans?'

'Kasakov and his wife will be travelling with five of his top-security personnel. He usually only takes a couple, but expecting revenge attacks from Ariff's people he is taking appropriate precautions. The dacha will be unoccupied prior to his arrival, but a local woman will clean it beforehand. I'll pass on his exact schedule the moment I have access to it.'

'Perfect,' Clarke said. 'I'll also need some more funds.'

'Of course. I shall make another donation to your account upon my return to Moscow.' Eltsina checked her watch. 'If that is all, Peter, I must be going.'

Clarke glanced around before saying, 'There is something else I need . . .'

Eltsina's perfectly plucked eyebrows arched. 'Is this one of those changes to a careful plan you are not fond of?'

'Touché.'

Clarke stopped and took a slim file from his overnight bag. He handed it to Eltsina, who finished her chocolate before opening the file. She spent a minute examining the file's contents.

'And who might this be?'

'A problem. He's the assassin my associate has used to get us to this point. He's been very useful, to all of us. However, that usefulness has expired, and while he continues to breathe he is an extreme liability to everything we've worked for.'

'And you want me to get rid of this problem?'

Clarke nodded.

'And just how am I supposed to have it done?'

'Use your new American friends,' Clarke said. 'They've proved themselves perfectly capable.'

'Why don't you take care of him yourself? We are old friends, but this seems like you are burdening me with your own trash when you should be the one disposing of it.'

'I can't be connected to it,' Clarke said. 'And I just don't have anyone who can take care of something like this. Remember, he's not just a liability to me but a threat to you also.' Clarke put a hand on Eltsina's arm. 'And don't forget my understanding in your need to alter our arrangement in regard to Ariff's premature demise. Getting rid of this problem for me is the price of that understanding.'

Eltsina frowned but nodded. 'You're a hard negotiator, Peter. But you have my agreement. How do you want it done?'

'Let's keep it simple, shall we? As soon as Kasakov is dead, have your American friends kill his killer.'

CHAPTER 47

Winnfield, Louisiana, USA

The American was forty years old – average height, average weight, brown-haired, brown-eyed, skin tanned. He wore sneakers, jeans, a white T-shirt. A ball cap covered his quarter-inch-long hair. Sunglasses hid his eyes. He had shaved that morning but already he could use another. His watch was a Casio G-Shock. His arms were hairy and hard with lean muscle. A faded tattoo was visible on his outer left bicep, half-covered by the sleeve of his T-shirt. A hilt of a dagger sat between the fletches of two crossed arrows. Across a banner beneath ran *De oppresso liber*.

He was in the garden of his Winnfield ranch, enjoying Johnny Cash on the radio and the smell of the twenty-ounce steak sizzling over a charcoal grill. The sun was hot and his white T-shirt was damp beneath his arms. In his kitchen, he mixed up a jug of Kool-Aid and added some to a waiting glass of Jim Bean on the rocks. Back in the garden, he sipped his concoction and turned the steak. Juices hissed.

The cell phone in his back pocket beeped. He had a new email. He read it, then read it again.

At his study computer, he opened up an internet browser to check the balance of an offshore bank account. He was pleased to see a very large donation had recently been made. The American loaded up another web page and entered an alphanumeric password into a dialogue box. He waited for a few seconds before the details of a shipment appeared. He entered a destination and was glad to see the shipment would arrive at the new location in adequate time. On a third website, he booked the flights.

By the time he returned to his steak he found it was over-cooked. He liked it rare, but he ate it well done regardless. He wasn't a wasteful man.

In his garage, he pushed aside the refrigerator and entered the nine-digit code into the digital lock face of the safe sunk into the concrete floor. He reached inside and removed two pre-packed sports bags and threw them into the passenger side of his pickup. He climbed behind the wheel and took out a charged cell phone that had never been used before and never would be again.

The American composed a message and sent it to two numbers.

CHAPTER 48

Sochi, Russia

Fine rain fell from a sky the colour of ash. Aside from the patter of raindrops, the forest was quiet. Victor knelt in the undergrowth. The ground was soft beneath his knee. He was on a highpoint that protruded from the slope of the hill, enabling him to see over the canopy that blanketed the hillside below. Mist enshrouded the trees. The rain was fine but relentless. Victor preferred the weather from an operational standpoint, even with the cold water trickling down his back. Better to be wet and unseen in the mist and rain than dry and visible. Binoculars provided him with a clear, albeit limited view of Kasakov's vacation dacha some seven hundred yards away to the west, at the base of the hill.

The mansion was located about three hundred yards inland from the eastern shore of the Black Sea. Woods surrounded the walled twenty-two-acre grounds, which included a guesthouse, swimming pool and the grand dacha itself, according to the plans Victor had been supplied with. From his vantage point,

Victor could see only the rear side's roof and some of the building's second storey, but most of the house, as well as the swimming pool and guesthouse that stood beside it, were hidden by the trees that dotted its grounds. They formed a useful privacy screen and a highly effective security measure. A narrow road led from the house, twisting north-west through the forest until it joined the highway running parallel to the coastline. The dacha was isolated, with no other buildings for at least half a mile in any direction. Again for privacy, but this feature made Victor's job far simpler.

The Black Sea coast was Russia's own Riviera with the region enjoying a sub-tropical climate. Warm and humid. Not today, Victor thought, as cold rain dripped from his nose. The closest town was Sochi, three miles south-east and famous for being home to one of Stalin's dachas. Victor had arrived on a cargo ship, travelling from Istanbul. The trip was uneventful and he had spent countless hours studying all the information he'd been given on Kasakov, his grand vacation home and Sochi. By the time the ship reached port, he knew everything he was going to about the strike point, terrain, weather, local population, transport links, police capabilities and his Ukrainian target.

A modest hotel near the port provided his accommodation. The room was small but came with a pleasant sea view. Adler Airport was located twelve miles due south along the coast from Sochi. Just as with the Bucharest contract, there had been an unremarkable sedan waiting for him in the long-stay parking lot of the airport with a trunk full of weapons.

Victor's employer had supplied everything requested. The dossier was the most detailed one yet. He had all the lead time he required. It was all as it should be. But the best way for the voice on the other side of the world to protect himself from Mossad was if Victor wasn't alive to tell them anything. And even if his employer wasn't planning on betraying him, the Kidon unit was still out there looking for him. Victor knew how to stay hidden as well as anyone, but no one was invisible.

Despite the two potential enemies, he had to concentrate on the job at hand. This could prove to be one of his most challenging and dangerous assignments. It was also one of the most unpalatable, despite the long list of heinous acts Vladimir Kasakov had committed during his long career and the numerous atrocities his weapons had been responsible for. Victor reminded himself he couldn't afford to be distracted by emotions he shouldn't be experiencing in the first place.

He carefully set his metal water bottle on the ground so it was standing up at the highest point of the outcrop and clear of vegetation, and descended the hillside. He moved slowly, carefully, gaze sweeping from left to right and back again. Every thirty yards he stopped and listened before moving on. He wore a green Gore-Tex jacket, Gore-Tex trousers and hiking boots. The woods were gloomy. The mist was thick in the air. Visibility was no more than twenty yards through the trees and thick underbrush. He approached the dacha's grounds from the east.

Raindrops pattered and splashed on leaves. He breathed in the cool air. It smelled of wet earth and decaying vegetation. Between the trees, he saw a wall up ahead. Made of stone and ten feet high, the wall formed a rough square around the property, with each section approximately one thousand feet in length. There was a single gate in the centre of the north wall, but covered by a security camera and therefore not worth tangling with when there were easier options. The plans made no mention of other electronic security measures along the wall, but Victor carefully checked anyway and wasn't surprised to find none. The boundary to the property was far too long to be effectively covered by cameras, and motion sensors would be frequently set off by wildlife or falling branches. Metal spikes topped the wall to create a barrier more than enough to stop a typical intruder.

Victor backed off to give himself a short run-up and sprinted at the wall. He jumped from a distance of four feet, hitting the wall with the ball of his right foot and using the momentum to propel himself vertical, doing the same with his left a split-second later to push himself even further before reaching upwards to grab the top edge. He pulled himself on to the top of the wall. Staying in a crouch, he stepped over the spikes, turned and lowered himself down the other side. He dropped the last few feet.

The house sat at the centre of the grounds, some two hundred and fifty yards away. The woods had been left as nature intended on the other side of the wall. It was quiet. The rain had stopped. Victor heard the rustle of leaves in the breeze and nothing else. He set off through the undergrowth, taking his time to reduce the noise he made, stopping regularly, always listening. The sodden ground squished underfoot. Leaves glistened.

As he was on reconnaissance the only weapon he carried was an MK23 handgun in the right side exterior pocket of his jacket. A suppressor in his left. He didn't anticipate using it, as

Kasakov wasn't due to arrive for another two days, but there was always the chance some of his people had travelled ahead of him. Even then, Victor would only use the gun as a last resort. Dead bodies left at the strike point tended to keep targets away.

The trees gave way to cultivated grounds after Victor had gone about two hundred yards. A six thousand square foot lawn led up to the rear of the dacha. The grass was very green and recently cut. A small wooden shed stood to the west of the lawn. The guesthouse lay to the east. A few trees were scattered across the grass. Their foliage had blocked Victor's view of the dacha from the highpoint.

At the far side of the lawn lay a swimming pool and beyond that the mansion itself, which was large but not huge: six bedrooms and just under four thousand square feet on its main level, according to the plans. The garage was big enough for four sedans. The odd light was on inside so Victor crouched within the tree line and used his binoculars to get a better look. He stayed watching until a woman passed an upstairs window. The dossier had stated the dacha would be cleaned and prepared at some point before Kasakov's arrival. He stayed watching for another half-hour but saw no one else.

He then used the binoculars to check the security cameras were where they were supposed to be. There were two where he expected to find them, each one positioned beneath the overhang of the roof so they had overlapping fields of view that covered the back of the house, patio, swimming pool and part of the lawn. They were small, high-tech, and would provide anyone watching the monitors with a clear picture.

Rain started to fall again. Victor continued through the

undergrowth, moving west towards the shed. Inside was probably grounds-keeping equipment and not much else, but there was no need to confirm that either way. The door was set facing the lawn, out of sight of the dacha. He circled back east through the trees and around the lawn to where the guesthouse was located. It was a two-storey detached cottage, close to the swimming pool and big enough to comfortably house a family of three in a nice suburban neighbourhood. The rain started back up.

Victor approached the rear of the cottage, emerging from the cover of the woods at the point with the least amount of open ground. He hurried across the twenty-foot-wide corner of lawn and paused with his back to the exterior wall. Listened.

There may have been no cameras here, but the cottage had its own alarm system. He peered through a few windows. Nothing of note. He circled the dacha through the woods surrounding it. There was about thirty feet of open space from the edge of the woods to the wall occupied by flower gardens. It was the same on the opposite side. At the front of the house there was a big driveway and lawn and then more woods.

Victor found a small car, most likely the housekeeper's, on the driveway. The front door of the dacha opened and the woman he'd seen pass the window appeared. She was young, not far over twenty, petite, wearing a big padded coat, her shoulders hunched up. The coat had no hood but she held a folded newspaper above her head as a shield against the rain. She rushed over to her car, leaving the mansion's front door open behind her. Victor watched as she smoked a cigarette and drank what he guessed was coffee from a thermos.

She wasn't facing the dacha and Victor knew he could easily sneak inside without her noticing, but not without taking off his muddy boots first, and there wasn't time for that. There was little point in exploring the house as Victor had no intention of getting up close and personal for this one. He knew from Bucharest how alert Kasakov's guards were.

The housekeeper smoked her cigarette right up to the filter and tipped the dregs of her coffee on to the drive, before hurrying back inside.

Victor stayed crouched for another hour until she finally left for the day. He watched her drive away, before making his way to the rear of the dacha.

Staying clear of the security cameras and their fields of view, Victor stepped out on to the lawn and got as close to the dacha as he dared. He turned and looked back towards the hill. The branches and leaves of the few trees on the lawn obscured his vision. He looked back to where the back door was located. Again, he looked at the hill, judging the angle.

The tree took seconds to climb after a short jump and pull up. Victor removed his knife from a pocket and opened it. He used the serrated part of the blade to saw through a thin branch. It fell to the lawn. He did the same with several others. Then again, up a second tree, then a third. When he was done, there were over a dozen thin branches scattered across the grass. Victor collected them up and dumped them individually throughout the woods. He returned to the first tree and climbed it. Squatting to achieve the right angle, he peered down to his left and saw the mansion's back door. He then took out his binoculars and looked right and up, through the tunnels of gaps he'd created in the foliage of the trees until he located his metal water bottle sitting on the protruding highpoint halfway up the hill. He cleared a couple of thin branches to improve his field of view and descended the tree. From the ground, the trees looked no different from before he'd tampered with them.

With his preparations complete, Victor headed back into the woods at the rear of the grounds. He followed his original trail back towards the wall. The paths he had made through the undergrowth were obvious to him but would be invisible by the time Kasakov and his bodyguards arrived. Until then no one would be around to notice them.

Someone noticed.

CHAPTER 49

Izolda Kasakov awoke from a nightmare with her heart thumping and her throat dry. She reached across to the other side of the bed to touch her husband and feel the safety of his presence, but instead found only empty bedclothes. She switched on a lamp and squinted against the light. She put her wrist to her forehead. It was damp with sweat.

'Vladimir?'

There was no response, no sound from the adjoining bathroom. She checked the time. They had gone to bed two hours before and she had been asleep soon after. The cool pillow next to hers told her Vladimir had been gone for a while. It wasn't like her husband to have trouble sleeping. He was a big bear of a man who slept easily and noisily. For the first few years of their marriage Izolda had used earplugs to block out his snoring. Now, she was so used to the loud, rhythmic sound that she sometimes couldn't sleep without him next to her.

Given his recent behaviour, Izolda wasn't wholly surprised he was having trouble sleeping. Something was going on.

Something he wasn't telling her about. He had not been his usual jovial self for several weeks now, and seemed always moody, self-absorbed and quick to anger. She had asked what was wrong but he kept assuring her it was nothing. She guessed it was about work, but didn't pry further, just as Vladimir kept his distance from Izolda's private life. They both had dark secrets the other didn't want to hear.

Her pulse finally slowed down to a normal beat. She couldn't remember the nightmare, only the fear it had evoked. Maybe the stress between her and Vladimir was doing more damage than she thought. Or perhaps it was the new guilt she carried. Either way she was unlikely to get back to sleep just yet.

Izolda slipped on her dressing gown and ventured out on to the landing. She loved Sochi, which was fortunate as it was one of the few vacation destinations that Vladimir was able to travel to without risk. The mansion was a large, lavish building, but nothing compared to the home she shared with Vladimir outside of Moscow. That house was huge beyond need or luxury. They had an entire wing that housed the full-time maid, chef, butler, driver, groundskeeper and bodyguards. The rest of the Moscow dacha was shared by just herself and Vladimir. She didn't know how many rooms there were and sometimes weeks could go by without her using some of them. Those bedrooms she and Vladimir had once designated as nurseries, she hadn't ventured into for years.

Izolda switched on lights as she went. She may have been a grown woman but she was on edge from the nightmare and being in an isolated dacha didn't help keep her imagination in check. Her slippers muffled her footsteps on the red oak flooring.

Faint light emanating from the study told her where she would find Vladimir. He looked up when she entered. He was sitting behind his desk, dressed in silk pyjamas, and facing the open door. Some men looked better as they aged; though Vladimir was perhaps not one of them, the grey in his hair did lend him a certain dignified presence, and the lines in his face added character to his somewhat blunt features. But he was still as strong and powerful as he had ever been.

It was the computer monitor that provided the light. Vladimir clicked the mouse and removed his earbuds.

'Izzy,' he said. 'I thought you were fast asleep.'

She leaned against the doorframe. 'I had a nightmare.'

'My poor baby.' He looked so concerned. 'What was it about?'

'I don't remember.'

'Isn't that the best way?'

She shrugged. 'What are you doing up at this time of night?'

An expression passed over Vladimir's face that was both happy and sad at the same time. 'Just work, my love. Just work.'

'Can't that wait until morning? We're on vacation, aren't we?'

'It's not urgent,' he said. 'But I couldn't get to sleep and thought I might as well make use of my insomnia. I hope I didn't wake you when I got out of bed.'

Izolda shook her head. 'No, no. I didn't realise you weren't there until the nightmare woke me. How long have you been up?'

'Not long.'

'Oh, I thought—'

Vladimir smiled and said, 'You looked so cute when I left. You were snoring.'

'*I was not.*'

'You were.'

'I don't snore.' She smiled, shyly. 'I'm a lady.'

'A very beautiful lady.'

She couldn't help but smile wider. 'I can't sleep if you're not there. Come back to bed, please.'

'Give me five minutes to finish up and I'll be in. How does that sound, my love?'

Kasakov watched Izolda turn and leave. He didn't like lying to his wife, but sometimes it was unavoidable. He was not working. Burliuk and Eltsina were running the business in his absence and he'd left instructions he was not to be disturbed under any circumstances. Burliuk had been opposed to Kasakov taking a vacation when they were in the middle of trying to repair the damage done by the many attacks the network had suffered in the past few weeks, but Kasakov had gone regardless. He didn't have the patience to deal with scared employees and North Koreans who were furious their order had been delayed, and even angrier to learn they would only receive eighteen fighter jets instead of the promised twenty. That mark to Kasakov's reputation would take a lot of work to repair.

He hadn't lied about his inability to sleep. However, it wasn't his business that kept him awake, nor was it his nephew's death; with Illarion avenged, he was finally at peace on that score. No, it was his wife who occupied Kasakov's thoughts. Her reluctance to concede to his advances had not gone unnoticed, nor had the increased frequency of shopping trips and salon visits and lunches with friends.

Her footsteps were too quiet for Kasakov to hear, so he waited a couple of minutes to make sure she wasn't going to suddenly reappear before reinserting his earbuds. He settled into his chair and clicked the mouse to continue the video. The recording had been made using a sophisticated camera, as Kasakov had requested, and both the picture quality and sound were excellent, even if the camerawork could have been better. Had it occurred to him beforehand he would have hired a professional cinematographer to handle the shoot. However, given the video's content, such an individual would probably have been impossible to find.

Kasakov had watched an hour of footage already and there was another two hours to go. He would check on Izolda shortly to make sure she was asleep. If she wasn't, he would climb into bed with her and wait until she was snoring again before returning to the video. This was the second time Kasakov had viewed it, and like any good movie he was able to appreciate it even more on a repeat viewing.

He blinked away tears and closed his eyes to picture Illarion's face while through the earbuds flowed the exquisite screams of Ariff and his family.

CHAPTER 50

It had rained all week. Victor lay in the undergrowth that covered the outcrop. With the limited viewpoint over the back of the dacha, Victor hadn't seen the arms dealer arrive, but had become aware of Kasakov's guards patrolling the property. Soon afterwards, Victor glimpsed the Ukrainian as he passed one of the visible window on the second floor, but he didn't loiter long enough for Victor to put the binoculars down and shoot accurately. Victor hadn't expected to complete the contract with such a shot, but that was why he'd trimmed the trees that screened the house.

A very beautiful woman accompanied Kasakov, who from the dossier Victor knew to be his wife, Izolda. She was tall and slim, carrying herself with the confidence of a runway model. There were no other guests. Victor counted five bodyguards in total, just as he'd been told there would be. They slept in the guesthouse in shifts, so there were always at least three awake and ready. As in Minsk, they weren't particularly big, but spec ops and intelligence guys usually weren't. Each had the gait and manner of a serious operator, and the dossier stated that Kasakov had a penchant for hiring ex-Spetsnaz soldiers. Victor's last run-in with the Spetsnaz was not something he was eager to repeat.

He lay in a shallow between two trees on the highpoint. With binoculars, he continuously watched the rear of the dacha. The branches he'd cleared provided a small corridor of space through the otherwise overlapping foliage of the three trees. The line of sight was far from ideal, but he could see the back entrance and a thin sliver of ground outside of it. A limited view, but enough to put a bullet into Kasakov should he use the door.

Victor had prepared the ground by removing stones and branches from where he would be lying and landscaping the soil flat. He knew he could be in the same spot for several days and every annoying lump and bump on the first day would be agony by the fifth. Any distraction had the potential to throw a shot and he wanted to squeeze the trigger just once and be gone.

Birds chirped above his head. They were used to his presence now, not scaring even when he was forced to move. A water-proof sheet stretched across the two trees formed a makeshift shelter. It only partially covered him, due to where he needed to lie, but it kept some of the rain off and allowed him to keep his weapons and equipment dry.

The CIA-supplied rifle Victor planned to kill Kasakov with was a Dakota T-76 Longbow chambered for .338 calibre Lapua Magnum ammunition. Victor wanted to be able to kill Kasakov from as far away as possible and, short of using a huge .50 calibre, a .338 offered the best range and power. The .338 Lapua Magnum was designed to penetrate five layers of military body armour at one thousand metres and have enough force left for a one-shot kill. Victor knew from painful experience the round's effectiveness against supposedly bulletproof glass.

As well as generating over five thousand pounds of muzzle energy, the Longbow was extremely accurate. The manufacturers even guaranteed .5 minutes of arc at fifteen hundred metres. It was an impressive claim but Victor would be shooting from half that. As long as he did his part, the Longbow would deliver.

He wouldn't be using a suppressor, to guarantee accuracy and killing ability, and a .338 made a lot of noise. The back door was seven hundred and twenty yards away so the sound of the shot would reach the dacha a little under two seconds after the bullet left the barrel. He could potentially get another two shots off before the noise reached the area, but Victor favoured doing things right the first time.

The Longbow came with a matte black finish that he'd sprayed with green and brown paint. He was dressed in the same green Gore-Tex clothes as he'd worn for his reconnaissance of the dacha's grounds. They hadn't been washed and Victor hadn't bathed. He didn't want the smell of soap and shampoo to alert the local wildlife and give him away if Kasakov's bodyguards were extra diligent and patrolled outside of the mansion's grounds.

A nearby rucksack contained rations and other equipment. In the pockets of his tactical harness were full magazines, a torch, waterproof matches, binoculars, compass, GPS reader and a combat knife. He had a bottle and plastic bags to serve as a toilet. There was no way of knowing when Kasakov might appear within Victor's limited target area and he couldn't afford to move in case the call of nature coincided with that moment.

Should things go wrong, either with the kill or the extraction, Victor had two other guns to assist him. Strapped to his right thigh was a tactical holster containing the Heckler & Koch MK23. Near to the rucksack was an MP7A1 with a forty-round box magazine. The MK23 was a fine handgun, designed to meet the requirements of US Special Operations forces. It fired the .45 ACP cartridge and had a twelve-round capacity. The gun was very accurate, considered match grade, capable of two-inch groups at fifty yards. The .45 ACP also struck with substantial stopping power but was naturally subsonic and almost silent when shot from a suppressor.

The MP7, also made by Heckler & Koch, fell somewhere between a sub-machine gun and an assault rifle, and had the designation of a personal defence weapon. In Victor's opinion such a designation was an awkward one. There was nothing defensive about the gun. The MP7 was all about offence. Lightweight at 4.19 pounds, and just over twenty-three inches in length with the stock collapsed, the gun was effective beyond four hundred yards. It was chambered for the high velocity 4.6 x 30 mm round, which dismissed lead and brass in favour of a hardened steel penetrator, making it better suited for use against targets in body armour than the traditional pistol-calibre ammunition used in regular sub-machine guns.

Kasakov's men had worn body armour in Bucharest and if Victor had to tangle with them he didn't want his bullets lodging in their vests. Using a suppressor would have been pointless with the high-velocity ammunition and using subsonic rounds would have countered the benefits of using the MP7 in the first place.

So far, Kasakov hadn't stepped outside the back door, which wasn't surprising as it had rained continuously since the Ukrainian's arrival. Lying in wait for hour after hour was boring, but Victor did not let his concentration lapse. With his restricted line of sight, he needed to stay focused at all times. The second after Kasakov fell he would be fleeing north-easterly through the trees, hiking two miles around the hillside to where his getaway vehicle was hidden off road, beneath a net covered with leaves, branches and earth.

His diet consisted of nuts, chocolate and supplement pills. He wanted maximum calories and protein in a minimum of food to limit time spent with a plastic bag. He had brought a one-gallon water bottle, which was set up with a funnel to catch rainwater to top up as he drank. Water purification tablets would be mixed with his urine if it didn't rain enough to keep him hydrated.

He flexed his muscles regularly and adjusted his prone position every hour to keep from getting too stiff and to help against the inevitable aches. As Kasakov was less likely to emerge through the back door during the night, this was when Victor slept. He had a small air cushion to lay his head on, but no sleeping bag or tent. Such things were great for keeping warm and dry but not for aiding fast movement if surprised. He slept for a few hours at a time, always to be awoken by some sound or cramp.

There had been no sign of Kasakov's men patrolling the woods outside the dacha's walls, but there was a lot of wood-

397

land and Spetsnaz guys knew how to keep a low profile. Victor wouldn't expect to see them unless they were close by. He kept the MP7 within reach for just such an occasion.

It hadn't rained this morning and the air was dry and relatively warm. The weather forecast he'd read before beginning his wait had predicted clear skies and hot temperatures, and from what he could see of the sky through the canopy, it looked blue and clear. If the forecast was accurate, hopefully it would be warm enough to go for a swim in the outside pool. Even if only Izolda liked to swim, her husband was more than likely to step outside to at least accompany her. Victor's preference wasn't to kill targets in front of loved ones, but this time it might be unavoidable. He had to take the first opportunity that came his way. Because there might not be a second.

Victor threw some nuts into his mouth and waited.

Nearby, a man watched. He was an American. He wore Universal Camouflage Pattern military fatigues, jungle boots and head sock. Over his jacket, he wore a hooded poncho customised to form a ghillie suit. Sewn and glued on to the poncho was a fine nylon net. Attached to the net were rough six-inch burlap flaps of varying shades of green and brown. Twigs and leaves were distributed among the flaps and held in place with dried mud. Burlap flaps were also glued to the arms and legs of his fatigues. A thick layer of camouflage grease covered his face and hands.

Four days before he had discovered a thin path of squashed detritus in the grounds of the dacha and knew exactly who had created the trail. It had led him to the hide he now watched.

The target, though unaware he was being observed, was alert and skilled. Even with the aid of the ghillie suit, which broke up the American's silhouette in three dimensions and made him all but invisible, he kept low in the undergrowth and didn't risk getting any closer.

The American was armed with a Heckler & Koch MP5SD-N1 camouflaged with green and brown paint and using leaves and branches as stencils to break up the weapon's lines. The N1 variant of the sub-machine gun featured a retractable metal butt stock, three-round burst trigger group and a stainless-steel integrated suppressor made by Knight Armament Company. As close to silent as any firearm could hope to get, it was the perfect weapon for a close-quarters engagement. A single squeeze of the trigger could put three 9 mm Parabellums in the target, and although the stopping power of the 9 mm round was significantly reduced flying at subsonic speeds, the overlapping of the hydrostatic shock waves on internal organs due to three bullets hitting the target almost at the same time more than made up for it.

'This is Cowboy Daddy,' a gravelly voice said through his earpiece, 'Cowboy Gamma, gimme a sitrep. Over.'

Another voice answered, 'Cowboy Gamma. I'm ten metres south-east of the guesthouse. No sign of Mr and Mrs VIP yet. A gorilla is on patrol near the swimming pool. Over.'

'Copy that, Cowboy Gamma,' the gravelly voice replied. 'Let me know when you have eyes on Mr and Mrs VIP. What's the target's status, Cowboy Bravo? Over.'

'Cowboy Bravo. The target is awake and having himself some breakfast. He has absolutely no idea his ticket is gonna get punched. Over.'

CHAPTER 51

Kasakov stirred from his sleep and groaned. His face was buried in a big goose-down pillow. One of Izolda's slender arms was draped across his waist. He lay still for a minute, enjoying the intimate feel of his wife's limb, the softness of her skin, the warmth of her flesh. When Kasakov rolled on to his back, the movement roused a sleepy moan from his wife. He gently kissed her on the forehead, the tip of her little nose, and then finally on the lips. She smiled and kissed him back. He found her especially beautiful first thing in the morning when only he got to see her.

'What time is it?' she asked, eyes still closed.

'Just before eight.'

'Wow,' she said with raised eyebrows, 'and you're still here in bed. I'm honoured.'

'I'm on vacation, aren't I?'

'Does that mean you won't answer the phone when Yuliya and Tomasz call?'

'I'll do my best. How does that sound?'

She grunted. They kissed again.

Kasakov sat up and yawned. 'What would you like for breakfast, my love?'

She stroked his wide chest. 'Hmm, your famous scrambled eggs, please. Plus orange juice and some melon. And coffee, lots of coffee.'

'A veritable banquet.' He scratched the back of his head. 'What might I receive in return for preparing such a feast?'

Izolda gave a cheeky grin. 'You get the pleasure of making it and bringing it to your gorgeous wife.'

'Ah,' Kasakov said, 'sustenance enough for any man.'

'You had better believe it.'

He climbed out of bed and opened the drapes. The dacha's master bedroom was at the front of the house and the window provided a breathtaking view of the Black Sea. Kasakov stretched as he stared outwards at gulls circling near the shoreline.

This was his favourite part of the country. Sochi had sandy beaches, the climate was as hot as it got in Russia, and the nearby Caucasus Mountains offered excellent skiing. Kasakov came with Izolda at least a couple of times a year, though he kept away from the tourist-heavy city itself, as well as the havens where Russia's elite frivolously spent their wealth. He preferred the isolation his dacha provided. It had its own private beach, accessible via a path through the woods, where he could relax without the bother of other people, and especially their children.

He'd bought the house when the international efforts to bring him down started to pick up momentum. He hadn't left the country for any purpose other than the most important business trips since then; the risks were so great that even those trips were growing less frequent, and only then to nations who wouldn't go running to the UN.

'What's the weather like?' Izolda asked.

'Blue sky, sunshine,' Kasakov answered. 'It's going to be nice for once.'

'Great,' Izolda said. 'I think I might have a swim after breakfast.'

Victor glimpsed a blur passing by one of the mansion's visible upstairs windows, which he recognised to be Kasakov's wife by the slightness of the silhouette. Kasakov's large frame followed a moment later, but again did so too fast to risk a shot, especially when the temperature was continuing to rise and the sky remained clear of rainclouds. Another ten degrees and it would be perfect weather to use the swimming pool.

The Dakota Longbow lay directly next to Victor, shielded from the elements by a waterproof sheet weighed down with small rocks. When the time came, it would take but a split second to whip the sheet away and prepare for the shot. The sight was already set for the distance. There was little wind at the moment. Maybe two and a half miles per hour.

Aside from the pleasant chirping of the birds above his head, there was no other sound. In other circumstances, Victor would have enjoyed camping in the forest. Maybe one day he would come back to Sochi and do just that, only far away from here.

He used a straw to drink some water while he watched the dacha. Soon the job would be complete and Victor's obligation to his nameless employer finally over.

One squeeze of the trigger and he would be a free man again.

The American using the call sign Cowboy Bravo remained kneeling in the undergrowth approximately twenty yards to the right of the target's position. From his elevation and angle, the man in the ghillie suit could only see the target's legs, elbows and half of the binoculars. The rest of him was hidden by the undergrowth, trees and rain sheet, but there was no need to keep a more complete view. The American saw enough to maintain eyes on the target.

He only needed to see more when the order came to complete the kill.

The American's earpiece crackled. 'This is Cowboy Daddy. Gimme a sitrep, Cowboys. Over.'

Another voice whispered, 'Cowboy Gamma, I'm eight metres south-west of the main building, alongside the shed. I can see Mr and Mrs VIP through the kitchen window, fixing coffee. Two gorillas are out and about. Mrs VIP is wearing a swimsuit, over.'

'This is Cowboy Bravo,' the man in the ghillie suit answered. 'I'm exactly nineteen metres north of the target. Ready and waiting. Over.'

'Copy that,' Cowboy Daddy replied. 'Cowboy Gamma, maintain your visual on Mr VIP. When he drops, you let us know and we can finish up here. If our boy is waiting for Mr VIP to step outside, today could be the day. Maintain focus, Bravo. Out.'

The American was patient but looked forward to fulfilling the mission. It would be simple.

One squeeze of the trigger and the target was a dead man.

*

Izolda finished her breakfast and kissed her husband on the cheek. They were sitting side by side at the breakfast bar of the dacha's kitchen.

'That was divine, Vladimir,' she said. 'Thank you.'

Kasakov nodded and slurped some coffee. 'Always a pleasure.'

She wrapped her thin arms around his huge shoulders, stretching to lock her fingers together. She kissed him again. 'I'm so glad we came away. I wasn't sure it was such a good idea with how strained things have been between us recently, but it's been wonderful.'

'And now the sun is shining it will only get better.'

She grinned. 'It's a shame we can't live here. It's much nicer here than in Moscow. There's no noise, no stress, no distractions. Just the two of us. In Moscow I have to share you with all your business associates, and you've been so busy lately it's as if you'd forgotten I even existed.'

He covered her hands with his. 'I could never forget about you.'

'I didn't mean it quite like that. I just meant you've been so distracted it's lovely to have your full attention again. I've finally got you all to myself and I'm going to make the most of it.'

'Is that right?'

She raised her eyebrows. 'Oh yes.'

'Well,' Kasakov began, 'I'm glad it's nice to have my attention again, because you're going to be getting a lot more of it.'

She eyed him suspiciously. 'And what does that mean?'

He took a deep breath and said, 'I think it's about time I took a step back from the business.'

She released him from the hug and turned on her stool to

better face him. Instead of looking happy, the way he'd hoped she would look, she appeared unconvinced. 'Really?'

Kasakov nodded. 'Why not? We have so much money it would take forever just to count it all. And besides, I'm tired of it all. I'm so tired.'

Izolda was shaking her head, not in disagreement but disbelief. 'I don't know what to say. This is so sudden.'

'I've spent my whole life planning for every last detail. It's about time I was spontaneous.'

'What will you do with your company?'

Kasakov shrugged. 'Tomasz and Yuliya can handle things without me. I'll still own it, of course, but they can run it. I've got a horrible feeling they could do a better job than me anyway.'

'You really mean this, don't you?'

He nodded. 'It's taken a long time, but I've come to understand that some things really are more important than money or power. I never want to lose you, Izzy.'

She was silent for a moment. 'You're not going to lose me.' She didn't look at him when she said, 'Why would you even say that?'

He gently stroked her cheek. 'I'm not a fool, my love. I know I haven't been the husband you deserve. I've allowed things to come between us. My company, Illarion's death, our *problem*.' He swallowed heavily and she squeezed his hand. 'Things have happened recently that have altered my perspective somewhat. I won't go into the details; all you need to know is that I've changed. And, I think it's about time I acknowledged that our problem is really my problem. These days, doctors can fix anything. And if not, there are other ways to conceive. It's not too late.' Kasakov pulled Izolda close to him and held her tightly. 'I'm so sorry I pushed you away.'

He felt her tears on his shoulder.

Just after nine a.m. Victor watched Izolda Kasakov emerge through the dacha's back door. She was a vision wearing a patterned silk kimono, wide-brimmed hat, and large sunglasses. Her feet were bare, toenails ruby red. She carried a glass of what looked like iced tea with a slice of lime. She sucked the iced tea through a long straw and approached the swimming pool, disappearing from Victor's line of sight. He imagined her taking a seat on one of the sun loungers while she finished her tea. No sign of Kasakov.

Victor cracked his neck and sipped some more water. The temperature was in the low seventies by now, even under the shade of the forest canopy. The breeze was still light and helped keep Victor cool. Birds sang overhead. Victor's ornithology knowledge was basic at best and he had no idea of the species, but he found their chirping especially pleasant and it helped relax him while he continued his long wait.

An hour passed, then two. Izolda Kasakov re-entered Victor's field of view. This time she was wearing nothing other than a black swimsuit. Her hair was damp and hung past her shoulder blades. She entered the house, closing the back door behind her.

As midday came and went, the temperature continued to rise. Victor wiped the sweat from his eyes with a sleeve. The breeze had picked up, but it was still hot. The heat made him feel tired but he remained focused. At random intervals he grabbed the rifle and centred the reticule over the doorway so when it came to it the movement would be fast and fluid.

At two p.m. Izolda appeared again. She was in her swimsuit still, but now a shawl wrapped around her waist covered her legs. She carried a plate topped with a salad. Again, no Kasakov. Izolda left the back door open. Perhaps for her husband to follow.

Victor hadn't seen Kasakov since he passed the window hours before. For all he knew, the Ukrainian could have gone out for the day, but guesswork was inherently problematic. Victor had faith in his plan. Whether it took an hour or a week, Kasakov would eventually step out of the dacha's back door.

Twenty minutes later, Izolda stepped back into view and stood in the open doorway. A bodyguard walked past her, patrolling the grounds, doing circuits of the mansion. He was armed with a compact AK74SU and wearing a level III Kevlar vest over his T-shirt. He spent longer than was tactically prudent checking out Mrs Kasakov as he went by. Victor couldn't help but smile. Even the best bodyguards money could buy were still only human.

From the way Izolda was leaning against the doorframe and gesticulating, Victor could tell she was talking with someone he took to be her husband. With his spare hand, Victor pulled the sheet off the Dakota and drew the rifle closer.

A silhouette appeared on the far side of Izolda.

Immediately Victor examined the sway of the tree branches on the lawn behind the house, estimating there was a ten mile an hour crosswind. He knew that with the .338 calibre round that would equate to around a twenty-five-inch displacement at seven hundred yards. He exchanged the binoculars for the rifle, adjusted the windage dial on the Longbow's scope to compensate for the displacement, and positioned himself so his right eye was an inch from the eyepiece. He closed his left.

The American with the call sign Cowboy Bravo watched as the target readied the rifle, and said into his throat mic, 'Cowboy Bravo. The target has taken up his weapon. This doesn't look like a drill. I think he's getting ready to shoot. Over.'

'Cowboy Daddy. Roger that, Bravo. Can you confirm that Mr VIP is exposed, Gamma? Over.'

'This is Cowboy Gamma. Hold on, I lost sight of Mr and Mrs VIP to avoid a gorilla. I'm re-establishing a visual. I can hear them talking. Yes, I can see him in the kitchen near the door. He's approaching it now. Looks like he's going to step outside. He's definitely going to step outside the door. Over.'

'Copy that, Cowboy Bravo,' Cowboy Daddy's gravelly voice answered. 'When he does, you can bet your bottom dollar our boy is going to drop that son of a bitch with one through the cranium. This is it. Be ready. I'm moving into killing range from the south of the target. Do the same from the north, Cowboy Bravo. Out.'

The American rose from his kneeling position and carefully approached the target, moving in a semicircle to come at him from behind. He released the safety on his MP5 and checked the selector was switched to three-round burst.

The silhouette behind Izolda stepped out of the shadows. Vladimir Kasakov was stripped to the waist and wearing long swimming shorts. His huge torso was covered in hair. His wife blocked a good deal of him, but Victor centred the reticule between Kasakov's eyebrows and breathed slow and steady. His heart rate fell. He concentrated on its rhythm, timing himself, finger poised to squeeze in the pause between beats, ready for when Izolda had moved out of the way.

Victor watched as she took a glass of iced tea from her husband and then stepped backwards and away from the door to allow Kasakov to exit. The big Ukrainian emerged through the doorway.

The birds stopped singing above Victor.

He squeezed the Longbow's trigger.

CHAPTER 52

Something whizzed past the right side of Kasakov's head, followed by a loud *thunk*, as if a nail had been hammered into the wood. He flinched in surprise, but didn't understand what any of it meant. He put a hand to his ear and turned on the spot, confused.

'Are you okay?' Izolda asked.

'Yes,' Kasakov replied. 'I think a wasp flew past me.' He stared, confused, at a small hole in the doorframe. The edges were frayed. 'Has this hole always . . . ?'

A sound like thunder rolled over them.

Kasakov and Izolda looked at each other.

'What was that?' she asked, sipping some iced tea and looking skyward.

Kasakov looked too. There were a few clouds, but certainly no storm clouds. What caused the thunder?

'Maybe it was a plane,' Izolda suggested.

A window shattered to Kasakov's left and Izolda let out a surprised yelp. She dropped her glass and it shattered on the paving slabs. Shards of glass and ice cubes scattered across the ground. Iced tea spread out in a puddle.

Brickwork exploded. Kasakov flinched as fragments pelted his arm and back.

A second sound like thunder echoed. Concern spread across Kasakov's face.

'*What the hell?*'

One of their bodyguards came running around the side of the dacha.

'*GET DOWN,*' he yelled, gesturing frantically with both hands, '*GET DOWN.*'

Izolda screamed. Kasakov cursed himself for being slow to understand and charged in his wife's direction. He threw her to the ground and lay on top to shield her.

Another gunshot filled the air.

So close to the fired rifle, the sound of the gunshots was loud enough to sting the ears of the American with the call sign Cowboy Bravo. He was barely ten feet behind the target, the iron sights of the MP5 lined up to put a triangle of rounds through his spine when the command was given, which should be any second now.

'*Cowboy Gamma, this is Cowboy Daddy,*' a voice spat through his earpiece. '*Shots have been fired. Gimme me a fuckin' sitrep. Over.*'

'He missed,' Cowboy Gamma replied. 'Goddamn missed with all three shots. Mr and Mrs VIP have realised what's happening and are on the ground. Bodyguards are securing them. Over.'

'*Shit,*' Cowboy Daddy said back. 'I thought this guy was

411

supposed to be good. Cowboy Bravo, hold your position. Do not shoot, repeat, do not shoot the asshole. We can't kill our target until he kills his own. Out.'

Victor lost sight of Kasakov and his wife. They both hit the deck soon after the third shot had drilled a hole in the dacha's brickwork. At least three bodyguards were now on scene, shielding their protectees until it was safe to get them out of the area. They were looking Victor's way as the hillside was the most logical place for a sniper to be positioned, but he was too far away to be spotted. In return, Victor couldn't see even a square inch of Kasakov.

He grabbed the MP7 and sprinted forward in the dacha's direction.

Cowboy Bravo whispered into his throat-mic, 'This is Cowboy Bravo. The target has ditched the rifle and is on the move towards the mansion with an SMG. Looks like he's going to do this from up close and personal. Over.'

'Roger that,' Cowboy Daddy replied. 'Follow him and maintain a visual. Out.'

The American rounded the two trees where the target had been lying, and gave chase down the steep front of the highpoint. The target was running fast, heading west down the hillside, maybe fifteen yards ahead, darting through the undergrowth, crushing shrubs and bending and snapping slim branches as he ran.

The hillside was relatively steep with jutting protrusions of rock and jagged steps covered in a thick layer of soil and detritus.

Thin-trunked trees rose into the sky all around him. Between them shrubs and other plant life competed for the light filtering through the canopy. Moss spread across tree trunks, fallen branches and rocky areas. Victor sprinted as fast as he could without stumbling, dodging trees, ducking branches, jumping rocks.

He spotted a fallen tree up ahead – saw it was perfect – and manoeuvred towards where it lay. He leaped up and over it, dropped down on the other side, spun around and into a firing position.

As he expected, a shape was running through the trees behind him, sixteen yards out, following Victor's path, hard to see at first, half-hidden by trees, blending well into the surrounding vegetation due to a ghillie suit, but unmistakably a man with an MP5SD.

The sudden turn took Victor's pursuer completely by surprise.

Automatic gunfire echoed through the forest.

The man in the ghillie suit danced momentarily as he was struck by a burst of 4.7 mm high-velocity rounds, then fell out of sight, leaving a mist of blood hanging in the air.

Victor's gaze swept from left to right, knowing there would be more of them. He saw another blur of movement through the undergrowth. Another man in a ghillie suit, twenty yards away at Victor's ten o'clock. The underbrush was thick and tall around him. Like the first man, the fact he was running gave Victor the chance to distinguish him from the surrounding vegetation. The second man had a half-second extra to react over the other guy and was dropping low as Victor fired, 4.6 mm bullets missing and blowing bark from a nearby tree.

The man shot back. There was virtually no noise or muzzle flash due to the fat integrated suppressor of the MP5SD. Bullets zipped over Victor's head. He crouched lower, maximising the cover of the fallen tree. He shot back, again missing, but this time hitting close enough to convince the shooter to back off into harder cover.

Victor had his left forearm resting on the horizontal tree trunk, gaze fixed along the MP7's sights at the area in which the gunman had disappeared. If he backtracked up the hill, Victor would see him, but if he moved laterally, the gunman could stay hidden in the mass of shrubs and tall plants. The trees there were thin but plentiful. Victor's eyes flicked towards any swaying limb or falling leaf.

He knew he was fortunate to still be alive. If the guy Victor had shot hadn't disturbed the birds in the trees above the high-point and stopped them singing, Victor would have put a .338 Lapua Magnum through Kasakov's skull as planned, and in return would have been shot where he lay. After noticing the sudden quiet Victor understood he was no longer alone and that he still breathed was a clear sign whoever disturbed the birds was waiting for Kasakov to die before acting.

One down. Another close by. Victor didn't know how many there were in total, but there had to be at least one more he hadn't encountered keeping a visual on Kasakov to confirm when he was dead. Which meant that one was now behind Victor, but maybe almost seven hundred yards away. He could forget about him for the moment.

Three bullets plugged holes in the fallen tree just beneath his arm. He didn't see the muzzle flash – the MP5SD's suppressor substantially reduced it. He couldn't see the shooter either. The ghillie suit guy was so well camouflaged he was almost invisible. Victor shot a burst back, ejected shell cases ricocheting off the tree trunk, and got his head down behind it. He pushed a hand through the plant life and scooped up some damp soil. He rubbed it over his face and neck, closing his eyes to make sure his eyelids weren't missed out.

He knew his attackers weren't Mossad. Kidon assassins would have just grabbed him while he slept and taken him someplace dark and quiet to slice every last shred of information from him. They obviously weren't Kasakov's men either. Any other enemies Victor had wouldn't have been waiting for him to kill Kasakov first. There was only one person who would want both Kasakov and Victor dead.

He emptied his mind of the thought. He had to concentrate. Adrenalin was flooding Victor's veins and he breathed slow and steady to control its effects. He needed his pulse lower than his body wanted it. A rapid heart rate would help him run faster, but it wasn't going to keep his aim steady.

More bullets slammed into the tree trunk shielding him. Splinters of wood and pieces of bark were blasted into the air and rained down over him. He stayed where he was, knowing subsonic 9 mm rounds had no chance of penetrating through the thick trunk. Even his supersonic armour-piercing rounds wouldn't, but the MP7 easily out-ranged an MP5SD. The problem was that contacts in this kind of terrain were almost exclusively from very close range. With the trees and undergrowth restricting line of sight to sub thirty yards, Victor couldn't make his fire superiority pay off. The virtually silent weapon of his attacker, with its almost eliminated muzzle flash, was far better suited to the fight than Victor's own gun.

He shuffled to his left until he was close enough to the stump of the fallen tree to pop his head and gun around the side and out of cover. His gaze scanned the area where he'd last seen his enemy, but before he could spot the shooter, rounds were coming his way, slicing through foliage, thudding into the ground. He rolled back into cover.

The gunman was firing from an elevated position, twenty-five yards out, and was perfectly camouflaged. Any time Victor emerged out of cover he would take longer to acquire his target than his enemy would. And in Victor's experience, whoever shot second in a firefight died first. If he was going to make it out of this, he needed to take away at least one of his attacker's advantages before the third shooter got involved.

He jumped up, ran, weaving between the trees, veering right and east in a wide curve taking him back up the hill, the muscles in his legs burning as they powered him forward. Bullets followed him, blasting off bark and chopping down thin branches, but the trees and undergrowth were great concealment and cover, and he was a fast target.

When he was at the same elevation as his attacker, Victor dived to the ground behind a thick tree. He then shuffled backwards and then sideways through the undergrowth, moving two yards further up the hill. The gunman wasn't going to stay in the same place for long and if he moved, he would ascend, not descend.

Victor inched forward, crawling with his knees and elbows. The ground was rocky. The woods were quiet. He heard the gentle rustle of leaves, his own breathing and nothing else. So low to the ground, the dense vegetation concealed him completely but also impeded his view. He positioned himself so he could peer through the tangle of plants and branches to see the shooter's last known location. Victor set his gaze along the sights of the MP7 and waited.

Ten seconds later, he saw movement. He couldn't see the guy in the ghillie suit but he saw a healthy leaf float to the ground. Victor squeezed the MP7's trigger, unleashing three bursts of 4.6 mm rounds into the thicket. He watched twigs and leaves shred but couldn't see if he'd hit his target.

Rounds whizzing over his head gave him the answer. From Victor's position, the shooter was impossible to see. He couldn't see any undergrowth damaged by the bullets' paths either. Foliage exploded next to Victor's head. He fired again, fanning bullets across the thicket, aiming low, knowing the gunman would be close to the ground like he was. The return fire stopped. At the very least, he'd forced his enemy to keep his head down too.

He strained to see where the firing had come from, but this guy was too good and too well hidden. He was keeping still and low, not relying on the ghillie suit to keep him unseen but making the best of the terrain as well. Professional, former military, experienced. Highly trained.

Against such an opponent, if nothing changed, there was only one possible result. Victor crawled backwards again until he was in the cover of a shallow depression. Thick roots protruded from the earth around him. He wiped sweat from his eyes and reloaded the MP7. The magazine wasn't empty, but there were only maybe six or seven rounds left. It was hard to keep an exact count on automatic. He had three magazines in total and slid the mostly empty mag back into his harness in case those six or seven rounds turned out to be the difference between life and death.

The shooter had shot seven identical bursts in a short time frame. MP5s had a three-round burst setting, so twenty-one rounds had been fired so far. Nine left, if he hadn't reloaded by now, which he probably hadn't as nine was almost a third of a mag. Three bursts remaining. Not as few as Victor would like, but it would have to do. If the shooter had in fact reloaded this was going to be a short run.

Victor turned around, got up into a crouch, and sprinted out from cover, moving north along the hillside, weaving as much as he could. He heard the rapid clicks of the SMG firing behind him and bullets tearing through vegetation.

He kept running north. Branches snagged his clothes and scratched his face. More rounds flew his way, ripping through leaves, slamming into tree trunks. Fragments of bark bounced off the back of his neck.

Then the firing stopped suddenly and Victor knew the guy was out of ammo. He powered on. The trees were less densely set but the undergrowth was thicker, slowing him down. A knee-high layer utterly covered the ground. Shrubs and saplings taller than Victor emerged from the carpet of plant life.

His getaway vehicle was two miles away. The gunman couldn't reload and run at the same pace as Victor, but he wouldn't chase with an empty weapon. That few seconds' lead would be enough for Victor to get out of his enemy's range and safely to the car. He wanted to get hold of his attacker to interrogate him for information, but playing hide and seek with a skilled operator dressed in a ghillie suit and armed with a suppressed weapon was a game Victor couldn't hope to win.

The shooter would have reloaded by now and had another

thirty rounds to play with, but he was forty or fifty yards away. In range of the MP5SD, but Victor was out of sight with too much vegetation in the way to make a shot at that distance. He was home free.

Movement caught Victor's eye – the sway of branches not caused by the breeze.

The third gunman appeared, twenty yards ahead, weapon raised, turning Victor's way.

CHAPTER 53

Spotting the swaying branches gave Victor enough warning to throw himself to the ground before the shooting started. Virtually silent again. Blasted leaves and chunks of shrubbery dropped down over his back and head. He rolled to his left, down the hillside for the quickest way to get out of the line of fire.

The new arrival had covered the distance fast, coordinating his movements with the other shooter through headsets so he could cut Victor off. But sprinting seven hundred yards through a forest and up a hill, with a ten-foot-high wall to scale in between, would have taken something out of the gunman, regardless of his fitness levels. His heart rate would be sky high, and his aim comparatively poor. Not that he needed to be a good shot to keep Victor pinned while the other shooter closed in.

With one twenty yards ahead, another maybe forty yards behind but closing fast, Victor had only two directions left to go. Going left meant giving his attackers the higher ground, and five hundred yards away was a wall he couldn't climb before taking bullets in the back, and beyond it five armed bodyguards. Right meant running against elevation up the hill, and a slow target became a dead one fast. But he couldn't stay where he was either. Not when every passing second gave the other gunman time to catch up and get into killing range.

Victor chose right, ran, keeping low. Rounds from the newly arrived attacker ripped through the undergrowth as he moved, but far enough away to tell him the shooter was either less adept than his partner or his accuracy was greatly suffering from a thumping heart and too much adrenalin. Victor pumped his legs as hard as he could, fighting gravity as he scrambled up the hill, knowing that if he tripped or slowed, his enemy wouldn't keep missing. Victor almost slipped on a mossy stretch of rock, but kept sprinting until he reached a tree big enough to take cover behind. He stood side-on to maximise its protection while he took huge gulps of air. He'd out-manoeuvred one attacker, but couldn't out-manoeuvre two capable of communicating with each other.

The tree had a trunk that split into two, protruding from the earth at a forty-five-degree angle. The twin trunks twisted over and under each other. Victor positioned himself behind the thickest part of the trunks and peered through the gap between them. A lizard scurried away.

He glimpsed the second gunman hurrying his way, closing while his target was cowering behind cover. The gunman was about thirty yards out, half-buried in the underbrush, weapon up and ready, pointing in Victor's direction. He was camouflaged in a ghillie suit and had an MP5SD just like the other two. With his left shoulder against the tree trunks, Victor quickly leaned out of cover and squeezed off a burst. The guy dived from sight.

Victor turned around, knowing the first shooter would take the opportunity to close the distance. It took a second to spot him, moving from tree to tree, low but fast, rushing but composed. Victor fired just as the gunman went out of sight behind a mass of low-hanging branches. Armour-piercing rounds blasted through the foliage. Victor hadn't expected to hit either man – hitting fast-moving targets in a heavy-cover environment was never going to be easy – but he knew they'd try and get nearer while they thought he was focused on hiding, and moving men in ghillie suits weren't as hard to see as stationary ones.

Having gained a few extra seconds while they were taking cover, Victor used it to again sprint up the hill, once more getting behind a tree as soon as one big enough presented itself. He felt himself tiring, his chest heaving, the lactic acid in his muscles building. All it would take to get a bullet in the back was being in the open for a second too long.

Victor breathed heavily, tasting the dirt and sweat on his lips. He fought the instinct to entrench himself and fight back, knowing they were still too far apart to engage at the same time, and if he stayed in the one place for too long he would be outflanked. He had to keep moving, otherwise he'd never make it out of the woods alive. His only chance was to find a small cliff, some boulders or a crevasse – any terrain feature that he could use to even up the firefight. He steeled himself for another sprint.

Leaves crackled overhead. Branches swayed. He heard something hard clatter on a tree trunk and crash into the undergrowth further up the hill, maybe five yards east.

Victor threw himself to the ground an instant before the grenade exploded.

Soil and plant life flew through the air. Hot slivers of metal slammed into the tree trunk above where Victor lay. Bark sizzled.

He breathed in the acrid smell of high explosive. He wasn't injured, despite his close proximity to the blast. Lethal radius for a modern fragmentation grenade was about five and a half yards, and injury radius around sixteen yards, but the path of shrapnel rises as it travels outwards and Victor had been lower than the grenade.

He lay still, hoping to convince the two gunmen he'd been killed and therefore draw them out of cover. He heard the clatter of another grenade sailing through the branches above him. He watched it fall out of sight three yards up the hill, and pressed himself prone, hands clamped over his ears. The grenade exploded and more soil and decimated foliage blasted outwards, more shrapnel ripped through the undergrowth. Smoke swirled in the air.

They weren't going to be convinced of his death quite so easily. Another couple of yards closer and the elevation wouldn't save him. The sound of a third grenade tearing through vegetation kept him from getting up and running. It sounded lower, closer.

It thumped into the ground two feet from Victor's face.

A typical fragmentation grenade had a three- to five-second fuse. One second of flight time left two to four seconds before it shredded Victor's skull with red-hot shards of steel moving at high velocity, and disintegrated what was left of his head with the overpressure wave. Two to four seconds, if the thrower hadn't cooked it off first. Not enough time to get up and out of lethal radius.

Only one choice remained.

Victor grabbed the grenade and hurled it in the direction it had come from, snapped his arm back, heard the huge boom three seconds later, felt the whoosh of air from the concussion flow over him, and heard shrapnel pelt the tree shielding him. His ears rang.

He doubted either of his enemies had been caught in the blast, but their close proximity to it would have surprised, if not disorientated, them. And that was all the distraction he needed.

Victor jumped to his feet and ran, not up this time but to the south along the hillside, in the direction of the highpoint, a plan taking shape in his mind.

He ran for two seconds before he heard the muffled clicks of an MP5SD firing – probably the first gunman, who was to Victor's right, to the west, with the second too far to the north to have a line of sight. Victor sprinted along the even gradient, another five yards, ten, his heart beating faster and faster, the burn in his legs growing more intense, fighting against the thick undergrowth, dodging around trees. The shooting stopped and he knew he'd disappeared out of the shooter's line of sight. Both would give chase, but Victor wanted them to follow. After another twenty yards, he paused briefly behind a mossy boulder, blind-fired some rounds in the direction he'd come from to slow his pursuers, and sprinted again. He jumped over vines twisting their way along the ground. After forty yards, he threw himself down to the forest floor where clumps of woody shrubs grew among the taller trees, swivelled around and reloaded the MP7. He sucked in a lungful of warm air.

Now, to the east, twenty-five yards up the hillside, Victor could see the outcrop from which he'd fired the Longbow. He wasn't interested in the rifle – at close range it was worthless – but the highpoint served as a perfect marker. He moved up into a crouch. He couldn't hear the two guys rushing through the undergrowth, so they were coming after him at a cautious speed – expecting an ambush – which gave him some time. If they thought he was going back to his hide, even better.

He looked around, spotted blood glistening on a tree trunk where he'd expected to find it. At the foot of the tree, the guy he'd shot lay on his back, arms and legs splayed outwards. There were four tiny holes in his chest. Not a bad grouping, considering Victor's limited time to aim. He stripped the corpse of the hooded poncho covered in burlap flaps and vegetation, and slipped it on. He then took the man's headset and radio. Victor clipped the radio to his own harness, fitted the headset in place, flipped up the poncho's hood and swapped his weapon for the dead guy's MP5SD.

Now things were a little more even.

Victor crept forward, settled into a mass of shrubs, kneeling to the side of a tree and waited. He tipped his head forward to make best use of the hood. Five seconds went by, then ten. Twenty.

A gravelly voice whispered through his earpiece. He spoke in English: American, Southern accent. 'This is Cowboy Daddy. I'm at his hide. He's not here. Gamma, do you see anything? Over.'

The reply came a second later. Another Southern accent, more pronounced. 'Cowboy Gamma. Negative. Over.'

'What's your position?'

There was a slight pause before the second guy said, 'I'm about twenty metres to the west, coming up to the base of the outcrop. Over.'

Thank you very much.

'Copy that. Keep 'em peeled. Out.'

Victor repositioned himself and stared into the undergrowth. He saw a slim branch tremble about fifteen yards to his eleven o'clock, near to the lowest point of the highpoint. The gunman moved slowly, keeping low, and would have been invisible in the ghillie suit had Victor not known exactly where to look. The guy's head turned Victor's way but he didn't see him, thanks to the stolen poncho. It may not have been as effective as a full ghillie suit with burlap attached to legs and arms as well, but his enemies were expecting Victor to be far more visible. Victor lined up the MP5SD's iron sights over the gunman's centre mass and thumbed the selector to single shot.

Fired once. Twice. A double tap.

The suppressed *clicks* echoed quietly in the trees. The man in the ghillie suit fell backward into the undergrowth. Victor approached quickly, moving from tree to tree in case the shooter called Cowboy Daddy heard the shots and moved to investigate from the higher ground. Victor saw the corpse lying on the forest floor, two bullet holes over his heart.

'Cowboy Gamma, were those shots? Over,' a voice asked through Victor's earpiece.

'Roger that,' Victor said back, imitating the dead guy's strong Southern twang. 'I got him.'

Victor waited, hoping his impersonation was a good one. His gaze was fixed east toward his hide. The elevation was too steep to see it, but he should be able to spot the gunman if he came this way.

'Good man,' the response finally came. 'The Cowboys rustle another steer.'

'*Oh* yeah,' Victor said.

'But listen up, ' the one called Cowboy Daddy said, 'we have a predicament here. This boy didn't drop his target before we killed him, which means our client is going to be mighty pissed off. I don't know about you, but I want another cheque. So let's see if we can't rub out Mr VIP ourselves. Over.'

'Copy that. Over,' Victor said back.

'Haul your ass back over that wall and try to get eyes on Mr VIP. If you see him, you take him out. Kill 'em all, if you got to. I'll get behind our boy's rifle, see if I can shoot better than him. We've gotta be fast if we're gonna fix this. Out.'

Victor waited for a ten count and crept north twenty yards before heading east and up the hill for thirty more. He approached his hide slowly, still cautious despite the instructions, but relaxing when he spotted the muzzle of his rifle tracking from left to right.

He moved around in a semicircle until he was behind the gunman and could see his legs poking out from under the protective sheeting. Ten careful steps brought Victor within five feet of the gunman's boots.

'This is Cowboy Daddy,' the guy with the rifle said. 'I can't see shit from up here. No wonder the prick missed. Cowboy Gamma, get there as fast as you can and take that fucker down. How far out are you? Over.'

Victor was too close to risk even whispering a response, so he stayed silent as he crept closer.

'Cowboy Gamma, this is Cowboy Daddy. Confirm your position. Over.'

Victor crept forward until he was inches from the man's feet. He nudged the sole of one boot and darted around the tree to the right, out of sight. He was on the other side of the tree, and behind the gunman, by the time the guy had scrambled to his feet to investigate what had just happened. Sometimes the simplest tricks were the best.

Victor smashed the butt of the MP5 into the back of the man's head where the spine met the skull. He collapsed forward, limbs limp, and was still.

CHAPTER 54

Victor threw some water over his captive's face. The American awoke suddenly, eyes snapping open, grimacing through the pain in the back of his head but evaluating the situation at the same time. He was sitting with his back against a mossy tree, arms stretched backwards around the trunk, wrists tied together on the other side. He pulled against the restraints.

'Don't bother,' Victor said. 'I used to be a Boy Scout.'

The guy stopped struggling. He'd been stripped of his headset, weapons and tactical harness. Victor had found nothing useful except some hard candy. He'd taken the green ones and left everything else. The American seemed groggy but without lasting damage, which was good because the brainstem was the most vulnerable part of the skull and a four-pound gun smashing against it wasn't conducive to coherency.

Victor squatted down and sat on his haunches. His captive looked at him with contempt, but Victor could sense the fear that lay just beyond the bravado. The guy looked to be around the forty mark, brown hair and eyes, muscular and athletic. His hair was very short, his face tanned, crow's feet etched deeply into his skin. He hadn't shaved or washed for a few days. He smelled pretty bad, but Victor guessed he smelled no better himself.

The air was hot even in the shade. Victor poured some water over his face and head. The water was lukewarm but still refreshing. He said, 'I'm sure I don't have to tell you there is an easy way to do this and a hard way.'

The American glared at him.

'I can see you're a tough guy,' Victor said. 'You're well trained. The tattoo on your arm says *De oppresso liber:* "To liberate the oppressed".' Victor sipped some water. 'That's the motto of the United States Army Special Forces.'

The American didn't respond.

'No point trying to deny it. It doesn't matter either way. I'll bet if I looked I'd find similar tats on the other two. They're both dead, by the way.'

The American was silent.

Victor said, 'I'm guessing you were all part of the same A-team back in SF. Must have been a real tight group to be doing this now. I can tell by the lines around your eyes you've spent a lot of time squinting in the sun. So you're an Iraq and Afghanistan veteran. Haven't long been out, maybe two or three years tops. Likely did some work as a private security contractor back in Baghdad or Kabul. Paid a lot better than it did in SF, but your talents were wasted guarding diplomats and news crews. It's frustrating to feel the skills you spent a lifetime honing being eroded through disuse, isn't it?'

The American didn't answer.

'But then someone you knew from the Army,' Victor

continued, 'who got out before you did, offers you a different kind of private-sector job. Kind of like what you used to do for Uncle Sam, only it paid better than even babysitting reporters. Given its nature, you were hesitant, maybe even said no to start with, but your friend convinced you this was a bad guy so you would actually be doing some good. And it worked out great. So great, you ended up doing another, and another, and before long that's all you're doing. Each time the money goes up and the voice in the back of your head gets quieter and quieter until you can't even remember what it used to say.' Victor paused. 'Before you know it, you're a contract killer.'

The guy stared at him, confused and more than a little uneasy. 'What's your point?'

'Bet you still think of yourself as a merc, though,' Victor added. 'Take it from me, another year and you wouldn't have bothered trying to lie to yourself. And, to answer your question, my point is that now your teammates are dead, I know you better than anyone. Because I used to be you. And I also know it's only your job to be my enemy. There's nothing personal between us.'

The American's eyes hardened. 'Except you killed my two buddies.'

Victor nodded. 'In self-defence. You've lost guys before. You got over it. This is no different. You'll get over it. But I can't wait that long. You need to decide right now if I'm just a job to you or if I'm your enemy.'

'Why?'

Victor stared at him. 'You know why.'

The American's head dropped forward and he took a heavy breath. When he looked back up he said, 'It's how you just put

431

it. This is a job. Nothing more. If things were reversed, I'd have done the same as you. No hard feelings.'

Victor motioned to the water bottle and the American nodded. Victor held the bottle so the American could use the straw. He took several swallows. Victor placed the bottle down.

'Who you are working for?'

The American frowned. 'Come on, man, you know I can't tell you that.'

Victor gave an understanding nod and took the combat knife from his tactical harness. 'I'm not a fan of torture,' he explained. 'Which isn't because I'm squeamish. You know as well as I do, the more blood you see, the less of an effect it has.' He touched a finger to the sharp point. 'The problem I have with torture is that I'm usually a very clean person and it can be such a messy business. I don't like making a mess, but sometimes it's simply unavoidable.'

The American's gaze was locked on the knife. 'We don't have to go there.'

'Then try again at answering my original question.'

The American shook his head. 'I don't know exactly.'

'That's not good enough.'

'Wait, Shane always dealt with the clients. No one else did. It was his job. I'm just a shooter. He was the boss.'

Victor raised an eyebrow. 'Your call sign was Cowboy *Daddy*.'

'Okay,' the guy said after a pause, 'okay.'

'You ran things, on and off the op. How did you do it? Dead drops, phone calls, online?'

'Did everything on computer. Safest that way. Different email account for each job. Half the money up front, other half after

432

the job was done. How I always do it. Less chance of clients fucking with you like that.'

Victor nodded. 'Which is why I do it the same way.'

He took a smartphone from his tactical harness and powered it on. He opened up a browser. The reception was perfect. Sochi's elite demanded it.

'Give me the details for the operational email account.'

'Won't work,' the American said. 'Can only access the job spec from my computer back home.'

'How would your buddies get paid the second half of the fee if you got killed?'

The American hesitated. 'I don't know what you mean.'

'Yes you do. You guys served and killed together in the military. You saved each other's lives. Nothing else creates a bond of friendship that strong. They were your buddies, like you said. And friends who watch each other's backs in combat never stop looking out for each other. You wouldn't leave them dangling if you took a bullet. If you used a safe, they'd know the combination; if you kept everything in a deposit box, they would have keys. A computer that only you could access would be no good to them. So, I'm asking you for the last time, before I start carving the truth from you: what are the details?'

The American looked away, finally defeated. 'Before we'd go on an op I'd give everyone the login info for the account I used. Just in case.'

'Like a good buddy.'

The American gave Victor the details and he logged into the account. There were five emails in the inbox from the anonymous client or broker. Victor read them in order. The first email was the offer of the job with the fee and window of opportunity. The next email included Victor's dossier. The following three were clarifications. He opened the attachment and read through the file.

Seven months back he'd read a similar document, but that had only contained a single sheet of paper – an estimation of his physical attributes and a photofit of his face. This dossier was considerably more extensive. It included accurate details on his height, weight, hair and eye colour. There was a list, though far from all-inclusive, of languages he spoke. A page described his combat capabilities and skills. Some of his identities were listed. The most telling inclusion was the photographs of his face, close-ups from the front and each profile. His hair was a clipped quarter-inch. There was dried blood on his forehead and other evidence of injuries. The photographs had been taken without his knowledge while he lay injured in hospital prior to his recruitment by the CIA. A substantial insurance policy for his employer. It was bad enough knowing his employer had betrayed him, without discovering that betrayal had been planned well in advance.

There was only one course of action to take in response.

The dossier went on to explain Victor's own contract for Kasakov and the requirements for Victor's demise. He was to be killed only after he had murdered the arms dealer. His body was then to be disposed of somewhere it would never be found. *Provide immediate confirmation upon elimination of target.*

The muscles in Victor's jaw flexed. 'How many other contracts have you performed for this client?'

The American shrugged as much as his position would allow. 'Just one.'

'Tell me about it.'

'Couple of weeks ago. In Beirut. Had to kidnap some Egyptian arms dealer and his wife and kids.'

A groove appeared between Victor's eyebrows. 'Egyptian arms dealer?'

'Yeah.'

'Name?'

'I don't know, man. Some rag name. You know how it is.'

'Baraa Ariff,' Victor said.

The American nodded. 'Yeah, that's it. How did you know?'

'Who did you deliver Ariff and his family to?'

'We didn't.'

'Then what did you do with them?'

The American looked awkward. 'What do you think? We killed 'em.'

'Why kidnap them if you were just going to kill them?'

'Client wanted them tortured and the whole thing filmed.'

Victor frowned. He tried not to imagine what that consisted of. 'What are the account details for the email address used for that job?'

'The account's been deactivated. After each job I—'

'I believe you,' Victor said with a nod. 'I do the same.'

He read through the emails again to get a feel for the American's word choice and tone before composing a confirmation of the kill. There was no point getting the American to choose the wording himself – either he would deliberately try and sabotage the message or his current stress level would unintentionally show through. Victor sent the confirmation.

His things were already packed and he had sterilised the area as much as he could. He powered off the phone, hoisted his rucksack on to his shoulders, and drew the MK23 from his thigh holster.

'*Whoa*,' the American said with wide eyes. 'What's that for?'

'I wasn't lying when I said there was nothing personal between us. But that was before I knew you'd killed children.' Victor released the safety catch and aimed the handgun between the American's eyes. 'Even people like us need limits.'

Clack. Clack.

CHAPTER 55

Bologna, Italy

Alberto Giordano sat outside one of his favourite little cafés in the heart of the old city, feeling the warmth of the sun on his back, sipping his espresso and enjoying the spectacle whenever pretty Bolognese women passed by. Giordano may have been a native of Rome, but he'd fallen in love with Bologna many years ago. It was a great city – vibrant, welcoming, entertaining, unspoiled and beautiful – and Giordano felt lucky his trade had brought him within its medieval walls. In his youth, he'd dreamed of being an artist, aspiring to create modern master-pieces to one day be as revered as those of the Renaissance masters he so admired. But it was hard to pay the bills as a struggling painter, and through a friend of a friend Giordano's dexterous skills had eventually found a more profitable use.

Another man might have been sad to think that all his boy-hood ambitions had been drowned in the harshness of reality, but it was hard for Giordano to be sad when life was so good.

A pair of shapely young women walked by, their heels

clattering on the cobbled surface of the side street, and Giordano politely clapped their passing. For some reason he had yet to work out, foreign women found such a compliment embarrassing or even rude, but Italians were rightfully pleased to have their efforts appreciated. These two were no exception and glanced and smiled Giordano's way as they whispered between themselves. Another time, and Giordano would have caught them up, but he had a client to meet after he'd finished his coffee. Instead, he made a flirty wave, and was happy to see it returned.

He had been the café's only outside patron until a man sat down at the table in front. A waiter appeared to take the man's order and Giordano gestured for the bill. He finished the last of his espresso and noticed the sun was no longer warming his back. He turned in his seat to find a woman sitting at the table directly behind him. He hadn't noticed her arrival and now saw why. She was plain of face and figure, with short, boyish hair. Her clothes were drab and hid anything about her that said she was a woman. Giordano turned back, irritated by the intrusion to his pleasant afternoon, and shuffled his chair so he was out of the new arrival's shade.

Giordano used his fingers to collect some crumbs of ciabatta from his plate to eat while he waited for the waiter to appear. A vehicle pulled up to the nearby kerb. He thought nothing of it, until he heard a sliding door open and noticed a shadow fall across his table. As he turned to investigate, he saw the man from the table in front leap from his seat. Giordano started and went to rise, but powerful hands grabbed his shoulders. He heard a fizz of electricity and felt a jarring pain originate in his lower back and wrack his entire body.

Giordano spasmed and toppled from his seat, but the powerful hands kept him from falling.

More hands grabbed his legs and he felt his paralysed body lifted up. He couldn't move, couldn't cry out, as he was slid into the back of a van. The door slammed shut behind him and he lay on the cold metal floor, aware of figures around him that he couldn't make out, and words in a language he did not understand.

The van pulled away and his hands were yanked together and plasticuffs wrapped around his wrists. He felt pain as they were pulled tight. Tape found its way over his mouth, and a sack covered his head.

'Struggle,' a female voice said in strangely accented Italian, 'and you'll be shocked again. Nod if you understand.' Giordano did. 'We're going somewhere to talk,' the voice continued. 'When we're there, if you answer our questions completely and truthfully, nothing bad will happen to you. Again, nod if you understand.'

He did, but Giordano knew a lie when he heard one.

Underneath the sack, he began to sob.

Giordano grimaced on the hard uneven metal of the van as it drove through the streets of Bologna. His lower back was sore – as if burned. His captors didn't speak again, either to him or to each other. He knew there were at least four of them: one to drive the van, the man who had sat in front of him at the café, the woman who had sat behind, and the strong one who had grabbed his shoulders. He didn't know who they were. He didn't know what they wanted.

There was no point struggling. At best they would just

electrocute him again. He didn't want to think what might be at the other end of the scale of punishments.

He figured it had been fifteen minutes before the van stopped. He tensed, terrified at what might happen next. Light filtered through the sack over his head as the van's sliding door was opened. Hands grabbed his limbs and pulled him out of the van. Giordano's feet found the floor and the hands kept him upright.

The woman's voice said, 'Remember, answer our questions in full and nothing bad will happen.'

He was led through what he guessed was some kind of deserted factory or warehouse. Their footsteps echoed. They walked quickly and Giordano struggled to keep up. The hands holding on to him made sure he didn't fall.

The woman said, 'Stop,' and Giordano did, and heard the sound of chains rattling.

They were wrapped around his wrists and a force above Giordano pulled his arms up until they were vertical, either side of his head, and only the balls of his feet touched the floor. The strain on his shoulders made him wince. He couldn't see anything. Tape was wrapped around his ankles, binding his feet together.

Wheels squeaked and something rattled across a bumpy floor. It stopped in front of Giordano and his pulse quickened and his breaths shortened in fear of what it might be.

The sack was pulled from his head and, despite the dim light, he squinted. It took a moment for his eyes to focus and he saw he was indeed inside a warehouse or factory. There was wide open space all around him, the extremes of the room lost in shadows and darkness.

In front of him stood a woman and a man. He recognised the woman's plain face and boyish hair from outside the café. In the dim light her features seemed even harsher. Giordano hadn't seen the man before. He was muscular and very tall, with a buzz cut and thick eyebrows that almost met in the middle. He stood without pose or expression, but violence seemed to radiate from him. Next to the woman was a rusty trolley, like a mechanic might use.

Resting on the trolley was a pair of pliers, bolt cutters, a variety of bladed instruments, a belt sander, a circular saw, and a blow torch.

Giordano let out a muffled cry.

The woman said, 'If you are honest with us, then we won't need to use of any of that.'

Giordano barely heard. His eyes were locked on the trolley. He pulled and yanked at his chains, achieving nothing more than lifting his feet from the floor and swinging gently.

The large man stepped forward and punched Giordano in the stomach. Pain flooded through his abdomen and he coughed and spluttered behind the tape sealing his mouth as he convulsed.

'We only require information,' the woman said, 'information that you have, Alberto. Give us that information and this can be over. Deny us, and this is only the beginning.'

When he had recovered, the large man ripped the tape away.

She ran her fingertips over the collection of blades and selected a box-cutting knife.

'No, please,' Giordano begged.

The woman raised the box cutter and stepped closer. Giordano screamed and tried to get further away from the blade. The large man grabbed his legs to hold him steady. Giordano continued screaming as the woman used the knife to cut through his T-shirt from waist to neck. She pulled it open to reveal his bare flesh beneath and pressed the blade to the skin of his stomach. The skin indented but the pressure wasn't enough to split it. Yet.

Giordano was paralysed with terror. Tears streamed from his eyes.

The woman produced a grainy picture and said, 'Where is this man?'

'I don't know, I swear.'

'You're lying,' she said, and Giordano felt the blade press harder against his flesh. 'He was here in Bologna with you four weeks ago. You met with him twice. Your people have already confirmed it.'

'But I don't know where he's gone,' Giordano shouted, trying to get away from the knife. 'I don't.'

'Why did he visit you? What did he want?'

'Information.'

'On what?'

'He had a camera. He wanted me to track its origin.'

'Did you?'

'I gave him the name of a company – Lancet Incorporated – that's all I found.'

The woman exchanged words with the large man, speaking in the language Giordano didn't understand.

'What else did you give him?' the woman asked.

'Nothing. I swear.'

The woman's eyes examined Giordano. 'I know you're loyal to him, but I see you are also afraid of him. Aren't you, Alberto?'

Giordano didn't answer.

'You don't have to confirm it,' she said. 'I find that amusing. I find it amusing that you would dare lie to me when I have the power to inflict upon you the most horrific pain imaginable.'

'I'm not lying,' Giordano dared to say.

'Of course you aren't.'

In one quick action, the woman dragged the blade of the box cutter down the Italian's abdomen. The skin bloomed open. Blood poured out of the wound.

Giordano wailed.

He thrashed and bucked against his chains and the large man holding his legs.

'You are a master forger,' the woman said, talking loudly to be heard over Giordano's screams. 'What did you make for him? Identification? A passport?'

'*YES*,' Giordano managed to yell through his cries of pain. '*A passport. I made him a passport.*'

'That's better,' the woman said in a pleased tone. She placed the box-cutting knife down on the trolley, and turned away from Giordano. 'That's much better. What is the name on the passport you constructed for this man?'

'Tolento Lombardi,' he said to her back.

'Remember when I told you if you were truthful, I wouldn't hurt you?' she asked without turning back around. Before Giordano could answer, she added, 'Unfortunately, you chose to lie to me. And now I can't believe anything you say.'

Giordano grimaced from the agony in his stomach. He could feel rivulets of warm blood trickling down his stomach. Sweat covered his whole body. 'I'm sorry. Please, I won't lie again. *Please.*'

'Some people believe torture to be ineffective,' the woman explained, her back still to Giordano. 'But it is only ineffective if the person administrating it is unlearned. I have studied the art for more than a decade, all over the world, learning every technique imaginable, both modern and ancient. But, alas, I rarely get to use my talents.' The woman finally turned around, the blow torch in hand. 'So, Alberto, I'm particularly glad that you chose to lie to me. Thank you for that.'

There was a *whoosh* as she sparked the flame.

CHAPTER 56

Moscow, Russia

Yuliya Eltsina stood inside one of the many warehouses owned by the organisation. Even though the arms-trafficking company was huge in size, there was no office building or central hub. The business employed a structure not dissimilar to a terrorist network with cells operating largely independently from one another. Each cell received its orders from a member higher up the chain, who in turn answered to an executive governed by the board, of which Burliuk and Eltsina were the equivalent of VPs. Kasakov, of course, sat at the top of the table as CEO. Until now.

Of the seven members of the board, only five could make it to her meeting. The others were stationed too far away to arrive in time, but would be contacted afterwards to be informed of the new changes. The power rush Eltsina was feeling made her hands shake. She had never felt so alive.

The warehouse was empty and was nothing more than part of the organisation's façade of legitimacy. The floor was clean and shiny, reflecting the glow of fluorescent tube lights hanging overhead as white lines that ran from wall to wall. Metal pillars supported the ceiling. Air-conditioning units hung unused. At one end, the huge roll-up door was open to allow the various cars of the board members to enter. In a loose semicircle were two Bentleys, a Rolls-Royce, a Zil limousine and three BMWs.

Burliuk and the five members of the board were standing in a loose group. Their drivers and bodyguards waited at the far end of the warehouse, out of earshot. The board members were all smartly dressed, as Kasakov always demanded. Most had grey hair. Most were overweight. They were a bland group of men who were as ruthless as they were greedy. All were chauvinists and it had taken Eltsina years to garner enough respect from them for this moment to be possible. She knew that so long as they were convinced she could make them even wealthier, she would have their support.

'Gentlemen,' she began, 'I'm sorry to call everyone here like this, but I have some very bad news for you all.' She looked at the floor and then around the warehouse as if she was struggling with what to say next. Her voice broke as she said, 'Vladimir is dead.'

Silence. Disbelief passed over their faces, then shock.

'What do you mean?' one asked.

'How? When?' Burliuk demanded, and fumbled for his asthma inhaler.

Eltsina tried her best to look pained, but not too pained, else they would see her as a weak-willed woman. 'I understand it happened earlier today. While on vacation with Izolda, he was shot and killed.'

A particularly fat board member scoffed. 'Impossible. I don't believe it.'

'It's true,' Eltsina assured.

'What about Izolda?' Burliuk asked, desperation in his voice. 'Is she safe?'

'As I understand it.'

Mumbles of astonishment and outrage passed around the group. Burliuk looked more shocked than distraught, just as she had expected. He was probably already rehearsing what he was going to say as he stepped forward to take over from Kasakov.

'As you all know,' Eltsina added, 'Baraa Ariff has been at war with Vladimir for some weeks now. We have lost hundreds of millions of dollars and many employees due to his unprecedented attacks. But by murdering Vladimir, he has cost us even more.'

She averted her eyes and swallowed heavily. Don't overdo it, she told herself.

'But how could he? Ariff's dead,' a board member shouted.

There were mutterings of agreement.

'I'm afraid Ariff must have sent his assassins before he was himself killed,' Eltsina explained. 'Else his lieutenants did it for revenge.'

There were nods and curses. Burliuk was looking at her, but his expression was unreadable.

'We will have time to grieve for Vladimir,' she said, 'but he built this empire with his own hands and it would enrage him to see it crumble in his absence. We must rebuild and become stronger than ever before.'

'Yes.'

'Hear, hear.'

'To that aim,' Eltsina continued, 'we must act decisively and with speed, lest others step into the vacuum left by Vladimir.'

'Agreed,' a board member said. 'Any delay only weakens us.'

The fat board member added, 'We need to show the world we are still number one, with or without Vladimir.'

'Then we must have a new leader.'

'But who?'

Eltsina let the silence build for a moment before she said, 'Of course Tomasz is the natural heir to Vladimir's throne.' She cast a glance at Burliuk. 'He was closer to Vladimir than all of us combined, and had been at his side the longest.'

Nods of agreement.

'But,' Eltsina added with a careful look to each of the board members she had lied to or manipulated over the past month, 'he thirsted for Ariff's blood as much as Vladimir, and together they brought Ariff's assassins to our doors.'

The faces of the board members told Eltsina everything she needed to know. None would have dared say what she had just said, but they all agreed with it, or at least had been convinced by Eltsina's lies and exaggerations. Burliuk stared hard at Eltsina, but still didn't speak. He was too smart to rush blindly into a retort until he knew exactly what was happening.

'We cannot have the same recklessness take us forward,' she said. 'So I propose that, in the absence of a more suitable candidate, I be the one to take over from Vladimir. If the honourable board agrees, naturally.'

The board members looked at each other. The braver ones looked at Burliuk too. They may have been rich, powerful men, but at heart each one was a coward.

Eventually one nodded. 'Yes,' he said. 'Yuliya should take over.'

'Agreed,' another said.

Like dominoes falling, the other three all expressed their approval. Eltsina resisted smiling and looked at Burliuk. A trace of fear crept into his expression. 'Do you have anything you'd like to say, Tomasz?' Eltsina asked. She felt dizzy with power. The adrenalin flowing through her veins felt divine. She said, 'Don't you have anything to say at all?'

'I do,' a deep voice answered.

It echoed around the warehouse. Everyone turned to see Kasakov emerge from one of the doors that lined the factory walls. Five bodyguards followed.

Eltsina gasped. She couldn't believe what she was seeing. Kasakov strode towards her – huge, imposing, alive. Terrifying. Eltsina limply reached for her pistol.

Before her hand was even around the grip, Kasakov's elite guards had their own weapons out and were shouting at Eltsina to stop. She showed her palms.

'I don't understand,' she managed to say as Kasakov grew closer.

'You don't need to understand,' Kasakov said, and punched her with a massive straight right that struck Eltsina on the side of the face, fracturing both cheek and jawbone and sending her crashing to the floor, unconscious.

Kasakov grimaced and shook his hand several times. He faced the board members.

'Gentlemen,' he began, 'I apologise for the deception, but I assure you the juvenile theatrics were necessary. I told just two people where I was vacationing: Tomasz and Yuliya. Yet someone tried to kill me there. I'm sure, after Yuliya's little speech, you will now understand who that person was.'

Eltsina, jaw broken and barely conscious, managed to mumble incoherently.

'Quiet, my sweet,' Kasakov said. 'You'll have plenty of time to make noise later.' He smiled and his shadow fell across the woman's face. 'And you thought what I did to Ariff was so very cruel.'

It was almost midnight by the time Kasakov and Burliuk arrived at Kasakov's home. Sheets lined the floor of the hallway. Everywhere were piles of bricks, metal beams, screws, tools and stacks of four-inch-thick sheets of laminated glass and polycarbonate. Each window in the dacha was being replaced with the best bullet-resistant glass money could buy. Motion detectors and cameras were being fitted in every room. Kasakov's dacha had always been secure and well guarded, but now it was being transformed into a fortress.

'You'll have to excuse the mess,' Kasakov said to Burliuk as they reached the top of the staircase, 'but I think you'll understand it's about time I upgraded my security. My guards didn't try to take your inhaler, did they?' Burliuk shook his head and Kasakov smiled. 'Be glad they didn't insist on giving you a cavity search.'

An armed bodyguard was stationed on the landing, overlooking the staircase. Another stood at the bottom. One either end of the long hallway. Kasakov led Burliuk inside his study and closed the door.

'Take a seat, Tomasz.'

Burliuk did.

'Izolda is downstairs,' Kasakov said, taking a seat behind his desk. 'She's taken the assassination attempt surprisingly well, I think. She's a strong woman, but I've already left her for too long with just guards for company.'

'Take some time off,' Burliuk said, 'stay with Izolda. Take care of your wife, and let me take care of everything else.'

Kasakov smiled at that. 'That's my plan, my old friend. But tell me, Tomasz, what's the latest with the North Koreans? I assume it's bad news.'

'I'm sorry to say they've withdrawn the MiG order and gone with the Indians.'

'I thought they would,' Kasakov admitted. 'For all their bluster, those people are scared of their own shadow. It's their loss, not mine.'

'If only that were true. That deal was vital for us, not only in monetary terms but for our reputation. It will be a long time before we are trusted again. And who else is there to sell to? How many conflicts are fought with tanks and jets today? War has changed. This is the era of the terrorist and the guerrilla. Rifles and IEDs are their weapons.'

'You're right, of course,' Kasakov agreed, 'but I still don't care. How much money and power is enough?'

'I don't understand.'

'I'm retiring.'

Burliuk struggled to respond for a moment, before asking, 'Since when?'

'I've been thinking about it for a little while, but when I found out I was going to be a father the decision was made for me.'

'*What?*'

Kasakov stood. 'Izolda's pregnant. We're going to have a baby. Finally.'

Burliuk's mouth fell open. He struggled with how to respond.

'Your manners are terrible,' Kasakov remarked. 'This is usually the point where you offer congratulations.'

'Sorry, Vladimir. Congratulations. I'm just shocked, that's all.'

He stood and they embraced. Kasakov squeezed his friend hard, but Burliuk's return hug was limp.

'You've taken me by complete surprise.'

They stepped back from each other. 'Not as surprised as I was, or Izolda for that matter. After the attack, Izolda complained of stomach pains. You see, when the shooting started I threw her to the ground. I thought I must have hurt her. We went to a hospital and they ran some tests.' Kasakov smiled. 'But she wasn't hurt at all. You should see her, Tomasz. She's so happy, so happy. All she's ever wanted is to be a mother. Now, she will be.'

'She'll make a wonderful mother.'

'I know. And I'll do my best as a father. I won't treat the child any different than I would my own.'

Burliuk's eyes widened in surprise. 'Excuse me?'

'Did you not wonder why Izolda and I have been without a son or daughter for so long? We've never spoken of it, but I don't believe you haven't been curious. The reason is that I can't father children, Tomasz. Of course, I never told anyone. Me and Izolda never even spoke of it until very recently, though she must have known for years, always afraid to bring it up for fear of my reaction.'

Burliuk was shaking his head. He used his inhaler. 'If you're not the father, then who is?'

'My first thought was that it might be you.'

He coughed. '*Excuse me?*'

'You should know me well enough by now to know I am no fool, my friend. I've seen the way you look at Izolda. The way you've always looked at her.'

Burliuk showed his palms. 'Vladimir, I have never, *ever*—'

Kasakov made another dismissive gesture. 'I believe you. You're in love with her, I know that. It was just a foolish idea, and one I dismissed quickly. I know Izolda thinks of you like a brother. She wouldn't betray me with you. Someone else, yes. You, never.'

Burliuk's eyes narrowed a fraction. He looked away.

'I'm going to play along with the deception,' Kasakov said. 'I won't let on I know the child isn't mine. I don't blame Izolda for what she's done. If I had been strong enough to admit to my problem, we could have received help long ago. I'm doing this for Izolda. Not for me.'

'Very noble,' Burliuk muttered.

Kasakov stood in front of Burliuk and rubbed his friend's arms. 'Are you sad for me, Tomasz? Or for yourself?'

Burliuk said nothing.

'It must hurt to have desired Izolda all these years while she shared my bed. It must hurt even more now that you know she chose another man, not you, with whom to lie. Maybe several men, for all I know.'

'Vladimir—'

'Don't say anything. Let me speak. You've been at my side for all these years. My one true friend. You're the only person in the entire world, besides my wife, who I could trust.' Kasakov rubbed Burliuk's shoulders. 'It occurs to me that we still know nothing about who tried to kill me in Bucharest.'

'Eltsina, surely. She said—'

Kasakov shook his head. 'Only under the most extreme pain

453

did she admit to hiring that sniper. However, her plan relied on you and I being discredited by the war with Ariff. Killing me before the war would not have achieved that. You would have been chosen to head the empire, not her. So, no. It wasn't Yuliya.' Kasakov squeezed Burliuk's shoulders. 'You, however, were most keen that I should personally go to Bucharest to negotiate with the North Korean broker. Why would you do that when they were willing to come to Moscow?'

Burliuk reached to again take out his inhaler. 'Vladimir, I—'

Kasakov's huge hands enveloped Burliuk's neck and squeezed. Burliuk gasped and dropped the inhaler to grab at Kasakov's wrists, pulling with all his strength. Kasakov's hands didn't move.

'I spoke to your friend Danil Petrenko just before he disappeared in Barcelona,' Kasakov said. 'He told me about what went on in Minsk that time. About your deal with Gabir Yamout. You put him in touch with Petrenko and Yamout did you a favour. I wonder what that could have been. Maybe he put you in touch with a killer. One who could never be traced back to yourself.'

'No . . .' Burliuk managed to croak.

'I know you've never shared Eltsina's ambition,' Kasakov stated, 'so why else, I ask myself, if not to take over my empire, would you want me dead? The answer is obvious. For Izolda, of course. But I would never have believed you could do that to me, until just now. When I told you of Izolda's affair you could not disguise the depth of your anger. Then I knew.'

Kasakov squeezed harder. The blood vessels in Burliuk's face stood out beneath his reddening skin. He wheezed, breathless, punching desperately at Kasakov, who didn't try to slip the blows, accepting each one as the price of forty years of friendship.

'If only you hit like a heavyweight, Tomasz.'

Burliuk's lips were turning blue. His eyes bulged. The toes of his shoes scratched at the floorboards.

'In a way, I don't blame you,' Kasakov admitted. 'You did see her first, all those long years ago, but for all your good looks she chose me, not you. Had that been reversed I would surely have done the same as you to make her mine. Only I, of course, would not have failed.'

Burliuk's arms flopped to his sides, his legs slackened and his head tilted forward. Kasakov kept his own arms straight, supporting Burliuk's weight, holding him upright for a long time after his heart stopped.

Kasakov then called his security to dispose of his best friend's body and went downstairs to look at nursery colour schemes with his wife.

CHAPTER 57

Washington, DC, USA

Procter pulled into the parking lot of a burger joint that had seen better days. The square of cracked asphalt at the rear looked no better. Procter spotted a blue Lincoln Town Car reverse-parked at the far end and headed towards it. No other vehicles were near the car. They were all parked closer to the restaurant itself. Customers never walked further than they had to. Procter stopped his Buick alongside the Lincoln, nose to tail. The night air smelled of exhaust fumes and grease.

Procter already had his window lowered. Clarke buzzed down his own.

'Evening, Roland.'

Procter's expression was hard, dejected. 'Tesseract failed to kill Kasakov.'

Clarke let out some air. He said nothing, but his disappointment was palpable. It seemed as if there was a little fear mixed in as well.

'The word's all over the Agency that someone tried to take him out two days ago. Kasakov was on vacation. Multiple bodies have been found near to his Sochi dacha.'

Clarke looked at Procter. 'Is Tesseract dead?'

'There are three as yet unidentified corpses. I've seen the pictures. He's not among them.'

Clarke stared across the parking lot. He was the most distressed Procter could ever remember seeing him. It wasn't the anger Procter had been expecting. Clarke hadn't raised his voice, hadn't thrown across any accusations.

'Looks like you were right about him all along,' Procter said, as sympathetically as he knew how. 'That's twice now he's failed and created an almighty mess in the process. I'm sorry I didn't listen to you earlier.'

'Let me assure you I take no pleasure in being proved right. Do you know what went wrong?'

Procter made a face and shrugged his shoulders. 'Not a clue. Tesseract hasn't reported in. But what does it matter? I've got no choice now. I'm pulling the plug. We'll never get Kasakov. Not after this. Not after two assassination attempts in as many months. He'll surround himself with nothing short of a small army. If we want him, we're gonna have to drop a cruise missile on Moscow.' Procter shook his head. 'All this heat on us, all these questions being asked, and for what gain? Kasakov is alive and well and we didn't even get our war, we got a skirmish.'

Clarke said, 'This should be our last meeting for a while.'

'Agreed.'

'What about Tesseract?'

'We'll have to get rid of him.'

'How?' Clarke asked.

'The contingency,' Procter explained. 'That boy has a lot of enemies, don't forget. Most notably in the SVR.'

'Efficient.'

Procter nodded. 'We don't have to get our hands dirty. We simply hand over his file, maybe say where he's going to be. Anonymously, of course. The Russians are a lot better than us when it comes to making problems disappear.'

An hour later, Procter sat slumped in the chair of his study on the second floor of his Georgetown home. He wasn't a big drinker, usually, but he was rapidly making his way through a bottle of Merlot. Everything he had worked so hard to achieve had fallen apart.

Patricia was watching soaps in bed and Roland Jnr was thankfully asleep, so Procter could stress in peace and quiet. Self-pity wasn't usually something he wallowed in, but this time he figured he had a right to. What could he have done differently? He replayed the past few weeks in his head, the months and years beforehand. The plan had seemed like a good one. It came with a real risk of failure, sure, but Procter had expected success. After all, he had the right backer in Clarke, the right triggerman in Tesseract. It should have worked.

He drank some more wine. It dribbled down his chin and he wiped it away with the back of his wrist. On the screen of his computer monitor was Tesseract's file. There wasn't much information on the guy, but there was enough to enable the right people to track him down. Procter didn't want to send it; as the man who'd brought Tesseract on to the op, the buck stopped with him, but the assassin had drawn a lot of attention, too much attention to allow him to carry on walking around.

Procter composed an email from an untraceable account and attached Tesseract's file. He knew just who in the SVR to send the file to.

He drained the last of his glass and wiped his mouth. His finger hovered above the left mouse button. *Sorry, my man.*

The computer beeped at him before he could click the button. Incoming VoIP call. Procter's eyebrows rose, and after a second's deliberation, he accepted it.

'I was just thinking about you,' he said.

The voice that came through the computer's speaker spoke in English but Procter couldn't place the accent. It was vaguely American at times, British at others, but also neither. He had no idea where Tesseract was from.

'You have exactly one minute to convince me you had nothing to do with what occurred on Friday.' Tesseract's voice was low and chilling. 'Then I'm hanging up and getting on the next flight to the States. You can guess what happens after that.'

Procter frowned, considered. 'What the hell are you talking about?'

'Fifty-seven seconds left.'

Procter sat up in his seat. He gathered his thoughts. 'If something happened, you need to stop playing games and just tell me what it is.'

'Fifty seconds.'

'*Jesus*, what the hell is this? You can't be serious. I don't know what you're talking about.'

'Forty-six seconds.'

'Okay,' Procter said. 'Someone came after you, right? That's why you're pissed. You think it was me. It wasn't. I swear.'

'Thirty-seven seconds.'

'All right, you need more convincing than that. I don't know what to say if I don't know what happened.'

'Thirty-one seconds.'

Procter grabbed hold of the desk with both hands. He leaned forward. 'Come on, cut me some slack here, I'm trying my best. Someone came after you, we've established that. You think it was me. Okay, so, that means they did so while you were on the Kasakov contract. Right? They were waiting for you, so you think I set you up.'

'Eighteen seconds.'

Procter stood. 'I understand why you would think that. But I didn't. You have to believe me. I know how good you are. I know what happened last time someone set you up. I don't want you coming after me.'

Tesseract's voice cut right through Procter. 'I am coming after you. Nine seconds.'

'Please.' Procter shoved his fingers through his hair. 'You have to believe me.'

'Seven seconds.'

'*Don't hang up*. We can work this out. I just need more time to figure out what happened.'

'Three seconds.'

'*SHIT*.' Procter slammed a palm down on the desk. 'Don't do this.'

'Two seconds.'

Procter took a huge breath. 'Okay, you win, my name's

Roland Procter. I work for the Central Intelligence Agency. I'm the Associate Deputy Director for National Clandestine Services. I've a wife and two kids. We live in DC. Georgetown.'

There was no response.

'You already know what I look like,' Procter continued. 'Now you know my name, my position and where I live. It would have taken you a month to find me before, now you can find me in a day.' He paused, caught back his breath. 'If I set you up, would I have told you that?'

Silence. Procter breathed heavily. His heart thumped hard inside his ribcage.

'All right,' Tesseract answered eventually. 'I believe you.'

Procter let out a massive sigh. He put a hand to his chest. 'Christ, my heart's beating fast.'

'No blasphemy, remember?'

Procter fell backwards in his chair. He wiped sweat from his forehead with the back of his hand. 'You need to tell me what happened.'

Tesseract said, 'For days I'd been waiting for Kasakov to be in just the right place to make the shot. A moment before I squeezed the trigger, I realised I was being watched. There was a team: three pros. American. Ex-Special Forces. They were waiting for me to kill Kasakov. The second I did, they would have killed me too. Otherwise Kasakov would be dead now and you wouldn't be considering how best to remove me. Only someone who knew I was in Sochi could have sent that team.'

Procter remained silent.

'That someone gave them a dossier on me. A dossier that

included pictures taken in the hospital before we met. So, if it wasn't you who set me up, who was it?'

Procter pinched the skin between his eyes and said, 'My partner. No one but him and me knew you were going to kill Kasakov, or had access to those pictures.'

'Name?'

'No,' Procter said. 'I won't do that.'

'You should seriously reconsider that stance.'

'Listen, I don't know why all this has happened, but I'm not handing him over to be killed. He's my friend.'

'Not much of a friend. He betrayed you too.'

Procter sat up. 'He was just trying to protect us both. It was stupid, but I get why he did it. I'll talk to him. You're not touching him. So, forget about that.'

'I interrogated the kill team's leader,' Tesseract added. 'He told me that before they were hired to kill me they'd completed another job for the same client. In Beirut. They kidnapped Baraa Ariff and his family, tortured and killed them. And filmed it.'

'What?' was all Procter could manage to say.

'Now, that doesn't sound to me like a typical assassination. But it does sound like the kind of thing someone would have done for revenge if that someone really hated Ariff. Every job I've done for you has revolved around him and Kasakov. At the start of all this you had me save Kasakov's life, otherwise with Kasakov dead it might have been hard to convince Ariff that it was Kasakov who sent me after Yamout in Minsk. And I imagine the specific explosives I used to kill Farkas somehow convinced Kasakov to go after Ariff. I've got to hand it to you, it was a decent plan: trick the world's biggest trafficker of small

462

arms and the biggest dealer in heavy munitions to wage war on each other.'

'It was a good plan,' Procter corrected.

'Then why did your partner send the American kill team after Ariff? Surely you would have sent me to kill whoever survived the war. You didn't just want Ariff and Kasakov to kill each other. You could have sent me to do that weeks ago. You wanted them to bludgeon each other's networks first, damaging the arms trade instead of simply removing its replaceable figureheads. So it makes no sense for your partner to have acted against Ariff at that time. Unless he had some reason for wanting Ariff to lose the war, not Kasakov. He's not in league with Kasakov himself, however, because Kasakov wouldn't send a team to kill me only after I've already killed him. So, it'll be one of his lieutenants, hoping to take over from Kasakov after I'd killed him. I'm sorry to be the one to tell you, but your friend has been playing you this whole time.'

Procter put his face in his hands and pulled his fingers down over his eyes and cheeks.

'Are you quite sure you don't want to tell me who he is?'

When Procter spoke his voice was quiet, deliberate. 'I'll deal with him.'

'You better had,' Tesseract said. 'Because I've got some more bad news for you.'

'Let's hear it.'

'You were wrong when you said it would take a month for me to find you.'

'What?'

'It took forty-eight hours. Not as many places selling steak

463

sandwiches within lunchtime driving distance from Langley as you might think. I stopped by Nelson's Diner this afternoon. The staff were very helpful when I told them I wanted to find my long-lost uncle. I can see why you like their food. Very tasty, but every day? That's not good for your arteries. With your weight you should be more careful and get plenty of exercise. I'll email you a workout programme.'

Procter's eyes were wide. '*What?*'

'I'd check under your Buick before you next start the engine. Make sure you cut the green wire, not the blue.'

The line disconnected.

Procter shot up from his seat, went to the window and heaved the blind open. His car sat on the driveway as usual. Nothing appeared suspicious. In the garage he grabbed a set of clippers and a flashlight and hurried out front. He lay on his back and used the flashlight to check under the car. Sure enough, there was a bomb set beneath the driver's seat, wires linked to the starter motor.

Procter took a huge breath, held it, and cut the green wire.

Nothing happened. He exhaled and carefully removed the device.

Back in his study, he put a hand to his chest. It was a long time before his pulse steadied. He poured out the last of the wine and drank it down. In one short conversation his life had been turned upside down. Clarke had betrayed him. Tesseract had threatened to kill him. He didn't take kindly to either.

A click of the mouse re-opened the email he had been about to send. He scratched his chin for a moment. Tesseract was a dangerous operator, unpredictable. Procter had believed he could control him, but he had just been proved very wrong. If he clicked the mouse, Tesseract wouldn't be able to put any more bombs beneath his car.

But, under the circumstances, that had been almost understandable. And dammit, Procter was starting to like the guy.

He deleted the email and got up to find another bottle of wine.

CHAPTER 58

Potomac River, Virginia, USA

The fish thrashing wildly on the end of the line was a small-mouth bass. Clarke reeled it in with a modicum of triumph. It wasn't particularly big – maybe twelve inches long, maybe three pounds – but a catch was a catch. He sat alone in his fishing boat, feeling the morning sun on his bare forearms and face. There was little wind. The water was calm. Trees lined the river-banks. No one else was in sight.

Clarke's dad had taught him fishing at a young age and though Clarke didn't fish often, he did enjoy it when he found the time. Good for the blood pressure too, his physician often told him. Clarke held up the smallie to take a good look. Its mouth opened and closed continuously in a futile effort to breathe.

'You are one ugly fish,' he said.

He threw it back in and took a can of Heineken from his cool box. He held it against his forehead before popping the tab. He took a drink. It was cold and crisp and momentarily helped

Clarke forget that he'd almost succeeded in doing the impossible and regulating the arms trade. But he hadn't. Clarke took another long drink.

His cell rang. He was surprised to see the caller was Procter.

Clarke answered it and said, 'I thought we were going to stay away from each other for a while.'

'This can't wait,' Procter replied. 'Where are you?'

Clarke found Procter waiting by his car, dressed in his office suit and sunglasses. It was parked on the side of a rural lane, a couple of hundred yards from the riverbank. No one was nearby. Procter looked pissed.

'You screwed me, Peter. You really screwed me.'

'I beg your pardon.'

Procter stormed closer. 'Don't even try and deny it. I know what you've been doing this whole time.'

'I've been fishing.'

Procter smirked. 'Nice. I'm glad you've kept your sense of humour, but I'm talking about your little arrangement with Yuliya Eltsina.'

Clarke did well to keep the colour in his face. 'Say again.'

'You had a team go after Tesseract while he was on the Kasakov job, to protect us from the Mossad threat, didn't you? I'm not happy about that, Peter, but I can understand it, even if in sending them you stopped Tesseract killing Kasakov. Funny thing is, it turns out this was the team who kidnapped Ariff and his family. What are the odds?'

Clarke held up his hands. 'I don't know where you're getting your information from, but it's wrong.'

467

Procter shook his head. He was furious. 'Want to tell me why you were at Heathrow two weeks ago at the same time as Yuliya Eltsina? Did you think I wouldn't find out? I'm offended you think so little of me.'

'Roland, please . . .'

'Shut up, Peter. Just shut the hell up. All this time you've been using me. You were never on my side, were you? What were you really trying to do, help Eltsina seize power?'

Clarke took a breath. He squinted into the sun. 'That was only half of it.'

'What was the other half? Don't tell me you did all this for a blowjob.'

'Don't be ridiculous. After she was in control of Kasakov's empire she would only sell arms to buyers I approved.'

Procter's eyes went wide. 'And you believed that?'

'Yes,' Clarke snapped. 'Of course I did. I've known Yuliya since the height of the Cold War. I trust her. And Roland, your plan would never have worked. Eventually Kasakov and Ariff would have worked out they'd been tricked. At that point the war would have stopped and we would have achieved nothing. My way would have enabled Eltsina to take over Ariff's network too. She would have been the single most important trafficker of small arms as well as heavy munitions, answerable to me. Me. I could have made sure the supplies of weapons to America's enemies ran dry and were never replaced. It would have achieved both our goals.'

'You should have told me.'

Clarke laughed. 'Roland, you're as stubborn as a grease stain. You would never have agreed to doing it my way.'

'Be that as it may, that didn't give you the right to lie to me and go behind my back. I'm guessing you told your boys to kill Callo too.'

Clarke shrugged. 'Keeping him alive was an unnecessary risk. And his death made the ploy more convincing, even you agreed on that.'

'You're not the least bit sorry, are you?' Procter accused.

'I'm sorry the plan didn't work,' Clarke said. 'I'm not sorry I tried to do some good. Our friendship means a lot to me, but not as much as saving American lives.'

Procter turned and walked away. 'Our friendship is over, Peter.'

'Roland,' Clarke called. 'Don't be so melodramatic.'

Procter didn't look back.

Thirty minutes later, Clarke was back on the river and tossing his line out once more. He'd tried to get hold of Eltsina but the Russian hadn't answered. She was either avoiding Clarke, on the run, or dead. Any of the three was just as likely as the others, but Clarke guessed the explanation was the latter. Eltsina had warned Clarke what could happen if Kasakov suffered another attack.

Would Kasakov have extracted any information from her first? If Eltsina had been killed for failing in her role as Kasakov's intelligence officer, then chances were she would have simply been executed. However, if Eltsina's plans had somehow been revealed then surely Kasakov would have made her suffer first. At which point she would scream out anything to make the pain stop.

Assuming Kasakov knew Clarke's name, would he make a move against a member of the US government? Unlikely, because of the fear of possible retaliation, but Clarke kept his .45 calibre Taurus nearby at all times, just in case.

He sighed, thinking about Procter. Clarke had never been happy using his friend the way he had, but it was unavoidable. Not that it mattered now.

The unmistakable noise of an outboard motor decimated the tranquillity. It grew louder and the boat itself appeared, rounding a bend in the river. The vessel was travelling faster than it really should and Clarke felt his own boat begin to rock with the newly created waves. He watched as the boat veered his way. There were two guys onboard. One waved at Clarke.

Clarke adjusted his sunglasses and glanced at the Taurus near his feet. Always better to have a gun and not need one than to need one and not have it, he thought. He tucked the weapon into the back of his shorts. He stood up as the boat grew nearer.

'Help you, boys?' he asked.

The two guys were in their twenties, carrying the unmistakable air of purebred hicks. The guy who waved had his left arm in a makeshift sling. He grimaced.

'My buddy hurt his arm,' the guy at the motor said. 'Think his wrist might be broken.'

'Ouch,' Clarke said. 'How'd you do that?'

The guy with the sling shrugged and looked sheepish. 'Fell over trying to reel in a big 'un.'

'Hope you got it.'

The guy shook his head.

'Too bad,' Clarke said, feeling better about the twelve-incher.

'Sorry to disturb your fishin', mister,' the guy at the motor said. 'But you got a first-aid kit? Maybe some aspirin?'

'Sure,' Clarke said. 'But ibuprofen is probably better for your needs.'

He turned to fetch his first-aid box. When he turned around, both guys were standing. They didn't look like hicks any more. The guy with the sling no longer had a sling. Instead, he had a silenced automatic pistol in his right hand. The other guy had one too. Both pointed Clarke's way.

'What is this?' he asked, though he knew the answer.

Clarke thought about the Taurus in the back of his shorts. No way he could get to it, let alone get it out. He tried to stay calm but panic overtook him. He shook his head from side to side.

The guy without the sling looked to the other guy, who nodded and said, 'Compliments of Vladimir Kasakov.'

Clarke felt the agony of the first bullet hitting him just below the ribcage.

After that, he felt nothing.

CHAPTER 59

Sofia, Bulgaria

Victor had been in the city for twenty-four hours after returning from the US, via Canada. He'd done the same on the way in to American too, to avoid the fingerprinting and photographing of flying directly. He sat at his hotel-room desk and used his new laptop to make the scheduled call with Procter.

The line connected and Procter said, 'My partner is dead.'

'I didn't think you had it in you.'

'I didn't,' Procter admitted, voice strained, 'but someone else did.'

'I can't say I'm sorry about that,' Victor said.

'He was a good man.'

'I'll take your word for it.'

'Do,' Procter insisted.

'I hope you're not going to ask me to avenge him.'

'No,' Procter said. 'I wouldn't, even if I wanted to. He made his bed. Now he's lying in it.'

'Where does that leave us?'

'Well, I'm still a little sore about the bomb you left under my car.'

'I told you which wire to cut, didn't I?'

'Yeah, you did. So I guess we're even. I take it you got my message about Mossad looking for you in Barcelona?'

'I did. And I haven't been there in years.'

'There we go then. They're chasing shadows. Keep your head down and it will stay that way. Resources are already being diverted at the Agency. Soon, neither of us will have to worry. And I don't know about you, but I'm going to take a vacation. I fancy somewhere hot and remote.'

'Sounds nice.'

'You should do the same. You can afford it. I've paid you the second half of the Kasakov fee.'

'I'm surprised.'

'You only failed because of the intervention of my associate. That's not your fault. I've done the same with the Yamout job. You could not have foreseen Mossad's involvement.'

'I appreciate the gesture.'

'That's a clever way of thanking me without actually having to say thank you.'

'I thought so too.'

There was a pause, and Victor felt Procter's smile. 'So, my man. We're done. You went after Kasakov, as agreed, and I'm a man of my word. You're no longer obligated to me. You're a free man. Enjoy your retirement. It's yours if you want it.'

Victor ignored the comment, for now. He said, 'Tell me something: why go after Kasakov and Ariff the way you did?'

'What do you mean?'

'Why do it under the radar, using someone like me instead of a CIA team? Kasakov and Ariff can't be popular in Washington.'

'They're not,' Procter agreed. 'But Kasakov has been the Kremlin's golden boy for a long time now. He's made them billions in sales. If there was any hint of the CIA's hand in his death there would be one hell of a shitstorm from Moscow. Would such a shitstorm bother me? No, sir. But Capitol Hill doesn't share my sentiments. With Ariff the prime suspect, however, it's a different story.'

'That's one half of it.'

'I don't follow.'

'Surely it would have been better to send a snatch-and-grab team after Ariff once you knew where he was hiding out. He could still have taken the blame for Kasakov's death, but you could hand him over to the ICC on war crimes charges and score a major PR coup.' Victor paused. 'Unless Ariff being grilled by prosecutors was something you very much did not want to happen. What did he have on you?'

There was a moment of silence before Procter said, 'I used to run Ariff, back in the day. It's no secret the CIA supplied Afghan Mujahideen with Stingers to knock Soviet choppers out of the skies in the eighties. But I was the guy on the ground who got those missiles into 'Stan by using Ariff, who already had donkey trains carrying AKs across the border from Pakistan.'

'Why would that matter now?'

'Because even before Ariff was supplying guns and components for IEDS to America's enemies in Iraq and Afghanistan, he was a known scumbag. Back then he supplied the PLO, Black September, Hezbollah, and every other terrorist organisation from Tripoli to Tehran. The explosives that blew up the Marine barracks in Lebanon in '83 were from Ariff. I knew all that, but I still used him, without CIA consent. We live in a post-911 world, my man, and Ariff dropping my name at The Hague would have caused me a heap of hurt. So, yeah, I got something out of all this too. Satisfied?'

'Surprisingly, yes.'

'You've got your answers now, and you've got your freedom.' Procter said, 'So, is this where we go our separate ways?'

Victor had spent the last few days thinking about little else. Procter had withheld information from him, creating extra problems, extra risks. But he had revealed his identity to prove Victor could trust him. That meant a lot.

He said, 'I don't feel the same pressing need to part company I felt before.'

'I hoped you'd say that. But I didn't expect you to.'

'When my actions become predictable, my life will fall into the past tense.'

'Does this mean that you finally trust me?'

'Let's not get ahead of ourselves.'

Another pause, maybe for another smile, before Procter said, 'I'll contact you when I need you again.'

'Which will be?'

'I don't know. Could be a while.'

'Suits me,' Victor said. 'It's been a long two months.'

'For you and me both.' Procter paused a moment and said. 'Take care.'

The line disconnected. Victor opened up an internet browser and accessed his other email accounts. He had another email from Alonso and two from other brokers. The contracts offered were for high figures and low risks. They would be simple to complete without Procter's knowledge.

Victor deleted the emails and deactivated the accounts.

For the first time in a long time he felt truly relaxed. He made a phone call.

Adrianna answered with a cheery, '*Allo*.'

'It's Emmanuel,' Victor said. 'How do you fancy a day in Sofia?'

CHAPTER 60

Victor met Adrianna in the lobby of the Grand Hotel Sofia. The large marble, granite and glass-fronted hotel was located in the centre of the city, overlooking the City Garden. He'd changed hotels after she'd agreed to meet him as his previous modest accommodation would not have met with Adrianna's approval. She wore a long flowing dress that seemed to float across her figure as she wheeled an overnight suitcase behind her. Her wavy brown hair hung loose and sunglasses rested on top of her head.

'You look so different,' she announced as Victor approached. 'I love the tan and longer hair. Very sexy.'

She flicked a lock of hair for emphasis before they embraced and kissed. Victor was careful to pull away before her hands could drift down his back to where an FN Five-seveN handgun was tucked into his waistband.

'You've lost some weight,' he said.

She beamed. 'You noticed.'

He hadn't. 'How was your flight?'

'A pleasure.' She took a tourist guide from her handbag. 'I've been learning all about Sofia.'

Once they'd dropped her case off in Victor's room and freshened up, they set out to explore Sofia. The City Art Gallery was close to the hotel, so they began there, discussing the exhibits and which they liked and why. Afterwards they used the city's yellow trams to visit some of Sofia's many historic Orthodox churches, of which the highlight was the impressive Alexander Nevsky Cathedral with its one hundred and fifty feet high gold-domed basilica.

Aside from the odd communist era tower blocks scarring the skyline, Sofia was a typically beautiful historic European capital. Victor liked the juxtaposition of architectural styles – Western and Central European, neoclassical and Stalinist, Roman and Byzantine. The ever-changing architecture gave each tree-lined street its own unique identity and feel. The roads of the city centre seemed to be almost entirely paved with yellow cobblestones.

'From Vienna,' Adrianna was quick to tell him.

It may have been Adrianna's first visit, but Victor had been a couple of times before, and had always found Bulgarians to be almost universally friendly and welcoming. This time was no different. He liked the climate too, warm but not hot, maybe seventy degrees today.

They ate a late lunch at one of Sofia's many open-air cafés, where they enjoyed the sun on their faces and the frenetic chatter of the surrounding locals. Victor knew enough of the language to get by and taught Adrianna the odd phrase. Together they tried to follow some of the lightning-fast conversations of those surrounding them, always quickly failing and adding their own fictitious translations.

'He's dumping her,' Adrianna explained as they slyly watched a couple of middle-aged Bulgarians arguing, 'because her breath smells like old socks.'

He smiled as, out of habit, he watched the crowd for shadows.

As evening came they returned to the hotel to wash and change. Chopin's Andante Spianato et Grande Polonaise in E-flat major flowed through the room's radio as Victor buttoned his shirt with one hand. The fingers of his other hand gently moved to the music, pressing imaginary keys.

Adrianna, fixing in earrings, noticed him. 'Do you play?'

'I haven't in months.' He finished buttoning his shirt with both hands.

'Any reason why?'

'I just haven't had the opportunity.'

He couldn't help but picture his most prized possessions, a nineteenth-century Vose & Sons Square Grand piano, which was now only ashes.

'I think there's a piano in one of the hotel bars. I'm sure they'd let you, if we ask.'

'I'll be too rusty. I don't want to embarrass myself,' he said, using the pretence of shyness to hide the fact that years of trying to remain unnoticed had conditioned him to find such acts as publically playing a piano to be an impossibility.

He finished getting ready, and while Adrianna was in the bathroom, tucked his gun into the waistband over his right hip. He would make sure she walked on his left side only.

'What do you think?' Adrianna said as she emerged back into the bedroom.

She looked gorgeous in a black evening gown, pashmina wrapped around her shoulders, and her hair tied up.

Victor didn't disappoint, and said, 'Stunning.'

Her glossy lips formed a huge smile.

The National Theatre was only a block away from the hotel. Elegant uplights bathed the grand early twentieth-century building in a golden glow. At the box office, Victor collected tickets for a performance of Puccini's *Turandot*. They sat in a box on the south-west wall and watched the performance with opera glasses, Adrianna enraptured by the spectacle and moved to the point of tears by the arias. Afterwards, they walked through the gardens set before the opera house while they discussed the performance.

Other opera-goers did the same, and tourists snapped photographs of the theatre. Couples sat on stone benches and held hands.

Adrianna linked her right arm with Victor's left and said, 'I've had such a wonderful day. Thank you for inviting me here.'

'My pleasure,' Victor replied.

'After Linz, I wasn't sure we were going to see each other any more.'

'What made you think that?'

She took a moment to answer, either struggling to articulate her thoughts or just hesitant of what she was about to say. 'I'm not sure really, but you seemed so different the last time I saw you. Like a different you. I wasn't sure if I would fit in with the change, that's all.'

'I didn't know I had changed,' he said, without meaning it.

'Oh, don't worry,' she replied, hearing a tone he hadn't

intended her to. 'I think it's a positive thing.' She examined him, and ran slim fingers through his hair. 'Definitely a good change.'

He smiled to show he agreed, even if he didn't. 'I'm glad you think so. And I take it you're happy I called?'

She smiled and lightly hit him on the arm. 'Of course I am.'

They walked some more.

'Excuse me,' a woman said in British-accented English, stepping into their path.

She was in her late twenties, accompanied by a man who looked thirty, presumably her boyfriend or husband. They were both in casual clothes, jeans, T-shirts, athletics shoes. The guy's hair was dark, the woman's blonde. She had a camera in hand. They were both smiling. Big, excitable grins. Tourists.

'Excuse me,' the woman said again, speaking slowly, deliberately, as if to a child, long spaces between each word, drawing out each syllable for emphasis, 'would you take a picture of us, please?' She made a big deal of pointing at the camera and then to her boyfriend and herself.

'Sure, of course,' Victor said back.

He would have thought it impossible, but their smiles grew wider. 'Oh, you speak English. Great. Thank you *so* much.'

Adrianna said, 'You're British, right?'

The blonde woman made a small laugh. 'Is it that obvious?'

Victor raised an eyebrow. 'British people have a certain way of speaking abroad.'

'We do, don't we? Thanks again for doing this.'

He said, 'It's no trouble,' even though it was. Had he been alone he would have pretended not to speak the language and moved on. He didn't like any contact that was not on his terms, but he didn't want to show that in front of Adrianna.

The female tourist handed over her camera. 'If you could get it so the opera house is in the background, that would be great.'

'No problem.'

He gestured. 'You might want to move closer together.'

'Oh yeah, sure.'

She leaned closer to her boyfriend, wrapping her arms around him as though he might run away if she didn't hang on tight. He put his arm around her shoulder, though somewhat stiffly. British reserve.

Victor stepped back and went down to one knee to get them both in the centre of the frame, with the opera house in the background, said, 'Say cheese.' and took the photo. He handed back the camera. 'Your first photo in Sofia,' he noted from the camera's display. 'I'm honoured.'

The couple looked at the image. 'Oh, that's perfect. Thank you *so* much.' She nudged the boyfriend. 'Wait 'til Andy and Meg see this.'

With lots more thank-yous the couple departed, leaving Adrianna and Victor alone again. Adrianna took his hands in hers.

'Those two made a cute pair,' she said, 'didn't they?'

Victor nodded. He wasn't sure what was cute and what wasn't.

'I can imagine them old and grey and still just as in love.'

Victor nodded again. He found it impossible to imagine such things.

She rubbed his arms. 'Do you ever think about settling down, Emmanuel; finding yourself a nice wife to pass you your slippers?'

482

'Do wives still fetch their husbands' slippers?'

'I don't know,' she said with a shrug. 'I guess for the right man they might.'

There wasn't anything in her eyes Victor couldn't read. He asked, 'What would you like to do now?'

'I'm not sure. Are you hungry yet?'

'I could eat if you're ready for dinner.'

'I've been ready for dinner for the last two hours. This diet is killing me.'

Victor knew a good Indian restaurant about twenty minutes' walk north, but Adrianna was too hungry to wait so they took a cab. He had aloo tika ragda to start, followed by paneer makhani. Adrianna started with bhel puri and then ate mushroom matar hara pyaz. The food was excellent, aromatic and flavoursome but without being excessively spicy. For dessert they both ordered mango ice cream. It came in a cone shape. After their meal they drank milky Indian tea while Adrianna talked about the possibility of going back to university.

'I'm thinking about getting a PhD,' she explained. 'I miss studying. Reading History at Cambridge was one of the best times of my life. I miss books. I miss being academic. I hardly ever even get time to read the paper these days. It sounds overly dramatic, I know, but sometimes I feel like I'm letting my intelligence slip away.'

'It sounds like you've already made up your mind.'

'It does, doesn't it? I think I have.'

'Would you go back to Cambridge to study or somewhere new?'

Mentioning Cambridge made him remember the British

483

couple. Specifically, the blonde woman. Tourists didn't usually ask him to take pictures. Victor gave off a subtle leave-me-alone vibe that most people subconsciously heeded, but it didn't always work. He could only go so far with negative body language. If he was too unapproachable, people would remember him. Better to be the kind of man some people were happy to talk to, than the kind of rude man no one forgot. And in Adrianna's company he would seem more approachable.

She asked, 'What's wrong?'

'I can't hide anything from you, can I?' he said, again surprised that she could read him so well. 'I was just thinking about work. Sorry.'

'Want to talk about it?'

He shook his head. 'Work is boring. Let's talk about you. So, Cambridge?'

'I'm not sure. I did love it there, but maybe somewhere different would be good. I'm all for new experiences.'

He nodded and enthused as she talked about her plans, but all the while he replayed the incident with the tourists in his mind. There was nothing suspicious about either of them. The guy hadn't spoken, but he seemed shy compared to his outgoing partner. No, it wasn't the tourists that were bothering him, it was himself, for his inability to lower his guard and take a picture for a couple of dumb tourists without feeling exposed because they had taken him by surprise. He wondered how he had become this facsimile of a person – a jigsaw with pieces missing – and if it would ever be any different.

Adrianna continued, 'Columbia University is very highly regarded, of course, and I absolutely adore New York. Though I'd run the risk of doing more shopping than studying.'

Victor nodded and sipped his tea, telling himself that his paranoia was excessively keen in this instance. Mossad were chasing leads in Barcelona, according to Procter. There was nothing for them to find there that would lead to Bulgaria.

'You're the first person I've told about this,' Adrianna added with a shy smile.

Victor said, 'I'm honoured,' and immediately remembered saying the same words to the British woman. He'd commented on having taken their first picture in Sofia, according to the camera's display. The woman had not responded to his remark. Not a single word or even gesture. A personable tourist, as she clearly had shown herself to be, would have replied with some kind of explanation. Maybe they had only just arrived, or it was a new memory stick in the camera. But nothing.

Victor cursed himself for not understanding sooner.

He didn't know how, whether they'd somehow tracked him or followed Adrianna to him. But it didn't matter. All that mattered now was that they had found him.

The Kidon were in Sofia.

The charade with the camera must have been to make a positive ID. With his longer hair, tan and beard he looked notably different from the man caught on camera a month before. They had needed to get close to make sure he was really their target. It was brazen, risky, but they hadn't been aware Victor knew they were after him.

Procter had been wrong about Barcelona, or maybe his intel had just been out of date. Across from Victor, Adrianna continued to talk about universities and studying, completely unaware of the mortal danger they were both in.

They were being watched at this very moment, Victor knew.

He detected no shadows in the restaurant, which would be unnecessarily close, but they would be waiting outside, ready to follow him and Adrianna when they left.

He had an advantage – they had no idea he was on to them. When would they strike? He didn't know. Probably not at his hotel. Hotels were notoriously difficult places for actions to go down – he knew that better than most – but that wouldn't stop Kidon operatives. Mossad had successfully pulled off more hotel assassinations than anyone else. But they didn't want to kill him – at least not yet. Otherwise they could have gunned him down outside the opera house the minute he'd been identified. They wanted answers first. They wanted to know who he was and who sent him and why. A kidnapping was more difficult than an assassination, so they would have to make an attempt on the streets, somewhere with the fewest possible witnesses to see him bundled into a van.

So long as Adrianna was with him Victor couldn't escape the Kidon. Alone, he might have a chance.

'So you see,' he became aware Adrianna was saying, 'I can't quite decide between Columbia or Cambridge.' She laughed. 'Maybe I'll do a PhD at both.'

'It's a tough decision,' Victor said. He stood. 'Excuse me for a minute.'

He headed to the restrooms, knowing the Kidon watchers outside would see him go, but they wouldn't be worried because Adrianna was still sitting at the table, awaiting his return. While she sat there, Victor gained time.

The restaurant's bathroom was compact and clean. A small window was set high in the back wall above the furthest stall. Victor entered it, knocked the lid down on the toilet, stood on

486

it, worked the latch, and opened the window. Cool air flowed in and over his face. He peered into the alleyway beyond. It was dark but empty. The Kidon were watching the front. There was no reason to watch the back.

In three minutes they would start to wonder, in five they would begin to worry. By six, they would send someone inside to check. But with a six-minute head start he would be long gone, in a cab or on a bus, heading out of town. They wouldn't catch him.

Their attention would turn to Adrianna as a solid link to him, even if she was anything but. They wouldn't believe that she knew nothing about him. They would have to be convinced. He tried not to picture what they might do to her to extract information she didn't have.

But together they couldn't avoid them, and if Victor sent her away first it would only make them suspicious and any chance he had of escaping would vanish.

Victor didn't have true friends. He cared about no one. It was one of the ways that kept him alive. His relationship with Adrianna was an act they both played, and she played it for money, nothing more. She used him like he used her. There was nothing else between them, nothing to stop him now.

He climbed through the window and into the night.

CHAPTER 61

Adrianna checked her watch. Emmanuel had been gone for over four minutes. She sipped her milky tea while observing the other diners around her. There were lots of couples, the odd family, everyone enjoying the food and having a good time. Indian waiters and waitresses effortlessly glided around the tightly packed tables, taking orders and delivering food with graceful ease.

She'd probably had one glass of rosé too many with dinner and was feeling a little less composed than she would normally prefer to operate, but she was having a good time. That wasn't an act. Her dinner had been delicious, the best meal she'd had in a long time. The mushroom matar hara pyaz was divine; so creamy. And the mango ice cream was just the thing to freshen the breath afterwards.

She finished the last of her tea while she thought about Emmanuel. The man of mystery, tall and lean, scars covering his athlete's body, always alert, never truly relaxing, and with a falseness in his smile and a deadness in his eyes she pretended not to see. She wanted to give him a hug – a real hug – but that was a dangerous path to take with a client. Even if Emmanuel had always been a dream client. Always the perfect gentlemen. Always paid without a fuss. Never got jealous of her other clients. Never hit her. Never tried to make their arrangement into something it wasn't. Never made her feel like a whore.

A young, smiling waiter stopped by her table and asked if she'd like anything else. She declined. After he'd gone Adrianna checked her watch again. Emmanuel had been gone over six minutes now.

She noticed a man entering the restaurant. He was slight of build, with pale skin and curly black hair. He seemed particularly underdressed in jeans and a nylon jacket, and waved a hand to dismiss a waitress's offer to seat him. Adrianna watched him as he headed for the restroom. He looked vaguely familiar, as if she'd seen him before but only in passing. Had he been on the same flight, or in the crowd at the airport when she landed? He glanced her way out of the corner of his eye, and Adrianna averted her own gaze so as not to be caught watching.

She turned her thoughts away from him, whoever he was, and back to Emmanuel. Adrianna had a strange feeling he wasn't coming back, ridiculous as that idea was. It was just that extra glass of wine playing with her, she knew, but maybe she'd scared him off with all that talk of him being different last time they met. Had she upset him by claiming he'd changed? She should have known better than to get that personal with a client. The kind of men who paid her for company didn't want her analysing them, especially a man as private and particular as Emmanuel.

Adrianna silently cursed herself for saying anything. Why had she? She knew the answer. Whatever the act they played, after

Linz she had thought – no, feared – she wouldn't see Emmanuel again.

Now that fear had returned. Again she checked her watch. Seven minutes. She wondered how long she should wait, and whether anyone would notice if she left without her date.

The man in the nylon jacket emerged from the bathroom. He looked flustered and drew a cell phone from a pocket as he hurried across the restaurant floor towards the door. She felt him looking at her again, but she was used to men looking her way. Not all of them knew how to do so without making it obvious.

The smiling waiter noticed her gesture and drifted over.

'Anything else, madam?'

She shook her head. 'Can I get the bill, please?'

'Of course.'

A moment later a long leather folder was on the table and Adrianna opened her handbag to retrieve her purse. She withdrew a credit card.

'Sorry I was so long.'

Adrianna looked up to see Emmanuel taking his seat opposite her. She hadn't even noticed his approach. She felt equal parts relief and foolishness, but a large part of her work was maintaining her cool, whatever the situation.

'Were you gone a long time?' she asked. 'I can't say I noticed. I had the waiter bring the bill.'

'Forget about that,' he said, leaning closer. 'I want you to listen to me very carefully, Adrianna. You must believe everything I tell you and do exactly as I say, without questions.'

He looked so serious it was almost funny. 'Okay,' she said, putting on an overly serious expression of her own. 'I'm listening.'

Emmanuel said, 'After we've finished talking, I want you to get up and go to the ladies' restroom. Go into the far stall, put down the toilet seat and take off your shoes.'

'My shoes?'

He ignored her. 'Then stand on the toilet and open the window in the wall. If it won't open then you'll need to break it and use your handbag to clear out the glass. The next part will be difficult, but you have to do it as fast as you can. Don't worry about getting dirty. You have to hurry.'

'I don't understand.'

'Listen to me, Adrianna, you don't need to understand. There isn't time to make you understand. You just need to do exactly what I'm telling you. You need to climb through the window and out into the alley on the other side. The drop isn't far and I've put some cardboard boxes on the ground outside that will break your fall so you don't hurt yourself. You'll find yourself in an alleyway. You must go left and then left again. You'll come out on to a side street. A taxi will be waiting for you. Get into the back and sit directly behind the driver. Tell him to go straight to the airport. On the way, take out your cell phone and throw it out of the window. Tell the—'

'My phone. Why? What's going on? You're scaring me.'

'Tell him to hurry,' Emmanuel continued. 'Tell the driver you'll pay him double if he steps on it. Show him the money if you have to. At the airport take out as much cash from an ATM as you can. Then get the first flight out, whatever it is, wherever it's going. When you arrive at your destination, take another flight, the next available flight. It doesn't matter where to. When you arrive you can go wherever you wish, but take a train or bus. Pay in cash. Don't use any credit cards again.'

Tears welled in her eyes. She didn't understand. Emmanuel was a whole other person. Intense. Frightening.

He grabbed a napkin and scribbled down a long number, an alphanumeric one and the name and address of a bank. 'This is a numbered account. The balance of it is now yours. It should keep you going for a few years if you're careful. Are you paying attention?'

'Yes, yes. But I don't—'

'This last part is very important. You can't go back to Geneva. You can't go home. You have to stay moving. You can't contact any of your friends or clients. And you can't contact your brother in America. You can't have anything to do with your old life.'

She felt nauseous. 'How . . . how do you know about David?'

'Listen to me, Adrianna. You're in a lot of danger. That's my fault, and I'm so sorry, but you have to do exactly what I'm telling you if I'm to protect you.' He wrote another number on the napkin. 'Call this number in a week's time. Hopefully, I'll have left a message to say everything's okay and you can go home, or I'll have left instructions. I'll use a code so you know it's from me.'

'What code?'

He shook his head. 'If I give you one now they'll make me tell it to them. But you'll know it's from me, all right? If there is no message, or there is no code or the message asks you to meet me somewhere, you must ignore it and not call the number back under any circumstances. In which case you'll never be able to go back home.' He paused. 'And whatever happens, you won't see me again.'

She couldn't stop the tears. She reached out a hand to touch his.

'Stop crying,' he said. 'Stop it right now. If they see you crying, they'll know.'

'Who? Who will see? Who will know? Who will make you tell?'

'Put that napkin in your bag and don't lose it. It's time to go.'

'I don't want to.'

'Do you remember everything I've said?'

'I don't understand why you're doing this.' She squeezed his hand, seeking comfort. 'Who will see? Emmanuel, what is going on?'

He snapped his hand away.

'*Go,*' he snarled.

'Who are you?' she asked, wide-eyed.

'Someone you don't want to know.'

Adrianna folded up the napkin, subtly dabbed her eyes, stood and headed for the ladies' room. She didn't look back. Victor was glad of that. He didn't want to see her face and the terror he'd put there. She pushed open the door to the restrooms. Then she was gone, for ever.

He finished his cold tea and paid the bill with cash, including a one hundred per cent tip. Better the waiter got his money than Mossad.

If he left this instant it might confuse them for him to be without Adrianna, and that might buy Victor enough time to create some distance. But if he left now, watchers in the area might notice a taxi and the woman who sat sobbing in the back. While

493

he remained here at his table, Adrianna was sure to make it to the airport safely.

After ten minutes they would know for certain she wasn't going to return, and that she must have snuck out the back. And that fact would tell them that Victor knew they were out there and he would have lost his only advantage. It would be too late to catch up with Adrianna, but they would take him at the first available opportunity.

When his watch showed it had been eleven minutes since Adrianna's departure, Victor stood, unbuttoned his suit jacket, and stepped outside.

CHAPTER 62

The air was cool. The sky was cloudless. There was a full moon. The Indian restaurant stood just outside Sofia's centre, in a dense commercial neighbourhood. The street out front was busy in the daytime, but at this time of night few establishments were open and the street was quiet. Pedestrians were sparse. The storefronts on the opposite side of the street were all dark. Some had security grilles. Cars were parked on either side of the road, but there was little traffic. Victor examined every person.

He went left because it would take him into central Sofia. More people there, more cars, more buses. More options. Plus there was access to Sofia's metro system. It was relatively small and new, but he needed as many escape options as possible. He couldn't know where or when the Kidon would strike and he needed terrain that would make their job more difficult while at the same time offering him the most advantages. A taxi was no good. He would be even easier to follow than on foot, and all they would have to do was get a car in front and a car behind and that would be it. He walked at a hurried pace. There was no point trying to act casual. They knew he knew.

He walked for four minutes along the same street. People walked ahead of him, behind him, on the opposite side of the road. Mostly men, the odd couple. No single women. He crossed over the street and looked in store windows to check the reflections of anyone walking behind on the far side of the road. No one, but there was a man and a woman on the same side as him. Not the couple with the camera. That would have been too obvious. These both looked in their thirties, both in reasonable shape, unremarkable clothes. Potentials.

He stood with his hand near his waistband, within a short distance of the gun tucked there. The couple didn't react and walked straight past him.

He walked some more. After two minutes the couple stopped under a bus shelter and sat down. A perfectly normal action or a smart way to step out of the game now their target was behind them and out of sight. Victor kept the same pace as he passed. He used what windows he could to keep watching but within seconds he'd gone too far to get an angle.

Cars rolled by intermittently in both directions. Victor walked towards the flow of traffic on the near lane so a Kidon vehicle couldn't come up behind him. Traffic was light. Too light for a van to roll up next to him without warning. The cars that went by were mostly small European sedans. He saw a blue four-door Peugeot that looked familiar, but it was hard to be sure.

He checked his watch. Adrianna should be almost at the airport by now. It was close to the city. Even if the Kidon had sent people there after realising what was happening, they wouldn't catch up that lead. He willed her to do exactly as instructed and take the first flight out, whatever it may be.

He watched the unmistakable shape of a minivan approaching. It seemed to slow as it neared. He looked to the row of stores to his left. No alleyways or side streets. No flimsy doors or unbarred windows. He tensed in readiness. His best bet would be to sprint across the road the second the van got close, adopt a shooting stance, kill the driver and keep shooting until his gun clicked empty and he felt the burning sting of a bullet penetrating his flesh.

But the van drove by without slowing. In minutes Victor was the only pedestrian in sight and the space between passing vehicles grew enough to cause him concern. He had to get off the street. He took the next turning that presented itself.

Victor walked along the side street, down another when he reached an intersection. The streets were darker, quieter, narrower. Far less people. He was still heading into the city centre, but taking a less direct route. It started to rain lightly. He walked two miles in twenty-seven minutes, darting down alleyways, doubling back, doing everything possible to lose them, but knowing they were near and he was only delaying the inevitable.

He pictured Adrianna now in a departure lounge, if not safely in a seat and fastening her belt. She would be traumatised, but she was safe. In time she would learn to deal with her fear. He hoped she could one day forgive him, but he knew how he'd spoken to her would make that a false hope. If he had been comforting and understanding, then maybe. But he had been harsh and uncaring because he'd had to make her afraid to save her life.

He kept his hands outside of his pockets and his jacket open. He paid attention to every sound, every shadow. Each time he heard an engine he calculated how far away it was and in which direction it was heading. Every person he saw, he absorbed their manner, age, looks, build, clothes, evaluating the probability of them being a Kidon operative.

The street Victor walked down had a cobbled surface and five-storey buildings flanking either side. To Victor's left was paving with a low kerb. To his right there was no sidewalk. The buildings were drab grey brick. Signs for stores fronted by security gates provided muted colour. The rain was fine and cold. No wind.

There was one other person on the street. Fifty yards ahead, at the intersection, a woman stood talking on a cell phone. She paced back and forth beneath the glow of a streetlamp. Victor's footsteps echoed. Few lights were on in the windows above the closed stores.

He felt the urge to light a cigarette and wished he still smoked. If his mental map of Sofia was accurate, there was a metro station about a block away. A few minutes and he would be in the relative safety of a clean, modern carriage. He would ride it to the train station and take any train he could. He was so close.

He noticed footsteps behind him. Someone had just turned on to the street on the opposite side of the road – a man, by the weight of the footsteps and the time between them.

Victor walked on. He felt a prickling at the back of his neck. Including himself, there were three people on the street now. A lot for a quiet street at that time of night. The woman continued to talk into her phone. She hadn't looked at him once.

He increased his pace. There were no alleyways leading off the street except back the way he had come. The intersection was forty yards away. The woman beneath the streetlight was short and slender. Flat practical shoes.

Victor looked up. No one at any windows or on any rooftops. He heard the rumble of an approaching engine. The footsteps behind him hadn't grown quieter. They should have. The walker was matching his pace.

A car turned into the street from the intersection ahead. Its headlights swept over the woman. Victor averted his eyes to preserve his night vision. The car crawled his way at fifteen miles per hour. It was a plain sedan. A Peugeot. Blue. Four doors. The nearside windows were all up. It didn't slow down or speed up. Victor's right hand hovered over the FN's grip. The Peugeot passed him on his right side.

Another car pulled into the road. Victor heard the Peugeot behind him slow down. As it did, the woman put away her phone and turned in his direction. She was twenty yards away. She had short boyish hair and a plain face. Victor glanced over his shoulder. The man walking on the opposite side of the street was tall, six-four, and strongly built. Buzz cut. The shadows hid any other details. The Peugeot was slowing down further behind him as the second car accelerated hard.

Two cars, two pedestrians. Victor couldn't keep eyes on them all. Which was the point.

He snapped his gaze back to the woman, and needing no other evidence, drew his gun. The woman was already reaching into her coat to do the same. Victor didn't need to look back to know the big guy across the street would be readying his own weapon. Positioned on opposite sides of the street meant they could safely shoot at him without endangering the other.

Headlights swept in his direction, momentarily blinding Victor as he took a shot. The crack from the unsuppressed Five-seveN echoed between the overlooking buildings.

He didn't see if he'd hit, and had no opportunity to check as the second car hurtled closer, straight at him. Another French sedan. A Renault. Ten yards away, then five. There was only time to fire at the driver or jump out of the way. If he killed the driver, it wouldn't stop the car slamming into him. Victor leapt right, into the road.

The car roared past where he'd been standing, and Victor rolled on the asphalt, absorbing the energy that would otherwise induce injury.

Doors were opening before the Renault had even stopped. Two people charged out. A woman from the passenger seat, a man from the back. Victor rose into a kneel, drawing a bead on the man, who was closer, but shouts from the big guy on the far side of the street and the woman with the plain face stopped him squeezing the trigger. Covered from two angles, there was nothing Victor could do. If he fired, he died.

The FN clattered on the road surface and Victor showed his palms.

The Peugeot had stopped sixty yards at the end of the street to block off the intersection from other vehicles. The Renault was less than ten yards away.

He recognised the woman now hurrying towards him from the Renault's open passenger door. She looked markedly different with a gun instead of a camera, the friendly smile

500

replaced by a cold stare. She covered him from a distance of five feet. The driver stayed behind the wheel. The man from the back had a pale, gaunt face and held the same gun. Beretta 92FS. Suppressed. Victor glanced over his shoulder to see the slender woman with the plain face remained stationary near the streetlamp, in a combat stance, gun aimed at his back.

The man with the Beretta aimed it at Victor and shouted, '*Don't move.*'

He spoke in Russian, just as Victor had spoken in Minsk.

The big guy approached. He was strongly muscled but a lean two hundred and twenty pounds. No excess bulk. Loose trousers, open sports jacket, T-shirt beneath. He searched Victor, locating the all-ceramic folding knife in seconds and tossing it away.

'Hands,' he demanded.

Victor held them out, shoulder-width apart. The big guy grabbed Victor's wrists. The strength of the grip was huge. The guy looped plasticuffs around both of Victor's wrists and fastened it tight enough for the skin to bulge white around the straps.

He took Victor by the right triceps, pulled him to the car. Victor didn't let the pain show or resist as he was thrown into the back of the Renault. The big guy gave some order in Hebrew and the original two from the car climbed in – the man on to the seat next to Victor, the woman into the passenger seat. The short woman under the streetlight slipped her gun away, and rushed over to the Peugeot, climbing into the back. The big guy got into the passenger seat.

Already Victor could feel the tingling in his hands caused by the blocked circulation. He sat himself upright. He was behind the driver. The guy on the back seat with him kept as much distance between them as possible, but didn't take his gaze off Victor. He kept his gun pointed at Victor at all times. The Beretta was chambered for 9 mm rounds, double action, safety off, hammer cocked. All he had to do was squeeze and Victor would take one in the sternum. The Israeli held the gun in his right hand and kept it parallel to his chest. It was too far away for Victor to risk grabbing, even if his hands weren't bound.

The blonde woman in the passenger seat turned to face him. She had a triumphant expression on her face. 'Put on your seat belt.'

She spoke with her British accent. She probably had been British, originally. Victor held up his bound wrists.

She smirked. 'That won't stop you.'

Victor reached behind his left shoulder and pulled the belt across his chest and fastened it. He did so as awkwardly as he could. When it clicked in place, the woman in the passenger seat turned away. She said something in Hebrew to the driver. None of the three Israelis in the car had on their belts to ensure speed of movement while he in turn was locked in place.

The Renault pulled away, following close to the Peugeot. Rehearsed moves. The driver kept the car a little above the speed limit, like anyone else who didn't want a ticket and who had nothing to hide. They drove through the narrow streets of Sofia, staying directly behind the lead car at all times. The passenger periodically looked back to check on Victor. The Israeli on the back seat didn't look away once.

Victor felt the adrenalin in his system speed up his heart rate. His pulse thundered in his ears. He looked up, staring through the window to his left. He saw the twinkling of lights in the night sky from an ascending plane and watched until those lights had disappeared into the darkness.

CHAPTER 63

The pain in Victor's wrists continued to build. His wrists were locked together, skin to skin. The tingling sensation in his hands worsened. He could make fists with his hands but precious few other movements. Soon they would be too numb to move.

They took a right turn then two lefts, bringing the car out of the backstreets and on to a wide avenue. Traffic lights glowed up ahead. Red glimmered through the raindrops on the windshield.

The Renault slowed down and stopped. Victor could reach the door handle and be rolling on to the road before anyone could react, but a Kidon team was too professional to leave the child lock disengaged. He could try anyway – on the minute chance the lock was malfunctioning – but Victor didn't want to make them even more alert by trying something destined to fail. Instead, he sat passive, defeated. His only chance was for them to underestimate him.

His knees pressed against the back of the driver's seat. He was a tall, the other fake tourist, and had the seat back to compensate for his long legs. There was little room for Victor to manoeuvre. He looked to his right, at the guy with the gun. The Israeli had a slim build and pale face beneath dark curly hair. He wore jeans and a nylon jacket. He was calm if not relaxed. The muzzle of the Beretta was slightly inclined, angled at Victor's centre mass. The guy looked like he very much wanted to squeeze the trigger, but his orders would be to only shoot if absolutely necessary. A dead man couldn't talk, after all.

The light changed and the Renault pulled away, one car length behind the Peugeot, maintaining formation, but without looking like it. They drove in silence. The radio was off. No one spoke. The woman in the passenger seat turned to look at Victor again, this time smiling to herself, and looked away. It was becoming difficult to move his fingers.

He couldn't see his watch, but he was good keeping track of time without one. Nine minutes had passed since he'd been captured. The scene outside his window changed as they left central Sofia. He saw factories and warehouses, open-air car showrooms, apartment blocks, areas of wasteland. Wherever they were taking him, he sensed it was close. When he reached it his chances of escape would drastically reduce.

The Israeli in the nylon jacket on the back seat continued to stare. He blinked regularly, keeping his eyes moist, removing the need to involuntarily blink at the wrong moment. Even if Victor could somehow get close enough to avoid the gun, he couldn't disarm the man while his hands were tied and the seat belt locked him in place. And that was before the woman in the passenger seat got involved. Similarly, Victor couldn't attack the driver while under the watchful gaze of the guy on the back seat. Maybe when the car stopped at their destination he would have a window of opportunity. The problem with that was the second car full of Kidon assassins that would have stopped too.

He took a deep breath, running multiple scenarios through his head. They all ended the same way.

The Renault continued its relentless drive. They joined a highway. The weather worsened. Rain pelted the car. Streams of water ran down the windows. Windshield wipers swung rhythmically back and forth. The pain in Victor's wrists intensified to a throbbing agony. The Israeli to his right continued to stare.

The woman in the passenger seat turned her head to look at him again.

'By the way,' she said, 'thank you for the photograph. It'll make a great souvenir. I look really good in it.'

Victor raised an eyebrow. 'And they say the camera never lies.'

She smirked.

The driver said a word in Hebrew and the woman quickly turned back. She stiffened in her seat and said something. The driver nodded in response. Victor saw headlights approaching fast on the opposite lane. He immediately saw why it had caused a reaction. A police cruiser, lights flashing, siren's wail beating back the sound of the weather, responding to a call.

The woman said something else, probably intended to calm herself as well as the two men. Victor inhaled and rocked his head from side to side to crack his neck. Ready.

He watched the woman's head turn to the right to follow the car as it sped past. It was habit, human nature. Everyone looked when a cop car rolled by. Especially when there was something to hide.

The Israeli on the back seat looked too. Human nature. His gaze left Victor. Just for a second.

A second too long.

Victor leaned forward, raised his hands, hooked them over the driver's head, and tugged them sharply back. The hard edge of the plastic strap dug into the bridge of the Israeli's nose. Victor's wrists covered his eyes.

The driver cried out in pain, surprise, and panic as he lost his vision. The Renault swerved as he took one hand off the wheel and pulled at Victor's wrist. But Victor had two arms against one, leverage and the will to survive. He sawed the plastic strap deeper into the driver's nose. Blood ran down his face.

The guy in the back and the woman in the passenger seat both yelled at Victor to let the driver go as they fought against the force of the swerving car. Victor, knees pressing into the seat and his wrists locked around the driver's face, kept himself steady. They weren't wearing seat belts either. He was.

Victor pulled backward harder, the plastic strap cutting deeper into the driver's nose. The man yelled in pain and fear as his head was forced against the headrest. The Israeli in the back tried to keep the Beretta trained on Victor, but he wasn't firing. Killing Victor was the last resort. He didn't want to have to explain to his masters why their investigation had permanently ended, and with the car swerving, it wouldn't take much to throw a shot off far enough to hit the driver instead.

The passenger turned in her seat. She had her own gun out and pointed at Victor. She had a better angle on him, but the swerving car was having more of an effect on her. She couldn't keep still or her aim steady.

'*Let go of him*,' she shouted. '*RIGHT NOW.*'

Victor's gaze flicked between her and the guy in the back. He felt the car slowing. Nails drew blood from his skin but he didn't let go. The driver screamed in Hebrew. Horns sounded from other cars on the highway. They were nearing an exit. If the driver took it, they could stop the car. Then it was over. The driver couldn't see, but one of the other two could call out instructions.

Victor wrenched his hands downward, shearing skin from the driver's nose, hooking the plastic strap under his chin, and pulled them against his neck. Victor's wrists pressed into the flesh either side of the driver's throat. He choked.

The car swerved again. Harder. The woman fell across the stick shift. The guy in the back tilted Victor's way, completely off balance. The Israeli reached out with his left hand, pressing his palm into the centre back seat to halt his fall before he got too close to Victor. Too late.

Victor released the driver, brought his hands back, grabbed hold of the Israeli's wrist, wrenched him closer, let go, and smashed his right elbow into the guy's face. Then twice more. The Israeli sagged on the seat, stunned and disorientated.

The passenger pulled herself back upright, swivelled her head in Victor's direction. Her gun began to rise.

Victor grabbed the stunned Israeli's right hand with his own two, heaved the arm up to tilt the Beretta in the correct direction as much as he could, and squeezed the guy's finger down on to the trigger.

The suppressed *clack* was loud inside the car. The bullet caught the driver in the side of his ribcage, halfway between his armpit and hip. The car swerved again as the woman fired, throwing her aim. A hole blew through the back window.

Pebbles of glass struck the back of Victor's head. Wind and rain rushed inside.

The Renault careered into the other lane, hitting an SUV side-on. The force pushed Victor against the door to his left and he lost his grip on the Beretta. It dropped into the foot well behind the driver's seat and between Victor's feet. The dazed Israeli fell against him. Metal shrieked against metal. The driver groaned.

Horns blared. Other cars swerved out of the way. The woman grasped the wheel, one hand keeping the Renault from crashing while trying to retrieve her own gun, dropped in the impact, with the other. The guy in the back grabbed at Victor, who threw a sideways head butt into his already bloodied face, took hold of his jacket and shoved him between the front seats and into the woman.

Her hand was forced away from the wheel and the car swerved sharply. Tyres squealed against wet asphalt. Victor tried to grab the Beretta in the foot well but didn't have the room with his legs in front of him and in the way. The driver slumped across the wheel, his weight turning it to the right this time. The woman seized the steering wheel again, this time with both hands, heaving it back to straighten the Renault out.

The Israeli between the seats twisted himself around and punched at Victor. The guy's position was bad, and they didn't connect with enough force to slow Victor down. He released the seat belt and drove his right elbow into his attacker's stomach, then again, fingers locked together, left arm adding to the strength of the right. The Israeli gasped and doubled over. Victor hurled him on to the back seat, grabbed the driver's headrest for support, swivelled in his seat, and kicked the

Israeli in the neck while his head lolled back. Victor felt the larynx crush beneath his heel. The Israeli choked and grasped at his throat.

Without his legs in the way, Victor reached down into the foot well. The woman in the passenger seat saw what he was doing, let go of the steering wheel and scrambled for her own weapon lying between the slumped-over driver's thighs.

Victor's eyes locked with hers.

With no one holding the wheel, the Renault swerved erratically, causing the Beretta to slide around in the foot well, evading Victor's stilted grasp. Rain lashed the back of his head. The woman pulled her gun out from between the driver's legs as Victor felt cool metal in his fingers, grabbed the Beretta, lifted it up in both hands.

He watched as the woman brought her arms back to get the trajectory. She had to make half the distance he had.

He fired first, without aiming, squeezing the trigger rapidly, gun below seat level, angled upwards.

Nine millimetre bullets tore through the transmission box and the passenger seat and hit her in the thigh and hip. She screamed and flailed backward. Victor kept firing, increasing the angle, bloody bullet holes appearing in her stomach then chest. The gun fell from her fingers.

The car swerved right again. A horn blared. Victor saw oncoming headlights glimmering through the raindrops on the windshield. He swivelled back around and pushed his feet into the foot well. With his bound hands, he reached over his left shoulder and snatched the seat-belt buckle.

The sound of the horn's continuous blaring and rubber screeching on wet asphalt filled Victor's ears. He pulled the buckle across his torso. The lights glowed brighter, closer. He pushed the buckle into the clasp and heard it *click* in place.

The sudden collision sent Victor hurtling forward. The seat belt locked against him. The breath shot out from his lungs. His head smashed into the headrest. He heard metal screech and crumple. Glass shattered.

He fell back into the seat and grimaced. The driver lay limp against the steering wheel. The Israeli in the back had broken the passenger seat in the crash and lay slumped against it. He made slow, sucking breaths. Blood glistened across his face and streamed from his chin. The woman's body was crushed beneath the seat. Her unblinking eyes stared at Victor.

He coughed and unfastened the seat belt. He used the Beretta to smash out the cracked window next to him, pulled himself through the opening and dropped down on to the cold and wet road surface.

He hauled himself to his feet and staggered away from the car. The Renault had crashed head-on into a similarly sized sedan. The driver of that car had been wearing his seat belt and Victor saw him rubbing the back of his neck.

Around Victor large warehouses and factories lined the four-lane highway. Other vehicles had stopped as far as he could see, behind him and ahead. A van had crashed through a chain-link fence. A few people were getting out of their cars. All eyes were on Victor.

Someone from a nearby Ford opened his door and headed Victor's way. Victor ignored him and everyone else, spotted the blue Peugeot stopping fifty yards further back along the road. The Renault must have overtaken it in the chaos of the struggle.

Victor dropped to one knee, used his left hand to support the

511

right as best as he could, lined up the Beretta's iron sights over the glass of the windshield.

Cracks spread through the windshield as Victor fired at the Peugeot. He couldn't see if he'd hit any of the Kidon, but he continued to shoot regardless. The Samaritan near to Victor fell over backwards in shock and fear. He scrambled away.

Four Israelis from the Peugeot – the big guy, two other men and the short woman with boyish hair – rushed out from the car and adopted firing positions of their own, but Victor was already running. He wasn't going to win a four-on-one gunfight with Mossad assassins even if his hands weren't bound together.

He sprinted in the opposite direction.

CHAPTER 64

Victor ran, cuffed wrists hovering before his chest, Beretta in both hands. He veered off the highway, across the parking space in front of a row of workshops, down an alleyway between buildings. It was narrow, dark, long, not much more than five feet wide from wall to wall, sheltered from the rain. He dodged around boxes and rubbish, eyes scanning for anything that could cut the strap between his wrists. He could barely see. He tripped on something metal, stumbled, grazing his arm against the rough brick as he kept himself upright.

The alleyway opened out to a wide expanse of asphalt, behind it a stretch of wasteland. He saw moonlight shining off a chain-link fence between the two. He was at the back of the row of workshops, all closed for the night. The only way to go was over the fence and across the wasteland beyond, but he wouldn't make it over the fence if the Israelis from the Peugeot followed him.

He turned and positioned himself so his left shoulder was against the wall to the left of the alley's opening. Six seconds passed before he heard the sound of a pursuer entering the alley. Victor gave it two seconds, enough time for someone to get far enough down the alley to trap themselves.

With his hands bound, he couldn't just hold his gun arm around the corner and squeeze, so he twisted to the left as he stepped out to the right, realising his mistake as the moonlight cast his shadow on to the far wall of the alley ahead of him.

A gun fired first, a snapshot before Victor had fully revealed himself, the bullet blowing a chunk from the brickwork.

Victor lurched to the side, squeezing off a shot of his own, knowing it had missed without needing to look. He hurried along the wall, away from the alley, walking backwards, gun up, but doubting the assassin would continue forward. He or she would backtrack and find another way around the buildings. The others could already be doing the same as the one in the alley. If Victor let them flank him, it was over.

He put two rounds into the very corner of the alley mouth to make sure his attacker did double back. Then he sprinted for the fence, running awkwardly, unable to pump with his arms, expecting a bullet in the back at any moment. Reaching the fence, Victor tossed the gun over while he was still running, leapt, grabbed hold of the metal links halfway up, pushing with his feet. He climbed the last few feet, one hand clutching on to the links while the fingers of the other hand stretched to take hold a few links up. He repeated the process rapidly, urgently, scrambling all the time with his feet.

Razor wire topped the fence but he had no choice. Holding on to the top links, he swung his right elbow up and hooked it over the wire. Edges of metal sliced through his clothes and skin. Victor ignored the pain, pushed up with his legs, got his left elbow over too and hauled the rest of his body up and over the fence.

He let go and dropped down to the other side. The razor wire shredded the sleeves of his jacket and shirt and the skin beneath. His feet hit the ground and he immediately went into a roll to disperse the impact. The earth was rocky and wet from the rain.

His fingers were slick with rainwater and blood. He couldn't feel them. He located the gun, scooped it up into both hands, turned and rose to one knee. On the other side of the fence, the row of workshops stood seventy yards away. Moonlight sparkled off thousands of falling raindrops. Victor saw no one.

He heard a faint muffled shot and saw the sparks as the bullet clipped a fence post, but couldn't see the shooter. There was too much cover, too many shadows. The assassin could be anywhere, approaching in the darkness to take a shot at closer range, while the others did the same. He heard another shot, but from a different origin, and heard the bullet strike the ground nearby.

Victor jumped to his feet and ran, hoping that the two shooters were the sum total of his pursuers, but knowing a third was probably circling around some other way to intercept him, leaving the remaining assassin to check the Renault for survivors, manage evidence, call for backup. Maybe Victor had been lucky and scored a hit with his shots at the Peugeot, leaving one of his enemies injured. Maybe, but Victor didn't believe in luck.

There was enough light to see the ground but not the many shallow ruts and rocks that littered it. He stumbled and staggered, unable to use his arms for balance, knowing any Israelis following him would cover the distance faster than he could.

He saw a factory up ahead. No lights. As he neared, he could make out gaping holes in its sloped corrugated roof. Abandoned. Derelict. No chance of finding a car to steal, but more chance of locating something sharp to cut the plasticuffs.

He sprinted on. The rain soaked his clothes, hair and skin. The wasteland crested and then sloped down before it gave way to a flat area of asphalt set around the factory itself. Grass grew through cracks in the ground. The factory was several hundred feet long and thirty high to the start of a sloping roof that rose and peaked after another twenty. The walls were made of brick, set all the way along with huge rectangular windows comprised of dozens of smaller panes, many broken.

Victor ran up to the factory and rushed along the edge of the building, crouching low, looking for a way inside. Outside, the Israeli's numerical superiority would win without question. Inside, he might be able to avoid them, or hide long enough to force a withdrawal. If he could get his hands free. The windows were no good as an entry point. He would have to smash more to create a big enough gap, and with bound wrists, wouldn't be able to pull himself up to get through them. All the time, the Kidon assassins were closing.

He found a set of double doors. He checked the padlock. Stainless steel and sturdy. Even if he fired all four of his precious remaining bullets he wouldn't get through it. He moved on.

He dared to glance back, but couldn't see his pursuers. They wouldn't be able to see him either, but they would have heard him kicking the door. After a few more seconds, he found another door, this time a single. It had been reinforced with a padlock too, but some enterprising person had smashed in the lower half of the door. Victor silently thanked delinquents everywhere and got on his hands and knees. He crawled through the gap. Splinters of wood snagged his jacket.

It was cold inside. It might have been cold outside but he hadn't noticed. He was in a huge expanse of almost empty space that had once served as the main factory floor. Rain fell through gaping holes in a sloping corrugated roof supported by huge metal pillars. Large puddles spread across the floor beneath and bounced back the moonlight.

Some grass and plant life grew where light and rain regularly reached. Metal pipes, pieces of wood and sheets of plastic were scattered around. Visibility was good for an interior at night, but some areas in deep shadow were utterly black.

Victor hurried away from the door. He heard glass smash and knew one of the huge windows was being used as an entry point. Another assassin would be following directly behind Victor, and in seconds, crawl under the door. He could wait to ambush his pursuer, but that would keep Victor occupied long enough for the second or third Israeli to kill him from behind. No time to find something to saw through the straps. There were several exits leading deeper into the factory. Victor lurched through the closest.

He strained to see in the darkness; the further he went the less light there was. He didn't know where the corridor led, but he had to keep moving. Water dripped on him from somewhere above. He passed an interior door, tried it, found it locked, and carried on. He turned a corner, pressed his back against the wall for a moment, breathing heavily.

Victor forced himself to carry on. The light increased as the corridor opened up into a courtyard, overlooked on all sides by tall factory walls. There was only one way out, on the far side of the courtyard. A metal door streaked with rust. It was padlocked. Impenetrable. The walls were too tall and sheer to climb. No way out.

He turned around, rushed back down the corridor. He found the interior door again, kicked it open. In his peripheral vision he caught a glimpse of a moving form before he dashed through the doorway.

On the other side, moonlight shining through the decaying roof illuminated the large space. He made out the shapes of machinery, crates, tools, shelving, a conveyor belt, barrels. There were huge empty metal shelves along one wall, an abandoned forklift set before them. Victor backed off into the darkness.

He needed to find a way out. The Israelis would know that, and one of their number would be sprinting around the exterior of the factory to cover the far side from which Victor had entered. Were all three to follow him inside, and he managed to get back outside, he would be home free. They wouldn't make that mistake.

He stayed away from the dim beams of light filtering through the roof, to protect his night vision as well as to stay hidden. On the end of each row of shelves was a circular mirror to aid driving the forklift. Most were smashed.

Large crates were stacked in several rows and piles. Victor squatted down behind them, breathing hard, and used a jacket sleeve to wipe some sweat and rain from his face. He felt along the floor, hoping to find something sharp to cut the plasticuffs, but there was nothing.

He peered around the crates, saw a tall figure enter the room, quickly sidestepping away from the door. Victor squeezed off a shot, but he wasn't fast enough and the Israeli disappeared into cover.

A shot sounded from somewhere unseen and wood exploded as bullets punctured one of the crates. Victor backed off. He couldn't see the assassin, and couldn't risk exchanging fire if he did. His wrists were still bound, and the Beretta had just three rounds remaining.

There was a passageway to Victor's left, which he guessed would take him back to the main factory floor. He made a break for it, sprinting out of cover, trusting to speed. A bullet pinged off machinery.

He made it, didn't slow down, running along the wide corridor, seeing the huge broken windows in the distance. He ran out into the main factory floor, veered right to take him out of the immediate line of sight of anyone following him. Victor didn't know if the second assassin was nearby. He had to risk it.

There was no time to fumble in the dark for something sharp to cut the straps so Victor tucked the Beretta into his waistband, grabbed a pipe from the floor and swung it at a corner of one of the metal pillars. It made a loud *clang*. He swung it three more times, hitting the pillar in exactly the same spot. He dropped the pipe and rubbed the strap between his wrists against where he'd smashed away paint, rust and grime to reveal cold steel beneath. He felt the heat of friction as he frantically sawed.

The clang of the pipe hitting the pillar would tell his enemies exactly where to find him, but he had no choice. If he wanted to live, he needed his hands back. He sawed harder, expecting the searing agony of a bullet's impact at any moment.

The strap snapped. Finally, he was free.

Victor scrambled away, avoiding the swathes of light cutting through the air and reflecting off rain drops. When he reached the shelter of a rusty staircase leading up to a split-level lost in the darkness, he stopped, turned, and drew the Beretta. His hands were still numb and his wrists tingling, but it felt good to have independent movement again.

He heard footsteps crunching grit and other debris, but couldn't see the source. He had to move. Every moment he stayed under the split-level gave the other assassins time to close in and flank him. There was an interior doorway about thirty feet away; he approached it, keeping close to the wall, stepping as slowly and quietly as he could. He couldn't see where he was treading, and knew that one wrong footfall could give away his position. He would have taken off his shoes, but the floor was so littered with sharp objects he would have sliced his feet to shreds by the time he made it to the door.

Victor stopped ten feet from the doorway. There was too much light around it to move closer without revealing himself. His enemy could be watching the doorway, figuring he would head that way, and ready to shoot the second Victor moved into the light.

He took a breath, preparing to sprint and trust to speed again. He didn't have a lot of choice.

Something brushed Victor's ear. He flinched, reached a hand up and found a flake of rust on his shoulder. Instinctively, his head tilted backwards, looking up. He saw nothing but knew the split-level was twenty-plus feet above his head. Something up there had caused the flake of rust to fall.

The second assassin. As Victor had thought, they knew where he was hiding, and while one waited on the factory floor, the second was seeking to flank, not from the left or right, but from above.

Victor pivoted in the direction of the staircase. The Israeli above would have to come down that way, into the light. Victor stepped forward and to the side to get a better angle on the staircase. If he could kill this one, that left only one inside with him. Those were Victor's kind of odds.

He knocked something with his shoe. It skidded into a puddle and splashed. Not loud, but loud enough in the silence.

A suppressor clacked and a bullet buried itself in the floor a couple of feet away. Another splashed into the puddle.

The shots came from above, firing through the wooden floorboards of the split level, impossible to tell exactly where from just two shots. Victor remained perfectly still, willing the Israeli to shoot again and give away his position. The assassin fired a third shot, then a fourth.

The final one hit the floor close enough for Victor to feel pieces of exploded concrete strike his shins. Moonlight glowed through a hole above. Victor calculated the trajectory and squeezed off a round. He heard it tear through wood. There was a grunt, a stumble. Victor tracked the sound and risked another shot. A second of silence before something small and hard hit the floorboards.

Something big and heavy followed. Dead, or maybe just wounded. Or pretending.

One round left in the Beretta. One too few to risk another blind shot, especially with another foe nearby. Victor felt around on the floor, found a heavy bolt, and hurled it at the open doorway. He was sprinting the instant the bolt clattered on the other side, knowing the Israeli on the factory floor couldn't help but be distracted by it, if only for a moment. Victor reached the staircase and ascended fast. He heard movement below him as the assassin responded, moving to get a shot, and Victor flinched as a bullet struck the metal handrail behind him, but he made it to the top of the stairs and dived through a doorway on to the split-level.

He was in a derelict office. Moonlight shone through a wide, smashed-out window. Victor jumped to his feet and, gun up, moved quickly across the space. The time for stealth had passed. If the Israeli up here was dead, it didn't matter. If he was still alive and wounded, Victor wanted to get to him before he could recover sufficiently to retrieve his weapon, and before the assassin below arrived. There was no furniture except for a dented filing cabinet against one wall. The drawers had all been removed and stood, upside down, on the floor. Makeshift stools. Crushed beer cans and broken bottles were spread across the floor.

Through another door, Victor emerged into a larger office, some kind of briefing room, perhaps. The carpet had been stripped to expose the floorboards. Rain fell through holes in the roof. There were piles of broken chairs and other junk, rusting filing cabinets lying on their sides, plastic water-cooler bottles scattered around. Too dark to see the bullets holes in the floor. There were two doors at the far end.

No dead or injured assassin.

Victor froze, knowing he couldn't backtrack and go down the staircase. If the Israeli from the factory floor was still down there, he or she would have an easy time shooting Victor as he descended. He had to keep moving forward, knowing at least one assassin was waiting for him.

He stepped around the junk. There was nowhere for anyone to hide, but there were two doorways that led out of the room. Both open. An ambush could be waiting for him on the other side of either. At least two assassins close by.

One bullet.

CHAPTER 65

As Victor approached the doorways he saw the closest wasn't an option. Junk packed the room beyond – broken chairs, boxes and other trash created an impassable blockage. Victor headed towards the second.

He walked down the hallway beyond, slowly, cautiously, one silent footstep after the next. The light was dim but abundant enough that he could see the details of the walls – old peeling paper, wires hanging where light fixtures had been removed, holes for hooks. The carpet had been stripped from the floor but some underlay was left over the floorboards. The roof above had yet to breach and the floor was dry.

There were two closed doors, the nearest to his left, the furthest to the right, before the hallway opened up to another area. Based on the width of the split-level, he imagined the closed doors would lead to small offices. Beyond the open space up ahead would be the other staircase. The cool air that flowed gently his way told him a large opening lay ahead, maybe a smashed-out window. He heard the relentless patter of rain hitting hard surfaces.

Victor ignored the doors. A Kidon assassin would not have trapped him- or herself in a small office with only one exit. He or she would be in the area at the end of the corridor or somewhere beyond.

Twelve more steps and he was almost in the open area. A rotting couch and a water cooler with no bottle revealed it as having once been a reception room or lounge. Rain soaked the floorboards beneath a huge hole in the ceiling. The couch had no cushions, bare springs visible and rusty.

A doorless entranceway on the opposite side of the lounge led to a kitchen. Victor could see the remnants of white-painted units and cabinets. He stepped quickly into the open area, first looking left, then right, sweeping with the Beretta as he did. No sign of an assassin and nowhere for one to hide. Shards of glass from broken bottles and crushed cans were scattered across the floor. Through an open door to Victor's right, he saw a metal balcony and another staircase.

The door leading to the balcony was open fully, letting in a swathe of dim light from the night sky above. Pieces of glass jutted from the door around the square hole that had once been a window.

Victor stepped forward again so he could see further into the kitchen and get a better angle on the balcony, but there were still blind spots that would only be revealed if he moved closer to one, presenting his back to the other. He knew there had to be an assassin hiding in one of the locations, but which one?

The open staircase door could have been like that before – nothing to do with his enemies – or maybe it was open to lure Victor towards it, so he could be ambushed from behind. Or maybe an assassin was on the balcony, figuring that Victor would think it a trap and head to the kitchen. Beyond that was double and triple bluff, a never-ending stream of potential deception. Tactics didn't come into it. Experience didn't help. In the end it was a straight fifty-fifty.

He had to pick one, fast. He couldn't hang around. The second Kidon assassin would be closing. The third one from outside could even have been called in, now Victor was trapped on the split-level.

He headed to the staircase door so that if he was wrong and the assassin attacked from the kitchen they would come out of hiding with the moonlight in their eyes. Victor approached side-on so that he could keep looking left towards the kitchen.

Eighteen inches from the balcony, he stopped. Any closer and he would give himself away an instant before he had a visual on his enemy. At the same time, Victor would reveal himself to anyone in the kitchen. And he couldn't be looking in both directions at once.

He grabbed the balcony door and flung it shut, creating an obstacle and combined warning system if he was wrong. Before he'd let go of the door, he was spinning round, aiming at the kitchen doorway.

He wasn't wrong.

The short woman with the plain face and boyish hair emerged from the darkness beyond, gun up, a two-handed grip, arms bent slightly at the elbow. She was already squinting, in preparation for looking into the light, expecting to see Victor's back.

He fired first, at centre mass, not risking his last round on a headshot on a fast-moving target in the dark.

The expended shell case clinked quietly on the floorboards.

The Israeli let out a dull cry, staggered backward, and fell into the kitchen. She wasn't dead – he guessed due to a concealed Kevlar vest. A subsonic 9 mm would not have penetrated it, but the blunt-force trauma to the sternum had stunned her, paralysing her diaphragm and leaving her gasping for breath.

Victor hurried over to complete the kill and take her weapon and radio if she had one, but he heard a noise, to his left – from the hallway where he'd entered – spun around and hurled the empty Beretta at the open doorway.

The gun clipped the six-four Israeli on the forehead as he appeared out of the shadows. The forehead was the hardest part of the skull, but even empty the Beretta weighed almost two pounds.

The assassin reeled from the impact, arms flailing, giving Victor time to close the distance. Using his left hand, he grabbed the Israeli's own Beretta while there was only one hand gripping it, hooked his thumb around the end of the index finger through the trigger guard, and squeezed the guy's nail against the hard edge of metal, at the same time twisting the hand back on itself and against the joint.

The Israeli released his weapon. Victor caught it by the barrel in his right hand, tried to reposition his grip, but the assassin shouldered Victor first, knocking him into the wall, pinning him there with his size and strength, trapping Victor's arms so he couldn't attack. His enemy was only a couple of inches taller, but forty pounds of muscle heavier. The Israeli slammed a forearm down on Victor's wrist, and he dropped the gun before it could be ripped from his hand. It clattered on the wet floorboards.

Victor's weight was on his left leg so he lifted his right,

wrapped it around his enemy's own load-bearing leg and wrenched it off the floor.

The Israeli fell, landing on his back, Victor on top of him, rolling away, going for the gun, on his hands and knees, cutting himself on broken glass.

He grabbed the Beretta and spun around.

The assassin threw himself at Victor before he could take aim, knocking the gun aside and punching Victor clean in the face. The Israeli didn't get his full power behind it, but the fist caught Victor on the jaw and sent a huge jolt of pain and disorientation through him. The gun was torn from his hand with ease.

Victor grabbed a handful of broken glass from the floor and smashed it into his enemy's face as the muzzle twisted Victor's way. The assassin grunted, knocked sideways, shards of glass buried in his cheek and forehead.

A hard kick to the wrist forced him to drop the Beretta and it skidded across the floorboards. Victor jumped to his feet and moved, circling his enemy, towards the gun. The Israeli stood just as fast, stepped laterally into Victor's path, blocking him before he could get close to the weapon.

The assassin charged forward, arms out, ready to grapple – two hundred and twenty pounds of strength and skill. Victor timed the attack, waiting until the Israeli's head inevitably dipped to grab him below his centre of gravity, and brought his knee up into his enemy's face. It caught him under the jaw, but the Israeli's momentum carried him forward regardless and he collided with Victor, slamming him backward into a wall. Plaster cracked. Victor elbowed the Israeli on the back of his head but the blow wasn't hard enough to stop him grabbing

Victor and spinning him around – off the wall – and hurling him.

He hit the floor, cracking wet floorboards, and rolled backward over his head and on to his feet. Blood, rain and sweat covered the Israeli's face. Moonlight glimmered against the shards of glass buried in his cheek.

Victor took a series of deep breaths. Hand-to-hand combat was exhausting against a similarly sized enemy, let alone a bigger, stronger one. The female assassin writhed on the floor of the kitchen, still winded, but she wouldn't be for much longer. Victor spotted the gun. It was too far to get to before his opponent was upon him. Victor read the assassin's expression well enough. He wasn't going to risk it either. But he didn't need to.

The Israeli grabbed a shard of glass from a broken window of the staircase door, held it like a knife. It was slim and narrow, five inches long. He gripped it tightly, not caring that it was cutting into his palm and fingers.

He attacked with fast thrusts to Victor's abdomen, not wanting to risk breaking the glass against ribs. Victor dodged to the left, maximising the distance between himself and the right-handed attacker. The Israeli turned with Victor, slashed at his neck. Victor ducked beneath the blade and darted away.

His enemy was composed, patient, maintaining his range advantage by keeping the shard out before him, arm almost fully extended. His arms were longer anyway, but with the extra inches of glass Victor's own reach was far too short to deliver a meaningful blow without bringing himself too close to the makeshift knife.

He backed away, circling, using the space of the lounge. He

glanced around quickly, looking for weapons. The couch was obviously no good, the water cooler too big and heavy to wield. The rest of the shards around the smashed window were too small to be effective weapons.

Victor dodged the assassin's attacks, always circling, waiting for an opportunity to strike back, but he was running out of room as the Israeli slowly forced him closer to the wall. Sweat and rainwater ran into Victor's eyes. He blinked it away. Lactic acid made his muscles ache.

He faked a stumble and the Israeli lunged to take advantage, his momentum carrying him forward an extra step, giving Victor enough time to sidestep out of the way and grab the assassin's right hand in his own. Victor squeezed, hard.

The Israeli grunted, blood oozing out between his knuckles as his hand was contracted against the sharp edges of the glass shard.

The assassin threw his free elbow, striking Victor on the temple before he could twist his head away. The blow destroyed his equilibrium. His whole body sagged.

The Israeli pulled his right hand free, dropping the glass shard, and it landed on the floor, intact, slick with blood. Hands grabbed Victor's shirt and shoved him backward, off balance and dazed from the blow to the temple. The assassin set his feet, planted his shoulder into Victor's chest, twisted his hips and pushed with his legs, throwing Victor to the floor.

He hit the floorboards hard, awkwardly, reacting too slow to break the fall. His head span. The Israeli scrambled on top of him, knees either side of his hips, grabbing the shard of glass in his left hand.

It came down fast, point racing to penetrate Victor's face. His senses cleared in time for him to grab the wrist with both hands, halting the shard two inches above his left eye.

Immediately the Israeli brought his injured right hand to add extra strength. The right hand was badly sliced and couldn't be fully employed, but he didn't need it. He was stronger, heavier and had the advantages of position and gravity. Victor's arms shook under the pressure. The shard descended towards his eye. Victor couldn't stop it, only slow it down. The assassin's face was directly above his own, cheek and forehead embedded with glass.

Victor set his left foot down outside his opponent's right knee and pushed up with his hips, trying to roll to the left, but the Israeli's legs were too strong and easily resisted the move. Victor tried to slam his knee into his enemy's kidneys, but the assassin's position was good and Victor couldn't get enough strength behind the blows to be effective.

The shard continued downward, now less than an inch from his eyeball. With it came the Israeli's face, ever closer to Victor's. Blood from the wounded hand ran down the edge of the glass. The point continued its inevitable descent. The burn in Victor's muscles intensified exponentially with every passing second.

Glass sparkled above Victor's eye. When he blinked, his lashes brushed the tip. The Israeli's own eyes were wide, eager for the kill. His face was mere inches above his hands as he leaned over to make maximum use of his weight. Sweat and blood dripped down on to Victor's skin. The pain in his elbows was horrific. The tip of the glass was moments away from piercing his cornea and plunging through the eye socket and down into his brain.

Victor felt the strength in his wounded right arm failing. Two seconds left alive.

One.

He rolled his head to the left and at the same time stopped resisting. The glass shard came down in a straight line, hard and fast before the assassin could adjust. The tip caught Victor on the side of the head, in the hairline, slicing through his scalp and ear in a line that followed around his skull and down into the floor.

The Israeli fell forward, but reacted in time to stop his face colliding with Victor's. Blood poured from the wound on the side of Victor's head. The tip of the shard was buried in a wet floorboard next to him. Both his arms were pinned between himself and the Israeli. He didn't have the strength to pull them free. It would be easy to finish him off now his arms were trapped.

But the Israeli was exactly where Victor wanted him.

Skin split, cartilage ripped, and bone crushed between Victor's teeth as he bit his enemy's nose off.

Blood splashed down over Victor and the assassin screamed. Loud. Shrill. He threw himself backwards, tearing the last shreds of tissue that linked the end of his nose to his face.

Victor spat out the nose and rose to his feet. The assassin stumbled backwards, agony and shock and horror controlling his actions, hands pressed to his face, blood gushing out between his fingers. Screaming.

Victor rushed for the Beretta, but before he got to it, he caught movement in his peripheral vision. From the kitchen.

The female assassin – recovered enough to move – was scrambling for her own gun. And she was going to reach it first.

Victor changed direction, shoving the screaming Israeli out of the way, flung open the balcony door and charged down the staircase. He heard a muted gunshot behind him, heard glass shatter, and leapt down the remaining steps.

He landed and powered forward, stumbling to keep his balance, knowing by the time the woman was on her feet and through the balcony door he would be lost in the darkness.

She fired anyway, hoping for a blind hit as she fanned rounds, the rapid *clacks* echoing throughout the factory. Bullets whizzed through the air, thudded into the ground, or pinged off pillars and machinery. Victor didn't slow down, sprinting in a straight line for speed because the screams of the noseless Israeli drowned out Victor's footsteps and because the main factory area was massive and the odds of a tiny bullet passing through the same space as him at the same time were negligible.

Victor reached the wall with the huge windows, found the one that was smashed out by his enemies to gain entry earlier, and hauled himself up and through it. He dropped down outside. Raindrops bounced off his face.

The third assassin would either be covering the opposite side of the factory exterior, or responding to the screams of his brethren. Victor ran. He ran back the way he had come. He ran up the incline. He ran across the wasteland.

He heard sirens. On the other side of the row of workshops would be cops and ambulances. A risk, but given the choice between arrest and death, Victor would take the former every time. The chain-link fence was hard to climb with his weakened limbs, and he added more gashes to his legs and arms getting over the razor wire.

On the other side, fatigue overwhelmed him and he fell down

to his knees. Rainwater mixed with blood on Victor's face. He tilted his head backwards and let the rain fill his mouth before spitting out the blood and remains of flesh and cartilage.

He put a hand to the cut on his head. There was too much adrenalin in his veins for him to feel the pain. The top of his ear was still there, but only just. The glass had slit the superficial temporal artery on the side of his skull – the main source of the blood – but it wasn't going to kill him. He used the rain to wash his face and head.

When he felt a semblance of his strength returning, he stood, keeping a palm pressed over the wound to stem some of the bleeding as he walked parallel to the workshops. Through alleys and gaps between buildings he saw the flash of police cruiser lights. Any surviving Israelis would have fled the scene before the cops had arrived. Witnesses would no doubt be telling crazed stories of guns and shooting. Eventually the area would be secured and searched, but by the time the factory was searched, the Kidon assassins would be long gone.

Victor hurried away, rain pelting his head and drenching his clothes. Within fifteen minutes he was a mile away, on the outskirts of Sofia, walking along a quiet street. He paid a homeless guy fifty euros for his woollen hat before catching a bus. Victor sat at the back, with the cut side of his head pressing against the cold window glass to keep pressure on the wound, and looking like just another tired and soaked traveller. There were five people on the bus. Nobody paid Victor any attention.

The pain intensified as the adrenalin faded away. He checked his watch. A little after midnight. A new day. Wounded but alive, with the remaining members of the Kidon team far behind him. The Israelis wouldn't be looking for him now. They would be extracting, just like him, trying to put as much distance as possible between themselves and the failed kidnapping. They wouldn't want to tangle with the Bulgarian authorities any more than he did.

Before the day was out the surviving members of the team would be back in Israel, trying to work out what went so wrong. In the coming days there would be reports to write, bodies to recover, funerals to attend, a nose to reconstruct. For the time being, they were no threat to him, but Victor knew the danger hadn't passed. After tonight, more than ever before, Mossad would want his blood. They could get in line.

The reflection in the glass stared back at Victor. The eyes were unblinking black orbs set in a face without expression, distorted by raindrops. A translucent spectre hovering over the world beyond.

The bus headed out of the city. To where, he didn't know. He didn't much care. Victor closed his eyes, and let sleep take him.

ACKNOWLEDGEMENTS

As with my first novel, I owe thanks to many different people. Firstly to my incomparable editor, Daniel Mallory, and the wonderful and hard working men and women at Little, Brown – Hannah Clark, Richard Collins, Hannah Hargrave, Anne O'Brien, Thalia Proctor, Kate Webster, Tom Webster and everyone in the Sales team. I couldn't ask for a more talented and dedicated bunch behind me.

I can't thank enough my legendary agent, Phillip Patterson, for booking me a seat on this fantastic journey and for keeping me pointed in the right direction. Thanks also to the tireless efforts of Isabella Floris and Luke Speed at Marjacq.

Thank you to my parents, Susan & Roger, and my sister Emma for all the support and enthusiasm. My brother Michael's ongoing contribution cannot be overstated, and my debt of gratitude to him grows larger all the time.

Finally thanks to Emmalene Knowles, Mag Leahy, Paul Mathews and Chris Wright for the numerous helpful comments and suggestions.

DISCOVER
THE MAN
BEHIND THE
ACTION
TOM WOOD

© Charlie Hopkinson

🐦 @TheTomWood
f facebook.com/tomwoodbooks
tomwoodbooks.com